THE WILD ADVENTURES OF

KING KONG

VS.

TARZAN

By

WILL MURRAY

Illustrated by

Joe DeVito

Altus Press • 2016

THANKS TO

Gary A. Buckingham, P.E., Edgar Rice Burroughs, Inc.,
Col. Richard M. Cooper (Ret.), Joe DeVito, DeVito ArtWorks LLC,
Dannie Festa, Theresa Henderson, Dave McDonnell, Henoch Neethling,
Dafydd Neal Dyar, Jeff Deischer, Ray Riethmeier, and Jim Sullos

COVER ILLUSTRATION COMMISSIONED BY
Richard Burchfield

First Edition — November 2016

DESIGNED BY
Matthew Moring/Altus Press

Like us on Facebook: "The Wild Adventures of Tarzan" and "The Wild Adventures of King Kong"

www.adventuresinbronze.com

Printed in the United States of America

Set in Caslon.

For Two Dreamers Whose Jungle
Trails Were Destined to Meet...

Merian C. Cooper
&
Edgar Rice Burroughs

Giants Who Begat Giants

King Kong Vs. Tarzan

Chapter 1

SKULL MOUNTAIN shook in the lunar light.

The earth trembled. Leafy jungle crowns jerked and danced in sympathy. Coconuts cascaded downward, hopping and rolling away like frightened animals. Even the lowering sky seemed to quake in fear.

Beyond the half-open gates of the great stockade wall, a force of nature was astride the night. A fanged mouth beyond imagination yawned like a sticky cavern and gave vent to a mighty roar.

Atop the wall, dark-skinned natives lifted their crude pitch-and-palm-frond torches as if to fend off the approach of the lumbering, unseen thing.

"Kong… Kong… Kong… Kong," they chanted. It was a dirge. A dirge of death older than time itself. It foretold the coming of the beast-god, undisputed monarch of Skull Mountain Island.

Across the Plain of the Altar rolled his roaring. The heavens themselves seemed to take up the cry, for out of the clouds rumbled a peal of thunder. Low, reverberant, somehow timid in contrast to the enraged vocalizations of the hairy mountain called Kong.

No eye could measure his exact height. No ear could withstand his punishing roar. Nothing made by man or machine could stand before him. For he was Kong the mighty. Unconquered by dinosaur. Seemingly unconquerable by man.

Ann Darrow heard those hellish roars and her brave heart quailed.

"Jack!" she cried. "He's behind us."

"Buck up, Ann," Jack Driscoll returned. "We can outrun the brute. At least, we'll have to. Now, come on!"

They pressed on, pushing through sticky jungle undergrowth, rife with sharp, serrated ferns and alive with noxious insects that made Jersey "canaries" seem like mere bothersome gnats.

Ann Darrow, blonde hair wet from the lagoon into which she and her companion had plunged to escape the prehistoric terrors of Kong's domain, her pale frock in flimsy tatters, clung to Jack Driscoll, First Mate of the tramp freighter, *Wanderer*— and her rescuer.

Grimacing, Driscoll ignored his right arm, which hung useless where Kong had manhandled him. Yet he had not gotten the worst of it. The First Mate had seen burly natives mangled into broke-boned pretzels in the monster's black, leather-padded paws.

Up ahead, across the ebony sward of the Plain of the Altar, loomed the massive wall, its battlements alive with swaying natives, faces unreal beneath their high-held torches.

They picked up their stumbling pace.

"Almost there, baby," Driscoll encouraged.

"Almost... there," gasped Ann, throwing a fearful look over her bare shoulder.

"Almost...."

A sob caught in her throat. For a bestial growl cut through the night air. Kong was somewhere behind, seeking, prowling, hunting... *her*.

Up ahead, a familiar gravelly voice echoed.

"*Yo-o-oh!* It's Miss Ann. And the mate."

"Lumpy!" hissed Driscoll. Turning, he hefted Ann into his battered arms, unmindful of the lancing pain, and stumbled toward the terrible altar where shadowy forms had gathered.

Human forms. The shore party of the *Wanderer*. But they might as well have been angels.

Old Lumpy, the ship's cook, was calling to the others. Eagerly, they started toward his outcry. Then the voice of Captain Englehorn came, loud and distinct, speaking in his native tongue.

"Gott sei Dank!"

"Jack!" That was Carl Denham's boisterous voice. "By God! Didn't I tell you Jack could bring her back if anyone could?"

Panting and out of energy, Jack and Ann stumbled into the outstretched arms of their friends. It was as if a nightmare had been dispelled by astringent moonlight. A hundred questions were barked, but Lumpy cut through the guff.

"Lively! Some of you mudhens take Miss Ann from the mate before he falls in his tracks. Can't you see he's dead beat?"

"Give her to me!" Denham bellowed.

As Denham relieved Driscoll of his beautiful burden, the Skipper yanked a flat flask from a pocket and offered it to his first mate, saying gruffly, "Do you good."

Driscoll took a long pull and his rangy frame shuddered. Crewmen began slapping him on the back.

"Good man, Mr. Driscoll."

"Good man, my eye!" snapped Lumpy. "Great man!"

They had laid Ann Darrow on a bed of their coats, where she refused the remnants of the flask. Her face in the moonlight was like a frozen pearl, blue eyes stark with a fading fear.

"Oh, Jack!" she sobbed. "We're really back!"

"Now! Now!" soothed Englehorn. "Of course, you're back. And we'll have you on the ship in no time."

"Cry away, honey," Driscoll whispered sympathetically. "After all you've been through, you've got a good cry coming."

Ann released her pent-up emotions in a teary flood. Her moon-washed shoulders shook. It became very quiet.

"It's the first time I've seen even a tear from her," Driscoll breathed in wonder.

So absorbed was the shore party by the amazing development, not a member of the crew noticed dark man-shadows stirring beyond the huddled knot of humanity they represented.

Out of the jungle slipped individual figures, then small groups, coming from the direction of the grass-hut village lying in the brooding shadow of Skull Mountain. Alerted by a solitary native woman who dared to steal a glance from the door of her hut and then vanish to alert her fellow tribesmen, they approached. Before long, the chief and the witch doctor were creeping toward the open council square, followed by others.

Still others began climbing the great wall, seeking its high battlements, carrying torches which they lit upon reaching the broad parapet.

Captain Englehorn perceived the moving mass of men and fixed them with his steely gaze.

"*Bado!*" he snapped. "Stop!"

Sailors pressed closer to him, forming a protective circle. But the curious natives did not advance further. They only stared dumfounded at Ann's prostrate and still living form.

"Kong… Kong… Kong… Kong… Kong… Kong," they chanted.

Denham growled, "That is just what *I* want to know, too. What about Kong?"

"What about him?" Driscoll returned hotly.

"I came here to make a moving picture," replied Denham. "But Kong is worth all the movies in the world. Now that Jack and Ann are safe, I—want—that—*Beast!*"

The assembled shore party of the *Wanderer* regarded Carl Denham in mute disbelief. Voices exploded.

"What?"

"He's crazy!"

"Don't he know when he's got enough?"

"I need it," insisted Denham. "We got our bombs. If we catch Kong, capture him alive—"

Driscoll exploded, "No! Kong is miles away. In his lair. And that's on top of a cliff an army couldn't get at."

"Not if he chooses to stay up there," the filmmaker allowed. His brown eyes grew steadily more crafty. "But will he choose?"

"Why not?" challenged Driscoll.

The two men locked stern gazes.

"Because we've got what Kong wants," bit out Denham. "You're the man who knows that, Jack, as well as I."

Driscoll frowned like a thundercloud getting set to unleash a deluge. "Something he'll never get again, Denham," he said forcefully. "If you're planning to—"

"To use Ann as bait?" finished Denham. "Not a bit. You know better than that, Jack. But you know, too, and so does everybody else, that when I start a thing—I *finish* it!"

No one spoke. All eyes were on Carl Denham. Ann Darrow looked at him, as if seeing the dynamic director for the first time, and questioning what manner of man he was after all.

The filmmaker searched the stiff faces of those who surrounded him, challenging their regard, man for man. "Well!" he rapped out. "I started to get my hands on Kong. And I'm going to see it through. The Beast has seen Beauty, so I won't have to use bait. He'll come without any. His instinct, the instinct of the Beast, is telling him to stay safe in his mountain. But the memory of Beauty is in him. That's stronger than instinct. And he will come."

Jack Driscoll gathered Ann in his strong good arm.

"I'm taking her back to the ship," he said firmly.

Another silence followed, and for all the expression they held, their faces painted by the flaring torches might have been cut from marble.

Suddenly, the monotonous chanting of the islanders broke, then twisted into a terrified shout.

"Kong! Kong!"

High on the protection of the log wall, a weird thunder resounded. It was not authored by any storm cloud, but emerged from the equally elemental throat of the fearsome beast-god, Kong.

Hearing this, Ann emitted a piercing scream and buried her face in Driscoll's strong shoulder. The First Mate drew her more closely.

"He's followed her!" Driscoll shouted.

Turning to the others, Denham bellowed, "Close that gate. Bar it!"

Half the crew raced for the great stockade gate. Natives on the ground, wild-eyed, followed to pitch in.

Soon, they were straining to close the double gate. Feet digging in the dirt for traction, they put their backs and shoulders into it. The massive log doors began to creak in complaint as they were pushed inexorably closed.

High above, the torchlight threw flickering reddish glare into the jungle, making leafy shadows leap and squirm like shadowy serpents.

The ground began to drum as if something monstrous was pounding the earth.

It was the sound of monster feet eating up distance, slapping the shaking ground as the Beast approached, not running, but striding along purposefully.

Came another roar, and their eyes lanced about until they spotted something moving, approaching, lumbering, too big to be believed, too swift to be possible.

Firebrands picked out a pair of red-rimmed eyes mounted in a head standing taller than the highest tree. Dark as the devil, it was, but the searching eyes gleamed a golden amber.

From the torch-lit line of natives emerged whimpering sounds of panic. Some dropped their firebrands. Others leapt from the battlements, unmindful of the bone-breaking fall that awaited them. Terror of Kong had seized their superstitious minds.

Jack Driscoll pulled Ann to the safety of the huts, while

Denham rushed forward to reinforce the sailors straining to close the gate.

It was nearly shut now, but not soon enough. For Kong, bounding along, threw himself against the barrier. The gate shuddered. Men fell back, yelping.

A colossal arm slipped through the crack, groped about, and seized a retreating sailor. The terrified man's outcry was silenced by squeezing fingers. A dark fist raised the unlucky one and dashed his flailing figure against the barrier door.

At that juncture, the natives who had taken charge of the wooden bars expressed themselves in a defeated wail and fled unashamed. For this was Kong!

The bristling brute threw one mighty shoulder against the log barricade, forcing the doors open, ripping great iron hinges off their mountings.

Ponderously, inexorably, with an almost majestic groaning, the gates were pushed apart.

Sailors scrambled for safety as feet larger than motorboats descended upon the milling mass of natives, squeezing them of their vital juices as if they were nothing more than grapes caught in a cruel winepress.

Moonlight framed the mountainous beast who stood holding the gates apart, half crouched, his inhumanly intelligent eyes sweeping the dark native hut before him.

Denham lifted his voice, shouting, "The bombs! The bombs!"

The stupendous size of Kong made his voice crack in awe.

Pushing forward, Kong moved into the cluster of grass huts and commenced pulling them apart as if they were nut shells containing delicious sweetmeats.

The last of the natives dropped their torches and fled the wall, but the simian creature had no interest in them. They were familiar forms, and he was looking for hair the color of polished gold.

Stooping often, Kong examined the interior of hut after hut, grunting and making noises consistent with animal anger and frustration. His broad nostrils flared as he sought a familiar, tantalizing scent.

By this time, Denham had torn open the packing crates, began distributing the powerful gas bombs among the shore party, while Jack Driscoll rushed white-faced Ann through the effulgent moonlight toward the sandy beach where the boats stood.

"He hasn't seen us yet," Denham assured the sailors while Kong continued to dismantle the village in a vain quest for the sacrificial bride who had escaped him. "You men break back to Driscoll. I'll follow. If Kong chases, I'll bomb him, but I'd rather not—yet. So many huts might stop the drift of the gas cloud."

The shore party dispersed, Denham following on their heels, looking backward warily and often, fear of the apish giant uppermost in their minds.

Yet another hut crumbled beneath Kong's probing fingers and the screams that lifted into the night told of a hapless family who were being crushed by the baffled brute. The sounds ceased with an awful finality.

Wiping bloody paws on his dark fur, Kong straightened, bullet head swiveling, feral eyes probing the night.

They fell upon two figures flitting through the moonlight, racing for the water. A flash of gold caused Kong's glowering bloodshot orbs to brighten.

Hairy fists lifted, he began beating upon his chest, whereupon the behemoth fell into a shambling half-crouch and raced for the dancing moonglade.

Seeing this, Denham shouted a sharp command. Snappily, the sailors took up positions blocking the creature's advance.

In his rough hands, Denham held two of the great egg-shaped gas bombs. Lumpy hefted two more. Made of brittle cast-iron, they were forged so that upon impact, the thin metal shells would shatter, releasing their potent chemical contents, which would vaporize instantly.

They set up a skirmish line as Kong loomed closer.

No one ever remembered who threw the first gas bomb. But it was Denham. The film director must have played football in his youth. For the unwieldy gas bomb landed perfectly in Kong's path, then broke. Greyish vapor rolled from the shattered shell casing, and ghostly tendrils began crawling up Kong's massive legs.

Denham took several steps back and heaved again. Kong charged through a fresh cloud of suffocating trichloride gas, and then a third mushy explosion gave up a greyish pall that blocked his path.

Stumbling, Kong vented a deep cry of challenge that twisted into a strangling cough. The black-haired brute hesitated, staggering. Small deep-set eyes grew stricken.

Shaking a fist, Denham gave an exultant cry, "What did I tell you?"

Sensing victory, he stepped in and flung another bomb. It sailed high, smashing against Kong's massive barrel chest, its liquid contents splashing and evaporating into another hazy cloud of choking vapor.

The gorilla-like titan twisted, one hirsute hand swinging around, grazing Denham and knocking him flat.

Laboriously, Kong reached out with both paws for the golden-haired girl huddling in the gunwales of a beached dory only yards away, protected by Driscoll's sheltering body.

Something like a groan escaped his leathery lips.

Then, blunt fingers groping, the beast-god of Skull Mountain Island swayed, swung about in a drunken, staggering circle and crashed into the gritty sand of the beach.

Lunar light painted his hairy form so that it appeared that Kong's bristled hide consisted of threads of silver mixed with iron.

Except for the slow pulse of lungs and ribs crackling with respiration, Kong did not move.

Every man of the shore party watched the fallen hulk in rapt wonder. Their stunned eyes were strange, as if they could not believe the size of the monster—or that they had conquered it.

Finally, Captain Englehorn cleared his throat and directed, "Man the boats. We'll get out of this."

The Skipper made his way to Denham's side, helping him to his feet.

"Are you hurt?"

Shaking his aching head, Denham laughed roughly. "Me? Not a bit! Come on, we've got him."

"We'd best get back to the ship, Mr. Denham."

"Sure. Send some of the crew. Tell 'em to fetch anchor chains and tools."

"You don't dare—"

"Why not? He'll be out for hours. Snap to it."

"What are you going to do?"

"Chain him up, and build a raft to float him out to the ship and the steel chamber in the hold."

"No chain will hold… that."

Carl Denham squared his blocky shoulders, his boisterous spirits expanding.

"We'll give him more than chains," he barked. "He's always been king of his world. He's got something to learn. Something man can teach any animal. That's fear! That will hold him, if the chains alone won't."

Drunk on the heady wine of victory, Carl Denham took hold of the Skipper's bony shoulders and shook him exultantly.

"Don't you understand? We got the biggest capture in the world! There's a million in it! And I'm going to share it with all of you. Listen! A few months from now it'll be up in lights on Broadway. The spectacle nobody will miss. King Kong! The Eighth Wonder!"

Chapter 2

D AWN WAS searing the grim summit of Skull Mountain as they finished the immense raft, built of split logs, balsa blocks and bamboo, whose frame consisted of sawn timbers scavenged from towering trees that Kong had toppled in his elemental fury, as well as pieces of the great double doors that had come loose when the beast breached it. The deep hollows creating the empty eye sockets of the unnatural granite death's-head formation dominated its forbidding rock countenance. Those shadowy stone pits seemed to be staring off into space.

The beast-god of Skull Mountain Island lay asprawl, draped in heavy chain where scrub grass edged up against the beach. The native men were crowded around, fearful yet curious. Captain Englehorn was explaining to them the way of things in their own language.

"If you help us drag Kong to the raft," he was saying, "we will carry him away from Skull Island, where he will never terrorize you again. Savvy?"

"Lord Kong god of Skull Island," intoned the chief.

"No more. Kong is our slave."

The notion of the mighty Kong reduced to being the slave of any man was astonishing to the natives. It showed in their coffee-colored faces, the manner in which their jaws hung slack. Nervous eyes lanced in the direction of the recumbent monster that was neither man nor ape, but something beyond both.

Viewed up close, the ship's master could make out things in

the monster's bristling fur than had escaped their notice before. Silver and grey hairs mixed in with the black ones. Numerous scars bespoke of victories long past. And on the creature's forearms, blood seeped from open wounds where the sharp teeth of a Tyrannosaur had recently taken their awful toll.

"*Gott in Himmel*," muttered Englehorn. "How old must this creature be?"

Over by the raft, Jack Driscoll was giving Carl Denham a hard time in no uncertain terms.

"This was your scheme all along, wasn't it?" the First Mate demanded. "To capture that prehistoric ape."

Denham stuck out his chest. "What of it? It's my expedition, my show. I had the hold outfitted for whatever we might capture and drag back to civilization. So we bagged Kong. That makes Carl Denham a better man than Frank Buck, doesn't it?"

"We almost lost Ann in the doing of it," growled Driscoll.

Denham waved the complaint away with a careless hand. "Aw, that plucky little kid was in no special danger."

"That's a lie and you know it!" raged Driscoll, balling his fists.

Denham rammed his jaw forward belligerently. "You see here, First Mate Driscoll, I'm bossing this operation. What I say goes. Get me? I chartered the *Wanderer*. Captain Englehorn works for me and you work for Englehorn. As first officer, you don't get any more say-so than that."

Driscoll fumed. "Even if you can lug that overgrown monkey onto the raft," he stated tightly, "do you really think the ship's cranes will be strong enough to lift him into the cargo hold?"

"We'll soon enough see, now won't we?" snapped Denham with the conviction of a determined man, one to whom no obstacle was too daunting.

Captain Englehorn came up on them, saying, "It's all settled. The natives will help with the hauling. They possess strong backs and a burning desire to not be around Kong when he comes to."

"How long do you suppose that will be?" Driscoll asked, snapping back to ship's business.

Denham scratched his head. "Hard to say. We got a few more hours, at least."

"Let's hope it's enough," Driscoll barked.

They had wound the great anchor chains around Kong's hairy wrists and ankles, and men of both races took up the weighty links, draping them across their bare shoulders.

Jack Driscoll ramrodded the work gang, calling out orders, which Englehorn translated into the native tongue.

And so, the dragging commenced. Much of it was over rain-slick grass and the rest beach sand, so there was positive traction at the start. The fine-ground sand produced only a modest hindrance, thanks to the cushion of coarse hair covering Kong.

"This is how they built the pyramids of Egypt!" Denham boasted. "By the sweat of their brows."

Kong breathed laboriously, oblivious to his fate. Breezes off the lagoon played with his stiff and seemingly lifeless hair, and set nearby palm crowns rustling with a dry, macabre muttering.

ANN DARROW watched from the starboard rail of the *Wanderer* in the company of Lumpy the cook and Ignatz, Lumpy's pet monkey, who was eyeing Kong with chattering fascination. Ann's sunburned features were still tense from her ordeal.

"Do you think they will succeed?" she asked breathlessly.

"Startin' to appear that way, damn it," spat Lumpy, scratching his hairless head. He was attired in his habitual frayed trousers. Bare to the waist, his stringy muscles and lath-thin ribs made him look as if he were held together by baling wire. The top of his bald skull was so sunburnt that it resembled an angry light bulb.

"What do you mean?" asked Ann. "Are you afraid those chains won't hold him?"

"No, Miss Darrow. I'm afraid that they will. And we'll have

to transit half of the Indian Ocean and all of the Atlantic with that big beast in the ship's belly."

"It's a fearful thought," agreed Ann, grimacing.

"You ain't kiddin'! Who do you think is gonna have to *feed* that overgrown gorilla all them choppy nautical miles!"

In spite of herself, Ann Darrow laughed. Then, a troubled thought crossed her smooth brow, darkening her expression.

"What will they feed him, Lumpy? He's enormous."

"That's another worry I just inherited," sighed the cook. "No one planned for a prize this big. I'll bet that behemoth of a baboon eats half his weight every darned day."

The thought of such a voracious appetite made Ann shiver despite her best efforts. Turning away, she sought the comfort of her private cabin amidships.

A LABORIOUS hour had crawled by. The equatorial sun continued its climb toward noon. Here and there, great winged forms took to the air. Pterodactyls, their hatchet-shaped heads craned about on spindly necks, blood-red eyes seeking prey.

The work gang stood in the mud and silt of the cove now, bare feet digging ankle deep, chains splashing and sloshing as they hauled Kong onto the foundering raft. Or tried to.

It was futile. A ponderous foot all but shattered one corner of the raft and they had to stop while repairs were made. Sailorly oaths fouled the morning air.

"What if he wakes up in the middle of all this?" Driscoll asked his skipper.

"The chains might hold, or they might not..." allowed Englehorn ruminatively. He had taken a plug of tobacco into his mouth and was energetically masticating it. This was the only outward sign that the seasoned sea captain was agitated; normally, he was as placid as a cow.

"Then what?"

"No choice but to shoot the brute. I've got a Tommy gun in my cabin. That should settle him."

"I half hope it will. Hauling that monster all the way to New York port is inviting trouble. I never signed on for this."

"Denham won't listen to reason," Englehorn muttered. "He's got a fever that won't break."

Driscoll scowled. "Well, let's hope and pray we don't catch it in a fatal way. Get what I mean?"

Englehorn nodded somberly. He was an old man, and had sailed all seven seas, and many lesser bodies. But he had never run into a storm such as this, nor contemplated ferrying a cargo of the magnitude of Kong. But he had a contract with the brash filmmaker and, in the old salt's mind, it was as unbreakable as his word.

While repairs continued, Carl Denham strolled over, looking every inch a man determined to have his way.

"Listen! Once we get that super gorilla onto the ship, we're going to have to figure out a way to keep him alive all the way back to New York."

Englehorn eyed the filmmaker with a trace of resistance. "And how do you propose to do that, Mr. Denham?"

Another man would have been stopped cold by the question. Not Carl Denham.

"Well, when you come down to it, he's just an overgrown baboon, ain't he? Just thirty times bigger. What do monkeys eat? Bananas. Coconuts. Forage. Then he'll need water. That should do it!"

Englehorn looked dubious of countenance. "With all due respect, Mr. Denham, we don't know what this *Neanderthaler* subsists on."

Denham waved in the direction of the toiling, sweaty natives. "They'll tell you! But whatever it is, we'll need a ton of it. A literal ton. Hell, maybe two tons."

Acting as if he had solved the problem for all time, Carl Denham stormed off to supervise raft repairs.

After the filmmaker was out of earshot, Jack Driscoll said to his skipper, "Who does he think he is? And who does he think we are—miracle workers? To gather up a ton of food for that gargantuan chimpanzee is the work of a week. We don't have a week. We may not have a day."

Englehorn sighed. "I can't disagree with your thinking, my boy. But Mr. Denham is paying the freight on this voyage, and we will have to do our best to satisfy him."

"Satisfy him! I'd like to take a poke at him. I'd like to take several. But I suppose when he came to, Denham would be just as stubborn as before."

Englehorn rumbled, "If you're so dead-set on taking a poke at him, kindly hold off until we dock in Hoboken."

Turning worried eyes toward the great hairy brute sprawled over the makeshift raft, Jack Driscoll muttered, "From the look of things, making New York City is a pipe dream. It's three months back. How are we supposed to keep Kong knocked out all that way? We're practically out of gas bombs. I think there are four left."

"Well, Mr. Driscoll," Captain Englehorn said heavily, "I have no answers for you. I can only tell you that we must try. And we will try. The honor of the *Wanderer* rests upon our trying."

"It's suicide, I tell you," Driscoll said hotly. "It's madder than any voyage ever contemplated since Ahab. You know it. And I know it. Can't you talk sense into his thick skull?"

Englehorn eyed the lowering granite countenance of Skull Mountain rearing up behind the beach-fronting native village, and moved his tobacco plug around in his mouth.

"No more than I could appeal to *that*," he sighed. "If I could reach him, I would do so. But you know our situation. The *Wanderer* has been limping toward bankruptcy ever since the stock market crashed. She would've been sold at auction if it weren't for Carl Denham coming along with this mad enterprise." The Skipper eyed his first mate levelly. "These are sink-or-swim times, Mr. Driscoll. And for better or for worse, we must all learn to swim in unaccustomed and uncomfortable waters."

That ended the argument, so Jack Driscoll marched off to finish supervising the raft work.

AN HOUR later, the colossal raft was fully buoyant once more. And so the hauling resumed. Kong slumbered through it all, showing no signs of awakening. The possibility, however, hovered over the entire work gang. The perspiration that soaked their bodies was not entirely the work of the tropical sun. They worked with an iron will, but deep in their haunted eyes there was fear. It was a terrible thing to see, but it lent extra strength to their bones and muscles, and fortified their resolve to complete their preposterous task.

By dint of hauling and maneuvering the massive raft, they managed to get Kong's monster feet into the water, and carefully positioned the floundering raft beneath them.

Blocks of balsa wood had been hastily hacked and shaped by machete blades. Many were inserted into the interstices of the makeshift flotation device. Crew stood by to add more.

There were several terrible moments where they thought the monster's weight would be too much for the raft to bear. For no sooner was Kong jockeyed into position than he sank like the Rock of Gibraltar.

Whether it was the monster's own natural buoyancy, or the buoyancy of the raft, they never knew. But after beast and raft had slipped into the waters of the cove, both arose once more.

Kong was soaked to his bristling roots, but still he did not move. The trichloride gas had been potent stuff.

For fifteen long minutes, they watched for signs that the trauma of immersion had stirred the instinct for survival in the giant anthropoid. Instead, Kong floated serenely atop the fantastic log raft.

Carl Denham gave a triumphant shout and exclaimed, "There she floats! I told you it would work! Now all we have to do is float him out to the ship."

Jack Driscoll and Captain Englehorn exchanged uneasy glances, but neither man's expression changed a particle.

"That's all we have to do," parroted Driscoll in an undertone. "Just float that monster out through the breakwater rocks our ship can't safely navigate, and winch him up into the hold. That's all. Shouldn't take more than ten minutes. A half-hour, tops."

Driscoll's laugh was low and ragged; edgy desperation threaded it.

By this juncture, the natives who had lived their entire lives in awe of the powerful Kong were equally impressed by the white men who had come far beyond the blue horizon which formed the boundary of their life experience and knowledge.

They had seen their beast-god brought low, and now Kong was being floated off as if he were mere felled lumber. It was astounding. At the same time, they did not care to be around when the dreaded Kong again opened his eyes.

So they ran their dugouts into the water and, using the vine and grass ropes that they had woven by hand, lashed their canoes to the edges of the raft, and prepared to paddle Kong out through the treacherous shoals to the waiting tramp steamer.

Turning to his first mate, Captain Englehorn advised, "We'll use the motor launch to guide the raft along; the natives and their paddles should help us steer clear of the rocks."

Driscoll grunted. "You make it sound as easy as baking an apple pie."

"That's enough, Mr. Driscoll," said Englehorn stiffly. "We have committed to this enterprise, and we must see it through."

"Even if it costs every man-jack of the crew their miserable lives," Driscoll muttered. "I understand, Skipper. I'm on your side. We got a job to do and we'll do it, come hell or high water—and maybe worse than that."

While they maneuvered the motor launch into position at the head of the sprawling raft, a strange figure floated out of the jungle, and watched the proceedings intently with thin eyes.

This figure was short in stature, dressed in barbaric finery, and stood so still no human eye perceived her. For it was an old woman, her age impossible to guess, her ancient features a webwork of wrinkles in which only the opal-black eyes seemed to harbor vitality.

She was not as dark as many of the natives of Skull Mountain Island, although her skin possessed a weathered and tanned hue that suggested she was a native of this lost island. She belonged to another category entirely, one possessing high cheekbones and wise eyes. Her hair was a thin cloud resembling milkweed.

After absorbing all that she could, the ancient crone drifted down from the grassy verge on which she stood, her sandaled feet padding with the casual confidence of one who walked upon her native soil.

She had studied the white men intently, and by some instinct walked up to the one she felt would listen. It was not Captain Englehorn, nor was it Carl Denham.

Instead, she approached Jack Driscoll, who stood apart from the others, smoking a cigarette with furious intensity.

"You cannot do this blasphemy you contemplate," she said without preamble.

Driscoll turned, and the cigarette fell from his shocked lips.

"Who in mercy's name are you?" he demanded, stamping out the smoldering butt, lest it start a grass fire.

"I am called by many names, all of which means Storyteller. I am the keeper of the history of this island. This is the land of my ancestors, going back untold generations. We are called the Tagatu. Call me Penjaga."

Her English was strangely accented, the vowels too round and her consonants too flat, yet the old woman was understandable.

"You're not one of these local boys," remarked Driscoll thoughtfully.

"I am the—guardian of Kong."

Jack Driscoll couldn't help himself. He burst out laughing.

"You! You don't look like you could keep a parrot, never mind a thirty-foot gorilla. Say, how do you come to speak English?"

"You are not the first white men to brave Skull Mountain Island. Many have come. Most have perished here. Pirates. Seafarers. Common castaways."

Driscoll nodded to himself. "The old map Englehorn has in his cabin must've been made by one of those jokers. So what is it you want?"

Her voice turned threatening. "Leave this place. Abandon Kong. Go far away. Do not return. Tell no one. It will be better for all."

"I don't mind telling you, old woman," grunted Driscoll, his eyes windy. "You and I are in complete agreement. But I'm not running the show. And the decision's been made. Kong's shipping out with us. Nothing can stop that."

"Kong will not survive a journey of any duration."

"My sentiments exactly," clucked Driscoll. "But what can I do about it? Nothing! I'm just a cog in a machine that's about to break down from overload. Nothing you or I can do about it, either."

Penjaga the Storyteller regarded Jack Driscoll with her wise eyes for a very long time without speaking. Thin lips moved as if trembling on the edge of speech, but she kept her counsel. All during this, she studied the First Mate's features, as if measuring every square inch of his sun-and-windburned epidermis.

When at last she spoke, Penjaga had changed her portentous tone.

"Kong will not survive long in your hands. He has wounds that need mending. Wounds I know how to heal. But I can help him overcome your foolishness. Heed me, and I will help you white men keep him alive for as long as necessary."

"You can!" Driscoll returned brusquely. "Mind telling me how?"

Dangling from a leather belt was a faded green pouch that looked as if it were sewn of dinosaur skin. Reaching down, the old woman lifted it into view and said, "I possess herbs that will keep him drowsy and weak, as well as a needle and catgut with which to sew up his wounds. I know how to tame the great one."

"Is that right?" barked Driscoll.

"Yes. I speak the truth. My people knew all there is to know about Kong. My ancestors long ago built the great Wall that contained Kong. To preserve his life, I will share this knowledge with you."

Up to this point, Jack Driscoll had not been taking the old woman seriously. But hearing her steady tones slowly altered his thinking.

"Do you know what the big ape likes to eat?"

Penjaga nodded. "I do. And if you wish to carry him to a faraway land, you will require this knowledge. Also, you will need me to direct my people while you are here. Therefore, I make you this bargain. Take me with you, and I will keep Kong alive."

"What's in it for you?"

"I told you. I am the lawful guardian of Kong. I am also the storyteller of my people. Kong's story is intertwined with that of my people. I must keep it safe and see events to their end if we are to survive. For Kong's fate will influence our destiny. I am old, but my tale—and that of my people—is not yet concluded. I will go with you, and together we will keep Kong alive."

"Well," said Driscoll ironically, "if you put it that way, I guess it's settled then."

The old woman failed to detect the humor in the First Mate's voice. "Yes, it is settled. Penjaga will go where Kong goes."

The seriousness with which the old woman presented herself infiltrated Jack Driscoll's skeptical mind. But it was the practicality of her offer that in the end persuaded him.

"Why don't you follow me?" he told her in a suddenly sober tone of voice. "Let me introduce you to some fellows. I'm getting the idea that you might come in handy after all…."

Chapter 3

"CAPTAIN ENGLEHORN, I have someone you might like to meet," announced First Mate Driscoll as he approached the sandy shore where the work party was engaged in determining the safest route through the lagoon fronting Skull Mountain's brooding rock countenance.

The Skipper and Carl Denham were having words over the task at hand. They turned, and various expressions rode their startled features.

"Well, what have we here?" rumbled Englehorn, wintry eyes crinkling at sight of the old woman.

"Says she's the guardian of Kong," returned Driscoll. "Calls herself Penjaga. Claims she can help us."

Carl Denham made a skeptical noise deep in his throat, demanding, "How is it she speaks our lingo?"

But Captain Englehorn proved wiser. "Ma'am, how can you help us?" he inquired.

"You have put Kong to sleep. I can keep him that way for as long as necessary."

"With what, your magic juju stick?" snorted Denham, planting both hammy fists on his hips.

Penjaga riveted the filmmaker with such a cold look that he immediately swallowed his derision.

"She also says she can help us to feed him," added Driscoll.

"Well, now that's something that perks up my interest," admitted Denham. He strolled up to the old woman, towering over her. "Spill it, what does the big bruiser eat?"

"Kong is the lord of Skull Mountain Island," Penjaga said severely. "He eats whatever he wishes."

"Be specific; we haven't time for riddles."

"Kong enjoys bamboo. Coconut. Plantain. Crabs and turtles. The flesh of certain lizards. Many plants and grasses. I will point them out to you. You must gather up all you can. His appetite is very great."

Driscoll said, "From what she says, we'll have to fill every cargo hold, and squeeze the surplus into the coal bunkers, as well. Then there will be no room for Kong."

Penjaga interrupted, "You white men know how to fish?"

"Of course we do!" Denham burst out. "What do you take us for?"

The old crone did not answer that; possibly she did not understand what was meant. But her stiff expression suggested otherwise.

"Kong will eat fish. He may not always like the taste of cold flesh. But if you are willing to fish, he will eat what you give to him."

Thinking of practicalities, First Mate Driscoll said, "It will be worse than the Augean stables in that hold after only a few weeks out."

"We will worry about that later," snapped Denham. "Let's get to it. First, we've got to steer that raft through those nasty rocks."

It was a daunting prospect, for Skull Mountain Island was surrounded by rocky reefs and shoals which formed a natural barrier around the mist-shrouded island that was all-but-unknown to modern mariners.

There was a gap in the stony breakers choking the lagoon, which they had first reached in their dories. That was one thing. Maneuvering the great raft and its slumbering occupant through those treacherous granite fangs was not work for the faint-hearted.

"We'll concern ourselves with his forage after the creature is safely in the hold," decided Captain Englehorn. "If we can't load him on board, we won't need to feed him."

That made perfect sense to everyone. Even Carl Denham did not disagree.

The survivors of the shore party waded out into the water, eyeing the sleeping Kong with undiminished nervousness. The brute slept on, oblivious to everything. If ever a mountain slept, Kong was that mountain. But his nearness reminded them of a dormant volcano. Should it rumble back to life, all would be lost....

They reached the motor launch, which had been maneuvered about until it bobbed at the head of the immense raft. Climbing into the rocking boat first, Driscoll assisted the old woman aboard.

Giving the motor a spin, Jack Driscoll took the tiller firmly in hand. The dory began muttering forward, her stern foaming.

On either side, uneasy-eyed natives manning their dugouts started paddling in an eerily synchronized manner. It seemed as if they had been practicing for this day all of their lives.

The raft lurched, moving ahead. Kong was leaving his ancient home.

In the bow, Carl Denham asked Captain Englehorn, "How much do you think he weighs?"

"I would judge better than ten tons. Possibly fifteen."

"Will the ship's cranes manage that load?"

Englehorn shook his grizzled head. "Individually, I doubt it. But working together, we have a chance."

"I don't like to hear that kind of talk," snapped the burly showman.

"What kind of talk?" returned the Skipper shortly. "This is a practical matter."

"Where I come from," Denham asserted, stabbing his chest with one thumb for emphasis, "it's do or die. My whole career is at stake. Get me? Every dime I own is sunk into this enterprise."

Englehorn nodded silently. "And the lives of my crew and the future of my ship are equally at risk."

"Exactly! That's why we can't fail. It's not in the cards, and we can't afford it. So let's start thinking positively, shall we?"

"You have a point, Mr. Denham," allowed Englehorn. "You have a point. We must exclude failure from our vocabulary."

Denham beamed broadly. "Well, now we are talking!"

"Especially if we want to survive," murmured Englehorn half under his breath.

Denham suddenly lost his enthusiasm. The Captain's quiet words were chilling. But the ambitious moviemaker did not dwell on them. He simply fell silent and stayed that way for a very long time.

AS THE bizarre procession approached the black rocks, a pair of pterodactyls glided by.

Swooping, they dipped and cavorted in the air, beady red eyes stabbing downward.

Driscoll watched them warily. From past experience, he knew the great winged creatures to be fish eaters. Swooping close to the chop, they spied silvery scales near the surface and plunged in their needle beaks in unexpectedly, to pluck a squirming meal from the surrounding waters. But these specimens did not appear interested in breakfast.

Their avid orbs were upon Kong. Only Kong.

"I don't like the way they're eyeing us," muttered the First Mate to his captain.

"Think nothing of it," returned Englehorn. "Prehistoric vultures, nothing more. Nothing less."

Abruptly, one dipped a wing. Like a membranous kite catching a downdraft, the angular creature flashed overhead, casting a morning shadow as large as a small airplane.

Everyone ducked, fearing an attack. It was good that they did so, for their clothes were soon spattered by a malodorous goo that was unpleasantly hot.

At the tiller, his broad back to the trailing raft, Jack Driscoll got the worst of it.

"What is this!" he roared, shucking off his uniform jacket. Before he could examine it, a second load of guano plopped down atop Kong's unprotected chest, forcing natives and white men alike to duck.

Giving off shrill cries, the two pterodactyls, having relieved themselves on their former antagonist, sailed off, whip-thin tails making them resemble bat-winged devils of Earth's prehistoric past.

The natives shook their dark fists at the retreating forms, and the chief took up his war spear and cast it all in one smooth, continuous motion. It missed, but not by very much. One pterodactyl veered wildly at the sound of the missile hissing past.

"What were you saying a minute ago, Mr. Driscoll?" Englehorn said tartly. "Something about the Augean stables...."

"They're giving Kong a sendoff fitting for their age-old feud!" crowed Denham. "Well, that's all over and done with now. Kong is ours!"

"Kong belongs to no one," murmured Penjaga who, alone of the dory occupants, had not been soiled by the pterodactyl's final insult to the former monarch of Skull Mountain Island.

AS THE equatorial sun continued climbing toward the noon hour, vapor arose from the inert mountain of hair and muscle-meat that was Kong.

It was an eerie sight, for the monster lay unmoving, except for the slow and rhythmic rise and fall of his massive chest. His nostrils distended with every slow exhalation; otherwise Kong did not stir.

At sight of the ghostly mist arising from the hairy ogre, the natives of Skull Mountain Island showed their superstitious side.

"Kong! Kong!"

"What were they jabbering, Captain?" asked Jack Driscoll.

Englehorn explained, "They think Kong is dying, and that mist is the soul of the creature escaping his mortal body."

Denham grunted, "Haven't they ever seen tropical steam rising before?"

"Of course they have," snapped Driscoll. "But they've never seen Kong in this condition, and the steam is going to work on their imagination."

Captain Englehorn turned to the natives in their dugout canoes and made explanations in their own language. The natives soon subsided, and it was well that they did so. The work that lay ahead was daunting and difficult.

At the tiller, First Mate Driscoll carefully guided the boat through the breakwater rocks, navigating with an iron-handed calm that would have impressed any sailor on earth.

When necessary, he pointed starboard or port, whereby the natives could change the pitch of their paddling so as to keep the great raft and its anthropoid cargo on course.

All the while, Kong's hirsute form gave up ghostly tendrils of vapor.

"Losing that water weight," commented Denham, "might make Kong easier to lift."

Captain Englehorn remarked, "You may be right at that, Mr. Denham. The test that lies before us is a dangerous one."

"Aw, we'll get it done!"

Englehorn said nothing to this. He was measuring the distance between the motor launch and the *Wanderer,* whose angular profile stood out beyond the outermost shoal rock. He reckoned it to be less than three-quarters of a nautical mile.

Threading the black rocks proved to be the least of it. A great deal of the credit went to Jack Driscoll, who knew just enough of the treachery of Skull Mountain Lagoon to shear off from the half-submerged reefs before he encountered them.

When at last they put the stony fangs behind them, Denham turned and whistled low in open admiration. "Snappy job of navigating. I'll give you that, Driscoll."

The First Mate did not respond in any kind. His searching eyes were cast on the deck of the *Wanderer*, which boasted an A-frame derrick capable of lifting cargo weighing several tons. But that was cargo secured in boxes and bales, not living meat and bone distributed along a thirty-foot tall frame.

Driscoll knew that he would need both booms if he hoped to hoist Kong aboard.

Now came the first truly difficult portion of the transfer.

Captain Englehorn took command at this point. First, he gave his first mate a chopping hand signal. No words were necessary.

Driscoll cut the outboard motor, and gestured to the native canoe-men to cease paddling.

Englehorn backed that command with quick words in their language.

Clear of the rocks, the great raft slowed, jostling the motor launch. It was moving along under its own momentum now, and all hands got to work cutting away the lashings.

Driscoll was the first to chop away at the launch towline rope. There was no time to do anything fancier. Engaging the outboard motor, he sent the launch scooting ahead and out of the way of the still-traveling raft.

While he was departing, the natives cut and hacked away at their grass and vine ropes, freeing themselves of the great log contraption. Once this was done, one by one, they pushed their dugouts away, using the blunt end of their war spears.

This was smoothly accomplished. Very quickly, the colossal raft was bobbing along, unguided by man.

Separating, the small vessels stood off while their occupants watched the raft's gliding progress. The raft was on a direct heading for the port side of the *Wanderer*. The only question remained: did it have sufficient momentum to make contact with the rust-streaked hull?

As they observed the raft's progress, it seemed for a long time that the matter could go either way. The vaporous condensation evaporating off the drying fur of Kong was greatly diminished now. The tropical heat had evaporated the greater portion of seawater which had infiltrated the monster's coarse black fur.

At last, the raft bumped the *Wanderer*, jarring her only a little. The great flotation arrangement of tarred logs and bamboo crosspieces bounced backward, but not by very much. Mere feet, not yards. It held together—not a certain thing until that carefully controlled collision.

"Smooth work," commented Denham. He was beaming. The dynamic director was seeing the possibilities while all others were concentrating on the peril of the mad undertaking.

Starting up the launch motor, Driscoll piloted the lean craft toward the rusty old tramper, while Englehorn waved the natives back, calling to them in their own language primitive expressions of gratitude. In truth, the old salt did not want the natives clambering onto his ship, for fear that they might overrun it.

Showing expressions that mingled relief with disappointment, the natives rapidly turned their dugouts around and made for land—and for the familiar safety of their wooded island with its great stockade wall and brooding skull knob overlooking all.

As Jack Driscoll sent the launch sweeping around, he measured the situation. Kong's great form was evenly distributed upon the buoyant framework. The raft was oriented with Kong's massive feet pointed at the old freighter's hull. Exactly as planned.

To Captain Englehorn, he suggested, "If we can drop lines

to the raft, we can jockey it around until Kong's head is pointed toward the stern."

"That would be the best way of lifting the brute," admitted Englehorn.

Denham remarked, "If you drop a line to the chain linking his ankle bracelets, and another to his wrist chain, I'll bet fifty bucks that the Beast goes up in one smooth pull."

Driscoll shook his head. "No, that raft will serve as a pallet. We'll hoist up the raft, and Kong will come up with it."

Glowering, Denham charged back to the dory's stern and demanded, "What if the damn raft breaks? Did you think of that?"

"I did," returned Driscoll firmly. "I thought of that a lot. But those cranes are designed for cargo, not something the size of a Greek cyclops. Better to lift the raft, and hope she holds, than risk Kong pulling down our booms if his unsecured weight shifts and becomes unmanageable."

"But he's not strapped down!"

"We'll see what we can do about that," Driscoll said.

Denham was not satisfied. He whirled on Captain Englehorn, bellowing, "I don't like the way this is shaping up. I don't think it's safe!"

The Skipper said methodically, "I agree with you, Mr. Denham. It is patently not safe. But Mr. Driscoll is correct in his estimation. The raft will provide stability, and stability is the thing we most value in moving loads."

"Kong is not a load!" barked back Denham. "Kong is worth a million bucks. And I won't lose him just because that raft is more convenient for your work crew."

Carl Denham and Captain Englehorn locked gazes, which seemed to strike sparks in the morning air.

The Skipper was a long time in responding, and when he did so, his tone was subdued but firm.

"I am sorry, Mr. Denham. I am the master of this vessel, and Mr. Driscoll is the best first mate I have ever known. If his professional judgment is that the raft will hold, I must abide by it. For that is my judgment, as well."

"Now listen here!" Denham erupted.

"The matter is closed, Mr. Denham," snapped Englehorn. "I will not have the *Wanderer* capsize if the loading goes amiss."

"I tell you, that raft won't hold!" Denham complained.

"Then I suggest you return to the island until my crew sorts out the matter."

By this time, Carl Denham's face was a shade of red verging dangerously close to purple. He looked as if he was on the threshold of an apoplectic stroke.

But the film director knew when he was licked. Captain Englehorn was not going to budge in this particular instance, and no power on earth could move him off his convictions.

"If it's all the same to you," Denham said in a dispirited voice. "I'll stick around and watch. It's only my future at stake, after all."

"Watch," rejoined the Captain, "but do not interfere. You may be a capable director of cameramen and actors, but we will direct ship's operations without interference."

Behind Carl Denham's back, First Mate Driscoll fought to keep his smile of satisfaction under control. This was the first time in three months that the hard-charging filmmaker had not gotten his way by bluster and demand. Jack Driscoll sincerely hoped this was the beginning of a trend.

Chapter 4

JACK DRISCOLL maneuvered the muttering motor launch to the *Wanderer's* scabby stern, and one by one, the shore party went up the Jacob's ladder, Captain Englehorn first.

There was some discussion about lowering a boatswain's chair with which to hoist up the old woman named Penjaga but, while the advisability of getting her to sit balanced on what amounted to a jury-rigged plank was argued, the passenger in question pushed two startled sailors aside and clambered up the accommodation ladder with the bony agility of a monkey a fraction of her years.

"She don't let nothing stop her, does she?" a sailor remarked to Driscoll.

"No, she does not," returned the First Mate, pushing the sailor to go next.

Driscoll clambered up last. When he reached the deck, Driscoll was met by the boatswain, Beaumont by name.

The man's eyes were round from studying the recumbent form of Kong, whose bristling black coat of hair was marred by numerous wounds and healed scars suggestive of ferocious past battles. One livid line burned down the right cheek, and a deeper one was gouged into the beast's right shoulder. His massive fingers resembled monster talons, the fingernails freshly cracked and broken from combat with the Tyrannosaurus rex.

The boatswain's leathery features looked a few shades paler than when Driscoll last laid eyes on him.

"Mean lookin' brute, ain't he?" he remarked dryly.

"I'll tell a man!" Driscoll returned gruffly. "And it's our job to yank him on board and keep him tied down."

The boatswain was not entirely surprised, as he barely flinched at this information. "What port will we drop him off at?"

Driscoll gave him a withering stare. "Hoboken—where do you think?"

"I was kinda hoping for Madagascar," admitted the seaman. "Do you think we can haul him all that way?"

"I'm getting damn tired of that question!" Suppressing his anger at the prospect before him, Driscoll snarled, "I'm not yet sure we can get him on board this hooker. Now here's the lay of it. We'll have to secure Kong to the raft, then hook the raft up to the lifting arm. Hoist the raft up, clear the well deck, then lower him into the Number Three hold, and that will be that."

"That will be something, all right," whistled the boatswain. "But if any crew can do it, ours can."

"That's the spirit, Boats!" returned Driscoll. Fishing into his coat for a pack of cigarettes, he carefully lit one, as if preparing himself for the ordeal ahead. His arm still throbbed from his near-fatal brush with Kong; fortunately, no bone had been broken, merely wrenched.

Quickly, seamen went down ropes, landed on the raft, and tiptoed around the recumbent monster. One sailor staggered, seemed about to faint.

Driscoll called down, "What's the matter with him?"

"This big ape stinks to high heaven!" hollered back the boatswain.

"It's that gas!" snapped Driscoll. "The stuff we knocked him out with. It's still in his fur. Evaporation is releasing it. Get back up here, Boats. He'll need time to dry off."

Hearing this exchange, Carl Denham charged up, his ruddy face growing pale.

"What's the holdup? We haven't all day!"

"Residual gas is seeping out of his fur," said Driscoll slowly. "It got to one of the men. We're going to have to let the monster cool off."

"Cool off! What if he wakes up?"

"If he wakes up, we'll have more on our hands than we will know what to do with. But until it's safe to be around him, Kong can't be properly secured."

Biting back his complaints, Denham stalked off in search of the captain—seeking an appeal that no doubt would fall on deaf ears, practicalities being what they were.

When he reappeared, it was evident that the bullheaded director had gotten nowhere with the Old Man. For Denham became busy setting up his bulky black Bell & Howell 2709 movie camera, beginning with the folding wooden tripod. He had already loaded a precious canister of film into the mechanism.

"Somebody let me know when the time comes," Denham bellowed to no one in particular. Then he found a shady spot in the shadow of a great tulip-mouthed deck ventilator, pulled his battered old campaign hat low over his forehead and sat down to take a nap.

Another hour passed until the sailors were able to brave the raft without keeling over.

Lifting his head, one flashed the O.K. sign, calling up, "Let's get to it!"

Driscoll gave orders to the boatswain, who relayed them to his work crew, and then the big derrick boom swung out and lowered its hook. In accordance with marine procedure, the radio mast had been lowered to the deck to avoid it being snapped by the swinging boom.

The deck gang was practiced in their skills. Lines were attached to the seesawing lifting-arm hook and run by the deck gang to safety hooks secured to eyebolts that had been installed into the framing timbers on dry land. Two men fixed these at the four points of the raft, while a second group worked hard to tie down the slumbering giant, paying special attention to his hairy arms and legs, moving them with crowbars to distribute the apish brute's weight evenly before making his limbs fast. Shackles had been hammered out of sheet steel by the ship's mechanical foreman and fitted around hairy wrists and ankles.

"The monster is secure!" called up the boatswain.

At the rail, Driscoll nodded and turned to the lifting arm. He gave the hand signal to the derrick operator and winch driver to commence hoisting.

Here is where the work was most perilous. The swinging derrick arm and steam donkey had to work in unison, not too fast, nor too slow, in order to keep the load balanced. A seasoned crew could hoist ordinary baled freight or crated cargo up to the level of the well deck, clearing its high steel sides without a hitch, while a freighter like the *Wanderer* was docked. But the old vessel was not snug in port, but anchored on the open ocean. Every wave and comber striking her rusty hull made every part of her sway drunkenly—derrick, anchoring deck and precariously balanced cargo.

Leaning over the rail, hoping for the best, Jack Driscoll watched the operation with his massive knuckles turning white as bone chips.

The raft began to shake, lift. It broke free of the chop with a rushing sound as water cascaded from every timber and lashing like a sea serpent drooling.

Four sailors—brave souls—stood at the eyebolts at the four corners of the raft, holding onto the hoisting cables, serving as lookouts, but also ready to move fast if the balance weight of the makeshift pallet shifted. Their job was to counterbalance any tipping—if they could.

"Look at the size of those mitts!" marveled one. "If he wakes up—"

"We'd be crushed to a pulp," finished another. "So let's skip talkin' about it. I've got enough jitters as it is."

There was not that much clearance between the edge of the raft and the scabby hull of the freighter, and twice the raft banged against the hull, giving everyone a start.

"Steady, boys, steady," cautioned Driscoll. "It's crazy, but it's working."

Almost as soon as the words were out of his mouth, there came a grunting sound, a splintering crack like dry thunder. Lightning, were it composed of wood and not energy, would make such a noise.

"Stop! Stop!" yelled Driscoll.

A lever was yanked, halting the steam winch. The frantic-faced First Mate peered over the rail to assess the damage.

"I can't see anything," he yelled down. "What broke?"

The two sailors released their cables and moved about, gingerly looking for fractures and breakage. One found something.

"One of the center logs split longitudinally," he called up.

"Holding?" yelled back Driscoll.

"So far."

"Good. Think it will bear the strain?"

The seaman shrugged his shoulders hopelessly. "Your guess is as good as mine, sir."

Captain Englehorn bustled up, and took his First Mate's terse report.

"Still time to abandon cargo, Cap'n," Driscoll concluded.

Captain Englehorn was long considering the matter. Carl Denham watched anxiously at a distance, for once afraid to interfere, lest the force of his belligerent personality tip things in the wrong direction for the wrong reasons.

"Mate," Englehorn said placidly, "resume hoisting. If she breaks apart, that will conclude operations."

At the stern where he was filming, Carl Denham overheard these words. He released a sigh of relief that was audible clear to the rust-stained bow.

Driscoll gave the order to resume hoisting. The winch driver engaged his controls. Gushing steam, the hammering steam donkey made whining sounds, and the raft lifted anew.

All ears were alert for any sound of warning—for the deck crew knew that they would hear trouble before they could see it.

The raft strained at many points, crackling like a distant fire. Twice, they were sure that something would snap from the uncommon stress. At one point, a sudden snarling and snapping told of a lashing that had parted explosively.

Yet the raft held.

"It's a miracle," breathed the boatswain to Driscoll.

Jack nodded. "That raft was designed to float, not bear Kong's weight unbuoyed by water."

As they watched, the crew retreating, the cargo derrick brought the ungainly contrivance above the momentarily level deck, and with exceeding care, shifted it until it started hovering over the open cargo hatchway amidships. This was Hold Number Three. The largest in the ship, it had been extended into Hold Number Four, doubling the size of either to over fifty feet, and had been lined with stainless steel.

The boatswain turned to Jack Driscoll and the First Mate nodded back.

At a signal, the raft was winched down into the hold, and the men who dropped down with it scrambled to release the safety hooks once the raft was firmly in place.

They were no fools. They rode the hooks back up onto deck, rather than remain in the darkness with the hairy beast-god from Skull Mountain Island.

Deck workers rushed to close the cargo hatch doors. Electric winches helped, the massive steel doors being too heavy for manpower alone, sealing Kong within. A massive tarpaulin was hastily unrolled over the hatch, and secured with long wooden battens, ensuring that the hold and its titanic occupant would be protected from the elements.

"She's all secure!" the seaman called out.

Carl Denham hurried over to them, shook their hands vigorously and seemed intent on shaking the hand of every crewman aboard the tramp freighter, promising bonuses in a hearty, overblown voice.

Driscoll turned to his boatswain and remarked dryly, "Now all we have to figure out is how to feed him."

"He looks like he could eat a ton of roughage a day," the boatswain said wonderingly.

"That he does," agreed Driscoll morosely. "And it won't be all bananas, Boats. That big gorilla eats meat. Dinosaurs. The Stegosaurus is lunch to him. For his supper, he'll want nothing less than a Tyrannosaurus Rex—raw."

"I draw the line at bringing dinosaurs aboard the ship," joked the boatswain.

"Maybe an Allosaurus will do," returned Driscoll without humor.

The First Mate walked away, leaving the boatswain blinking stupidly, wondering if he was going to have to hunt up a live Allosaurus.

Chapter 5

NO ALLOSAURUS was discovered by the foraging party led by a coxswain named Coldwell.

Armed with machetes and rifles, they collected palm fronds and all the greenery that could be harvested, as directed by First Mate Driscoll.

Coconuts and bananas grew in profusion upon Skull Mountain Island. The latter were huge freak plantains. Relying on their simple knowledge of anthropoids, they collected as many as they could. They picked only the greenest bananas, knowing that the longer they lasted, the better.

The work gang had some difficulty harvesting coconuts, owing to the coconut crab population of Skull Mountain Island. These hard-shelled monsters grew as large as dogs, and guarded their main food source jealously.

After a period of nervous uncertainty, the local natives, fully understanding the white men's intentions, pitched in. This assistance greatly accelerated the process.

Boatload after boatload of roughage was thus transported to the *Wanderer* and stowed away in the Number One Hold, forward of Hold Number Three, where Kong rested in his stainless steel sarcophagus, oblivious to the frantic shipboard activity centering on him.

Pacing the poop deck of the ramshackle freighter, Carl Denham watched these furious activities through a pair of binoculars lent to him by Jack Driscoll.

The First Mate had remained on board in the belief that his presence was needed in the event that something went amiss in Hold Number Three.

"When are we going to raise the hook?" Denham demanded of Driscoll.

"Not until we scour Skull Mountain Island for every pound of edible matter," returned Driscoll impatiently.

The film director snorted. "The longer we dawdle, the sooner he wakes up."

Driscoll snatched the binoculars from Denham's nervous hands and said, "He's bound to wake up sooner than later. And the more food we have to give him, the more content he'll be."

"Content! Kong can no more be content than you can wrestle a Stegosaurus with your bare hands. It's not in him, I tell you!"

"No," Driscoll admitted slowly, "I will grant you that. But between the need to feed him and the danger certain to come of his empty stomach, if we allow it, we have to steer a middle course. So we lay in sufficient food to get us to Madagascar or Africa. We'll re-provision there."

"What about meat! He eats meat, don't he?"

Driscoll shrugged. "More meat than we can keep fresh in this heat…."

Denham strode up and reclaimed the binoculars, saying, "You've got to use your imagination."

"Make yourself plain," invited Driscoll.

"There's got to be some creatures on that blasted island we can capture alive. Take them along with us."

"Live dinosaurs!" scoffed Driscoll. "That won't do. We have our hands full with Kong. We don't need anything else running wild aboard ship."

"Small ones," pressed the director. "They might be morsels to Kong, but after weeks of eating bananas and palm fronds, he'll probably welcome the taste of raw flesh."

Jack Driscoll eyed him skeptically. "You've got something more up your sleeve. Cough it up!"

Denham was scanning the tree line, picking out the brown forms of the natives, who had shinnied up assorted coconut palms, and were dropping the hairy fruit into waiting nets, while sailors on the ground fended off the coconut crabs with boathooks.

"I'm just thinking of Kong's well-being, that's all. Bananas and coconuts are like candy to him. All that greenery is nothing more than a tossed salad. Kong is a king. And kings eat meat. He's going to need a lot of meat."

"Which we can't provide under any circumstances. Whether dead or alive, dinosaurs are not proper cargo."

Denham kept scanning the trees, saying, "If Kong's stomach starts growling for red meat, cold fish isn't going to do the job."

"Well, it will have to," returned Driscoll sharply. "And that's that."

Captain Englehorn walked up at this point, drawn by the loud voices and demanded, "Gentlemen, what is the problem now?"

Driscoll said, "Aw, this director wants to take on a load of assorted dinosaurs, for when Kong feels up to a real meal. But I told him it was out of the question."

Englehorn regarded Denham steadily, and his thought processes could not be read in his steady sea-grey eyes.

At length, he remarked, "Mr. Denham, what have you in mind?"

"Just what I was telling your first mate here," Denham said hotly. "We can take on all the bamboo and coconuts and bananas your crew can load aboard. But it won't be enough. We need to do better by Kong. An animal will be satisfied if he's well fed three times a day. But you've got to give him what he craves. And you know what Kong craves. Raw, bloody meat. No question about it."

Captain Englehorn fingered his chin thoughtfully. He appeared to be unswayed by Denham's bluster. But his wintery eyes remained thoughtful.

"I do not doubt your thinking, Mr. Denham. But I am feeling that there is more than Kong's stomach at the center of your concerns."

Denham did not reply. He kept looking into the trees. His broad face grew intrigued.

A sailor and a coconut crab were having a tug of war. The monster crustacean had got hold of the curved end of a boathook in his great foreclaw. The sailor was trying to tug it free. The crab was winning.

"Take a look at this!" Denham said enthusiastically, handing over the binoculars. "What I wouldn't give to capture that set-to on film. Look at the size of that horny thing!"

Captain Englehorn followed Denham's pointing finger until he spied the struggle.

He trained the binoculars on the jungled spot. The Skipper's frown told that he had seen more noteworthy sights. He passed the binoculars over, but the First Mate showed no interest. He was studying Carl Denham, who was again scanning the man versus crab scuffle through the field glasses. His eyes narrowed craftily.

Abruptly, Jack spoke up. "I catch on now! Sure, I get your drift. If the big gorilla doesn't make it all the way across, a couple of dinosaurs on a leash would make a fair consolation prize. You could make a killing on a couple of Stegosaurs alone. Hell, there's a safer bet than Kong. And probably more controllable, too."

Slowly, Carl Denham lowered the binoculars and turned, saying, "It never hurts to have a couple extra aces up a man's sleeve." His grin was crooked and a little sheepish.

Jack Driscoll regarded him with no warmth whatsoever.

"Many a man went to his grave with an extra ace tucked up his sleeve," he said levelly. "Remember that, Denham."

"That will be enough, Mr. Driscoll," Captain Englehorn said

firmly. "Mr. Denham, I think we will see what we can do about corralling a dinosaur or two. Purely as a precaution."

Driscoll gazed at his skipper, and made a show of digging at his ears, as if to remove obstructions.

"I guess my hearing is going," he remarked. "Could've sworn I heard you give the order to round up some dinosaurs for Kong's breakfast."

"See to it immediately, Mr. Driscoll," ordered Captain Engle-horn, walking off thoughtfully, leaving Driscoll and Denham to share an awkward silence.

"Do you have any particular species in mind, Denham?" Driscoll asked eventually.

"Whatever you can catch—just as long as it's red-blooded," grinned Denham.

SINCE the foraging group was busy, First Mate Driscoll mustered a separate shore party to be equipped with rifles and belaying pins.

He assembled the men on the back deck, and explained the proposition to them.

His speech did not go over well.

"Catch 'em alive?" barked a young ordinary seaman named Jimmy. Barely out of his teens, he had braved the dangers of Skull Island before, and had worked up an appetite for more.

Driscoll nodded. "Those are the Old Man's orders."

"Can't be done," scoffed another merchant mariner.

Here, Jack Driscoll set aside his own misgivings, and his pride in his crew came to the fore.

"We captured Kong, didn't we?" he barked back. "If we can conquer that man-mountain of an ape, we can catch a few small dinosaurs in our nets."

Jimmy grinned cockily. "Sure, if they don't catch us in their teeth first!"

Driscoll was on the point of reprimanding his men when a

murmur of laughter ran around the shore party. It erased his reproving frown. The men were game. They would follow him into the triple horns of a charging Triceratops.

"All right, you farmers," he sang out. "Fall to. Put a dory over the side and get to it. The Old Man wants to set sail before we lose the light."

Chapter 6

THEY BEACHED the dory in a little notch of a cove north of the lagoon, out of sight of the village. Although they had enjoyed good relations with the natives, First Mate Jack Driscoll did not care to press his luck.

"No telling when those savages might turn on us, once it sinks in what we've done," he commented.

Young Jimmy whispered, "You don't think they're cannibals, do you?"

"I don't think they're anything of the sort," returned Driscoll. "I just don't want to take chances now that we've come this far."

Another sailor grunted. "This far? Hell's bells, Mate, we just barely begun. Think of all those sea miles back to Hoboken with the ship's belly full of slumbering ape flesh."

"Belay that kind of talk!" growled Driscoll. "I don't want to hear another word about that big monkey. Thinking about the trip home gives me nightmares as it is. Now we're out to bag a dinosaur. I'm not going to be too particular about what kind. Let's just surround something and be done with it."

The surrounding proved more challenging than first imagined.

During their sojourn on Skull Mountain Island, they had encountered an endlessly alarming procession of prehistoric monsters. A cavalcade of terror. Some of the creatures they happened upon belonged in no phylum or genus Twentieth Century scientists understood.

They knew that the great upright man-eaters would be too

much for them, so they moved through the jungle brush, seeking game that walked on four legs, not two.

The brush was hot and sticky, and gossamer-winged insects made the going miserable.

Jack Driscoll took the lead, as befitted his rank. In his hands he clutched a modern rifle, an elephant gun capable of discharging .577-caliber Nitro Express cartridges. This weapon was not fitted with ordinary shells, however. Every high-velocity round was a hollow lead form charged with a modern concoction of knockout chemicals, called a "mercy" bullet.

A professional hunter had developed them a few years ago to bag big game—specifically mountain gorillas. When fired into the meat of the animal's muscle, the powerful shell introduced the fast-spreading potion through a tiny hypodermic needle fixed at the bullet's otherwise-blunt tip. Unconsciousness followed in a matter of minutes.

How effective these mercy bullets would be against armored dinosaurs was an open question. Even Stegosaurs and the like had soft underbellies. It was just a matter of getting in a good first shot. If that failed, Driscoll also toted a .45-caliber pistol in his cartridge belt.

They were moving up a rise. The tropical sun beat down on them mercilessly.

"Wish I thought to bring along my pith helmet," cracked one sailor.

"I didn't know you owned one," Driscoll cracked back.

"I do. But it's not on the ship; it's back in the States. Sure wish I had it now. This sun has me beat."

"Less talking and more walking," suggested Driscoll. "Save your strength. Especially if we have to turn tail and run."

They soon topped the rise and the great tangled vastness of Skull Mountain Island lay before them.

They had seen enough pterodactyls gliding high on air currents to pay them no particular heed. The shore party's eyes were on the ground, and up in the trees.

The jungle is a funny place. It is packed full of life, teeming with activity, but even a careful observer would miss much of it—for a great deal took place out of sight.

Driscoll lifted a pair of field glasses and was searching for movement, flashes of color, unusual eyes. A sultry sea breeze made the crowns of the myriad trees quiver and tremble.

Everywhere bustled with movement—but no signs of crawling life.

Descending, they pressed on into the valley. Here and there stood ancient trees blasted by lightning bolts, alive with tropical termites devouring the punky wood.

Jimmy laughed. "Maybe Kong likes bugs. We should scoop up a bushel full."

No one commented. They were too busy being wary.

How long this stretch of jungle had thrived was anyone's guess. But it was clear that the natives never made any attempt to clear it, or even police it of fallen trees.

Where saplings fell, they simply deteriorated. Trees toppled in their advanced age, and so thick was the rain forest, some of the stout tree boles never quite fell to earth, but instead hung up in the sturdier branches of surrounding healthy trees.

They worked around these knots of little forests, picking paths possibly no civilized man had ever trod.

"You'd think we would've happened upon something by now," Jimmy remarked.

"Or something would happen upon *us*," another mariner said gravely.

"I don't fancy being eaten for my troubles," muttered a third.

"What did I tell you mudhens about talking out of turn?" barked Driscoll.

Voices fell silent, mouths sealed, and men breathed the humid air through their nostrils in an irregular way that signaled an increasing fatigue. The jungle was hard on these seamen who were accustomed to the flat decks of a freighter, and the reassuring pavement of modern cities.

Working through close-packed trees, blazing a trail, their eyes searched the branches of the forest canopy above, as well as the way all around. They missed little, but encountered nothing of consequence.

When the sailor bringing up the rear gave a wild jump and let out a screech, everyone turned, half expecting to see him wrapped in the coils of a constrictor snake.

Instead, the man had dropped his rifle and was slapping at his arms in panic.

Rushing up to him, Driscoll demanded, "What's eating you?"

The sailor was tugging at something on one arm and the Mate seized it, slapping the other's free hand away.

"Blister me!" Driscoll growled. "It's only a leech."

"Get it off me!"

Smoking was forbidden by the shore party because the smell of tobacco was sure to draw unwanted attention. But Driscoll pulled out a cigarette lighter, snapped at it twice, then applied the gaseous flame to the fat leech.

Curling up in pain, it released its vampire grip and fell to the ground, blackening as it perished.

"All right," said Driscoll. "Watch out for leeches. Now shake a leg."

IN TIME, they came upon an unusual line of mossy hills.

These sat in a vale where vivid green moss coated the twisted and gnarled trees and surrounding boulders. There was something uncanny about the way the moss had overtaken the surroundings. The pocket looked impossibly ancient, preternaturally prehistoric.

Driscoll called for a halt. His eyes went narrow, and creases corrugated his forehead.

"What is it?" hissed Jimmy, bright eyes widening in wonder.

The First Mate said slowly, "I'm not exactly sure. But take a gander at those hills."

Hills might have been too generous a term; perhaps they were better described as hillocks. But there were three of them set in an orderly row further up the valley.

They were perhaps twenty-five feet in circumference, more flat than tall, and almost evenly covered in bright green moss. Nothing more grew on them. That was what made suspicion glint in the First Mate's searching eyes.

"Funny nothing is growing on those little hills," remarked Driscoll.

"What do you mean, nothing? That's moss. It's sprouting pretty good."

"Right. But no ferns, no plants, no grass. Nothing else. Just moss. Seems unnatural to my eyes."

Now that it was pointed out to them, the faces of the shore party reflected their First Mate's careful suspicion.

"What do you say, Mate?" questioned one man. "Investigate— or give them a wide berth?"

Driscoll was a while in answering. He searched the three massed hills with his eyes, looking for he knew not what.

"Let's push on," he decided at last. "There's nothing for us on those hills."

The party pushed on, going in the opposite direction of the three strangely symmetrical hills of green moss.

The only inkling they had that they were walking into trouble was a humid odor. The smell was rank. It brought Jack Driscoll up short, and he dropped the destructive end of his powerful rifle to waist level, ready, he hoped, for any and everything, come what may.

"Smells like water buffalo," a sailor mumbled.

"Is that right?" muttered Driscoll. "When did you ever smell a water buffalo?"

"I think I'm smelling one now. At least I hope that's all that it is."

But it was no water buffalo.

Out of the bush, emerged a head. It was reptilian, and wavered low to the ground.

At first, the thing fooled them. They thought it was some great serpent, an equatorial python perhaps. It had that general look about it.

But then the thing pushed out of the underbrush, and they saw that the back was a mass of plates like dull-cut diamonds, while on either side two mismatched rows of spikes jutted out, discolored by dried blood.

Driscoll knew his dinosaurs. They had fascinated him as a child. And he had not forgotten what he'd learned.

"Ankylosaurus!" he burst out.

One of his crew, mishearing that word, growled, "Agreed. Let's ankle out of here."

Turning, the First Mate barked, "Stand your ground, you men. That's an Ankylosaurus, an armored dinosaur. It might be exactly what we want."

In the act of turning tail, the shore party reversed itself. Revolvers jumped out of holsters even though Driscoll had not given the command to draw weapons.

Bringing the rifle stock to a shoulder, Jack Driscoll lined up his sights with the thick forehead of the armored brute.

"Steady, men," he said quietly. "Here goes."

The powerful rifle kicked once, violently, and even though he stood ready for it, the First Mate was almost knocked off his feet. The Nitro Express was no mere sports rifle. Its recoil was five times that of a Springfield army rifle.

The scaly-plated head of the dinosaur flinched upon the impact of the mercy bullet—flinched, and did not otherwise react.

Lowering his rifle, Driscoll watched carefully, and disappointment made his sunburned face grow long and his cheeks hollow.

"He ain't keeling over, is he?" a sailor muttered darkly.

Driscoll shook his head. "Mercy bullets sometimes take a

while to work. The chemical is driven into the bloodstream through the puncture wound and has to take its course."

Minutes dragged past, and the Ankylosaurus, its dark eyes fixed upon the knot of humans, advanced on awkwardly splayed feet.

"Here he comes!" Jimmy yelled, dodging wildly.

The sound seemed to spook the dinosaur, for its stumpy legs began churning, and the ground shook. Soon the thing was charging in their direction.

Lifting his rifle again, Driscoll fired twice, but to no avail. The bullet seem to smash against the armor plate, harmlessly.

"Retreat! Retreat!"

No man-jack needed to hear it twice. They turned around and ran for all they were worth.

Plunging into the thick part of the jungle, they raced between trees where the creature could not follow.

Except that to their utter dismay, the Ankylosaurus *did* follow. The creature seemed oblivious to its own girth and size, for it shoved its small head between two tree trunks and, unmindful of the narrow space, tore on.

Its bony-spiked sides ripped and tore at bark and trunk. Trees groaned in agony. One toppled. One was all that was needed.

The determined Ankylosaurus continued its pursuit. More than one seaman decided that the top of a tree was safer than solid earth.

Young Jimmy managed to gain the crown of a particularly spectacular tree whose twisted limbs were slippery with age-accumulated moss. From this perch, he whipped out his revolver, rapidly emptying the cylinder downward.

Bullets broke the horny diamond-shaped armor, and the creature reacted violently. It possessed a short tail, which ended in a great knob like a primitive mallet. Laying this bulbous protuberance against the standing tree trunk, it began to hammer away violently.

The tree shook and shook, and the young sailor who thought

he was safe in its branches lost his revolver in his scramble to hold on for dear life.

He began yelling for help.

"Mate! Mate! This thing is trying to topple my perch!"

Hearing this, Driscoll got his scattered men organized and they moved in the direction of the commotion.

It was an unnerving sight, the Ankylosaurus hammering at the mossy tree trunk with its natural mace. The thing was enraged, and the ferocity of its tail made every man feel a little sick inside, recognizing what that knob could do to a human being.

"Hold this," said Driscoll, handing his rifle to one man. Removing his revolver from his holster, he lined up on the creature's small skull, and took careful aim.

Squeezing the trigger brought a loud pop and a great cloud of cordite smoke.

The Ankylosaurus staggered, shot through the brain. But it did not roll over. Driscoll fired again, twice more, and each bullet smashed home.

By reputation, dinosaurs are believed to be small-brained and on the stupid side. This creature might or might not have fit that description. But even shot through the brain, it was slow to give up its life.

It stood its ground. But the lashings of its violent tail slowed, then ceased. The thing quietly folded in its legs and came to rest, leaning against the battered tree trunk.

From his high perch, the hapless Jimmy called out, "Is it dead or not? Because I ain't coming down until someone certifies that it's a goner."

Keeping his weapon handy, Driscoll crept up on the thing, saw that the tail still twitched, but the armored sides of the creature were heaving with difficulty.

Showing more nerve than sense, the First Mate walked up to the head, carefully placed the muzzle of his revolver to one temple and fired a finishing round.

The dinosaur's head jerked as if whipped, then all animation seemed to ooze out of it.

Holstering his revolver, Driscoll called up hoarsely, "It's done for, Jimmy. Now get down out of that tree."

Jimmy must have had some quality in common with a cat for he found it easier to have ascended the tree than to descend it. He got most of the way down when he ran out of handy branches, took his chances and simply jumped. He landed hard.

Helping him to his feet, Driscoll growled, "You could've broken your legs doing that."

Jimmy grinned crookedly, "Aw, I knew you'd carry me back to the boat if I did anything stupid like that. Wouldn't you?"

"Dragged you, more likely. By the hair. And it would serve you right."

By this time, the shore party had collected itself and were looking to their First Mate for instructions.

Driscoll studied the dead monster with hands on hips. "This thing is too heavy to haul back to the boat, so the hunt goes on."

No crewman looked happy about that, but neither did they complain. Forming up behind the first officer, they made a single file and trudged along in his dusty wake.

When they got into the clear part of the valley floor, Driscoll noticed something peculiar.

"Hold up, you men," he hissed, waving them back. The First Mate was looking to the west, where the three little hills had loomed.

Someone hissed, "What is it? I don't see anything."

"Can't you count?" Driscoll snapped.

"Sure, up to twenty if I take my shoes off. What of it?"

"Take a gander at those three hills."

It took a moment to sink in only because their brains refused what their eyes perceived.

"Holy smoke!" Jimmy blurted out excitedly. "There's only two of them now!"

Chapter 7

I T WAS no trick of the jungle, no optical illusion created by
the relentlessly beating sun or the tangle of variegated greenery in profusion all around them.

Not twenty minutes before, three irregular hills had stood in
close formation, the sun making their mossy backs vivid. Now
there were but two.

"It ain't possible," a sailor undertoned. "Is it, Mate?"

Jack Driscoll scrutinized the two green humps. "No, it's not
possible. But there it is."

"But—what could've moved a whole hill? Could there be
another Kong?"

Advancing purposely, Driscoll said steadily, "Let's find out."

The others of the shore party swapped amazed expressions,
but any hesitancy rising in their chests was shoved down out
of sight. First Mate Driscoll strode on unafraid, and they could
do no less. Throwing off their reluctance, they crept along after
him, every man clutching his sidearm and every trigger finger
touching curved steel.

As he pushed ahead along the valley floor, Jack Driscoll
studied the two remaining hillocks. When he got within one
hundred yards, he lifted his powerful rifle and sent a charge
screaming skyward. The recoil brought fresh agony to the arm
Kong had manhandled, but he shrugged it off.

To the amazement of everyone except the First Mate, two
mossy humps reared up, exposing stubby legs as thick around

as tree stumps. From the northern end of each, strange beaked heads emerged, belligerent mouths falling agape.

Pistols came up, ready to discharge their deadly contents.

Hearing this, Driscoll instructed, "Hold your fire, men. Hold it, I say!"

The shore party held their fire, but kept their weapons trained on the stirring masses of green.

Ponderously, the bulky things revealed themselves, displaying their true nature. Four clawed legs dug into the dirt, seeking traction, while heavy eyelids opened to reveal dark orbs set in heads that slowly weaved back and forth.

Young Jimmy exclaimed, "Turtles! Those monsters are giant turtles."

Driscoll nodded. "Sea turtles from the looks of their flippers. They probably live a long time, maybe centuries, with moss growing on their backs, providing camouflage against the dinosaurs that might otherwise eat them."

The things were stupendous in size, although Kong would have dwarfed them.

Driscoll studied the rearing reptiles, his brain working fast.

Noticing this, a sailor drifted up and said, "You're wearing your scheming face, Mate."

Driscoll nodded silently. "That I am."

"What's hatching up there? Mind tellin' a fellow sailorman?"

"Those things are amphibious. If we could stampede one of them into the water, I might be able to knock it out with a mercy bullet or three."

Hearing this, the others gathered around, faces intrigued. One said, "You think we can winch one aboard the *Wanderer?*"

"Well, we wouldn't need to build a raft, would we? The thing is practically a living raft."

"It's a mad scheme you're hatching. But it's better than trying to lasso a berserk Tyrannosaur."

Driscoll began stalking around, keeping his distance from

the stirring creatures. Like a surveyor, he attempted to ascertain the quickest and clearest path to the sea.

After he was done, he rejoined his men and they fell into low conversation.

The plan was simple in design and proved to be uncomplicated in execution. They took up positions to the rear of one of the tortoises, and while out of sight of the great staring heads, they began firing in the air and shouting at the tops of their lungs.

That did the trick. The two tortoises began to flop their clawed flippers and dig into the dirt, moving with as much alacrity as their immense weight would permit.

One went north, but the other ran toward the sea—although the word "run" did not quite capture the locomotion of the amazing reptile.

If they had not been aquatic by nature, it would never have worked. But they were amphibious, and understood that safety lay in the water, so one reptile made a beeline for shore.

Following at a cautious distance, the men reloaded their revolvers and discharged them into the air periodically, which materially contributed to the creature's motivation.

At last it came to a rocky shelf, struggled to flipper itself along, and became stuck.

Low groans came from the shore party. Driscoll quieted them with a curt command.

"Find long branches, small saplings—anything you can. We're going to push and pull and lever that thing like old Archimedes."

The shore party scattered, came back lugging assortments of timber, and after these were sorted out, they went to work with a firm will.

The creature had gotten stuck on the flat underside of its shell, and its flippers were waving and beating helplessly, unable to propel it the last few yards. Its wise-eyed head looked out over the rocky edge into the heaving water, but the reptile could not make the plunge.

Using their wooden levers, the shore party pushed against the carapace, moving it ahead sometimes feet, sometimes inches, until the fore part of the turtle stood poised over open space.

"Enough pushing," Driscoll ordered. "Now it's time to make like Archimedes."

Large stones and small boulders were set down as fulcrums, and they applied their crude levers. Digging in under the underside of the shell, they set themselves.

His arms wrapped around his own picked pole, Driscoll called out, "I'm going to count to three. On the three, everybody give it their all."

They waited, then came the words. "One. Two. Three! *Heave-ho!*"

Every man moved as one. Two poles snapped. One merely splintered. But the combined effort was sufficient.

The great helpless tortoise lifted its hind quarters into the air, and slid down into the water.

Dropping their poles, they raced to the edge of the rocky shelf, peered downward.

The round reptile had landed properly right-side up and was splashing the water with its flippers, trying to orient itself toward open water.

"Quick!" Driscoll called out. "Where's my damn rifle?"

The coxswain came running with it, and Driscoll took the heavy weapon in hand.

Directing the barrel downward, Driscoll sighted on the thing's forehead, and fired three times in closely-spaced succession, agony again numbing one shoulder.

Soon, the flippers ceased their splashing. They began to wave feebly, ultimately subsiding.

As they watched, the great orbs slowly closed and the thing floated inert.

Ten minutes later, they were in the dory, pushed off and went muttering in the direction of the thing.

Their intention was to affix towlines to the creature's tail, but when they rounded the rocks, the turtle was no longer there.

"Where is it?" barked the coxswain.

Eyes raked the chop, but of course the creature could not have swam very far in such a short time.

The dory glided into the gathering waters before the truth dawned on them.

"Thar she blows!" Jimmy yelled, pointing downward.

Directly below them, visible in the clear waters, floated the thing.

"Maybe we can rig an anchor," a sailor said half-jokingly. "Use it like a fish hook."

"And what will we use for bait?" retorted Driscoll.

The sailor shrugged. "Search me. I guess we gotta start over, huh?"

Jack Driscoll took off his cap and looked as if he wanted to throw it up in the air in sheer frustration.

Instead, a light came into his eyes.

"When I was a kid back home in Connecticut," he said slowly. "I'd come across turtles like that one dug into the dirt after they laid their eggs. I'll bet my seaman's papers that if we hike back there, we can harvest a few."

"Mr. Denham won't like it much," warned Jimmy.

"No, he won't," snapped Driscoll, replacing his cap. "But we'll tell him they're dinosaur eggs. He'll be satisfied with that—until they hatch."

"Maybe we can convince Denham to sit on them himself!" Jimmy laughed.

Returning to land, they made their way back to the eerie vale of moss.

Two of the monster turtles had returned to their nests, but one stood empty.

Lugging a pair of burlap sacks from the dory, they crept up on the empty earthen crater. The nesting turtles watched them with ancient, expressionless eyes, but made no move to interfere.

Sixteen spotted eggs lay baking in the sun, half covered in dirt. Very round, almost like gigantic tennis balls, and just as white.

Hastily, they excavated these, breaking three in the process and cursing the work.

Finally, they filled one sack with six eggs.

"That's enough," decided Driscoll. "No sense pressing our luck. You two lug that sack between you and if you break one egg between here and the ship, I swear I'll make you drink the yolk raw."

"I hear drinking raw egg puts hair on a man's chest," observed young Jimmy.

"That goes double for you, Jimmy!" Driscoll barked. "And what would you know about manly hair, anyway? You've yet to wear out your first razor blade."

THE DECK crew lining the freighter's rail watched the returning dory with eager eyes. They groaned like a great single beast, then began hurling complaints down toward the First Mate.

"Where's your catch?" one jeered.

"We were hoping for a Brontosaurus," another jested. "A baby one."

Driscoll called up, "Quiet, you farmers! Just drop the lines and we'll take care of the rest. And be careful unpacking this sack when it reaches the hold. Contents are fragile."

A deck crane was all that was necessary for the hoisting. Once the burlap sack was stabilized, it went up without incident, and was swung into the Number One Hold, slick as a whistle. Two deck workers stood below to capture the burden and unhook it from the hook, whereupon the fragile cargo was stowed amid the plantains and bamboo in the tween decks, which would secure it from breakage.

The hatch doors were lowered by an electric winch.

Carl Denham watched the entire operation with a mixture of emotions tormenting his thick features. He walked up to Jack Driscoll and complained, "I ask you to fetch me a dinosaur and what do you bring back?"

"The biggest dinosaur eggs on record," Driscoll retorted. "And if it's not good enough for you, Mr. Denham, you can climb down into that hold and throw them back into the ocean. It's the best we could do under the circumstances. A lot more manageable than a herd of full-grown Ankylosaurs, which we couldn't have got into the dory anyway."

The vehemence of Jack Driscoll's voice seemed to slap down the filmmaker's fighting spirit. He took a step backward, and cocked a speculative eye at the Mate's glowering features.

Denham cracked a crooked grin.

"Ankylosaur, eh?"

Driscoll nodded. "We ran into a mean specimen—too mean. Had to kill it. But we scavenged some eggs. If we treat 'em right, they'll hatch out some entertaining playmates for Kong."

"I wonder if Kong likes Ankylosaur stew?" mused Denham. His laugh was a little ragged, but there was genuine humor in it.

Driscoll did not join him in his mirth. The First Mate's eyes went to the hatch doors of Hold Number Three, and the worry tugging at his sunburned features told that Jack Driscoll was contemplating what slept beneath those flat steel panels.

Chapter 8

I T WAS the shank of the afternoon when Captain Englehorn gave the order to weigh anchor and set sail.

A long rattling of chain commenced. A donkey engine drew complaining steel links through the bow hawse hole. The steam engines roared into life. The steel deck plates of the old freighter became busy with seamen going about their business.

As if to encourage their leaving, from the village situated at the forested foot of Skull Mountain, native drums took up a steady tattoo. The monotonous beating carried over the rippling water, seemed to join the throb of the engines, blending into a single albeit syncopated rhythm.

At the stern, Penjaga stood watching the shattered lumber battlements of the Wall recede into the afternoon mist that forever shrouded Skull Mountain Island. She might have been a displaced figurehead carved out of nutmeats, for she did not move. Her eyes were moist with deep emotion.

A pair of pterodactyls glided out, circled the rumbling ship, and followed it some distance.

"Look at that!" marveled Carl Denham, shading his eyes as he watched them circle majestically. "They sent an honor guard to see off Kong."

"They're just looking to drop a last load on his shaggy head," muttered Jack Driscoll.

"Vultures," said Captain Englehorn dismissively. "Nothing more. Nothing less."

After a time, the trailing creatures reached the limit of their overwater range and turned back, soon vanishing into the outlying mists.

From her position on the back deck, Penjaga watched the rounded knob of Skull Mountain as it was swallowed by the thickening ocean fog. Her expression was rapt.

That monstrous death's-head had brooded over her from the day she had been born of an unknown, long-dead mother. Now, she was beholding it for what she believed to be the final time.

High in the cavernous hollow behind those blind, stony eye sockets lay the lair of Kong, the only home the beast-god of Skull Mountain Island had ever known.

"No more," she murmured. "No more."

Ann Darrow had come out on deck, and drifted up to the ancient crone.

"What are you thinking?" she asked gently.

Penjaga paused to brush at one overfilled eye before turning to acknowledge the quiet inquiry.

"No more will Kong rule his rightful domain. No more will the treetops shake to his awesome roars. Why do they do this?"

"I have asked myself that same question a thousand times," Ann allowed. "They are men. They live to strive, to conquer all that they can. It's a kind of fever with them."

"They have captured Kong," spat Penjaga. "They have yet to conquer him."

"It is a mad scheme, I agree."

Her wise old eyes fixed upon Ann. "What do they intend to do with him?"

"They will put him on display in a great city," explained Ann. "That much I know. Gawkers will come from all over the country—the world, I imagine—just to catch a glimpse of him at a dime a look. Maybe Denham will charge a quarter."

"And after that?"

Ann blinked. "After what?"

"After the white men have drank their fill of his majesty."

"Why, there will be no end to it. Once Mr. Denham has milked Kong for all he is worth, I imagine that he will be turned over to a zoo, or perhaps go on tour."

These words meant nothing to the Storyteller of Skull Mountain Island. But she nodded as if she understood.

"Attend my words, Gold Hair. There will be an end to it. A terrible end. I cannot yet perceive it, but its shadows are already gathering in my mind. These forms are yet dark. Kong is not to be trifled with by mere mortal men. He is greater than Skull Mountain, mightier than the sky thunder. The great lizards quake at the pounding of his feet. Why do white men not fear him? Tell me that."

"They *do* fear him," admitted Ann.

"Not enough," intoned Penjaga, turning to capture a final glimpse of her fogbound island home. "Not nearly enough...."

The empty orbs of Skull Mountain disappeared in the thickening mists. Only the bald crown remained in view. Then it faded into a milky outline, and soon became visible no more.

Shivering despite the heat of the day, Ann Darrow went to her accommodations.

FOURTEEN knots. That was the top speed of the *Wanderer*. Fourteen knots meant raising Africa in three weeks and reaching the port of New York in just under as many months.

The old freighter sailed on a northwesterly heading, seeking to cross the equator and catch the northeastern trades of the upper Indian Ocean. This was the dry monsoon season, when the winds push the currents along at a westward clip. That was what the *Wanderer* sought. Those powerful westerly currents would add to the steady speed of her coal-fired steam engines.

This was not the way they had come to this desolate stretch of ocean far south of Ceylon. After setting sail from the port of New York, the *Wanderer* had rolled down beyond the Caribbean and taken the Panama Canal passage to the open Pacific.

With necessary stops along the way, they had made fair time. But that was back in December. This was now March. Matters were entirely different.

On the outbound leg, they had run empty. No cargo to speak of. Carl Denham had forbidden the simple economy of taking on outboard freight to be dropped off along route. The hard-driving film director insisted that the ship's passage not be slowed down by anything except austere necessity.

That meant docking in coaling ports like Honolulu and Yokohama. Provisioning in the Hawaiian Islands. A three-day layover to let the crew blow off steam. That was the limit.

It was the fastest passage to their mysterious destination, and they made excellent time thanks to the *Wanderer's* tireless engines.

Going back that way was another matter entirely. Captain Englehorn, Carl Denham and First Mate Driscoll had worked it out during the long, uneventful Pacific crossing.

"We will take advantage of the westerly currents, shoot up into the Red Sea, and make passage through the Suez Canal," Captain Englehorn had said between puffs of his ever-present pipe.

They were staring at a map spread out on a table in the ship's wardroom. The course was marked in red pencil.

Driscoll traced the route with a sturdy forefinger, explaining, "It's an easy drift across the Mediterranean and into the Atlantic Ocean, then straight on to New York City. If there's no trouble along the way, we'll be back in homeport in approximately three months."

"June?" Denham ruminated.

"Late June," Englehorn corrected.

"Well, that ought to work out just fine," said the filmmaker. "Whatever we have to show for this deal, it will be America's summer entertainment sensation."

It was a sound plan. But that was then. Before Kong.

Now it was March. March—the worst month of the tropical cyclone season. That was the least of their worries.

Greatest of their troubles was containing Kong.

Once again, Captain Englehorn and his first mate conferred in the solitude of the Master's cabin, amidships of the rushing vessel.

"Mr. Driscoll," began Englehorn, tamping his favorite brand of tobacco into his broad black pipe bowl, "I asked to speak with you without Mr. Denham being present. For we must work out in our minds solutions to the myriad problems with which we are now presented."

They stood around a simple deal table on which the original map tracing their intended course had been unfolded.

Englehorn's weather-withered finger tapped the chart impatiently.

"You will recall our intended course," he said, taking his first puff.

Driscoll grunted, "Well I do! I don't need a chart to remind me, either. It's burned into my brain."

"Well, burn it from your mind now. Because we may have to start over."

A troubled flicker touched the depths of Driscoll's windy eyes. He asked, "Spell it out for me, Skipper. I'm feeling a little dull-witted today. Must be the sun."

Tapping the portion of the red-ink line that bisected the Suez Canal, Englehorn said, "Here is our bottleneck, Mr. Driscoll."

"The canal?"

"The canal authorities—not to put too fine a point on it. We cannot expect to be passed through without the ship's cargo holds being inspected. We have no cargo manifest, a fact which will raise questions by itself."

"I hadn't thought of that on the way in, but you're right. There may be trouble."

The Captain took his fragrant pipe from his mouth. "No two

ways about it," snapped Englehorn. "There will be trouble. Trouble if we inform the canal authorities of this beast we are bearing into their waterway, and even more trouble if we fail to do so."

"I get it. You're afraid they'll turn us away, deny us passage."

Englehorn nodded. "That is the conundrum we must solve, Mr. Driscoll. If we radio ahead, would we be believed?"

It was evening, and eight-to-midnight first watch. The First Mate rubbed some of the sleep out of his eyes before he replied.

"No, I don't imagine that we would."

"If I know Mr. Denham, he will ask us to bluff our way through the canal. That would be disastrous."

"Especially if Kong is awake and growling like a bear. It's not like we could throw a tarp over him and pretend he's a heap of coal."

"No, we could not, Mr. Driscoll. So you see our dilemma."

"That I do, Cap'n. Damned if we do. Damned if we don't. And probably thrice damned for some reason I can't call to mind right now. It's a nasty fix all right. Probably the worst fix any sea captain ever faced since the days of Ahab."

"Or Cap'n Bligh," grunted Englehorn.

Driscoll stared at the *Wanderer's* master, searching his wintery face while he waited for the next shoe to drop.

The old seafarer appeared to be doing the same to his first mate. Neither man spoke for quite a while.

Finally, Driscoll spoke up, realizing that it was expected of him.

"The way I see it, Skipper, we're going to have to stay close to land all through the Indian Ocean passage, in case of trouble, but also to take on provisions once Kong wakes and starts looking around for food. We'll probably have to put in somewhere in North Africa to provision, if not before."

Englehorn nodded sagely. "So far your reasoning is sound, Mr. Driscoll. Pray continue."

Driscoll was studying the map, and his face grew increasingly troubled.

"If we're denied passage through the Suez Canal, we will have no choice but to turn back and run down the east coast of Africa and round the Cape of Good Hope, adding weeks to our passage."

Englehorn blew his words out in a stream of aromatic smoke. "Weeks we can ill afford."

Driscoll scratched the back of his head worriedly. "We can provision as often as necessary while we circumnavigate Africa, but once we push into the South Atlantic, it's going to be tough. We may have to throw that super gorilla overboard if matters get out of hand."

"Let us not get ahead of ourselves, Mr. Driscoll," admonished Englehorn. "Keep to the immediate problem. Do we forgo the Suez Canal, or do we risk bluffing our way through, as surely Mr. Denham will demand? Remember that upon Denham's success, our pay relies."

Driscoll sunburned features slackened. "Well, it's got me stumped. But the way I see it, we don't have to solve it tonight. It's only our first night out. For all we know, that overgrown monkey will perish before we clear the Indian Ocean."

"Well then, you agree with me that we will not raise the matter with Mr. Denham until absolutely necessary."

"Yes, sir. Wholeheartedly. No sense getting Denham riled up at the start. He'll have two or three oceans to be miserable in—once he realizes things are not going to go according to the original plan."

Englehorn nodded. "Then we will leave it there, Mr. Driscoll. Your advice is appreciated. Don't think it is not."

"Don't hand me that, Skipper!" said Driscoll, cracking a grin. "You knew what you were going to decide all along. Just wanted someone to agree with it."

Captain Englehorn took a long suck on his pipe, and let fragrant tobacco smoke billow out slowly.

"When we raise the matter with Mr. Denham," he concluded, "we will do it together."

"Not looking forward to that!" Driscoll admitted.

"In the meantime, we will steer a course for the Suez Canal. There will be plenty of time after we cross the equator to alter our course, as it seems we inevitably must."

"Suits me," muttered Driscoll. "Well, my watch is up. It's been a long day. Time for some shut-eye."

"Good night, Mr. Driscoll."

> *CAPTAIN'S Log*
> *Wednesday, March 15, 1933*
>
> *It is a fearful task that I must now undertake.*
>
> *We have secured in our main hold, a brute unlike anything spoken of by the naturalists going back to Charles Darwin. Savage, a force of nature in his own kingdom, the enormous ape that Carl Denham has dubbed King Kong lies sleeping.*
>
> *I am charged with ferrying this uncontrollable behemoth across nearly the greater breadth of the Indian Ocean and then somehow over the entirety of the Atlantic until we can finally drop our hook at homeport.*
>
> *Kong sleeps. But for how long? He must be fed, or else he will perish. But if he is properly fed, his strength is sure to return. Myself and my crew must find a middle course between these two extremes, lest the monster tear asunder his chains and doom us all.*
>
> *God in Heaven watch over the* Wanderer *as we embark upon the most perilous voyage since the days of Ulysses.*
>
> *I suspect that Ulysses had it better than we will. For he did not carry in his hold any of the monsters he eventually overcame....*

Chapter 9

FIVE DAYS out, Kong stirred for the first time.

The transit had been uneventful until then. The weather remained clear. It was the season of the dry monsoon. This produced a westward current that helped the *Wanderer* make better time than her standard fourteen knots.

"We have gained a day, as of today," Captain Englehorn told his first mate.

It was the morning of the fifth day and they were standing on the bridge, conning the horizon ahead of them.

"A good omen," remarked Driscoll, although in a guarded tone.

The Skipper nodded. "A fair omen. I put no stock in omens that are part of the natural order of things. I half expected to gain a day. I am satisfied. But not greatly encouraged."

"I take your point," admitted Driscoll.

"A day gained might turn into a week ahead of schedule, if this keeps up. But over a three-month transit, it is a drop in the proverbial bucket. We need more than drops, Mr. Driscoll. We will probably require a miracle."

Driscoll fell silent. The brightness of the day combined with the clearness of the sky had lifted his grumpy spirits. But now Captain Englehorn's salty practicality was lowering them again.

"How fares our slumbering passenger this morning?" the Skipper inquired.

"Sleeping like a big baby—or like Mount Vesuvius. Take your pick."

Englehorn emitted a short laugh. "I would venture to say that Kong belongs in the Krakatoa category. If he should erupt, more than this ship will shake."

Driscoll continued his report. "The hold no longer stinks to high heaven. Since Kong hasn't taken on any forage to release, it will stay that way a while. The deck crew have done an excellent job of keeping the space clean."

The Skipper nodded thoughtfully. "How much longer does the old woman say he will sleep on?"

A tiny notch of worry appeared between the Mate's salt-bleached eyebrows. "From the way Penjaga talks, it's hard to say. She's got a circular way of speech. Claims she can keep him asleep almost indefinitely, except for one thing."

Captain Englehorn was staring at what looked like a bank of smoke on the far horizon. "What do you make that haze out to be?" he asked.

Frowning, Driscoll lifted a pair of binoculars, and trained them on the horizon line. The smoke was intermittent, and difficult to make out.

"If there weren't so many of them," he ventured, "I would say I'm looking at a line of water spouts."

Captain Englehorn grunted out a laugh. "When you have been at sea as long as I have, you will see some marvels. Those are not water spouts, First Mate, but whales blowing. From this distance it rather resembles smoke, does it not?"

Driscoll trained the binoculars again, and gave the focusing screw an adjustment. He shook his head heavily. "Well, if there are whales cavorting out there, I sure can't see them."

"They're there, all right," asserted Englehorn. "Take my word for it or not, I have seen this sight many times. If you ever command your own vessel, Mr. Driscoll, you will do well to recognize phenomena at a distance, lest you divert course in the hope of rescuing an imaginary ship ablaze."

Just then Lumpy the cook came bounding up the companionway, knocked once but did not wait for leave to enter.

The ship's master and First Mate swung about, and were about to reprimand Lumpy when the latter began panting, "I think the big ape is rousing."

"Say again?" Driscoll demanded.

Lumpy scratched at the tight grey curls on his sweaty chest. "Kong! He's snorting and grunting. He ain't never done that before."

"Maybe he's having a nightmare," suggested Driscoll.

"Kong *is* a nightmare!" Lumpy exploded. "I went down to check on him. His face is twitching to beat the band. He might be fixin' to wake up."

Captain Englehorn turned to his first officer and asked, "What was that you were about to tell me about Kong sleeping indefinitely?"

Driscoll said, "I meant to finish my thought. According to the old woman, she could keep him asleep as long as necessary, except for the fact that Kong needs to be fed and hydrated. From what Lumpy is saying, we may be at that point."

Englehorn said, "Fetch the old woman and we will see about Kong's disposition."

Not quite comprehending, Lumpy clucked, "Disposition? He's a big gorilla! His disposition is *mean*."

A DOZEN minutes later, they were deep in the stainless steel vault that was the Number Three Hold, where Jack Driscoll was explaining the situation to Penjaga, who seemed not interested in his words.

The old woman was pacing around Kong's massive form, grabbing at clumps of his intensely black fur, testing to see if they were firmly rooted, and making muttering sounds that suggested concern.

Draped in heavy chain, the beast-god was stretched out upon the cumbersome raft of lumber and lashed-together odds and

ends. The Tyrannosaur tooth marks that scourged the anthropoid's massive arms were no longer leaking his life's fluid. Catgut
stitches had closed every one. Healing was progressing well.
His fingers nails, which had been cracked and broken in battle,
were slowly growing out.

Showing uncommon courage, Penjaga stepped onto Kong's
slowly heaving chest, and strode up to his great hairy head. The
monster's mouth yawned like a fanged cave ready to receive a
human sacrifice. The stink coming from it fouled the air.

Striding up to this on her sandaled feet, the Storyteller of
Skull Mountain Island sniffed at Kong's unpleasant breath,
noted the dryness of his cavernous mouth, and turned eyes dark
with a repressed resentment upon the others.

"Kong will need nourishment soon," she said flatly.

Driscoll asked, "How soon?"

"One day. Possibly two days. No more. His body fights my
herbs. Kong is losing strength. His muscles will melt away if
we are not wise in our husbandry of him."

"What do we do in the meantime?" Driscoll wanted to know.

"Pour water down his throat. Slowly. Carefully."

Jack Driscoll eyed Lumpy. "You heard the woman."

The bald old cook looked aghast. "Do you expect me to climb
up on that big bruiser's chest and throw water down his gullet?"

"You're the ship's cook. It's your job to feed all souls aboard."

Lumpy swallowed hard. Beads of perspiration popped up on
his wrinkled forehead. He tried swallowing, but his Adam's
apple didn't seem to work properly.

"Aye, Mr. Driscoll. But if I fall in, promise me you'll come
jumping after to pull me out."

Jack Driscoll laughed heartily. "Think of it as practice for
when it's time to actually feed Kong."

Grumbling, Lumpy went topside and was soon back, a pail
of slopping water in each thin-boned hand.

Penjaga stepped onto one of Kong's scarred and matted

shoulders and said, "Hand those to me. I will do what you fear to."

"My pleasure, ma'am," grinned Lumpy.

The old woman stooped, took ahold of one bucket by the wire handle and carefully used it to irrigate Kong's open mouth, only then pouring a libation down the throat. She was exceedingly careful in what she did.

Once the first bucket was empty, she handed it down and took the other, repeating the process without the preliminary moistening of Kong's mouth.

"Need more?" asked Lumpy helpfully.

"This will do," said Penjaga, climbing down off the monstrous mountain of tangled and matted hair.

Driscoll asked next, "When he does wake up, what's the best way to start his breakfast?"

"Green bamboo broth. I will teach this man how to prepare it. Kong must not have solid food until absolutely necessary."

Lumpy grinned foolishly. "That's a relief to hear. Part of my job is cleanin' this hold out. The drains will carry off any water he makes, but when his bowels let go, it's going to be a hell of a job to clean up."

The old crone from Skull Island regarded the white men without pity.

"You brought these troubles upon yourself," she said curtly. With a dismissive rustle of her strange skirts, Penjaga departed the hold.

Chapter 10

ON THE seventh day, the supine hulk called Kong twitched spasmodically.

Penjaga the Storyteller was summoned to the Number Three Hold. Driscoll remarked, "Might be time to whip up a batch of that bamboo soup."

Penjaga said nothing as she made a slow circuit of Kong's body, observing how the muscles of the shoulders and calves twitched intermittently. Sleeping dogs often behave that way, but this was new with Kong.

When she had completed one pacing circuit of her monstrous charge, the Storyteller drew up to the First Mate and looked up into his eyes, saying only, "Tell your cook to begin the broth. I will instruct him."

"Yes, ma'am," Driscoll said with a mock sincerity. The old woman seemed to think she was in charge of ship's affairs.

While Driscoll went aft to the galley, Penjaga drew from a pouch of dinosaur skin a ball of herbs, which had been dried in the sun of the afterdeck. She lit this with an arrangement of flint, placed the burning herbs in one of the dry water pails then, chanting an ancient song of her people, walked around Kong, swinging the bucket the way priests swing smoking incense censers at their church services.

The Number Three Hold soon filled with a sweet smoke reminiscent of sagebrush. The smoke wafted into Kong's broad nostrils. Before long, the twitching of his mighty form subsided. A calmness settled in and his breathing became less labored.

Lumpy the cook was used to being first cook, as well as second cook. A vessel the size of the *Wanderer* often had a second cook, but times were hard and cargo scarce. So Lumpy served in the dual capacity of first and second cook. He ran his kitchen the way Englehorn ran his wheelhouse. Brooking no guff or back-talk.

When the old woman from Skull Mountain Island began telling him how to whip up green bamboo broth, he was not happy.

"Boil the water slowly," she reprimanded. "Do not boil it so fast. The juice of the green bamboo must be brought out slowly."

"This is my galley!" snapped Lumpy. Perched upon his shoulder, Ignatz the monkey began chattering and scolding the old woman in imitation of his owner.

Penjaga fixed the monkey with her glare of iron, and chattered back in no recognizable language.

Hearing these sounds, Ignatz grabbed at the hair atop his tiny skull, and made a round mouth.

"Are you talking his language?" Lumpy demanded.

"I am scolding him back, no more and no less. Your monkey lacks manners."

"There's a lot of that going around this old hooker," sneered Lumpy. "Like I was saying, this is *my* galley. Butt out. Just tell me what to dump in the pot and I'll do the dumping."

"*Your* galley, but Kong is *my* charge. You will boil the green bamboo as I direct. I will hear no more of your stubbornness."

Flicking forefingers in the direction of Ignatz, she caused the little monkey to leap from the cook's shoulder and go scamper-ing off into an open cupboard, whereupon the tiny creature pulled the door shut, and huddled inside in utter silence.

"Never behaved like that before," muttered Lumpy. "Did you put a hex or something on him?"

"Boil the green bamboo mash properly, unless you want Kong's hunger pangs to shake this vessel into pieces," directed Penjaga.

The thought of the mighty ape flailing about in the Number Three cargo hold, shaking the ship at every joint, rivet and bulkhead seam, sobered Lumpy's recalcitrant mood.

"O.K., O.K. Have it your way then. Everybody thinks they're a cook…."

Penjaga hovered over the great stewpot, which was large enough to feed thirty men, sniffing the fumes as the young bamboo shoots slowly cooked. From time to time, she reached into one of her belt pouches and pulled forth what appeared to be herbs and spices, adding pinches here and there, sniffing again until her wrinkled face relaxed and her eyes softened in satisfaction.

Only by these signs did the Storyteller indicate that she was pleased with the progress of the steaming soup.

When the concoction was simmering, the gas stove was shut down and it was allowed to cool until it was merely warm.

From time to time, Penjaga dipped in a callused finger until she was satisfied as to the broth's temperature.

"Pour into buckets and carry them to Kong. I will feed him."

"I don't think we have that many buckets."

"Two buckets to start. Kong must be fed slowly and carefully, lest he awaken."

"Well, we can't have *that*, now can we?" Lumpy sniffed disdainfully.

THE FEEDING proceeded much the way that the old woman had watered Kong on the fifth day. She slopped the mushy stew into his mouth, carefully moistening the gums on the roof of the mouth and the tender orifices that did not look very tender at all.

When she had finished emptying the first bucket, Penjaga took the second and very, very carefully poured the warm mash down Kong's open throat, kneading his larynx, causing him to swallow reflexively.

The juicy bamboo broth went down easily, and brought forth no reaction from Kong.

Jack Driscoll was a silent witness to all this. He made a point of standing as far away as practical, just in case Kong began coughing and expelling the bamboo soup.

Turning to him, the old woman remarked, "It is going well. Better than expected."

"Good. How many buckets are you going to feed him?"

"I will feed Kong until the last one is empty. If my reckoning is true, this will sustain him for a week."

Driscoll frowned. "Will he need solid stuff?"

"We will see. We will see. Now fetch more broth."

"At your service, as always," the First Mate said dryly.

Crewmen brought the heavily-laden buckets in relays, and while Kong was being fed, Driscoll made a point of examining Kong's wrist and ankle shackles.

Wielding the rounded curve of a marlinspike, he slipped the steel tip under the shackles, and by this means judged that Kong was losing some of his mountainous mass.

Seeing this, the old woman demanded, "What are you doing?"

"These shackles were tight as a drum when they were placed on his wrists," returned Driscoll solemnly. "Now there's plenty of give. And here we are, only a week out. I don't like the trend of things. Not one bit."

Leaping off Kong's chest as lightly as if she were half her age, Penjaga stormed up to the First Mate, took hold of the marlinspike and wiggled it experimentally. Her wrinkled face gathered up like a twitching spider web.

"See?" said Driscoll. "At this rate, he'll be skin and bones before we reach Africa."

Penjaga was silent for a long time. Her wise eyes darted back and forth; evidently she was thinking.

"We may have to feed him fish sooner than I had planned," she mused.

"That's up to you. But in the meantime I'm going to have the shackles tightened."

"Use care," said Penjaga. "For if I fatten up Kong, they will have to be loosened again."

Driscoll nodded. "Believe me, I don't want to monkey with the shackles any more than I have to." He grew thoughtful. "Listen up, Penjaga. Give me the straight dope. Will Kong make it all the way to America? That's three moons. A long time."

"A long time for mortal man," said Penjaga. "But for Kong, who has lived longer than your ancestors, it is not a very long time at all. Still, he must be fed properly."

"You haven't answered my question," reminded Driscoll.

Penjaga studied his face. She compressed her thin lips until they almost disappeared.

"That is because I know not the answer," she said at last. "No one knows the answer."

"But what's your best guess?"

"I do not guess. I know things, or I do not know them. But I have a strong feeling." Her eyes were challenging.

Jack Driscoll stuck out his jaw. "Out with it then. What do you feel?"

"I feel," intoned Penjaga the Storyteller, "that Kong cannot survive a journey of three moons if he lies in chains the entire voyage."

"That is your final word?"

Her wise old eyes closed as if to end the conversation. "That is the final word of Penjaga."

Chapter 11

I T HAD been sweltering in the southern latitudes, but up in the northern Indian Ocean, it was not appreciably cooler.

The sultry warmth was a relief from the torrid heat they had experienced cleaving the waters away from Skull Mountain Island. It was no longer necessary for the crew to sleep out on the afterdeck, instead of their overheated bunks.

Nightfall was a relief. Nightfall was always welcome.

As a tropical moon rose, Jack Driscoll loitered by the poop deck, conversing with Ann Darrow in low, urgent whispers. Rushing of the sea against the *Wanderer's* scabby hull masked the sounds of their urgent exchange.

"Oh, Jack," she was saying, "I've been having the most frightful nightmares."

"About Kong?"

Ann nodded expressively. "Always Kong. He's like a dark, smothering shadow that has been cast over me, and refuses to depart."

"Buck up, kid! Once we hit the big town, old Kong will be Denham's problem."

Ann laid her golden head against Driscoll's broad shoulder and they fell silent, as lovers often do.

Driscoll frowned suddenly.

"What is it, Jack?" asked Ann, noticing.

"Denham. There's a hitch in the return voyage. I had wanted

to tell you, but it's coming to a head. And it's liable to bust loose anytime now."

Ann laid a pale palm against Jack's tropical pongo shirt, and implored, "What is it? Please tell me. I must know."

"The Skipper thinks we can't make passage via the Suez Canal. Authorities there won't let us through because of Kong. So we'll have to steam down to the southern tip of Africa, go clear around the bottom of the continent, then push north up the Atlantic Ocean."

"What does that mean?"

"It means," mused Driscoll, "the chances of Kong making it all that way through to landfall get slimmer and slimmer."

"Perhaps that is what is meant to be," sighed Ann. "He may be a brute, but now he is no better than a slave in chains. Bound for a fate that he did not seek out."

Driscoll eyed Ann's pale, distracted features and asked, "Are you going soft on me? After being caught up in that big gorilla's paw?"

Ann laughed shortly, "Perhaps I've been hanging around Ignatz too much. But the little monkey reminds me of a tiny human, and Kong makes me think the same."

"But only bigger, eh? Listen, Kong is cargo. Nothing more, nothing less. But valuable cargo. It's my job and the Skipper's to get him as far as wind and weather and King Neptune's moods allow. But that's the extent of it. His fate is up to...." Driscoll's voice trailed off.

"The Almighty?" prompted Ann.

"Oh, I was thinking of Carl Denham, who just *thinks* he's Almighty." Driscoll's eyes grew reflective. "Well, I guess Mr. Denham is soon to discover that he is not the master of old Kong's fate, any more than he is the master of this vessel. We'll be breaking the bad news to him tonight, I think."

"Denham will be livid."

"Right. That's why we put this off as long as possible. But

tonight's the night. Better go to your cabin, bolt the door. Denham's sure to be a wild man when it sinks in."

Taking Ann's slim shoulders in his heavy hands, Jack Driscoll gave her a chaste kiss on the forehead, spun her about, and sent her on her way with a gentle push.

"Don't let me see your face again until the storm blows over," he called after her.

The First Mate's boisterous voice carried. It brought Lumpy up from below.

"Did I hear something about a blow?" Lumpy demanded. He was wiping his soiled hands on an equally soiled apron.

"Figure of speech!" returned Driscoll. "Put it out of your mind, Lumpy. How's the big behemoth faring, by the way?"

"That old battle axe from the island thinks he'll have to be fed red meat in another day or two. No later. Mr. Driscoll, what are we going to do then?"

Driscoll gave Lumpy a hearty smack on his sun-reddened spine and said, "Shove it to the back of your cupboard, Lumpy. Forty-eight hours is a long time from now. Worry about it then. We've got to get through the next two days."

The wizened old cook looked around again, searched the evening skies with squinting eyes, and noted the fleecy clouds racing along in the moonlight.

"What's coming in the next two days?" he asked weakly.

"That storm I mentioned. Man-made. In fact, it's a one-man storm. His name is Denham. And he's about to blow his cork. He just doesn't know it yet!"

Lumpy made a puckered mouth and muttered, "From what I've seen of that guy, he pops his top quite regular."

"He sure does," Driscoll allowed. "But this time we may have to go fishing it out of the Indian Ocean, it's going to blow so high."

"Sky high, huh?" Lumpy said. "That should be a sight."

"Better go below, Lumpy. It may happen tonight. And you don't want to be around it."

Nodding to himself, Lumpy scuttled back down the companionway, disappearing into his galley, satisfied for the moment.

FIRST MATE DRISCOLL continued on his rounds, and finally climbed up to the wheelhouse where Captain Englehorn was studying the horizon ahead. There was not much to see. Darkness piled up on darkness. The lunar orb sprinkled sparkling moonglade in all directions, making the Indian Ocean a beautiful sight, as if loose stardust was dancing on a swell of black velvet.

Englehorn turned, unplugged his pipe from his tight mouth, and asked, "Have you seen Denham, Mr. Driscoll?"

Driscoll shook his head. "Not in the last few hours. But he likes to sleep during the day and prowl the decks at night. Guess he's a night owl."

Replacing his pipe, Englehorn nodded somberly.

"Are you thinking tonight's the night?" Driscoll probed.

"I am, Mr. Driscoll."

"In that case, why don't we just get it over with? No sense putting it off any longer."

"You have caught the trend of my thoughts perfectly, Mr. Driscoll. Helmsman, carry on."

"Aye, Cap'n," returned the helmsman, not taking his eyes off the way ahead, or his sunburned hands off the steering wheel.

Englehorn leading, they banged down the companion stairs and went in search of Carl Denham.

After a protracted search, they found him in the Number Three Hold. The showman was seated on a wooden crate, a hurricane lantern illuminating the cavern of steel. He was contemplating the creature he had dubbed King Kong.

Hearing the rattle of feet on the steel companionway steps, he stood up and called out, "Who is it?"

"Just the Skipper and me, Denham," announced Driscoll. "We have been looking for you."

"Well, you found me. What's the scuttlebutt?"

There was a jaunty ring in Denham's voice that told that he was in a good mood. They were loath to disturb that. The mercurial filmmaker's personality had come to remind them of the weather—sometimes calm, sometimes threatening, but always changeable.

Captain Englehorn took charge of the discussion. His pipe had gone out, and he fiddled with it, then decided that he needn't bother.

Instead, he used the curved stem as a pointer, and directed it at Denham's chest.

"Mr. Denham, I must speak to you about a grave matter."

Denham lost his jocular smile. His fingers sought his tropical jacket pockets, disappeared within, thumbs hooked outward, the only digits visible. He rocked back on his heels. "Well, let's hear it then."

Englehorn continued. "Mr. Driscoll and I have been discussing the challenges of our return voyage. And they are mounting."

"Mounting, eh? Kong has been snoozing the days away, and we haven't hit any weather. I hear we're making good speed, and are ahead of schedule. Isn't that so?"

The old seaman nodded. "As far as that goes, you have captured the situation. But we face a difficult decision, the three of us."

"I'm listening," Denham said tightly, pulling one hand out of a pocket.

"As you know, in order to make the best speed possible, our intended course is to transit the Red Sea and enter the Mediterranean by means of the Suez Canal."

Denham nodded. "I remember."

"That course was originally laid before we understood the nature of our cargo. It has dawned on Mr. Driscoll and me that we dare not enter the Suez Canal and expose the ship to official inspection without giving the canal authorities fair warning that we carry live cargo."

"Well, just tell them we got a big load of bananas and a bigger gorilla, and let it go at that."

"I wish it was as simple as that," asserted Englehorn. "But we risk the likelihood that the canal authorities will not let us pass, inasmuch as we are carrying dangerous cargo."

Taking a broad hand out of the other pocket, Denham waved in the direction of the slumbering mountain of fur and said, "Dangerous? He's sleeping like a baby! Better! He's like a little lamb."

"Now," asserted Driscoll. "But two weeks from tonight might be a different bucket of blood. Don't kid yourself—or us."

Denham subsided, searching the faces of the two ship's officers.

"What we are trying to tell you, Mr. Denham," continued Englehorn, "is that we must radio ahead to the Suez Canal authorities and provide them with the full particulars of our cargo, holding back nothing. Concealing no pertinent details whatsoever."

Denham considered this. At last, he said, "Fine by me. Radio ahead. Let's hear what they have to say."

"I am glad that you agree, Mr. Denham."

The filmmaker beamed a little too widely and said, "Well, why wouldn't I? We're all on the same boat, aren't we? The three of us are in this together. We've got to do things by the rule book in order to get to our destination safely."

"Good, good," said Englehorn. "I will have Sparky contact the Suez Canal authorities tonight. We should hear their answer before long."

Something in Carl Denham brought a twinge to his ruddy features. "Not so fast," he said. "Let's think this through. What do you suppose the canal authorities are going to wire back?"

Captain Englehorn took his pipe into his mouth and chewed

on the stem ruminatively. When he took it out, his mouth drooped at both corners.

"It is my belief," he said, "that the Suez Canal authorities will not believe a word of our wireless transmission."

Denham blinked. His soft brown eyes grew crafty.

"So we just sail into the canal and hope for the best, is that it?"

"Doubtful," returned Englehorn. "The authorities are not going to believe that we are carrying a thirty-foot terror weighing nearly ten tons. On our representations alone, they are not going to permit passage. And if they do, it will not be without a full inspection. In which case, we will almost certainly be turned back to fend for ourselves."

"Well, if they're going to be tough about it," said Denham heatedly, "don't radio ahead. We'll just take our chances. Try to bluff our way through. Don't give them a chance to say no. That's how it's done."

"If they do say no," murmured the Skipper evenly, "we will be turned back and forced to circumnavigate the entirety of Africa in order to reach the Atlantic Ocean. There are no two ways about that."

Denham's expression quivered. "What are you saying—we don't even try for the canal?"

"It is in my mind that this is our least undesirable course of action. For if we are turned back, we will have lost several days, if not a week. We cannot afford that. Kong cannot afford that."

Carl Denham was hot now. It wasn't the stifling heat of the hold. He yanked out a handkerchief, and was mopping his forehead in his increasing anxiety. The changeable weather of his emotional state was shifting before their eyes.

"They won't turn us back!" he exploded. "I'll bribe them if I have to. Nothing's going to stop me from getting this big monkey back to New York."

Driscoll inserted equally hotly, "See here, Denham. We have a hard choice to make here. We can't make it by getting hot under the collar. If you want us to try to transit the canal, you're going to have to live with the consequences. And they are predictable. The canal authorities will take one look at Kong, and they won't see the strength of his chains, they'll imagine what happens if they snap. Their minds will get to working, and they'll realize that if Kong busts loose while we are passing through, he'll sink the ship in one of the most important and busy waterways ever built, and possibly run amok on land."

More evenly, Captain Englehorn inserted, "There is also the matter of insurance. All ships transiting the Suez Canal must be insured by a local company. No reputable insurance company will stake their reputation on the freight we are carrying."

Carl Denham had no answer for that. Instead, he began stamping around in circles, muttering to himself.

"Authorities! Permits! Insurance! How I yearn for the days when a man could just bust loose, tear around and get what needs to be done, done."

Wheeling, he faced the *Wanderer's* officers. "In my time, I've filmed lion stampedes in Africa, pythons in Siam, and other things I don't even want to talk about. My movies made money because I took risks, and damn the consequences."

Captain Englehorn kept his even tone. Only Driscoll saw that his temperature was rising slowly.

"If they deteriorate," he reminded, "the consequences would be the loss of my ship, my crew, not to mention your prize, Kong."

"We've got to risk the canal," he stormed. "Do you hear me? We've got to!"

Driscoll snapped back, "And what if the worst happens? You won't be getting your almighty super gorilla into port, but a dead ape, no better than a stuffed animal. And that's the best you could hope for. A corpse you can display for the yokels. Taxi dancers get a dime a dance. I'm sure Kong's cold corpse will fetch a quarter a throw. Aw, what does it matter? You don't care about Kong. You just want the money he'll rake in for you. Alive or dead, it amounts to the same heap of coins."

For a moment it seemed as if Carl Denham was willing to listen to reason. He stared over at Kong, whose hirsute chest was gently rising and falling in the dimness of the hold, and resumed talking to himself.

"Suppose I could get the big boy stuffed," he muttered. "With the right taxidermist doing the job, he'd be good for five or ten years. Hell, maybe twenty."

Denham chewed on his lower lip, suddenly shook off his morbid thoughts.

"No! What am I thinking? Kong alive and roaring is what the public wants to see. Alive, I tell you! I haven't come this far to settle for any less."

Shaking an angry finger at Captain Englehorn, he snarled, "Make your damned radio call. Let Suez know what we're planning to ram down their throat. Let me know what they tell you. We'll figure it out after we receive their reply."

"Very well, Mr. Denham," said Englehorn. "I will have Mr. Driscoll relay their answer once we have it in hand. Good night, sir."

Englehorn turned and went out via the companionway, but Jack Driscoll remained, studying Carl Denham thoughtfully.

"What are you staring at, Driscoll?" demanded the film-maker.

"I was just thinking that you're just the type of guy who's willing to risk anybody's skin to achieve your dream. And you don't care who might perish in the process."

Driscoll made fists, but kept them at his side and stepped up to the First Mate, practically putting his nose against the other's.

"Damn right I'm willing to take risks—any risk! Don't you see how big this is? Don't you see how we will astound the world? A hundred years from now they'll all be talking about King Kong, the *Wanderer* and Carl Denham—maybe even you if you keep your wits about you."

"My wits," said Jack Driscoll tightly, "are always about me. Remember that."

The First Mate turned to go. Denham called after him, "You accuse me of being willing to risk anybody's skin. Well, you're right about that. I would! I'm built that way. Don't forget that. But remember—I'm also willing to risk my *own* skin. Haven't I shown that? Haven't I?"

Climbing the companionway stairs, Jack Driscoll did not bother to reply. His opinion of Carl Denham was written in the grave lines of his face.

SPARKY the radioman received a reply from the Suez Canal authorities within an hour of sending out the wireless message.

He read it, whistled once and took the inscribed response up to the bridge and presented it to Captain Englehorn.

The First Mate was also present, awaiting the same reply.

As he read the succinct radiogram, the Skipper's iron-grey eyebrows drew together, creating a vertical knot in his seamed forehead.

> MESSAGE UNDERSTOOD. STOP. KINDLY SOBER UP BEFORE ATTEMPTING TRANSIT. STOP.

He handed the flimsy over to his first officer, who read the sparse sentences and said, "About what we should expect. So what do we do, Skipper?"

"We have our reply. There's no point in attempting to convince the authorities by radio that our ship is laden with what we claim it is. I leave it to you to inform Mr. Denham. Please advise him at once. Let him know our decision is irrevocable. *Wanderer* will not attempt to transit the canal. Instead we will turn south and hope for the best."

Saluting, Driscoll said, "Aye aye, Cap'n."

Jack Driscoll found Carl Denham in his cabin. It was by that time very late.

Knocking once, he heard Denham demand sleepily, "Who is it?"

"Driscoll. We have our answer from the canal authorities."

"Good or bad?"

"Depends on how you look at it, I suppose," admitted Driscoll dryly. "They assume we're all a bunch of rum-soaked sailors. We'll never convince them otherwise. Skipper says no choice but to turn south."

The First Mate braced himself for the cabin door to fly open and a human gale to come tearing out, blowing hot bluster in his face.

Instead, Carl Denham was very quiet. A minute passed, then two. Three.

Driscoll said, "Captain Englehorn asked me to inform you that his decision is irrevocable."

"Well, he's the ship's master, isn't he? If he's determined to turn south, then south it is. Don't let me get in your way. Just make all speed."

"Yes, Mr. Denham," said Driscoll, and walked away with relief written on his tight features. One fist was a hard knot of bone and ligament, which the First Mate was prepared to drive into Carl Denham's face if the filmmaker had flown out of control.

Regret vied for relief on Jack Driscoll's thoughtful face as he sought the bridge in order to inform Captain Englehorn that there would not be a one-man mutiny. At least, not tonight.

Chapter 12

THE NEXT morning Carl Denham showed up at mess in an amiable mood.

He was singing an old song, repeating the first verse, and not bothering with the rest.

"Oh, the monkeys have no tails in Zamboanga,

Oh, the monkeys have no tails,

They were bitten off by whales,

Oh, the monkeys have no tails in Zamboanga."

Lumpy was slinging hash and eggs and, noticing this performance, sidled over to Jack Driscoll, who was eating at a nook table alone in one corner.

"Who turned his crank?" he wanted to know.

"Beg pardon?" Driscoll asked.

The cook made a circular motion with one hand and said, "You know how they used to fire up the old jalopies with the hand crank. He looks like he got that exact treatment."

"He does, at that," Driscoll said slowly. Picking up his tray, he brought it over to Denham and asked, "Mind if I join you?"

The filmmaker grimaced wryly. "Why not? The food isn't so hot, so maybe the company will make up for it."

"I heard that!" scolded Lumpy. "And just for that, the next time I serve you, you'll get leftovers and like it!"

Denham laughed it off, so Driscoll asked, "You're in a jovial mood this morning."

"I try to be in a good mood every third or fourth morning. It breaks up the monotony of life."

"A good mood under the circumstances, I mean," added the First Mate pointedly.

A sly smile touched the director's lips. "Spell it out for me. You're leading up to something."

"We just lost a month."

"That's one way to look at it. But I slept on it. And the way I see it now, on this beautiful morning, we gained two and maybe three weeks from not fussing with the Suez Canal and being turned back like unwanted dogs."

Driscoll shook his head humorously. "You're an optimist, Denham. I'll give you that."

"A cockeyed optimist, and don't you forget it!" said Denham, shaking his fork in the First Mate's face. "You think I make my living shooting movies all around the world by letting life get me down? Let me tell you, I've been knocked down plenty of times, sure. Plenty of times. But I always get up. Get up and fight back. I slept on the problem, and now I'm fighting back. I need to get Kong home alive, intact and fit to put on display. Hell or high water may slap me in the puss, but giving up isn't in my nature. I'm not built that way."

A growing admiration came into Jack Driscoll's clear eyes and he allowed, "Well, if I were a betting man, I might put twenty bucks down on Carl Denham to get his way."

"That's the spirit! Full steam ahead and we'll make our run for New York. Watch if we don't beat every record in the maritime books."

Driscoll chuckled good-naturedly. "Now you're getting carried away with yourself. But go ahead. Maybe your enthusiasm will fire up the crew."

"Well, if it doesn't, the bonus I promised everybody should do the trick."

Jack Driscoll dug into his breakfast, and tried to keep the frown of worry off his face. He had not forgotten about that promised bonus, but he never completely believed in it, either. More than ever it looked like a mirage, always floating on the horizon, always seemingly within reach, forever approachable, yet invariably elusive.

After he finished, Driscoll brought his dirty plate over to Lumpy and asked, "Has Miss Darrow had breakfast yet?"

"I ain't seen her," admitted Lumpy.

"In that case, put together a plate of your best viands and I'll run it down to her cabin."

"Comin' right up!"

Lumpy piled a plate so full of scrambled eggs and hash browns that Driscoll eyed him suspiciously.

"Did you make too much vittles this morning—or are you trying to fatten her up?"

Lumpy shrugged. "She hasn't been eatin' much lately. You should encourage her."

"I think I'll do exactly that, Lumpy. Thanks."

Jack Driscoll carried a covered dish down on a composition tray and knocked on Ann Darrow's cabin door while balancing breakfast precariously in the other.

A muffled voice asked sleepily, "Who is it?"

"Breakfast. Open up if you're decent."

"One moment."

Ann Darrow answered the door in a yellow silk sleeping robe, her blonde hair disheveled, and the sand of sleepiness in her blue eyes.

Driscoll grinned. "You'd better have a sea appetite. Lumpy really piled it on for you."

"I haven't been very hungry lately," she confessed, opening the door wide for him.

Ann Darrow had been given the best accommodations the old steamer offered. It was cramped, with only one porthole for natural light, but there was a small deal table, on which Jack Driscoll set down the tray with a soft thud.

"You don't look like you got much shut-eye," he said solicitously.

Ann dropped into a chair, lifted the serving dish lid and made faces at the yellow-white mountain of scrambled eggs.

"These eggs of Lumpy's don't taste very fresh," she said wryly.

Driscoll chuckled. "Do you think we have a flock of chickens stashed in a stowage hold? Those eggs are powdered. That's all we have."

"They taste peculiar."

"Well, they *were* fresh—a month ago. And Lumpy does his best with them."

"Why do they call him that, by the way? Lumpy, I mean."

Driscoll let out a belly laugh. "No one told you that story? It's because of his mashed potatoes. They always have the mumps and the lumps! That's why they call him Lumpy."

Ann toyed with her eggs, put a gob into her mouth and rolled it around before chewing. Her expression indicated she did not care much for what her tongue encountered, so she swallowed without the formality of chewing.

"Now you've caught on!" Driscoll laughed. "Eat quick and be done with it."

Ann's slim fingers reached up and caught the Mate's sleeve. "Why don't you sit down, Jack? I could use the company."

"If only I could. But I have ship's matters to attend to. See you around."

As the First Mate turned to go, her hand drifted to his thick wrist and stayed him.

"Don't be in such a hurry," she implored. "Did you talk to Mr. Denham? What did he say?"

"He was madder than a boiled owl. But I guess he got over it because at breakfast, he was all sunshine. Give him a day or two and I imagine he'll cloud up all over again."

Ann laughed lightly. "Well, don't let him rain all over you."

Driscoll grinned good-naturedly. "Don't fret. I won't. Now

listen, I want you to keep to your cabin. We're probably going to start feeding Kong solid food today. No telling what might happen."

Ann Darrow's blue eyes grew clouded. "Kong. He's all I think about during the day, and all I dream about at night. The very thought of that foul thing sleeping below deck under this very cabin makes me feel like I'm sitting on top of a volcano."

"Plenty of us sort of feel that way," said Driscoll sympathetically. "But this Stromboli hasn't got much fire in his belly. Maybe solid food will change that. I don't know. But just the same, stick to your cabin in case it gets rough on the weather deck."

"I'll do that, Jack. Come visit me from time to time, won't you? I get lonely here cooped up all by myself."

"What about that old woman? I thought you two were bosom buddies by now."

"Penjaga likes to keep to herself, but we have become friends. It's just that…." Ann hesitated. "She's such a strange old duck. She speaks of Kong in a way a Moslem talks about Allah. She positively worships that awful creature. Worships him with a fervor that is almost religious."

"I know. I've seen it, too. But that's to the good. The old woman is our ticket home. What I mean is, she's helping us keep old Kong flat on his back and dead to the world."

"Mr. Denham must be mad to think you could ever control such a beast."

Driscoll's hand was on the cabin door now, and he was opening it.

"You have to admit, Carl Denham hasn't done so badly so far. I don't know if it's the luck of the Irish or what it is. But I'm beginning to believe he's going to get his way."

Ann Darrow scrutinized Jack Driscoll dubiously while a slippery segment of scrambled eggs slid down her throat.

"It is almost as if Carl Denham has cast a spell on everyone on the ship," she murmured.

Driscoll cocked a lopsided grin. "It's the spell of personality. He's got one of those magnetic ones. Hard to explain, but there it is. I'll be by with your lunch later on."

"If you bring more eggs, I will make you eat them!" taunted Ann mischievously.

Chapter 13

K ONG SLUMBERED.
His tangled fur was matted with sweat, and the odor arising from his disheveled bulk was growing foul.

Penjaga the Storyteller walked in a stately circle around the immense anthropoid, singing in a low, quavering voice. She might have been intoning a funeral dirge, for her words were not in English. But couched in the language of her vanished people, who were unknown to the civilized world.

Six times she circled the recumbent form, her narrow eyes darting quickly over the mountain of withered meat and damp fur, her pulsing throat never ceasing its morose song.

Only one word could be understood. It was a word repeated often. *Kong.*

"*Danna miquelon* Kong… *Danna miquelon* Kong… *tobaris* Kong…."

On the sixth and final circuit, the old woman laid her incense burner aside.

It rested atop the wooden crate on which Carl Denham had sat the previous night, smoking faintly, its aroma alternately pungent and repellent.

Down the steel companionway steps tramped heavy feet.

Penjaga did not turn toward the sound. She continued to study Kong.

Reaching the bottom of the steps, Jack Driscoll announced himself.

"It's me. Driscoll."

"I know it is you, Driscoll." She never called him Jack. She hardly ever addressed any of the crew by their names. It was as if such formalities were beneath her, that white people were anathema to her. For some reason, she gave the First Mate the courtesy of addressing him by name.

"How's old Kong?"

"Great Kong still breathes. But the heat and the lack of air of this metal chamber are sapping him of his vitality."

Frowning, Driscoll strode over, and gave the recumbent form careful study.

He fell to examining the thick soles of Kong's broad feet. The leathery pads showed signs of cracking. But he discerned no seepage of blood. Next, he felt of the bristled hair, and his palm came away moist.

"He's drenched," he observed.

Penjaga's thin lips grew firmly disapproving. "The sweat is pouring out of him. It is not a good sign."

Removing his peaked cap, Driscoll smoothed his hair, then wiped his perspiring forehead with a handkerchief. "I can see why. Maybe we will open the top hatch covers. Let some fresh air in."

"Strong sunlight might awaken him," Penjaga warned.

"Thought you had him sedated."

"His brain sleeps, but his body is awake." She looked up at him questioningly, dark eyes sharp as those of a bird's. "Do you understand the difference?"

Driscoll replaced his cap and said, "I suppose I do. His heart still beats and his lungs work normally. Blood is coursing through his veins just like it's supposed to."

Penjaga nodded sagely. "The heat is bringing all the juice out of his muscles. His brain is asleep, but his stomach craves something more than green bamboo juice. We will have to feed him solid food very soon."

"If you say so." Driscoll studied the monster's profile, noting that the nostrils twitched occasionally. He scowled. "What do you suppose the big brute is dreaming about? Food?"

"No," the Storyteller said flatly. "Home. Kong dreams of home. Kong yearns for his ancestors, who are no more."

Driscoll looked down at the old woman and asked shortly, "What about your people?"

"That is no concern of yours," she snapped. "Kong is my concern. Only Kong. There will never be another Kong. After us, there will be no more like us."

Driscoll's windy gaze turned speculative. "Is that why you came along?"

"You know why I came along, Driscoll."

"Yeah, I guess I do, at that. What do you propose feeding him to start with?"

"Have the one who cooks prepare a mash of bananas. We will start with bananas."

"What'll we wash it down with?"

"Coconut milk. Have the hairless man prepare two buckets of coconut milk. Tell him to take care to crack open the shells and gouge out the white coconut meat. Dry it in the sun. It will be useful later."

Driscoll grinned. "You want him to make copra, eh? This old tub has hauled loads of copra from Fiji to Madagascar. Don't have a lot of deck space for that purpose, but I'll see what we can do."

Penjaga added, "After one day of this, we will try fish."

"Fish?"

"Whole fish. Remove any fins or spines. We will push the fish down his throat, for they should slide without trouble."

Driscoll nodded. "I'll set a couple of boys to fishing. We'll see what they catch."

The old woman went to one leg of the great beast and examined the steel shackle around its hairy ankle. The moist fur there was tangled and matted, but she was feeling the shackle itself.

"Loose," she pronounced. "We must replenish what perspiration is carrying away."

"I can have the shackles tightened."

"Leave them be. If the feeding goes well, they will be tight again in three days."

"I'll see to it." Driscoll hesitated. He had his cap in his hands and was fussing with it.

"There is something on your mind," Penjaga told him, "that is reluctant to emerge from your mouth."

"There's a hitch with the route to New York. It's going to take longer."

"How many moons?"

"There's no telling. But it will be weeks more than our original estimate."

Sharp pains came into the old storyteller's eyes and she was slow to reply.

"The food will not last," she said firmly.

"We'll put into port somewhere and take on provisions. Don't worry. We won't let Kong starve."

Penjaga made a distasteful face, her withered lips pursing.

"You are starving him now. Holding him in a state of deprivation will keep Kong docile. Feeding him will stoke the fire that burns deep within him. That is your choice, Driscoll. To bank the fires or to feed them. If you do the first thing, Kong sleeps balanced between this world and the next. If you do the second thing, his awesome power will return, and no chains may hold him for very long."

Stubbornly, Jack Driscoll cocked his cap higher on his head and growled, "I hear what you say. I guess you're unofficial supercargo on this run. It's your job to help us do the balancing act of keeping the old boy from tipping in one direction or the other."

"You ask the impossible!" snapped Penjaga.

A voice hollered down from above, "Did somebody say my middle name?"

The rattle of heavy feet on the companion stairs announced the arrival of Carl Denham, who was grinning from ear to ear.

Driscoll declared, "I was just telling Penjaga here that we need to keep Kong from getting too fat or too lean, otherwise he will shrink out of the shackles, or burst them apart."

The showman stepped off the lower steps, sized up Kong's situation at a glance and said flatly, "We've been performing the impossible ever since we brought Kong to his knees. Who's to say we can't keep it up?"

Driscoll inclined his head toward the wooden crate and said, "Last I checked, we have only four gas bombs left. It'll be enough to put him down if he gets out of control. But once we play those cards, we have nothing else up our sleeves."

Carl Denham seemed not to hear those words. He was feeling through the damp fur of Kong's right arm and encountering the sharpness of tangible bone where before he had felt powerful muscle.

"Is he losing weight?"

"He is," admitted Driscoll. "He's parched and perspiring to beat the band. The old woman wants to start feeding him solid food before he wastes away."

"Well, she's got my vote! I need Kong hale and hardy for when I put him on display." Turning to the old woman, he exhorted, "Better fatten him up. He's got to look impressive for the public."

Penjaga said nothing, but her dark eyes bored into those of the stocky showman.

Driscoll interjected, "She's afraid if he gets too strong, he's liable to bust loose."

"Damned if we do, and twice-damned if we don't, huh?" mused Denham.

"That's about the size of it."

The filmmaker's broad face gathered in serious lines. "We'll take it day by day. Yeah, that's what we'll do. Day by day. The shackles can be tightened or loosened as needed. We'll just keep a close eye on them."

"Yes, sir," said Driscoll. "Now I've got to get about the business of ordering up old Kong some fresh chow."

Patting his midriff, Denham grunted, "Just don't feed him any of Lumpy's eggs. They're sure hard on a man's stomach; no telling what they'll do to an ape's belly."

"You and Miss Darrow are thinking alike now," laughed Driscoll, bounding up the stairs without waiting for Denham's riposte.

Carl Denham tore his eyes off Kong and faced Penjaga, remarking, "I guess we'll just have to keep old Kong company while his grub is being prepared."

Penjaga turned and presented the director with her back, making it plain that she preferred her own company.

"Say, if you're going to be that way about it," said Denham in an injured voice. "I'll just go topside and get some fresh air."

The director had gotten halfway up the companion steps when Penjaga's voice lifted, seizing him with surprising power.

"It is not too late to turn the ship around and restore Lord Kong to his rightful seat on Skull Mountain."

Without breaking stride, Denham hurled back, "Kong was the last of his breed back there. In New York he will be hailed as a king. I'm going to make the name of King Kong world famous. Just watch me!"

The door banged shut, cutting off the sunlight and throwing the hold into gloom.

"You think you are mightier than Kong," muttered Penjaga under her breath. "Kong will crush you... and you do not suspect this at all."

Chapter 14

THE FRESH mash of banana and shaved coconut went down smoothly and without evoking a gag reflex in Kong's enormous esophagus.

As before, Penjaga stood upon the black beast's barrel chest, pouring the mash in, followed by two buckets of thin coconut milk.

Carl Denham and Jack Driscoll monitored this operation in silence, but not without an understandable nervousness.

"This is making me sweat more than the heat of the hold," muttered the director.

"The old woman knows what she's doing, Denham," assured Driscoll, mopping his forehead.

"Well, what worries me is when Kong *really* needs food. That stomach of his must be as big as a boxcar. And we don't have a boxcar's worth of bananas and coconuts and whatnot on the ship."

"Have you seen the Number One Hold lately?" Driscoll retorted. "The crew is complaining that the *Wanderer* is no better than a banana boat now. And what happens if those dinosaur eggs hatch in this heat?"

"We'll cross that particular bridge when we happen along it," muttered Denham distractedly. "All she's got to do is keep him alive. Just alive. No more."

"Right," said the First Mate skeptically. "Just like maintaining the ship's boilers. Have you ventured into the engine room, Mr.

Denham? The black gang down there shovels coal all day and all night, just to keep this old rust bucket moving along at fourteen knots. Kong is like those boilers. He requires a lot of his own brand of coal. So far, all we've been doing is keeping him from expiring on us. That won't do for much longer. He'll need real fuel. And it will be the work of a dozen men to keep shoveling it down his gullet. That's what worries me."

"One day at a time, Driscoll, one day at a time…."

Lumpy stumbled down the stairs with another brimming pail of coconut milk, grumbling, "Has anybody seen my monk?"

"Ignatz?" Driscoll asked.

"Have you seen any other monkey around here?" scoffed Lumpy. Then he landed on the bottom step, kept himself from tripping and laid eyes upon Kong. The cook swallowed once very hard.

"Other than this black-souled behemoth, I mean," he added weakly.

Driscoll rushed over and took the bucket from him. Lumpy never approached Kong. More than any other crew member aboard the *Wanderer*, he seemed afraid of the slumbering monster.

"Your monkey doesn't come down here, and you know it," said Driscoll, toting the pail over to Kong, and carefully heaving it up. Penjaga accepted it without any expression of gratitude. She stepped carefully over to the open mouth of Kong, and the sound of coconut milk sloshing about could be heard.

"No sense in me dawdling here," said Lumpy. Staring at Kong, he asked, "How is he coming along?"

Denham grinned. "Like Grimm's Sleeping Beauty."

Lumpy made a grimace. "You mean sleeping *ugly*, don't you?"

"Call him what you will," returned Denham. "Kong may be worth his considerable weight in gold. Now go fetch more of his vittles."

Lumpy did not have to be asked twice. He scampered up the companionway, banging the door behind him.

Penjaga finished emptying the zinc pail, and listened attentively, her white-haired head cocked to one side like a curious cat while coconut milk gurgled down Kong's throat.

The mighty ape did not possess the distended stomach of a mountain gorilla. For he was something other than a modern anthropoid, perhaps some evolutionary atavism. His stomach was flatter than that of a gorilla, and covered with coarsely tangled hair. His nearly hairless chest resembled a black leather sofa. And most disquieting of all, his eyes were more human then simian. Around irises the color of honey, the bloodshot whites showed.

Penjaga padded over the stomach, got down on all fours and pressed one withered ear to the ape's bulging belly and listened intensively.

Her efforts were rewarded by a gurgle and growling.

When she stood up, Penjaga announced, "Kong may require fish sooner than expected."

Denham cracked a grin. "Any particular variety?"

"Small fish to begin with. Then larger ones. And coconut milk to wash them down with. Remove the heads, spines and the fins. Do this now."

Denham's features turned red with indignation. To Driscoll, he said, "Why do you let her boss you around like that? What does she think she is—first mate?"

"No," said Driscoll somberly. "She's the supercargo."

"Supercargo? Isn't that what they call the officer in charge of cargo?"

"Exactly right."

Carl Denham planted his meaty fists on his wide hips and said truculently, "See here. If anybody has a right to call himself the supercargo of this particular voyage, that worthy gentleman is myself."

"As far as I'm concerned," cracked Driscoll dryly, "you could split the duty. So long as it gets done."

"Well, it's getting done," the director said firmly.

"That's what matters, I suppose. I'll see to his food," said Driscoll, leaping for the companionway steps. He went up with all due speed and was soon lost from sight.

PENJAGA stood up, went back to Kong's head and stared into his broad simian face.

"His eyes flutter," she announced.

Carl Denham had taken a seat on the crate of gas bombs, but once he heard those words, he shot to his feet.

"You don't say!" he exclaimed. "He isn't waking up, is he?"

The old woman was hesitant to answer. She continued scrutinizing the prehistoric countenance.

Quickly, she said, "The incense."

Denham's avid eyes skated around the dim hold. Spotting the incense burner, he scooped it up and handed it to Penjaga, who took it with alacrity.

Alighting on his heaving chest with nervous speed, she began swinging the smoking thing under Kong's broad nostrils.

The intermittent fluttering of the monster's closed eyes abated, and finally settled down a period of spasmodic twitching.

"Kong's mind still sleeps. But his body is weary of rest. His body wants to rise, and stride about the earth. Kong does not know that he no longer strides the earth, lord of his domain."

"That's right," said Denham. "They called him the beast-god of Skull Mountain Island."

"*Tuane* Kong is the name the villagers gave him," corrected Penjaga. "It means Lord Kong."

Satisfied that the brute's slumber would continue unbroken, she walked off the chest, down the arm and stepped off just before reaching the shackled wrist.

She discovered that the bottoms of her feet were slick with perspiration. Wiping them dry against the deck floor, she slipped into her woven grass sandals and announced, "We must feed him. We will see about the air in this dungeon. It is too hot. Kong's juices are running out of his body, depleting his might."

Denham inserted, "Well, that's what we want, don't we? To keep him weak."

Penjaga shook her head slowly. "No, to keep Kong alive."

"What are you saying?"

The ancient Storyteller stared into Carl Denham's face, intoning, "The heat is worse. You face a choice now. Strong or weak. Alive or dead. You cannot have both."

Denham rocked back on his heels. "Is that how you see it?"

She shook her head. "No. That is how it is. We must replenish his vital juices, or Kong will die. See how he has withered since yesterday?"

The old Storyteller turned her attention to her stainless steel surroundings. "Water may not be enough to preserve him. The great doors must be opened. Kong is hot. His body swelters away. He must have cool air."

Denham frowned doubtfully. "Well, you'll have to settle for the sultry variety. It's over a hundred degrees up there on the weather deck."

Penjaga fixed Carl Denham with her ancient eyes. "It is not too late to turn this vessel around and restore Kong to his ancient home."

"In a pig's eye, I will!"

"It would be the wisest course of all. To think that he will survive such an arduous voyage is madness. Kong will surely die."

"You listen to me, you old bat. I've sunk every dime I have into this expedition. Sure, Kong might die. We might *all* die, for that matter! But if he kicks the bucket, I'm gutted and sunk. Sunk, you hear me? Why, I'd rather go down with the ship than turn around now."

"You lack wisdom, white man. And heart."

"Aw, you sound like Miss Darrow."

"The gold-haired one possesses more heart in one strand of her hair than you do in your entire body. Would that you had a shred of my wisdom and a strand of her gold in your heart, but you do not. Fetch food. I will do what I can. But I cannot work a miracle in the face of such stubbornness."

"Oh, stubborn, am I? You bet I'm stubborn. Listen to me. Kong is the last of his kind, ain't he?"

The old woman hesitated.

"Yes. The last of the ancient line of Kongs."

"In time, he'll kick the old bucket, just like any man or animal. There's no avoiding it. Back on that island, he'd perish and his bones would be picked clean by Tyrannosaurs and other scavengers. But in New York—if I can get him there—he'll be famous. King Kong, the Eighth Wonder of the World, the absolute last of his prehistoric species. Listen, it's been proven that animals taken from the wild live longer in captivity than in their natural jungles. The old boy might live another fifty years in civilization. We'll take good care of him, too."

"In chains."

"Sure, in chains. He's too colossal to be allowed to run loose. But when his time comes, no dinosaur will feast on his carcass. Kong will be dead, and his race extinct. But he'll live on in legend. Why, they might stuff and mount him, put the big fellow on exhibit in a famous museum."

Penjaga appeared unmoved; her withered mouth had acquired a contemptuous twist.

"You don't know what that is, do you?" murmured Denham, deflating.

"I care not for civilization and its ways. I care only about Kong."

"Well, that puts us in the same boat, don't it? I care about Kong. But in a different way. Listen, we got to work together on this thing. Keep Kong going. Find a way to keep him breathing all the way to America."

"Skull Mountain Island is where Kong belongs."

"Aw, I'm wasting good breath talking to you. O.K., I'll take care of everything. You may be supercargo on this old wreck, but I'm the charterer. That means I outrank you."

"Go," intoned Penjaga sadly. "Open the great doors. Let Kong breathe. If he must breathe his last, let that air be pure, even if it is not free."

"Is that all?" asked Denham, turning to go.

"Pray for Kong, if you know how to pray...."

"Sure, I'll do that little thing... maybe the Captain will say a rosary for him."

"Pray for protection," warned Penjaga, "for you have defiled Kong, and the gods who created him will surely visit their wrath upon you when they learn of his plight."

Carl Denham had no answer to that. Clutching his sweat-smeared campaign hat, he banged up the stairs, fit to be tied, muttering under his breath.

"That's what I get for trying to reason with a woman...."

As Denham sought the well deck, he heard the old woman fall into a low, sonorous chanting....

"*Danna miquelon* Kong... *Danna miquelon* Kong... *tobaris* Kong...."

Chapter 15

CARL DENHAM bumped into Jack Driscoll in the narrow part of the shelter deck where the deckhouse squeezes the port rail.

"What's eating you, Denham?" asked the First Mate.

"Aw, that old woman's in a lather. Kong's melting away, she claims. Wants the cargo hatches opened before the big monkey is put on solid food."

"Is that right? Well, after nearly a week of starvation rations and steam-bath conditions, maybe it's high time."

"Let's present this proposition to Englehorn," suggested Denham.

The two men climbed up to the flying bridge, where the Skipper was training his binoculars on the horizon off the port quarter.

Driscoll began, "Excuse us, Cap'n. Might we have a word with you?"

Dropping his glasses, Englehorn turned and asked, "What is it, gentlemen?"

Driscoll made his report. "The old woman from the island wants the cargo hatches opened to cool off Kong. Also, she thinks it's high time he goes on solid food."

Englehorn ruminated on this before replying.

"It won't take long to go through our supply of eatables," he pointed out.

"No, it won't," agreed Denham. "But she says he's wasting away to skin, bone and hide. Something has to be done."

The old ship's master had a plug of chewing tobacco tucked in one cheek. He moved it to the other one with his tongue while he considered the problem.

"Inasmuch as you are the charterer on this particular expedition," Englehorn said slowly, "I will abide by your wishes." Addressing Driscoll, he instructed, "Mate, open the top hatch and see what good that does."

"Aye aye, Skipper." Driscoll departed to execute the order.

That left Englehorn and Denham alone on the bridge.

"Mr. Denham," the old ship's master said, "this intolerable heat is putting pressure on the entire crew. Furthermore, sailing at this latitude means we are more liable to encounter tropical cyclones than our original course dictated."

"I know it's the season for them," Denham admitted. "But what are we going to do?" His brown eyes grew crafty. "Unless— unless you're willing to give the Suez Canal authorities another crack?"

Englehorn winced. "You're a man who never gives up, Mr. Denham. Not that I blame you much. Were I in your shoes, I would be thinking the same way. But Suez is lost to us as a solution. Our present course will take us to the northern tip of Madagascar. We may be able to provision there, presuming that Kong can stand the next leg of this trip."

Denham set his fists on his hips and stood with his legs apart, as he so often did when his mood shifted in a determined direction.

"Kong will stand it, all right. We'll do everything in our power to help him to. There's too much at stake. A lot is riding on the big baboon. The problem will be to feed him enough to keep him going without giving him the strength to make trouble."

"That will be up to you and the old woman," returned Englehorn diffidently. "I'm counting on you to find the proper balance. But I must warn you, if we run afoul of a tropical cyclone, I will be forced to order Kong unshackled and heaved into the water for the safety of both ship and crew."

"Now, wait a minute, Englehorn, who's running this expedition?"

"You are, Mr. Denham. There's no argument about that. But as master, I must put safety above all other considerations. Shifting cargo can capsize a vessel in foul weather. You know that as well as I do. There must be no misunderstanding on the score. I will do what I must to keep this vessel out of Davy Jones' Locker."

Denham flung back, "And I am bound and determined to get Kong to New York. Let there be no misunderstanding on *that* score, either."

Captain Englehorn nodded. Turning to the crashing bow, he raised his glasses to the horizon, and said, "We understand each other perfectly, Mr. Denham. Keep me informed on the situation in the Number Three cargo hold."

"I'll do exactly that," returned Denham, exiting the bridge and bounding down the accommodation ladder leading to the weather deck.

Shoving amidships, he found the deck crew already hard at work lifting the great cargo bay doors, which they did by means of an electric winch—the massive doors being too large to handle any other way.

Denham found Driscoll bossing his men, and said, "Snappy work. You didn't waste a minute."

"There isn't a minute to waste, Mr. Denham. We're about an hour before noon, and I want the sun to hit Kong as hard as it can. Burn off some of that foulness that sweat baked into his hide."

"We'll have to increase his water intake to make up for the sun beating down on him."

Driscoll nodded. "Thought of that already. I asked Lumpy to get busy. Hold on, there he is now."

The bald cook came bustling up, holding a bottle in each hand and asked, "What do you think about these?"

Denham took one bottle while Driscoll grabbed the other and they studied the labels.

"Clam juice!" burst out Denham. "What respectable monkey would drink clam juice?"

Lumpy said, "Well, this is my own private stock on account of I like to swig the stuff myself. Keeps my insides from churning when the seas get rough. Ignatz likes it, too, so I thought Kong might stand for a taste of it."

Driscoll said, "We'll ask Penjaga. She will be the last word on that. Say, Lumpy—did you ever find Ignatz?"

"No, ain't seen hide nor hair of him. Wonder where that varmint got to?"

Denham grunted, "Did you check Miss Darrow's cabin?"

Lumpy frowned, "No, why would I look there?"

The director laughed roughly, saying, "Didn't you notice that the two have taken a shine to one another? Don't be surprised if Driscoll asked the Skipper to perform a wedding ceremony. Why, it's 'Beauty and the Beast' in miniature."

Taking back his precious bottles of clam juice, Lumpy bowled forward to the deck house, and knocked on Ann Darrow's door.

The portal opened promptly. Ann appeared, looking radiant despite the heat. On the blonde's shoulder sat Ignatz, chattering away.

"Oh, there you are, you rascal!" Lumpy crowed. "I searched every scuttle, scupper, deck and even shone a light into the bilge and forepeak looking for your furry hide!"

Ann smiled sheepishly, saying, "Oh, were you looking for him? He came to my door of his own volition. Can you imagine that?"

"If Ignatz locked the Old Man out of his pilothouse, and took control of the *Wanderer*, it would scarce surprise me. That monkey has more mischief in him than a—" Lumpy hesitated.

"Than what?"

"A-a rainbarrel full of monkeys!" Lumpy said with exasperation.

Reaching out his gnarled hands, Lumpy waited for Ignatz to leap from his silken perch, and the small creature soon obliged, waving goodbye to Ann as his owner turned away without further conversation.

The way back to the galley took Lumpy past the decking over the Number Three Hold. There, he paused to look down the open hatchway to observe Kong laying supine in the vast vault that was like a great stainless steel sink.

Ignatz peered down, saw his fellow anthropoid lying there in chains, and began chattering excitedly.

Without warning, the little monkey hopped from Lumpy's left shoulder to the top of his bald head and down to his right shoulder and back again, seeming to shout imprecations.

"Settle down, will ya? You infernal goblin!" Lumpy complained.

Down below, Penjaga looked up and her eyes squeezed shut in the searing tropical sunlight.

"Kong must be fed fish," she called up.

Denham yelled down, "Hold your horses, you pushy battle axe. We'll get to that shortly."

Jack Driscoll inserted, "I have men running a seine net off the poop deck. We'll see their first catch before long."

THAT first catch proved to be a mixture of tuna and dorado.

Denham and Driscoll watched as the net was hauled up and hoisted onto the poop deck, where the live fish writhed and wriggled in their gasping death throes.

As the active net was untangled, Driscoll scrutinized the catch and remarked, "Some good sizes to start with here. You men take the smallest fish, dress them, and dump them in those buckets. Tote them down to the Number Three Hold. We'll handle the rest."

From the looks of the crewmen's faces, they did not relish the thought of going down into Number Three. But no one said anything. They just began collecting the smallest fish, dressed them on the deck, whose peeling plates soon went from rusty to blood red.

Buckets were quickly conveyed down into the hold by means of lowering them with a rope run through a pulley-and-tackle arrangement. A bucket was tied to each end of the long length of cordage so that when one slopping bucket was lowered, the empty pail would be raised to deck level for refilling. This was the idea of one industrious deckhand, who convinced Driscoll that it would save time and effort, which it did.

Once this operation commenced, Denham and Driscoll pounded down into the hold to oversee Penjaga's first attempt at feeding Kong solid meat.

By the time they reached the steel flooring, the old woman had dragged the first galvanized bucket up onto Kong's chest. Selecting the smallest fish possible, she inserted this into Kong's gaping mouth, pushing it down the throat with a gnarled walking stick.

The dressed fish went in, but did not seem to travel very far down Kong's gullet.

Denham called up, "How's the operation coming?"

"The fish is not slippery enough; bring cooking oil."

"I'll tend to it," said Driscoll, disappearing up the companion.

A short time later, he was back with a bottle of codfish oil, and a pail of lard, saying, "One of these ought to do the trick."

Penjaga accepted the bottle and applied it to the fish's severed stern, then used her walking stick the way a powder monkey would ram a gunpowder charge into an old-fashioned pirate cannon.

The fish disappeared down Kong's gullet, and the old woman kneaded the great creature's throat with her bare feet, helping the muscular contractions that naturally followed.

It was five minutes before she announced, "Kong has swallowed the fish."

She dashed the rest of the codfish oil into the bucket of fish and, using both hands, swished the piscatorial mess around until every fish was coated.

Thereafter, Kong accepted each morsel until the first bucket stood empty. Then Penjaga reached out for the second, which Driscoll handed up.

When that was empty, she croaked, "More fish."

Denham interrupted. "Hold on! He's had two buckets full. Isn't that plenty?"

"Kong has not had solid food in twice seven days. Bring more fish."

The entire catch ultimately went down Kong's throat, except for a few specimens that proved too large.

By this time, the crew had come down to open up the side hatch, which usually permitted cargo to be loaded sideways through the hull when the *Wanderer* put into port. It was not normally lowered while on the open sea, but the Indian Ocean was calm, and for the moment there was no danger.

The huge hatch door was lifted through a complicated arrangement of cranks and connecting rods regulated by worm gears. This took considerable muscle power to accomplish. Ponderously, the door lifted.

This brought in fresh air and sultry sea breezes that made the fur on King Kong's recumbent form swirl and twitch as if toyed with by fairy fingers.

Now that bright sunlight flooded the entire hold, they got a better look at Kong. All could see that the ordeal had ravaged him. Two weeks without solid food had produced clear signs of emaciation, which previously could be felt, but not clearly seen.

Driscoll said it first. "The poor son of a gun looks like he's at death's doorstep."

Hearing these words, Denham's face grew red, and he called up, "You men! Catch us more fish! We've got to feed this beast until his belly bursts."

Jack Driscoll eyed the excitable showman and remarked, "You don't have much hesitation when it comes to changing your mind, do you?"

"My mind," retorted Denham, "is fixed upon one idea. And I don't have to tell you what that is."

"No, you don't," said the First Mate sourly as he turned toward the companionway stairs, on his way up to urge the deck crew to resume fishing.

While he was climbing the rattling steps, Ignatz the monkey, who was loitering around on deck, took hold of one of the lines that dangled down into the hold and, teeth bared, slid down the cordage, unnoticed by anyone.

When he reached the floor, he dropped down to all fours, and very carefully, body trembling, approached the mountainous mass that was Kong....

Chapter 16

F OR TWO days, Kong digested his food. Two days in which the sun beat down upon him for hours at a time, while the moon bathed his nappy fur at night.

Penjaga oversaw every feeding. She resembled a witch doctor, attending to a patient possessed by evil spirits. She crawled all over Kong's great form, listening to the beat of his heart, the rhythm of his respiration, and the growls and gurgles emanating from his moving belly, while Ignatz scampered after her, copying every action in miniature.

All was as it should be.

This she communicated to Jack Driscoll at the dawn of the third day of solid food.

"Kong is regaining his natural strength," she informed the First Mate gravely.

Driscoll studied the black behemoth in the quickening light and asked, "I don't see a lot of difference…."

"His bowels have not moved. That means Kong is absorbing all the fish we have given him into his being."

Driscoll nodded, wincing. "I don't want to be around when that happens."

"Have the cook prepare more banana mash and green bamboo soup. And bring coconut meat."

"The husks should've dried out by now. But shouldn't we save it for when we need it? Copra keeps."

Penjaga asked, "How many days sail until we reach land?"

"Four, I reckon. Maybe five."

Penjaga nodded. "Keep the coconut meat safe. Fetch the rest."

So saying, the old woman from Skull Mountain Island returned to attending Kong. She wore a long comb of bone, which she took out of her cloudy hair, and used it to groom the great monster. The Storyteller had been doing this methodically over the last few days.

Driscoll watched her, noting the reverence with which she worked. It made him think of a primitive embalmer preparing a dead body for eternal rest.

To his surprise, Ignatz the monkey emerged from Kong's left armpit, chattered a moment or two, then scrambled atop Kong's slowly rising chest.

"What's he doing there?"

Penjaga said absently, "The little monkey has discovered his god. He performs oblations."

Driscoll cocked his peaked cap back and scratched at his own hair. "I'll be darned! Lumpy's been hunting for him for three days now. Why didn't you say something?"

"The monkey is where he should be," said Penjaga flatly.

Jack Driscoll squinted one eye skeptically while Ignatz dutifully copied Penjaga's grooming technique—except that he used his tiny fingers. He sought out knots and tangles and carefully undid them, smoothing and patting down patches of wiry black hair, trying to restore King Kong's coat to its natural orderly appearance.

Seeing this, Penjaga scuttled over to the crate where the gas bombs reposed, and removed the bottle of clam juice which stood on the lid. She brought this over and lifted it up for Ignatz to capture in both delicate hands.

The clever monkey eagerly unscrewed the lid, took a swig, then carried the open bottle to Kong's gaping maw.

Carefully, he poured out a libation, just enough to coat Kong's tongue and slide down his throat.

Then he capped the bottle and handed it back to Penjaga, who took possession of it.

Driscoll grunted. "Guess the clam juice came in handy, after all."

Without comment, Penjaga took a swig of the clam juice, apparently not minding that the tiny monkey had done the same.

Jack Driscoll started laughing, and it was as much a release from the endless tension of the voyage as it was a reaction to the popularity of Lumpy's otherwise unwanted clam juice.

The First Mate threw back his head, and allowed his hilarity to roll out, unrestrained.

A solitary raindrop, warm as a tear, struck his forehead. He started. As if the bony finger of the Grim Reaper had tapped him on the shoulder, Jack Driscoll threw his head forward, raised an open palm, and captured a second drop. A third splashed into the tiny puddle made by the second raindrop.

"Oh, hell!" he exploded.

Tearing up the companionway, he gained the weather deck, then made a beeline for the pilothouse.

By the time he got to it, the pattering of raindrops was turning the deck into a slippery obstacle course.

"Make way, make way!" he yelled at blocking sailors.

Opening the wheelhouse door, the First Mate threw himself in, demanding, "What about this rain?"

"Take a look for yourself," Captain Englehorn invited with his usual placidity.

Accepting the binoculars, Driscoll turned them in the direction of the port side. There were not many clouds above, and they were scattered. But the horizon line to the south was an ugly grey smear. It was dark. It was very dark.

"Squall line?" asked Driscoll.

"I believe so," rumbled Englehorn. "I have ordered the helmsman to change course in the northwesterly direction. We may be able to outrun it."

"At fourteen knots? Doubt it. But it's worth a try."

Englehorn sighed. "Madagascar is out of the question now. We will have to continue on to Africa."

"Well, dammit all to Hell. You want to tell Denham, or shall I?"

"No point in putting it off, my boy. I'll gladly transfer that duty and responsibility to you."

JACK DRISCOLL found Carl Denham in his cramped cabin.

One sharp knock brought the director's ruddy face to the door. Denham was unshaven, his hair tousled.

"What? I was planning on sleeping late, given that it's Sunday," complained the showman.

"The Skipper asked me to relay the latest weather report."

Craning his neck, Denham peered around, noticed the pattering raindrops and grunted, "You wake a man up to tell him that it's raining?"

"There's bad weather to the south," Driscoll rapped back. "Got to steer north and hope to avoid it."

The showman's features collapsed. "Not a cyclone, is it?"

"The only way to find out is to hit it. We're trying to avoid that."

"I get it. What does that do to our itinerary?"

"Well, Mr. Denham, it pretty much sinks it. We can't chance Madagascar at this point. We're going to have to add a few days and push on to Africa."

Shoving his jaw out, Denham growled, "Let me talk to Englehorn about that."

"If you're thinking to change his mind, don't trouble yourself. It's fixed like concrete. There's no changing it. We can't chance running smack into a tropical cyclone, not with Kong on board."

Denham disappeared for a moment. When he emerged, he

was tying a bathrobe around his striped pajamas, and stamped past Driscoll in bare feet, not bothering to insert them into a pair of sandals. After he stepped out onto deck, his naked soles splashed with every step.

Tearing up the bridge ladder, the dynamic director appeared upon the bridge and accosted Captain Englehorn in the wheelhouse.

"Driscoll gave me the dope," he said tightly. "So we're going on to Africa instead of Madagascar?"

"It's the only sensible course left to us, Mr. Denham," the Skipper said firmly.

"Any particular port in mind?"

Englehorn shook his head. "First order of business is to outrun this blow. We will see where that takes us. Landfall in Africa is very much the same below the desert regions. They'll be plenty of jungle. Where there is jungle, there will be bananas, coconuts and whatever else we need to feed Kong."

"Look here, Englehorn," asserted Denham. "I've been to Africa plenty of times, shooting pictures. See if you can raise Mombasa. Anywhere around Mombasa would be good."

"Why do you say that?" asked Jack Driscoll, curious. The First Mate had entered not long after Denham, and stood listening.

"I know people about Mombasa—fellows who like good American greenbacks. We can put in the port quietly, conduct our business on the sly and slip out again without any trouble."

"Without any trouble over Kong, you mean?" Englehorn returned.

Carl Denham grinned crookedly. "That's exactly what I mean, and you know it. Also, that area provides plenty of forage, even if we have to collect it ourselves."

Captain Englehorn nodded. "Mombasa is as good a port in a storm as any. We will do our best to shoot for it. But I can make no promises."

"I'll settle for that." The showman stretched his arms, and released a wide yawn. "After all this monotonous sailing, it'll be good to see dry land again. And Mombasa is a place I know well. Tramped around it many a time, shooting wild animals, looking for things just as wild as King Kong."

"What kind of things?" wondered Driscoll.

"A few years back," Denham said expansively, "I took a crew deep into the jungle east of Lake Victoria. Stories had come out of the jungle about a white man who lived with the apes. A white man who had been seen, but never photographed. A kind of a forest god. Something like Kong, yet very different."

Captain Englehorn was smoking his pipe this morning. He took it out of his mouth, and blew out a rolling cloud of aromatic tobacco fumes.

"I have heard tales of such a creature," he allowed. "But I never gave them much credit."

"That's the difference between you and me. No one believed that there existed a spot called Skull Mountain Island, or a Kong. But I did. And I ran them both down. It was the same with this Tarzan."

"Tarzan?" Driscoll asked.

"That's right. They call him Tarzan of the Apes, on account of the legend that he was raised by monkeys. Can you beat that? A white man raised by apes, until he became the king of an ape tribe."

"Balderdash!" snorted Driscoll.

"That's what I thought," returned Denham. "But I took a safari crew into the jungle, and we beat the bush for weeks. Once, I heard his bloodcurdling cry. It petrified my native porters. Why, half of them turned tail and ran off."

"But did you catch up with Tarzan?" demanded Driscoll.

Denham hesitated. His eyes narrowed, clouding over as if troubled memories were rising up in his brain.

"Well, I never got any footage, if that's what you mean," he grudgingly admitted.

"But did you catch up with this Tarzan?" pressed Driscoll.

"You might say," allowed Carl Denham in a calculatedly vague way, "Tarzan of the Apes caught up with me. That's a story for another time. Right now, I hear breakfast calling."

"Enjoy your eggs," Driscoll said dryly.

The look that came over Carl Denham's face was priceless. "Eggs again?"

"Lumpy says they're fresh this time."

"Yeah, I'm sure they are. Fresh out of the box!"

At that, Carl Denham exited the bridge. Once the sound of his bare feet could be heard slapping the bridge ladder, Driscoll turned to Captain Englehorn and said, "What a yarn! A white man raised by apes, living with them wild and free."

When Englehorn declined to join in his laughter, Driscoll asked, "Is something eating you, Skipper?"

A wintry gleam came into the old mariner's eyes. "I have heard tales of this Tarzan of the Apes. Heard them for many years."

"You don't put any stock in them, do you?"

"No more stock than I did in that map that brought us to Skull Mountain Island."

It took over a minute for Captain Englehorn's words to sink into Jack Driscoll's brain. When they did, he exploded, "Wait a minute! What did you just say?"

"Nothing, Mr. Driscoll. Nothing at all. Go about your morning business. I will attend to the job of steering clear of this storm, whatever it may be."

Firm of face, Jack Driscoll went down the companionway, grumbling, "By my way of thinking, this old tub is awash with apes!"

Chapter 17

BEFORE LONG, the *Wanderer* was rocking and heaving in a tropical downpour, her scuppers overflowing and her bulwarks apparently hemorrhaging rust.

This was no cyclone. Not yet. The wind picked up, and the pelting rain became raw. The crew scrambled to put the ship in proper order to weather the storm, whatever it might turn out to be.

The first order of business was to close the deck hatch, for the rain was fast turning the slumbering form of King Kong into a sodden mountain of fur.

"They'll be no fish for him today, that's for sure!" Lumpy howled as he pitched in.

"He's back to liquid rations," Driscoll hurled back.

"Anybody seen Ignatz?"

"Forgot to tell you, Lumpy. Ignatz has taken a liking to Kong. He's been sleeping in the big ape's fur, like he's some bug in an overgrown bearskin rug."

"You don't say! Imagine that! That mischievous little monk! I'll teach him."

The hatch clanged back into place and the winch was released, then the boom was restored to parking order.

"That's that," Driscoll said. "We'd better see to the hull hatch next. Before the seas make it impossible to close."

Captain Englehorn suddenly appeared, coming from one direction, while Carl Denham tripped up from another. Denham was still in his bathrobe, but seemed oblivious to the improper state of his attire.

"All secure, Skipper," reported Driscoll. "We'll see to the hull hatch next."

"Too dangerous," snapped Englehorn. "The seas are already getting rough."

"We can't leave it open for long. You know that as well as I."

"No, not for long," allowed the old seaman. "But for some time yet. Until we see which way the wind blows."

A meaningful glance passed between Captain Englehorn and his first officer. Carl Denham caught it, and his jaw fell open.

"I get it, I get it," he ground out. "You don't have to spell it out. If the going gets rough, you aim to jettison Kong like so much spoiled cargo, don't you?"

"Let us hope it doesn't come to that, Mr. Denham," said Englehorn carefully.

"Well, it better not!" snapped Denham. "It damn well better not. If Kong goes over the side, you might as well toss me after him. Everything I have is tied up with that big monkey."

"And everything I have, Mr. Denham," rejoined the master, "is tied up in this vessel. I will not lose her."

In his growing ire, the film director had lifted himself up on tiptoe, but now he was settling down to his normal height.

"We'll just see which way the wind blows!" he said belligerently.

Standing on the peeling weather deck, they permitted the rain to soak them thoroughly. Suddenly, Denham realized the state of his undress, and snapped, "Let me get myself decent."

He left them, rolling along toward the shelter deck, his head sunk between rolling shoulders.

Jack Driscoll sidled up to Englehorn and asked in a low voice, "Any news on the storm?"

Englehorn shook his head. "Sparky has been trying to raise

other ships in the area. But he has no reports. We will just have to press on and hope for the best."

"I'm thinking the best outcome is to lose this super gorilla."

"I will not disagree, Mr. Driscoll. But that is in the lap of the gods now. Mother Necessity will show us the way."

"If that's the way the wind blows, that's the way the wind blows," sighed Driscoll. "But if that *is* the way the wind blows, I don't know who will be wilder, Denham or Penjaga."

"That is not our concern, Mate. Now go about your duty, for I must be about mine."

As Captain Englehorn made a circuit of the weather deck, Jack Driscoll went to look in on Ann Darrow.

Ann had been keeping to her cabin, as instructed. Her worried face was pressed to the solitary porthole when she spied Jack Driscoll coming in her direction. Sad blue eyes coming to life, she disappeared from view.

Ann threw open the door before he could knock.

"Jack!" she cried. "What does this rain mean?"

"Trouble," admitted Driscoll. "But how much we don't know yet. Securing the ship now. We're going to make a run for the African coast. It's our best bet now."

"You mean it's your only hope."

Driscoll laughed roughly. "Yeah, that's what I mean, all right. It's Africa or bust now. About everything that could go wrong just started to go wrong." He doffed his cap, shook rain off it. "Nothing we can do about that. Just batten down and press on. Keep your chin up, Ann. I'll look in on you from time to time."

"Oh, Jack…."

Driscoll beat a hasty retreat before Ann could tear up. He went down to the Number Three Hold to inspect the situation there.

Kong lay upon his primitive lumber-and-bamboo-raft bed, hairy chest rising and falling in the grey light. The rain was slanting, but fortunately it was coming in from the direction of port. Very little precipitation entered the open hull hatch to add to the misery in Number Three.

Penjaga sat in the lee side of the wood crate housing the remaining gas bombs where the rain could not reach. Her eyes had been closed, but now they opened. The old woman stood up and directed her flinty gaze at the Mate. There was no warmth in them, but neither was there contempt.

"When will this portal be closed?" she demanded.

"There's no telling," admitted Driscoll. "The water is already too choppy to have the crew close it safely. We're going to leave it open for now."

Penjaga scrutinized his face carefully. "And if the storm grows worse? What will you do then? Will it not be harder to close the door then?"

"If not impossible," admitted the First Mate.

"What I see," intoned the Storyteller slowly, "I see very clearly. You will leave this portal open until you know for certain whether you can permit Kong to live or not."

Driscoll lowered his head, pushing back his cap visor sheepishly. "That's about the size of it. I'm sorry. Captain's orders. Now it's too dangerous for you to stay here. You have a cabin. It's time you used it."

A firm stubbornness caused the wrinkled webbing of the old woman's features to gather together. "I will remain here."

"If the ship starts tossing about violently," warned Driscoll, "you could go flying out into the open ocean. We wouldn't be able to rescue you."

She shook her head firmly, saying, "No. I will not obey you, Driscoll. This vessel rocks too much. Kong might awaken. His vitality is slowly returning. His eyes may open. I must be here if that happens. For who but Penjaga can put Kong to sleep should he awaken, his voice like thunder, his hands eager to wrest freedom from his ignominious chains?"

Jack Driscoll was shaking the rain off of his face as he listened.

"You make plenty of sense," he admitted. "O.K., then. You

can stay for a while. But if Kong shows signs of stirring, let out a yell loud enough that I can hear you. Understand?"

"I understand that should Kong awaken, his life might be forfeit."

"I didn't mean it that way!" snapped Driscoll. "That's a different decision. If this big ape wakes up, you'll have every opportunity to put him back to sleep with those herbs of yours. If he doesn't go back to sleep, well, that's a different pot of fish. Do we have an understanding?"

Penjaga nodded. "I will take you at your word, Driscoll."

"Good. I'll be listening for you. Don't hesitate to raise a fuss." Turning to go, he added dryly, "Not that you ever have hesitated to raise a fuss in the past."

As he climbed the companionway steps, Jack Driscoll looked back and saw Ignatz the monkey seated on Kong's sloping forehead, plucking at his closed eyelids, as if to entice the great creature into awakening.

"Knock that off, Ignatz," he shouted down. "Lumpy's looking for you. Better get topside."

Staring up, the little monkey began chattering. From somewhere, he lifted an empty bottle of clam juice, then flung it in Driscoll's general direction.

The bottle popped apart striking the steel stairs, and the First Mate shook a calloused fist at the tiny creature, saying, "I thought Lumpy broke you of that bad habit of throwing things at people."

Ignatz stuck out a long pink tongue and seemed to sneer up at the Mate.

"Don't get too big for your britches, you little scamp," Driscoll warned. "You're no Kong."

Chapter 18

THE *WANDERER* was a tramp of the sea.

Built just before the turn of the new century, her keel laid in the Bath Iron Works up in Maine, she was designed to wander from port to port, picking up and discharging cargo in ports as primitive as Bora Bora, and as sophisticated as Marseilles. She was as familiar with the nitrite docks of Chile as she was the jute and copra wharves of the South Seas. During the World War, she had briefly served as a Q-ship. Dozens of her sister ships had been sunk by German submarines during the great conflict, but the *Wanderer* had lived on to decline naturally.

Over thirty years old, she showed her age in her rusty innards, her fire-scorched steel deck, and in a ramshackle air of near obsolescence.

The *Wanderer* might have another ten seafaring years in her, but perhaps only half that. Her pulsing steam engines still ran on coal, while newer vessels of her type were built around Diesel power plants.

Through all that, she was as seaworthy a general cargo tramp afloat as any, thanks to her Isherwood framing construction. A three-island ship, five hundred feet caught her length. Boasting four holds when built, the enlarging of hold Number Three had reduced that number by one. The tramper was large enough to carry profitable cargo to any point on the globe, but not so large that she couldn't comfortably slide into the smaller, more disreputable ports of call when necessary.

Captain Wilhelm Englehorn was her owner, and although he had paid off the mortgage a decade before, and coal was cheap, it cost good money to roam the seven seas, taking on baled and crated freight and discharging it again at wharves and docks as elaborate as San Francisco and as rickety as Pago Pago.

In her day, the freighter had carried everything from calcium to coconuts. She had been profitable clear up to April of 1931. That was when the bottom fell out. There were hundreds just like her roaming the oceans of the world, and when the stock market crash and its aftermath finally caught up to the shipping business, profitable cargo became hard to come by. Especially cargo that justified paying a full crew to comb the out-of-the-way ports of the world increasingly impossible to come by. So the *Wanderer* became little better than a common banana boat, but banana cargoes didn't pay much.

She was too young to be sold for scrap, but too old to be fitted with modern engines and made competitive against newer vessels, whose owners were also scratching and scheming for loose cargo.

What would become of the ship and her complement was unknown. When Carl Denham had entered the picture, he had cash, a relentless, almost inhuman drive, and big ideas.

Since the advent of talkies, the film business was hungry for new sensations. In silent film days, it was enough to go out into the far corners of the world, set up a camera, and crank away. The public ate up moving pictures in distant and dangerous places that before they could see only in *National Geographic* in the form of still pictures.

It was an odd arrangement, the showman and the tramp freighter. But the *Wanderer* had carried Carl Denham from New York to Africa and Sumatra and elsewhere.

It had been a profitable arrangement. Until now.

Standing on the bridge, staring out into the night, Captain Englehorn reflected on the misadventure that was the expedition to Skull Mountain Island.

Their present precarious situation was all thanks to a curious map acquired from a Norwegian skipper in Singapore, and leading to a fogbound mystery island found on no marine chart.

Skull Mountain Island. Skull Island for short. Mysterious, prehistoric, shrouded in perpetual fogs—a place where evolution continues to run wild.

Captain Englehorn had lost nearly a third of his crew to the terrors of Skull Island. The hard-bitten ship's master had borne the brunt of those losses in the solitude of his captain's cabin. No one saw his true heart. For he would not show it. The captain of a tramp freighter often lorded over a crew of roughnecks and wharf rats. He could not afford to be too fussy about who crewed aboard such a vessel.

But the men of the *Wanderer* had been solid sailors, they had pulled their weight, and more than pulled their weight on Skull Mountain Island. That so many had perished in the jaws of prehistoric creatures was something that would weigh on Captain Englehorn's teutonic soul to the end of his days.

In the solitude of the bridge—for, being shorthanded, the morose skipper had the wheel to himself—Englehorn faced a difficulty as problematic as any encountered back on Skull Island.

If he did not deliver Kong to New York alive and healthy, Carl Denham would be broke, and the *Wanderer* would be left to fend for herself. Two years into the business depression, the cargo transport business showed no signs of turning around. The future looked bleak for merchant mariners the world over.

If he lost Kong, Captain Englehorn was convinced he would lose his ship. If he lost his ship, it would be the old sailors' home for him. No one was hiring ship masters teetering on the edge of retirement. Not in these hard times.

Englehorn cast back his mind to the days only a decade before when it was possible to hop from port to port, taking on cargo that filled warehouses and loading docks to capacity. The sea trade in those days was bustling. These days it seemed as if the maritime trade would never recover. In his salty heart, Englehorn felt as if the best part of his life now lay behind him, drowning in the foamy wake of his seafaring existence.

As for that tramper he called home, the *Wanderer* would become a sad derelict old hulk, destined to be sold for scrap. The thought was a tightening band of steel around his heart.

All day and into the night the rain had beat down, making the steel plates of the *Wanderer's* weather deck freckle and splash. Only hours before the temperature had exceeded one hundred degrees. Now, it was a sultry 82. Still hot, but not intolerable.

Past midnight, the radioman came up from his radio shack to report.

"What is it, Sparky?"

"Sir, reports from another ship confirm that it's a tropical cyclone, and she's coming this way."

"I will steer a more northerly course in that case. Thank you, Sparky."

"Yes, sir," said the radioman, ducking out into the rain.

The Captain strode over to the speaking tube, thumbed open the cap, then called down into the engine room, "Pour on more coal."

Deep in the bowels of the freighter, men who worked in dungarees whose pant legs had been torn off at the knees, hairy chests bare, their sweaty faces grimy, took shovels to heaps of coal and flung them madly into the firebox.

The *Wanderer* was doing fourteen knots. The same fourteen that she always paced, except when nature in the form of the fast-moving westward current provided otherwise.

The old ship might outpace the cyclone, or she might not. That was impossible to guess. She carried tons of extra coal in her forward bunkers, but those heaps were not subject to being thrown overboard in a crisis. Every lump was precious. For the old cargo vessel burned over three tons a day, and she had not resupplied since Yokohama.

By her normal standards, the *Wanderer* ran light, the only tonnage subject to being jettisoned was the cargo he dared not shove overboard, but neither could Englehorn afford to give the order to push Kong into the sea, all things considered.

His wind-weathered hands on the wooden wheel, Englehorn steered a steady course, and wondered if he was making his last run. Africa lay ahead, thirty-six hours or more.

Wilhelm Englehorn began to doubt that he would see Mombasa—tomorrow or any other day. A nagging fear gripped him. It was a coldness in his stomach. No amount of black coffee or fragrant tobacco smoke drowned it into insignificance.

Chapter 19

THE RELENTLESS rain had settled down by the four-to-eight p.m. dogwatch, which was a split watch during which the entire crew could be fed their supper in quick order.

Lumpy was dishing out hash as fast as he could. The men were taking their plates out onto the well deck to eat—the mess room being too hot and humid for comfortable dining.

Ann Darrow ate on the poop deck a comfortable distance above and behind the sweaty crew, wearing a sport frock and a sun hat so wide of brim that several times she had to grab at the crown to keep it from sailing away.

Jack Driscoll joined her, remarking, "I thought this dismal rain would never die down."

Ann smiled limply, for the long hours confined to her cabin had gotten her down.

"Are you afraid the crew will see us acting so chummy?"

"Hang the crew," muttered the Mate. "They could use practice in minding their own business."

"I don't know about that, Jack. They've been swell to me."

Jack Driscoll smiled fiercely. "That's because they're afraid of my fists. They know if they got fresh, I'd be splitting my knuckles against their thick skulls in short order."

"Tough talk, you hardboiled sailorman. How is Kong doing?"

"Holding his own. We've been giving him cold water and not much else. That will keep him hydrated, and out of mischief."

134

"Speaking of mischief," said Ann, "is Ignatz still tucked in with Kong?"

"That's right. Won't leave his side. They must be cousins, three or four times removed. Lumpy is beside himself, fussing about the galley without companionship."

"Well, it's only until—"

Driscoll shrugged. "Until we raise Mombasa, or we have to jettison the big gorilla."

"I shudder to think of consigning Kong to the Indian Ocean. Huge as he is, these waters are bigger."

"If it comes to that, it comes to that," said Driscoll resignedly.

Ann looked out upon the horizon to the south. It was a smoky grey mixed with black, as though some giant hand had smeared charcoal the length of the horizon.

"We seem to be outrunning the cyclone," she said hopefully.

Driscoll forked a lump of hash into his mouth and remarked, "You can never tell about these tropical cyclones. They're not the kind of twister you hear about in the far west. A tropical cyclone is more like a hurricane. They just don't call them that. But they move fast over water. One can sneak up on a boat and overwhelm her in no time."

"Well," Ann said slowly, "we seem to be keeping our distance from this one. I meant to ask, how is Penjaga keeping?"

The Mate scowled. "Won't leave the hold. Stands watch almost around the clock. She's losing weight, too. They both are."

Ann heaved a long sigh. "This mad venture of Denham's, it's becoming endless."

Driscoll nodded. "So far, just about everything that could go bad, has. It's even getting to Ignatz. The little scamp has gone native again. He's been pelting old Lumpy with assorted tin cans, just like he did before he was ship-broke of the habit."

"Oh, Jack, what do you mean?"

"Aw, Lumpy picked up Ignatz in Marrakech a while back.

Ignatz was half wild, I guess you could say. He liked to steal food and throw things at people. He threw a rock at Lumpy, beaned him pretty good. And Lumpy being Lumpy started throwing rocks back. Before you know it, the two of them were engaged in a young war. Lumpy got the worst of it. But when he returned from liberty, Lumpy had a monkey on his shoulder to go with the lumps on his skull. That's how he got his nickname."

"That's not what you told me the other day!" Ann cried. "You said it was after his lumpy mashed potatoes."

Driscoll barked out a laugh and grunted, "I heard it several ways. Lumpy's told different people other tall tales. The other one I heard was that he got the name because he was always complaining about the lumpy water the *Wanderer* kept running into."

Ann smiled radiantly. "He's a character, all right. How did Ignatz get his name?"

"From his behavior. Lumpy likes to read the funny papers whenever he pulls into port. He follows a comic strip called 'Krazy Kat.' In it, there's this cartoon mouse named Ignatz who likes to throw bricks at Krazy Kat. Since Lumpy made the little guy's acquaintance by being conked, it inspired him to call the monkey Ignatz. Not much more to it than that."

Ann laughed. "Does that make Lumpy Krazy Kat?"

Driscoll shrugged. "Crazy, at any rate. Most of the crew are a little bit off. Especially now, after Skull Island. And with something in the Number Three Hold that staggers the imagination."

Ann fell silent. Her blue eyes grew dreamy as they gazed out at the charcoal sky.

"Sometimes," she said slowly, "I listen to the throbbing of the engines and the gurgle of water against the hull, and I make myself forget that Kong lies under this dreary old deck. But I can't forget for very long. He sleeps, but he's got to awaken sometime."

Jack nodded almost imperceptibly. "Wake up, or perish. From what I hear, he's hovering between those two extremes."

Conversation had caused Ann to forget her meal. Coming out of her dreamy trance, she dug in while it was still warm, but seemed lost in thought.

Finishing up his hash, Jack watched her eat and marveled at her porcelain profile. Ann's fine-grained hair, always on the unruly side, resembled golden sea foam blowing in the steady southern breeze.

"We should make Mombasa tomorrow night," he remarked. "Probably late."

"Wake me, will you, Jack? I want to see dry land again. I ache for it. I'm so used to the rocking of this boat that standing on something that isn't moving but feels substantial seems like a faraway fantasy."

"I will, Ann. Promise."

Ann Darrow placed her head on his shoulder. She closed her eyes as if tired.

Driscoll fished out a cigarette and got it going. He smoked thoughtfully, enjoying the pre-storm quiet and the comforting warmth of Ann's nearness. His clear eyes grew uncharacteristically soft and reflective.

Smelling tobacco smoke, the blonde actress took the cigarette from the Mate's mouth, puffed twice, then returned it to Driscoll's parted lips.

Picking up a surprisingly long length of cordage from the deck, where some careless sailor had left it lying unstowed, Jack began tying it into a complicated knot that started with three flat coils of concentric line. He worked deftly, fingers manipulating the interlocking loops until they were positioned just so, flat on the deck.

When he judged the arrangement satisfactory, Driscoll pulled on the loose ends, yanking hard in opposite directions. The cluster of cordage abruptly snapped into a ball-shaped knot. Then he tied the ends into a bowline knot.

"You should go on the stage!" laughed Ann. "You'd give the Great Blackstone and Thurston the magician a run for their money."

"Aw, that was no magic trick," scoffed Driscoll. "Just expert knot-tying."

"It looks heavy," the blonde marveled. "What is it used for? Keeping soused sailors in line?"

"Oh, it has plenty of uses. Attach the bowline to a heaving rope and then throw the ball knot to another ship's deck, and you'll have yourself a handy lifeline. It's also used for decoration. Smugglers sometimes conceal gems in the core."

Ann eyed the Mate longingly. "If you were really a magician," she breathed, "when you untied that thing, a diamond ring would pop out." Then she laid her honeyed hair on his shoulder and a long sweet silence followed.

Carl Denham tramped up not long after, looking around purposefully. When he spied the First Mate, his eyes took on a fresh light, and he made a beeline for Jack Driscoll.

"Skipper wants to see you. Pronto."

"Know what he wants?" asked Jack, standing up as he helped Ann to her feet.

"I think he wants you up in the crow's nest. But let him tell you."

"Trouble?"

"Trouble, or whales. He's not sure."

Handing the hard cord ball to Ann, Jack said, "Hold onto this for me."

"Why?" asked Ann, weighing the heavy knot on her sunburnt hands.

Jack grinned. "It's called a monkey's fist. Maybe it will bring you luck."

DRISCOLL reported to the flying bridge, where Captain Englehorn was studying the southern horizon with his binoculars, wind whipping at his white uniform.

"What's this about whales?" he hailed.

The Skipper handed over the binoculars. "Take a look for yourself, Mr. Driscoll."

The First Mate did. He twisted the focusing screw, struggling to make out what the ship's master was pointing toward.

"I can't tell if what I'm looking at is weather or spouting whales," he admitted at last.

"Or something else," murmured Englehorn. "You got the best eyes of any man on this vessel, possibly excepting myself. Climb up in the crow's nest and take a good hard look. Let me know what you see."

"Aye, sir," said Driscoll, taking the binoculars over to the mast of the crow's nest. He went up the precarious ladder with the binoculars banging on his chest, popped the hatch, and squeezed into the narrow steel tub.

Finally, the First Mate stood up in the small enclosure. The fact of his height conferred upon Driscoll's conning a definite advantage. He studied the horizon, switching the lenses back and forth, and his face became hard as a rock.

He clambered down the rickety ladder as fast as safety would permit. After his feet slammed to the deck, Driscoll went charging for the flying bridge.

"Weather, or whales blowing?" asked the Skipper.

"Can't you read from my expression?"

"I can read that the news is not good, so let me have it plain."

"Water spouts. Three of them. Twisting and squirming like charcoal elephant trunks sucking up sea water."

"So I feared," said Englehorn heavily. "Do they seem to be coming our way?"

"I didn't stick around long enough to reckon it exactly. But we have to assume the worst though, don't we?"

Englehorn squinted in thought. "If water spouts are forming to the south of us, others could develop anywhere on our present course. Take a crew down to Number Three, and be ready to unshackle Kong upon my order."

"Denham will be wild if he sees us making ready to do that," warned Driscoll.

Captain Englehorn smoothed his mustache with a sun-reddened hand, and suggested, "Have Miss Darrow distract him."

"Good thinking," said Driscoll, racing for the stairs. At the top, he caught himself, and came down briskly but not madly, lest Carl Denham spot him and jump to correct conclusions.

Denham and Ann Darrow were still engaged in conversation when the First Mate broke in.

"Ann, since the rain has stopped, why don't you take Mr. Denham on a tour of some of the seldom-seen sights of the ship?"

Ann looked blank. Driscoll winked at her so that Denham could not see it.

"What are you driving at?" Denham said hotly. "I've been over every square inch of this barge. Twice! You know I have."

Driscoll made his grin lopsided. "But you've never been up in the crow's nest, have you?"

"Why would I do a fool thing like that? There's nothing up there. Not even crows."

"I have!" Ann said excitedly. "I'll be happy to show Mr. Denham the ship from high above."

"Say, what is this?" Denham said truculently. "A gag?"

Driscoll shook his head solemnly. "Captain thinks there's a whale spouting to the south. He thought you'd like to borrow these binoculars and take in that particular show."

Denham's skeptical features melted and his voice lost its resistance.

"Whales? You don't say? Well, since it's not raining, I might like that. It'll be kind of a diversion."

"Exactly," said Driscoll evenly, handing over the binoculars. "Think of it as a diversion."

Taking Denham by one hand, Ann led him off. Jack Driscoll watched them go, not taking his eyes off the pair until they were ascending the frail ladder to the crow's nest high over the deck.

When he deemed it safe to do so, the First Mate went about collecting deck workers, saying gruffly, "Come with me to Number Three Hold. We have to make like Mohammed and move a mountain."

Chapter 20

THE STEEL tub of the crow's nest rocked to the rolling and pitching of the *Wanderer* as the hardy freighter plowed through the choppy waves. The seas were running high, but surging crests were no trouble for the old tramper's rust-stained prow, which sliced through every foamy obstacle with indomitable intent.

The Skipper's binoculars passed between Ann Darrow and Carl Denham as they searched the lowering southern skies.

Denham looked around while Ann had the glasses and remarked, "Should be dark in another hour or so."

"I think I see them!" cried Ann suddenly.

"The whales, you mean?" returned Denham, craning his thick neck.

"I don't see the whales themselves, only their spouts. There must be at least three of them."

Denham grabbed the field glasses, training them on the smoky southern skies.

"If those are whales," he exclaimed, "they're monsters!"

"I've heard there are whales so big around they could swallow a small boat," said Ann lightly.

The showman seemed not to hear, for he was studying the rising, twisting forms far away.

"If I didn't know better, I would think I was looking at a bunch of Texas twisters," he mumbled.

"That can't be," said Ann quickly. "Jack said that tropical cyclones are more like hurricanes, not tornados or whatever."

Denham's eyebrows knitted together and he didn't take his eyes off the weather troubling this lonely stretch of the western Indian Ocean.

"I wonder…" he murmured.

"Wonder what?"

"If these might not be waterspouts."

"What are waterspouts?" wondered Ann.

"They're kind of like sea tornados. When one gets to circulating, it pulls up ocean water in a whirling column of air and H_2O. I may have tramped around the world, but I'm no sailorman. I've never seen a live waterspout, so I could be wrong."

"Let me see," requested Ann.

Taking the binoculars from Denham, she studied the phenomenon, and started a running commentary.

"I think they must be whales," she offered.

Denham snorted skeptically. "Surfacing whales would spit up a plume of water from their blowholes that die down quick. Then they start spouting again. Those devilish things are not collapsing into the water."

Now Ann's pale face grew worry lines as she realized the truth of the showman's gruff assertion.

"I'm sure Captain Englehorn can't be wrong," she said reassuringly. "He's lived his entire life on the sea."

Leaning on the rocking rail, the troubled filmmaker slowly rubbed his blunt chin, brown eyes narrowing. He began looking around, and his gaze fell upon the deck.

It looked suspiciously empty of crew.

"Where did everybody go?" he muttered.

Ann lowered the binoculars, offered brightly, "Isn't the view grand?"

"Huh? Oh, that. I guess you're used to it by now. First Mate has snuck you up here a bunch of times, hasn't he?"

Ann Darrow's cheeks turned a pale pink as she lowered the lids of her blue eyes.

"Oh, once or twice. The air is so much sweeter up here. No coal smoke or kerosene."

"Not tonight," grunted Denham. "It's as humid as the hot place." He studied her. "Speaking of sweet, Driscoll's pretty sweet on you. I guess you return the favor, eh?"

A dreamy look came into Ann's blue eyes, and they looked skyward. "Well, Jack hasn't exactly proposed yet, but he has hinted around the subject," she said timidly.

"He's a straight shooter," admitted Denham gruffly. "You might do better—if you spent a few years looking. But fate kind of threw us all together. So maybe destiny means for you to get hitched."

"I guess I have you to thank for that, right?"

Denham laughed roughly at the recollection. "When I first stumbled onto you that night in old New York, you tried to snitch an apple off a fruitier's sidewalk stall. If I hadn't stepped in, cops would've pinched you for sure. When you agreed to ship out with us, your whole life took a wild jump across half the globe. That's quite a reach you got there, sister."

Ann laughed musically. "I was so down and out I would've boiled my shoe soles and made a sandwich with the tongue for baloney if you hadn't happened along. That's how desperate I was. Now look at me! I'm in the crow's nest of the most reckless vessel ever to sail the Indian Ocean, with the greatest discovery man has ever made sleeping in the hold. A long way from my parents' ranch—or the Fort Lee movie studios, for that matter."

Mention of Kong caused a cloud to cross Denham's broad features.

"What I want to know is how that big baboon is doing. It's cooler now. That should help him."

Absently chewing at a lower lip, his suspicious eyes flicked to the closed hatch of the Number Three Hold.

"Dogwatch must be over by now. You'd think the decks would be crawling with crew, now that they've eaten."

"You forget we're shorthanded since we lost so many men back on that horrid island."

"Yeah, that we did," Denham said vaguely. His eyes casting about the ship, he noticed something strange off the starboard quarter.

It appeared to be a patch of ocean that was moving in a circular manner. As he watched, plumes of water bloomed forth, whipping about with growing violence.

"I'll be damned!" he barked out.

"What is it?" Ann asked anxiously.

"That water is behaving mighty peculiar."

A blunt finger indicated the direction of the phenomenon. Ann followed it with widening eyes. She saw the water starting to rise and swirl.

"Waterspout!" shouted Denham. Calling down over the metal rim of the crow's nest, he repeated the cry, "Waterspout off the starboard quarter. Waterspout! Waterspout!"

If the excitable showman expected deckhands to pour out of the forecastle and other shipboard crannies, he was disappointed.

Then he spotted Lumpy's bald skull coming up from the Number Three Hold, clutching Ignatz the monkey, who was chattering and fighting and trying to get out of his owner's bony clutches.

"It looks as if Lumpy has finally reclaimed his pet," Ann remarked lightly.

"Seems to me like that monk wants no part of the cook," grumbled Denham suspiciously. His fingers were back at his jaw and he was worrying it energetically.

Next, a sailor emerged, pulling Penjaga by one scrawny arm. She was also fighting and making angry noises that carried as high as her shrill words escalated.

"What on earth?" Ann said dully.

"*No!*" the old woman shrieked. "*You cannot do this!*"

Using his cupped hands to form a megaphone, Denham shouted, "What's going on down there?"

Hearing the rough voice, Penjaga lifted her anguished features and screamed, "*They are doing what you do not want them to do!*"

Denham roared, "Are they? Well, we'll see about that!"

Lifting the steel trapdoor, he charged down the ladder as if unafraid to fall to the hard steel plates of the lower bridge.

"Where you going?" Ann cried out.

"I'm going to see a man about a monkey!" ripped back Denham. "And he better listen to reason if he knows what's good for him...."

Chapter 21

JACK DRISCOLL was supervising the operation in the Number Three Cargo Hold amidships.

Freshening ocean winds were pushing into the open hatch, making the air breathable, but not rendering the task any more pleasant. The hold grew surprisingly cool in very short order.

Two pairs of deck workers were attempting to undo Kong's ankle shackles, and having a hard time of it.

"Step it up," barked the First Mate. "No telling how much time we have, but we don't want to find out the hard way that it's run out."

"Tryin', Mate," said one man. He was on one knee, and attempting to pry the makeshift shackle open. The things were not designed for easy adjustment. They had been crafted on the ship during the period when Kong was being rafted out to open water back at Skull Mountain Island.

The ship's master machinist had done the best he could, but his intent was to keep Kong in restraints until landfall. No one anticipated that there would be a need to open the shackles before reaching ultimate port.

A blunt blacksmith's hammer was being applied, and Kong's hairy right leg shook with every blow.

Above on the weather deck, Penjaga was screeching like an angry parrot, her words unintelligible, emotions rising and twisting.

Then a voice called down, "Mr. Driscoll! Mr. Denham is tearing along, hell for leather!"

"Now that's the last thing I need," grunted Driscoll. "Snap it up," he said again.

Striding over to the bottom of the companionway steps, the First Mate took a firm stance, legs apart, his burly body blocking the way as Carl Denham pounded down, his face red as a cooked beet, belligerent eyes striking sparks.

"What's going on down here?" he thundered.

"Orders," Driscoll said curtly. "We've got to jettison Kong. It's getting rough out there. We can't wait 'til the ship and its cargo are unmanageable."

"Over my dead body!"

"If it comes to that, it comes to that," grated Driscoll, refusing to budge.

"Step aside, Mr. Driscoll," warned Denham.

The First Mate took his fists off his hips, but kept them hard. His knuckles turned white against the rawness of his hands.

"Your presence is not needed during this operation," Driscoll said flatly. "Return topside. Captain's orders."

"Don't roughneck me," warned Denham. "I can knock a man down if I have to."

Driscoll scowled stormily. "You hit any member of my crew, and you'll be in the brig before you know it."

"I wasn't thinking past you," growled Denham, rolling up his sleeves one by one.

Turning his head, the First Mate called, "Keep working, you men. I'll handle this."

Driscoll lifted his fists. Too late.

Carl Denham didn't wait for the First Mate's head to swivel back in his direction. Setting himself, he drove out a meaty fist—and connected hard.

Caught by surprise, Jack Driscoll staggered back, brief sparks and stars exploding in his stunned eyes.

Bounding past, Denham sloped for the seamen belaboring Kong's ankle bracelets, and barked, "Belay that!"

One deck worker snapped back, "Don't talk like a sailor if you ain't one. Take my advice, brother."

Features working with rage, Denham reached down for the man's shoulders and set himself to haul the sailor to his feet. No sooner had he wrapped his fingers around the man's rough shirt than equally rough hands grabbed his shoulders, spun him around, and a fast-traveling fist rocked his jaw to one side.

Caught off-guard, Denham lost his footing and sprawled on the steel floor. He lay there dazed for a moment, lifted his suddenly shaggy head, then shook it violently. The expression on his face told that this was a mistake.

"In case you're wondering," Jack Driscoll told him firmly, "that's what they call a bolo punch. And if you stay flat on your back, you won't collect another."

"You can't do this, Driscoll," Denham spat thickly, red fluid leaking from his mouth. "Kong is everything I've got!"

"And this ship is all that's keeping us from the bottom of the Indian Ocean. I'm sorry, Mr. Denham. But we have to deep-six Kong. No choice in the matter. Captain's orders."

The ship had been steaming along on an even keel, but now it commenced rocking. Driscoll lifted his head and shouted, "Storm's getting closer. Let's get this finished!"

From the floor, Carl Denham groaned, "Not closer. It's here."

"What are you yakking about?" challenged Driscoll.

"Up in the crow's nest. I saw one forming."

"What?"

"Waterspout. Off the starboard quarter."

"You better not be lying, Denham."

"See for yourself, Mate."

Driscoll hesitated, then went flying up the companionway, gained the deck, and went to the high rail off to the starboard.

He had to crane his head to see over the bulwark against which tormented waves were sloshing over the deck.

The waterspout stood up like an elephant's trunk that had dipped down from some higher realm to quest about in a watery world. Churning mightily, it resembled a black tornado—but a foamy whirlwind composed of wind and water and not merely mad circular motion.

Driscoll lifted his voice in a crash of harsh words. *"Waterspout! Starboard quarter! All hands turn out! Waterspout!"*

Just then his anxious eyes went to the bridge. He could see that Captain Englehorn had already spied the ugly apparition.

Driscoll charged up the ladder as the master himself was spinning the helm wheel, attempting to evade the unpredictable threat, joining Englehorn.

"Where did *that* come from?" he said out loud.

The old seaman did not reply; he was too busy wrestling with his ship's great wheel, throwing the rudder to port. The vessel heeled drunkenly, changing course.

"Bad news, Cap'n," continued Driscoll. "We haven't even got his leg irons off."

"No time now," bit out the grizzled old mariner. "See if you can get the hull hatch shut. In another few minutes, we're going to be in for a pounding."

Driscoll slammed down the companionway stairs, and suddenly there was rain, lots of it. It rolled across the deck in drumming waves and the overhead skies were darkening faster. It was as if the sun was going down in a violent hurry.

Racing across the deck, Driscoll got down into the Number Three Hold and barked, "Forget it! Get the hull access door shut. We're in for it."

Every crewman in the hold went to work with a firm will. The hatch was closed by turning cranks that had long since acquired gobs and patches of rust. Having stood open for days in the salt air had not made the mechanism any more cooperative.

They struggled with the wheels and the handles, and the turning mechanism fought back. But finally they got the thing closed off. Darkness smothered the Number Three Cargo Hold.

On the stainless steel floor, unseen by anyone, Carl Denham smiled in broad relief.

Then the ship was jumping violently, and the noise of the rain against the hull sounded like rolling storms of buckshot drumming and drumming without end.

"We're in for it now," the showman said, sounding positively giddy about it.

IT WAS over within an hour.

Guided by Englehorn's sure hand, the *Wanderer* evaded the rampaging storm, and found a break in the rain, plunging for untroubled water like a floundering swimmer seeking dry land.

The waterspout had careened south, away from their course. And now the sun was going down, smoldering behind burning clouds.

The crew assembled on the foredeck, looking about and seeing that the way ahead was clear of weather.

Ann Darrow had long since come down from the crow's nest, and taken refuge in her cabin. Now she stirred about, to investigate the aftermath of the *Wanderer's* brush with disaster.

Jack went to her after he spotted Ann's blonde hair fluttering in the settling sea breeze.

"We made it," he said excitedly. "The worst is over!"

"What about Kong?" Ann asked breathlessly.

Driscoll laughed roughly. "Waterspout probably saved his life. At least for now. We had to close the hull hatch. If we can keep steaming along, we should reach Mombasa in short order."

Ann hugged herself and shivered despite or possibly because of the coolness of approaching evening. In one hand, she clutched the knot of cordage Driscoll had called a monkey's fist, as if clinging to a good luck talisman.

"I wish I knew whether that was a good thing or not," she sighed.

Driscoll shrugged carelessly. "Fate, I guess. It was plain fate. It's just not Kong's time. But it's probably only a reprieve."

"I held onto this thing all through the storm," she murmured. "For luck. Didn't someone write a famous story about a monkey's fist that granted wishes?"

"You're thinking of 'The Monkey's Paw,'" Jack told her gently. "And I was joking about that kind of knot being good luck."

"Joking or not," sighed Ann, "I held onto it for dear life. It gave me comfort." She smiled bravely. "Perhaps because it reminded me of the man who made it—hard and strong."

Jack cracked a self-conscious grin and remarked, "Maybe I spoke too soon."

Penjaga had been locked in the private cabin she rarely visited and, upon her release, her wrinkled face was like a stone, changeless and unmoving.

She strolled up to Jack Driscoll and asked no questions. Her eyes bored into his and she waited for the Mate to speak.

"Kong lives. We had to close the hatch to save the ship."

The old woman's facial expression changed not a particle. Her eyes took on a curious light. Where before they had been hard and bright as agates, now they were moist with tears that refused to flow.

"I will return to my watch."

Driscoll nodded. "Look, I can't say I'm sorry about how things turned out. I can't say I'm happy, either. Just know that if it comes down to saving the ship, Kong will be the first thing to go."

Penjaga firmed her withered lips, brushing past them.

"I'll go keep her company," Ann volunteered.

"With Kong?"

Ann hesitated. "Sometimes I lay awake thinking about that horrid beast. Perhaps if I face my fears, I will sleep better."

"Go ahead. Denham is down there, sleeping off a roundhouse punch. You might see to him, too."

"What happened to him?"

Driscoll laughed. "He took a poke at me and connected. So I socked him back. That makes us even. Make sure you tell him that. I don't want any more guff from him for the rest of the voyage. There'll be plenty enough trouble between here and New York."

Smiling bravely, Ann disappeared below while Driscoll went off to report to Captain Englehorn.

STEADY before his wheel, the grizzled skipper took in his first mate's report and nodded solemnly at the end of it.

"I want no more fisticuffs between you and Mr. Denham."

"It wasn't my idea," Driscoll declared. "But I think I settled the matter once and for all. Denham has no more beef with me. He's still got his Beast, and he's breathing."

Night was closing in and, as was his custom, the Skipper took the evening's plug of tobacco out of his mouth and disposed of it, then began filling his pipe.

"If all goes well," he undertoned, "by this time tomorrow, we will put into Mombasa."

"Let's hope nothing else goes wrong between now and then," said Driscoll. "We've had enough excitement."

Salty eyebrows gathering together, Englehorn nodded as he applied a wooden safety match to the bowl of his pipe, got it lit, and took an experimental draw.

The old seaman held the tobacco smoke in his lungs for a long time. When he expelled it, with the fragrant cloud came carefully-chosen words.

"I will count on you, Mr. Driscoll, to keep matters calm aboard my ship. That will be all."

"Sorry, sir," said the First Mate, departing.

Jack Driscoll made a point of seeking out Carl Denham, and asked, "How's your jaw?"

The director took the jaw in question in one hand, and gave it an experimental wiggle. "Not completely unhinged, if that's what you're asking. "How's yours?"

"Hanging properly and shipshape," reported Driscoll. "Listen, the Old Man wants no more trouble between us."

Denham looked as if he was thinking about that for a long time. Finally, he allowed, "I suppose we should shake on it."

"I consider us even. If you don't, I'll have to ask the Skipper about confining you to the brig on bread and water rations."

The boisterous showman laughed heartily. "Say, if you put it that way, I guess I'll have to shake hands with you. Not that I mind so much. But after seeing Kong melting away before my eyes, I have no appetite for short rations."

Jack Driscoll suppressed a grin, and the two men clasped hands as the sun set in a blaze of heliotrope and the waters of the Indian Ocean east of Mombasa slowly turned red as blood....

Chapter 22

THE NIGHT passed uneventfully.
The weather became calm, and the temperature dropped, thanks to a steady northwesterly sea breeze.

The starboard side hatch remained open all night, and the air circulated through the Number Three Hold, ruffling the furry form of Kong, steadily drying the residue of perspiration that had collected during the day.

Past the midnight hour Penjaga and Ann Darrow idled away the time conversing in whispered voices.

"When Kong looks at your hair," the Storyteller was saying, "he is reminded of the forebears from which he sprang. Your pale skin means nothing to him. But your hair is the color of the eyes of the Kongs of old. He will never again look into the eyes of those who came before. Dead, all dead...."

"His parents are dead?"

"Long dead. For Kong is older than your imagination would accept...."

Ann Darrow shivered, instinctively touching her golden locks.

"How long have you... known him?"

"I was little. A girl. It was long ago. Kong was young, too. His size was not what it is now. He was larger than the little monkey who worships him now. But he grew. Grew mightily. One day, he had become so large that he no longer recognized me, small as I was, large as he was. On that day, he nearly crushed me underfoot. I understood then that Kong walked above the world

155

of mortal men. A god he had become, a being whose roars were like thunder, whose throne was the hollow of Skull Mountain. The great lizards feared him by then. Thunderbolts shunned him. But I worshipped him. He was no more of this world than the Creator who fashioned him to battle the terrible lizards."

Ann stared wonderingly at the crone's cobwebbed profile. "If Kong is so old and you were a little girl when he was young, why, how old are you?"

"Old, old, old," murmured Penjaga. "Old." The word became a lament, an invocation of a lost world and an ancient time. "I am the last Storyteller of my line. I alone carry in my heart the history of my people. But I am not the last of my tribe. There are others, back on the island. But I have no one to pass the secrets to. With me, perishes the wisdom of a mighty nation, the one that built the mighty Wall that kept the demon lizards in check. Now look at it," she muttered darkly, thin eyes going to the pitch-covered raft on which Kong slept, portions of which had been constructed from the great doors broken by the beast-god after he had broken through them. "It is a broken bed, not an unshatterable bulwark. My ancestors would be sad and shamed to see this. I speak of the Tagatu, whose secrets I keep and whose Storyteller I am."

The blonde woman laid a gentle hand on Penjaga's bony shoulder.

"It's a long way to New York, yet," she said gently. "And the days are sometimes endless. I will be glad to hear the stories of your people. That is, if you want to share them with me."

Instead of answering directly, Penjaga began to croon a low, mournful song. Although she could comprehend not a word of it, Ann listened, enthralled.

The song went on and on, until gradually it dawned upon her that this was no song, no dirge, no lament, but the story of Penjaga's race sung as history. It was by turns sad and uplifting, mysterious and thrilling. But utterly incomprehensible.

Eventually, the old woman ran out of breath, or story, for her words sank into a doleful humming.

The humming exerted a somnambulant effect on Ann Darrow. She grew sleepy and excused yourself.

"I think I will repair to my cabin—as the Duchess once said," Ann remarked lightly.

The humor of the remark went over the elderly Storyteller's head, and she barely nodded saying, "Sleep well, Gold Hair. Of all who I have come in contact with, only you seem to possess an open heart."

Ann laughed self-consciously, saying, "I hope you're wrong about that. For Jack Driscoll and I are going to be married some day!"

"Driscoll possesses a true heart, even if he does not always see with it."

"Well, good night. I will see you in the morning." Ann paused, struck by a sudden impulse. "Oh, why don't I leave this with you?"

Penjaga looked at Ann's outstretched hand. It clutched the hard round knot Driscoll had made.

"What is that?"

"Jack calls it a monkey's fist," explained Ann. "It's supposed to bring luck."

"A talisman?" asked the Storyteller, accepting it in both withered hands.

Ann nodded. "I like to think it brought us safely through that storm. It's silly, I know, but…."

"You prayed to it?"

"I wished on it. Wished with all my heart."

Bowing her gauzy white head in gratitude, Penjaga intoned, "You possess a great kind heart. If this talisman did not possess power before, it does now. For you have imbued it with the gold of your heart. Thank you."

"Good night."

Ann floated up the companionway. The door to the well deck opened and closed, leaving Penjaga alone with the colossal beast-god of her people.

The moon was pouring its effulgence on the starboard side of the ship. Silver light filled the Number Three Hold where Kong slept. From time to time, he made snuffling noises, but this had been a common occurrence.

The creature's stomach grumbled, but this, too, was not unusual. Gargantuan gurgling and low growls told that his digestive tract was patiently processing his most recent meals.

As the Storyteller watched through narrowed slit eyes, she could tell that animal vitality was flowing back through Kong's recumbent frame.

Under her breath, Penjaga began chanting, calling his name, "Kong. Kong. Kong." This was followed by songs and prayers. She stood up, shaking her body, causing seashells and other decorative items at her throat and waist to rattle in sympathy. She spun the monkey's fist knot about her head, and around Kong's, as she moved and swayed.

"Kong. Kong. Kong."

As if in response, the enormous tawny eyes of the brute sprang open. Upward they gazed, staring at the steel hatches above.

A dry gasp was wrenched from the Storyteller's parched lips. She had been consumed by what an anthropologist might call an ecstatic dance, and seemed oblivious to her surroundings.

Kong made no detectable sound opening his orbs, but when they snapped wide, Penjaga stopped, turned, and her wise eyes went immediately to the creature's shaggy head. The monkey's fist knot fell from her fingers, landing with a dull thud.

She seemed to freeze, peered thinly for a moment, and then padded forward. Lifting her voice in a whisper, she asked, "Kong?"

But the behemoth did not respond. He continued staring upward, eyes unmoving, irises neither dilating nor contracting, just staring blankly as if sightless.

Reaching to the back of her belt, Penjaga found a pouch. It was not one of the pouches containing the herbs that had kept Kong sedated during the long weeks of the voyage westward. This was another pouch entirely.

From this she took a short bundle of what appeared to be sweetgrass or sage, and holding this in one hand, she lit the bundle with a striker until it was smoldering and shedding burning particles and greyish smoke that was pleasantly pungent.

Holding this aloft, the Storyteller commenced circling Kong, speaking in an increasing musical cadence, endeavoring to fill the huge hold with the sweet smoke of her dry bundle of jungle grasses.

"Kong, Kong, Kong," she intoned, her voice rising with each repetition.

Somewhere nestled in the mountainous fur of Kong, Ignatz the monkey awoke. He sat up, sniffed the smoky air, and was soon chattering excitedly.

As if in response, mighty Kong released a deep, bestial growl—one that reverberated throughout the Number Three Hold, rising to the weather deck through the chinks and joints of the overhead hatch.

Hearing this unfamiliar noise, Ignatz scampered to Kong's head and began tugging at his drying fur....

Chapter 23

A N ABLE seaman named O'Brien had the watch.
He was taking a turn around the weather deck when
the growl came rumbling out of the Number Three hatch.

Seaman O'Brien froze, and when the sound did not come
again, he crept toward the hatch. For there was no other spot
on the ship that could have produced such a bestial sound,
except the hold that held Kong.

Taking care not to step on the hatch doors themselves, O'Brien
knelt down and put one ear to the port side of the hatchway,
listening for a repetition of the terrible growling.

None came, but below he heard Ignatz the monkey chattering excitedly. "Better let him be," he muttered to himself. "Lumpy
will know what to do."

O'Brien found Lumpy in his bunk and roused him by barking,
"Wake up, you salty old sea dog!"

Lumpy demanded, "What do you want, you common scala-
wag?"

"Thought I heard a big dog growl coming from the Number
Three Hold hatch. When I listened again, all I heard was your
foolish monkey carrying on to beat the band."

"Who—Ignatz?"

"Do you know any other foolish monkeys on this old rust
bucket?"

Rather than reply, Lumpy jumped out of his bunk and hopped
into his trousers, not bothering with his shirt.

Together they raced for the hatch, and went down the companionway leading into Number Three.

Seaman O'Brien had a .45-caliber revolver that he toted in a cartridge belt about his waist. He had the weapon out.

Despite this, Lumpy led the way, eager to see what was troubling Ignatz.

When they reached the bottom step, Lumpy froze, and Seaman O'Brien almost went tumbling over him.

After they got their limbs untangled, Lumpy barked, "That mangy mutt has got his eyes open!"

O'Brien stared. Kong's immense orbs were wide open, staring upward, apparently oblivious to them both. Still, they were an unnerving sight.

"Should I shoot it?" he hissed.

Lumpy shook his hairless head. "If I thought it would do any good, I would say blaze away. But I don't think it would. We better fetch the Mate."

Up the companionway they raced, abandoning all stealth.

Below them, Penjaga continued filling the air with her bundle of smoking sweetgrass while Kong stared uncomprehendingly at the underside of the double hatch over his face.

JACK DRISCOLL tumbled out of his bunk, and belted on his own revolver, knowing that it would probably avail him very little, if at all.

"You heard a growl, you say?" he demanded of O'Brien.

"Sounded like thunder far away, except it came from inside the ship. But it didn't repeat. All I heard when I put my ear to the hatch door was that idiot monkey chattering like he was having a nightmare."

"If Kong has woke up on us," Driscoll grated, "we'll all be having a nightmare."

"His eyes were wide open, I can tell you that. They were as big as pie plates."

"Did he look your way?"

Lumpy answered that, saying, "We didn't stick around long enough to find out."

They pounded along the weather deck and the noise they made brought Carl Denham stumbling out of his cabin, looking as if he hadn't really slept.

"Trouble?" he demanded.

"In spades!" Driscoll flung back, not breaking his pace. "O'Brien here heard Kong growling and when he investigated, his eyes were wide open."

"O'Brien's or Kong's?"

"Who do you think?" snapped the Mate.

"That's trouble, all right," grumbled Denham, rushing to catch up.

The three men jammed through the doorway leading below, without waiting to alert the rest of the crew, most of whom were sleeping.

Reaching the bottom of the companion, they halted, and saw that it was all true.

Kong was growling, but it was not issuing from his cavernous mouth. The noises were coming from his stomach—along with gurgles and other sounds of digestive processing.

"Was that what you heard, O'Brien?" pressed Driscoll.

"No, not like that. It was louder, more of a rumble. I don't think his stomach did it."

Driscoll's eyes went to the shifting shape of Ignatz the monkey, who was tugging at Kong's hairy black jowls as if to awaken him.

Seeing this, Lumpy called out, "Ignatz, you crazy monk! Get down off of that thing right now!"

Turning to the sound of his master's voice, Ignatz eyed him with extreme anxiety, opened his rubbery mouth and began scolding like a squirrel. Then he returned to his endeavors.

"What do we do, Mate?" asked Lumpy. "Ignatz is tryin' to wake the brute up!"

Instead of answering, Driscoll strode over to Penjaga, who was immersed in her ritual, singing and chanting, oblivious to all.

Seizing her by one shoulder, Driscoll turned the Storyteller about, shook her with both hands, demanding, "What are you up to?"

Comprehension of her surroundings came into the woman's eyes, wise as a turtle's, but she croaked only, "Kong stirs."

Grabbing the bundle of half-burned sweetgrass, Jack Driscoll demanded, "This doesn't smell like the weeds you used to keep him on his back. What is this stuff?"

"It is medicine," snapped the Storyteller. "It is to keep Kong alive. He breathes the sweet smoke, and his soul remains in his body."

"Sounds like mumbo-jumbo," growled Driscoll suspiciously. "Are you sure this isn't some type of revival ritual?"

Penjaga said nothing. Just a few feet away, Kong's stomach gave a shortened growl.

"I don't trust her," muttered Denham. "We got to do something. I think he's getting ready to come back to life."

"If he does," said Driscoll tightly, "all hell will break loose. We'll be goners. Every sorry man-jack of us."

Lumpy was yelling at Ignatz and the small monkey was hectoring him back. He had his tiny paws wrapped around one of Kong's lower canines, and was pulling at it as if to compel the massive head to lift up.

Perhaps he was succeeding, or perhaps only Kong was coming around naturally.

Suddenly, the huge jaws sprang wide, and an even greater growl rumbled forth, causing everyone in the hold to freeze in place.

Except Carl Denham. The stocky showman was moving now, pounding for the wooden crate lying at Kong's hairy feet.

Falling on this, he shouted, "Everybody clear out. I'm going to use one of these things!"

With both hands, the showman extracted one of the remaining gas grenades, and bundled it over to where Kong's head lay atop the makeshift pallet.

Seeing that the others were still frozen in place, he yelled out again, "Didn't you hear me? Unless you want to go to sleep for the next two weeks, get up those stairs!"

"You heard him!" Jack Driscoll warned. And grabbing Penjaga in both arms, he carried her toward the companionway steps. She spat like a furious cat every step of the way.

Carl Denham showed that he possessed more than his ration of bravery then. While the others were jamming up the steel steps of the companion, he hopped onto Kong's shackled wrist, picked his way carefully up the shaggy arm, came to the shoulder and said to Ignatz, "You clear out, too!"

Ignatz pulled free a clump of Kong's stiff bristly hair and flung it in Denham's general direction.

"You had your chance, monk!" Denham hissed, bringing the gas grenade slamming down on King Kong's blunt nose, releasing billows of greyish fumes once the brittle cast-iron shell cracked like an oversized egg, as it was designed to do under sharp impact.

The stuff was supernaturally potent. Denham had time to throw himself clear, but by the time he hit the deck, the hazy stuff was all over him, and his feeble attempts to lift himself to his feet came to nothing.

Carl Denham collapsed like a deflated balloon. Ignatz the monkey stopped chattering in mid scold, and went limp, his long tail uncurling slowly.

For King Kong, the chemical gas was drawn into his lungs through his broad nostrils, and slowly and ponderously, his large bloodshot eyes closed.

The beast-god resumed his deathlike slumber.

Chapter 24

DAWN FOUND the *Wanderer* steaming through placid waters, the warmth of the the day was beginning to build up again.

The morning watch went about its usual routine. The crew had largely remained oblivious to the predawn misadventure down in Number Three.

One seaman remarked to another, "Did you hear that thunder last night?"

"Sure did. I kept expecting rain. But these decks are dry as a bone."

First Mate Jack Driscoll declined to enlighten his crew as to the true source of the post-midnight "thunder."

"Keep what happened to yourself," he told Lumpy and Seaman O'Brien just before breakfast was served. "Kong should sleep peacefully for the rest of the day, if not longer."

No one questioned the wisdom of this order. Least of all, Captain Englehorn.

Driscoll had decided to let the ship's master wake up of his own accord before apprising him of the near disaster. The Old Man looked as if he had passed beyond worry. His wintry eyes, grey as dirty ice, were opaque with a strange light.

"How can we expect to keep that monster under control clear across the Atlantic, never mind during the run down to the Cape of Good Hope?" he muttered loudly.

"I'll admit it looks pretty bleak," returned Driscoll. "But it's your call, Cap'n."

"What does Denham have to say about it?"

Driscoll laughed in spite of himself. "You'll have to ask him when he wakes up. The knockout gas laid him pretty low. But I'll admit he showed guts. And plenty of them, too."

Englehorn nodded sagely. "I have never questioned Carl Denham's courage. His common sense is another issue."

The First Mate had taken breakfast into the officers' wardroom, and sat with his superior while the old mariner ate methodically.

Making a face, Englehorn remarked, "Remind Lumpy to lay in a fresh store of eggs in Mombasa."

"Don't worry, it's at the top of my list, too."

Turning serious again, Englehorn stated, "From your description, it appears that feeding Kong substantial food is bound to work against us."

"I'm not a hundred percent sure of that, Skipper. I caught that old woman smoking up the hold with some pungent weeds I haven't smelled before."

"Meaning?"

Driscoll shrugged, saying, "Well, maybe she saw that Kong was getting his strength back, and was encouraging him along—if you know what I mean."

"If we feed Denham's Beast, he will turn on us. And if we fail to feed him properly, Kong will dwindle away to skin and bone, is that it?"

"That's about the size of it," admitted the Mate.

"Between the devil and the deep," mused Englehorn, frowning deeply.

"So what do we do, Cap'n?"

"At this present clip," the Skipper observed, "we will raise Mombasa around dusk. By my reckoning, that may be too many hours for comfort. Perhaps we should find a nice quiet inlet or cove."

"There go our fresh eggs…."

"It is my thinking, Mate," continued Englehorn, "that, if we put into a secluded spot, should anything happen when Kong awakens, we will be in a better position to be rid of the devil."

"I think I follow the wake of your thinking, Skipper," said Driscoll slowly.

"I imagine that you do. But I am still committed to serving Carl Denham's orders. But within reason. We will take on what provisions we can for ourselves, and for our strange cargo. We will lay in for a day, or perhaps three."

"Denham won't like that. He might not stand for it, for that matter."

"We will provision as best we can," continued Englehorn, "and we will feed Kong and see how he handles himself. If the situation remains under control, we will steam south as planned. But if this sleeping brute is on the verge of roaring back to life, I am not convinced our chains will hold him for very long, if at all."

Driscoll nodded. "I'm with you there, Skipper. I'm with you all the way."

"Go and see to it. Have the helmsman set a course for an anchorage sufficiently sheltered against any tropical storm. We still have that to be worried about as well."

"Aye aye, sir," said Driscoll, taking his leave.

The First Mate stopped by Ann Darrow's cabin, to check in on her.

Ann answered his short knock without delay. "Good morning, Jack."

Driscoll gave her chin a gentle chuck. "Sleep well?"

Ann smiled wanly. "No nightmares tonight, thank goodness. But I heard thunder."

Driscoll grinned reassuringly, "That particular storm has

passed. For now, at any rate. Would you like me to fetch your breakfast?"

"Not if it includes eggs," she said firmly.

"I'll see what Lumpy has whipped up this morning. Oh, by the way. We're not putting in at Mombasa after all. We're going to find a nice quiet anchorage."

Sleepy blue eyes sparkled with interest. "Oh?"

"Some of the crew are getting seasick. We think a little layover will settle their stomachs."

Ann's penciled brows shot up. "I didn't know your crew is subject to that malady."

"You'd be surprised," said Driscoll dryly, walking off.

Next stop was the bridge, where the Mate conferred with the helmsman. They studied their marine charts until they found a cove well north of Mombasa that seemed to suit their needs.

"Head straight for that point," Driscoll instructed. "All due speed. We should have clear weather the rest of the day."

While the helmsman was executing his orders, the First Mate came down off the bridge, then went below into the Number Three Hold.

As he pounded down the steel steps, Driscoll reflected that, had the side hatch not been open when the gas grenade had been uncorked, the narcotic gas would surely have crept up onto the shelter deck and knocked out a good portion of the crew, if not in fact the entire ship's complement. The stuff was that potent. Designed to fell a charging rhinoceros, it had taken several bombs to bring down King Kong back on Skull Mountain Island.

The noxious vapors had pretty well cleared out by now, the Mate's sense of smell told him.

Kong slumbered like the great invulnerable brute that he was, while Ignatz sprawled insensate on his fur-tangled left shoulder, resembling parent and infant offspring.

Driscoll found Carl Denham not far from Kong's right elbow,

flat on his back and mouth open. The formerly dynamic director was snoring, completely dead to the world.

Putting his hands on his hips, Driscoll muttered, "You are one sorry son of a sea cook."

Without further ado, Driscoll slammed down the crate lid over the remaining gas bombs. Walking back to Denham's slack form, he attempted to hoist him up onto his shoulders.

This proved to be more challenging than anticipated, so the Mate took hold of the heavy-set showman by his ankles, and dragged him to the foot of the companionway, maneuvered him up on the lower steps, then knelt down and managed to lift the sleeping man onto his shoulders, whereupon Driscoll went up the stairs slowly and carefully, bearing Carl Denham in a fireman's carry.

To any who inquired, Driscoll said of Denham, "He must have had a snootful of bathtub gin down there. Nothing serious. We'll let him sleep it off in his cabin."

Depositing the filmmaker onto his cabin bunk, Driscoll drew a black curtain over the porthole and closed the door after him, enjoying the prospect of Carl Denham staying out of his hair for the day.

The First Mate encountered Captain Englehorn as the master was walking toward the bridge to take charge of the vessel.

"All shipshape, sir," he reported. "Denham. Kong. The helmsman. All of it."

Englehorn nodded. "Carry on then, Mate. Be sure to let me know when Mr. Denham awakens."

Driscoll chuckled good-naturedly. "That's not likely to happen until we put into that anchorage. Denham got a face full of that trichloride witch's brew of his."

"Perhaps it will teach him something," sighed Englehorn heavily. "But I doubt it."

"And I'm sure of it!" laughed Driscoll, changing course for the ship's mess, his mind going to breakfast now that more urgent matters were settled for the morning.

Chapter 25

A MONKEY sat in a spreading pine tree on the shores of British East Africa, along the coastal strip known as the Protectorate of Kenya.

This little monkey was patiently picking grubs out of a hole in the tree, and eating them one by one.

He looked like any one of the numberless monkeys who inhabit the Dark Continent. But he was not. He was in his own way special. Although he gave every outward indication of being wild, he was in fact only half wild, having been tamed by man. One special man, in truth.

This monkey was busy gathering his breakfast when the rusty old steamer hove into view.

Coastwise cargo vessels were nothing new to this monkey, whose name was Nkima. He had seen many such in the course of his short life. This one was of no particular interest to him as it approached.

Only when it turned about, and presented its starboard side to land, did Nkima take special notice.

An enormous door hung open, revealing a rectangular cavity. Bright sunlight streamed through, illuminating the tremendous hold, which was lined with steel.

In this chamber, bound in chains, lay the largest gorilla little Nkima had ever beheld in his rather eventful existence.

At first, he blinked tiny eyes in disbelief, then squinted suspiciously at the queer sight.

Nkima was no stranger to gorillas, of course. They ranged the jungles and forests of his own stamping grounds. But the largest gorilla he had ever seen was no taller than an average man, and less tall even than the one man he respected most in all of his jungle habitat. This specimen was stupendous in size.

His appetite temporarily satiated, Nkima scampered down the bole of the tree, hopped onto the jungle floor, and began working his way toward shore, creeping on all fours, long tail curled like a quivering question mark.

Reaching a rocky ledge, he found a stone that was more flat than round, and sat down upon it, studying the ship and its exposed cargo for many long minutes, mouth open in mute wonder.

After careful study, and a great deal of cogitation, little Nkima decided that the giant gorilla was not what it seemed to be. This creature, even lying down, was enormous. He measured its length with his mind and his thought processes told him that this was a gorilla as tall as a tree.

Since no such gorilla had previously shambled into his experience, Nkima decided that it could be dismissed from consideration as a living creature.

What it was, was not clear to Nkima. True, men created things that were strange to behold. This might be one such construction of man, just as the great ship was.

Its purpose was unfathomable. And since monkeys are blessed or cursed with innate curiosity, Nkima continued staring at the creature that resembled a gorilla as tall as a tree, attempting to puzzle it out with his clever monkey brain.

More than an hour of this was sufficient. So Nkima turned and walked back into the jungle, looking for fresh novelty now that his curiosity had been exercised to its utmost.

He told himself that he must tell his good friend, Tarzan of the Apes, about this strange gorilla-thing when he next encountered the ape-man.

Tarzan, he was certain, would be very interested in this monster ape, even if it were not a living creature. For the Lord of the Jungle was always interested in the doings of man, whom Tarzan preferred to stay away from his forest realm.

Chapter 26

C ARL DENHAM floated back to wakefulness in jerky stages.

For half a day, he lay in his bunk like a log possessing regular respiration, and not much else in the way of animation. Before noon, he began to roll on his mattress, and before the afternoon was half along, the unconscious director was tossing and turning, moaning and groaning, as if caught in the throes of a distressing nightmare.

He might have remained so enthralled by restlessness and slumber in uneasy opposition, except that by the time six bells rolled around—signifying seven o'clock in the evening—the disoriented director managed to roll off his bunk, slamming his heavy body to the floor.

That did it. Denham's dazed eyes opened warily. He found himself staring at the ceiling without outward comprehension. It took several moments for his eyes to clear and his vision to come into focus, and when he sat up, the filmmaker was not immediately certain that this was in fact his own cabin.

Slowly, the events of the previous evening came back to him and the groggy showman began to berate himself, saying, "What a ripe jackass I've been."

It required considerable effort to climb to his feet. Denham was forced to throw himself back onto his mattress, because his legs lacked the nerve strength to hold him erect—never mind allow for stable locomotion.

Sunlight was streaming through the black-curtained porthole, and its strength and intensity suggested that the day was well along to its conclusion. A combination of thirst and hunger compelled the filmmaker to get up and feel his way along the cabin walls to the door and pull it open with surprising difficulty.

He forgot about the raised threshold designed to keep out deck wash. In exiting, Denham fell onto the deck rather noisily.

A deck worker happening along discovered him, and helped lift the unsteady showman to his feet saying, "Let me get you back to your bunk, Mr. Denham. You've had a tough go of it."

"Kong," mumbled Denham thickly. "What's become of Kong?"

"Sleeping like a lamb," he was told.

"Kong is no lamb," Denham said gruffly. Looking about, he asked thickly, "Where are we? The ship isn't moving, is it?"

"African coast. We found an anchorage. Laying over for a day or two."

Denham blinked stupidly. "This doesn't look like Mombasa…."

"We're north of Mombasa. Captain's orders."

"I need to talk to your skipper. Tell him so. I'm in no shape to climb to the bridge."

"I'll see to it, sir," said the sailor, helping Denham back onto his bunk.

A few minutes after the seaman departed, First Mate Driscoll popped his head in and asked, "Still woozy?"

"I've had weekend hangovers I enjoyed more," grunted Denham, holding his pounding head in both hands. "What are we doing anchored here?"

"Long story. But the short of it is we made a beeline for the safest anchorage so we can provision and take stock of matters."

"Kong?"

"Back in dreamland. That was sharp work, putting him down that way. No telling what would've happened if he'd started to rear up in earnest."

"Thanks. What I want to know is this: What are Englehorn's intentions? This isn't what we agreed on."

Driscoll said breezily, "It'll have to do. Captain wants to take stock of the entire enterprise. Particularly the disposition of Kong. We think that the old woman tried to wake him up on purpose. Since she's our best bet for keeping him alive, and docile, we've got to get a grip on her."

"You're not thinking of dumping Kong if things look bad, are you?"

"I'm not," the Mate said truthfully. "But we need to get the big fellow on a feeding regimen that will cut a middle course between him wasting away and getting too big for his britches."

Denham grunted. "I follow you. I'd give you an argument, if I had an argument in me. So you get no argument from me. Today. Tomorrow might be different. Savvy?"

"Savvy," Driscoll retorted. "I'll have Lumpy bring you some grub, so you can build your strength back up."

Denham groaned weakly. "Imagine that. Me and old Kong in the same miserable boat. Well, maybe I deserve some of it. I've been thinking that I've been a jackass."

"You're not alone in that thought," returned Driscoll without rancor.

"You could have at least given me the benefit of the doubt," cracked Denham. "I'm trying to be frank about everything."

"Save it for when you get your wits fully gathered about you. You don't sound like yourself. Let me see to your food and you can talk to the Skipper when you're both up to it."

"O.K., have it your way. Just see that Kong stays on an even keel until I get my sea legs back."

"That's the plan, all right," said Driscoll, closing the door behind him.

The First Mate found Lumpy in the galley, fussing with the limited possibilities for supper. Ignatz was fast asleep, curled up in a big mixing bowl, dead to the world.

Poking his head into the kitchen, Driscoll asked, "What have you got that will build up Mr. Denham's strength?"

"I have half a mind to cook up that monkey in this bowl, and make him eat it, tail, teeth, and sassy tongue!"

The Mate winced. "I thought Ignatz was like a second son to you."

"Well, ever since he met Kong, the scamp hardly knows me. It would serve both Denham and the monk right if I fed one to the other. Maybe Denham would have his fill of apes, and we can be rid of this hellish slumgullion." Abruptly, Lumpy exploded, "Slumgullion! That's what I'll whip up tonight."

"Slumgullion? Never heard of it."

"It's also known as hobo stew. Take some potatoes, some tomatoes, some rutabagas, celery sticks, a dash of this, a dollop of that, and you heat it up until it's all properly cooked. That's slumgullion."

"You left out the meat, didn't you?"

Inclining his undershot chin in the direction of the sleeping Ignatz, Lumpy growled, "I'm still contemplating the meat portion."

Driscoll said, "That little monkey won't feed the passengers, much less the crew. Maybe you should widen your horizons, at least as far as the tonight's meal goes."

Looking the First Mate directly in the eye, Lumpy suggested, "If you want to do better, why don't you send a couple of your bully boys onto land and have them bag some real game?"

Driscoll grinned. "I just might, at that. Stand by."

Lumpy shrugged carelessly. "Sure. Ignatz ain't going anywheres."

After conferring with Captain Englehorn, and receiving permission, Jack Driscoll put together a shore party and addressed them on the poop deck.

"We're going to provision. Bananas, bamboo and what have you for Kong. And some real meat for ourselves if we get lucky."

A throaty cheer went up, but it died under Driscoll's withering scowl.

"Order and discipline, you farmers!" he berated.

Sidearms were issued, and the men looked eager to stand on solid ground again. Although some of them might have been more eager to get as far away from Kong as possible. Though they had stood it well, Driscoll realized that it had been a nerve-racking voyage up to this point, and the crew were getting frayed around the edges.

Lowering a dory from its davits, they were soon rowing toward land, conserving kerosene by not engaging the outboard motor.

HIGH in a spreading nut tree, Nkima the monkey took notice. He had gotten bored with throwing sticks at assorted wildlife that happened by and was contemplating the long trek inland to the plantation of Tarzan when this new activity caught his interest.

Tarzan, decided Nkima, could wait. The news of the long ship carrying a monster gorilla fell into the category of jungle gossip. White men stepping onto the land, however, was another matter. Tarzan of the Apes did not like men from civilization intruding upon his preserves. Many were poachers, invading the jungle to take game that did not belong to them.

Nkima decided to observe them at length, so that he had something of substance to report to his friend and master.

Chapter 27

THE HUNT went well.

The shore party bagged a wild boar from the start. A big snorting bull, it had come charging out of the bush in their direction.

Two men with rifles dropped it with such alacrity that the boar kept traveling even though its legs and its brain were no longer connected.

When it finished sliding to a halt, the boar snorted noisily, seeming as if it wanted to lash out, but had no control over its great bulk.

Jack Driscoll finished it with a bullet to the brain, and said, "That ought to feed the whole crew for a couple of days, if not longer."

While they rigged up a sling with which to drag it to the beached dory, Driscoll ordered the others to harvest as many bananas and coconuts as practical.

"Don't go shinnying up any trees," he instructed. "Just forage for any dropped coconuts. We can come back later for more. And don't forget green bamboo. Hack off some short lengths. We'll add it to the pile."

Several of the men had come ashore equipped with cane knives, and they used these wickedly sharp blades to harvest bamboo.

So while one group dragged the dead boar to the dory, the

others worked in relays, fetching assorted roughage that would be suitable for the ravenous appetite that was Kong.

Driscoll said, "If you spot anything that looks like eggs, grab those, too."

But no eggs were discovered. Nor were they otherwise molested by the jungle inhabitants.

HIGH in the treetops, a little long-tailed monkey crept along, using great care not to be seen, observing their every move.

Nkima did not understand the tongue of white men, of course, and so did not know that they spoke of the giant gorilla lying in the hold of the ship anchored not far off as if it were alive.

Had he been able to understand their speech, Nkima would not have believed a syllable. For he was certain no such gorilla ever drew breath.

Only a few hours of daylight remained when the dory pushed off, heavily laden, and was rowed back to the *Wanderer*, lying a quarter mile off the African coast.

The heat of the day was not oppressive, but neither was it comfortable. The shore party was soaked in perspiration as much by the strenuousness of their efforts as by the beating tropical sun.

Lines were dropped, then secured, and an electric winch brought the dory back up to the ship's deck. Seamen rushed over to offload the heaping food stuffs.

The boar was another matter. It was one thing to muscle it over the gunwales. Quite another to lug it down to the galley.

Supervising this part of the operation, Lumpy suggested, "Why don't we just butcher it on the deck? Carry it down in pieces."

Driscoll considered this and decided, "I'll clear it with the Old Man. If the Skipper says that's how it will be done, then that's how it will be done."

Captain Englehorn, dozing in his cabin, was only too happy to give permission—the pleasant prospect of fresh meat softening his habitual resistance to unorthodox methods. But it had been an unorthodox expedition from the beginning.

Returning to the poop deck, Jack Driscoll announced, "Fetch your knives, boys. This ugly hog is about to be rendered on the spot."

A boisterous cheer went up as the men dispersed to get the appropriate cutting tools, leaving Lumpy to glumly contemplate the massive boar.

Noticing his demeanor, the First Mate asked, "What's eating you?"

"I guess I got to let that ungrateful monk live to squawk another day."

Driscoll laughed. "Ignatz wake up yet?"

"No. He just rolled over once. At least he's out of my hair."

"And out of Kong's!" laughed Driscoll.

Chapter 28

THAT EVENING, Lumpy served up a feast.

The air coming off the Indian Ocean was cool, and the wind steady. Along the shoreline, palm trees rustled like stiff paper in the distance. Lions roared, dull and throaty.

In celebration of their first night at anchor since the perilous crossing from Skull Mountain Island, Captain Englehorn abandoned ship decorum and permitted passengers and crew to eat together in the open air of the weather deck.

The mood was mixed among the crew, some mariners feeling justified seamanly pride in having successfully brought their formidable freight to within hailing distance of dry land, while others evinced an equally maritime concern that Kong was a Jonah or a jinx certain to bring disaster upon the officers and crew of the *Wanderer*.

Carl Denham took his meal on the raised poop deck, and was soon regaling intrigued crew members with details of his previous exploits, most of which were suspected of being exaggerated.

"Only four years ago," he was saying, "I plunged into the jungle not far from here on a quest for the legendary wild man whose existence has never been proven."

Denham paused, like the showman he was. He was building up his story in the telling.

A crewman deflated his egoistic balloon when he hollered

out, "Yeah, we know all about it. Some of us were on that ill-fated voyage."

"Say, who are you calling ill-fated?" returned Denham. "I got some swell footage on that jaunt. Don't tell me I didn't. Made a bundle, I did. Of course, that was before the crash...."

The director's boastful voice trailed off.

"Go ahead with your yarn," encouraged young Jimmy, who had not been with the *Wanderer* in those days.

"Sure, I was getting there," Denham said, regaining his expansive mood. "Anyway, as I was saying, stories had been coming out of this neck of the African woods of a white man who had gone native. They called him Tarzan. Tarzan of the Apes. Legend had it that he had grown up among a tribe of savage gorillas, the like of which no civilized man had ever beheld. I aimed to capture footage of Tarzan and his ape tribe."

Off to one side, in the shadow of a looming wide-mouthed deck ventilator, Ann Darrow turned to Jack Driscoll and asked, "Is that true? Is there really a wild man called Tarzan?"

Jack shrugged carelessly. "Only Denham knows. He went into the jungle with a cameraman. When they came back, Denham didn't want to talk about it. But let's hear his version. I understand that it changes from telling to telling."

Denham was saying, "I plunged into the jungle, taking only native porters and a cameraman. I went in deep, fellows. Deeper than any white man had ever ventured. I found tracks. Bare footprints. Human, but no African native ever made such tracks."

A seaman spoke up. "How can you tell? White skin and black make the same footprints."

"Aw, I've seen plenty of native footprints in my time. These did not belong to any black man. Mixed in with these were the tracks of wild apes whose footprints did not match any gorilla spoor I'd ever seen, except in size."

A ripple of laughter floated over the diners. A ribald voice asked, "Well, how many gorilla tracks have you seen in all?"

"Plenty!" insisted Denham.

"How many is that?" Jimmy demanded.

"I lost count," insisted Denham. "But let me tell my story."

"Sure, sure," a sailor chided. "But try not to get too tangled up in the details. Otherwise, someone might accuse you of exaggerating!"

More chuckling broke out. It brought a pained expression to the director's wide features.

"Say, haven't you ever seen any of my pictures? None of that stuff was staged. It was all the McCoy."

"G'wan," a skeptical voice snorted. "Tell us another."

"As I was saying," Denham went on truculently, "mixed in with the footprints of an ape species science hasn't recorded were those of a white man, as if he was traveling with them. In fact, he appeared to be leading the pack. I knew then that I had found Tarzan of the Apes. So I followed those tracks, me and my cameraman."

Denham paused, shifting from face to face, measuring the attention of his audience like the seasoned showman that he was.

"Night fell, boys. Still, we pressed on."

"Unafraid, were you?" said a mariner derisively.

"Sure," another jeered. "He's a regular Frank Buck, he is."

"You said it, sailor!" Denham snapped. "We had guns, and we were prepared to use them. We weren't afraid, just cautious. Finally, we came to some kind of camp in the jungle. There was a crackling campfire, just like you'd see in a native village. But there were no huts. Only gorillas. Gorillas and one white man wearing a loincloth and nothing else. It was the king of the apes, Tarzan. I saw him with my own eyes. He was real."

At last, Denham had his audience's rapt attention. His voice grew conspiratorial.

"We hung back in the bush, and my cameraman started rolling film. He captured ten minutes of footage, when out from behind us, a tiger charged! We scattered, the two of us. Ran for our lives, we did. Somehow we made it even with the great apes and their white leader tearing after us with mad abandon.

"Somehow we made it to the water intact, threw ourselves into our dinghy, and rowed out to open water like our lives depended on it. Some of you were there to pick us up out of the water. You saw how much we were shaking."

A seaman asked, "So where is the footage?"

"We lost it during the chase," Denham said glumly. "Many times I thought of going back, to see if I could shoot Tarzan of the Apes. And maybe I would have. But the map to Skull Island fell into my hands, and that changed everything."

"Crackling good yarn," Jimmy said with open approval.

"Well, I don't often tell it," Denham said with a trace of uncharacteristic humbleness.

Jack Driscoll called out, "There's only one problem with it."

"There's no problem with it, unless you mean the lost footage," returned Denham.

"From what I hear, tigers aren't native to Africa. So how could one have run you off?"

Carl Denham's facial expression quivered, but quickly recovered.

"Why, it was dark, maybe it wasn't a tiger. Might've been a panther, or a leopard, or some other big cat. It's a minor detail. But everything I told you was true."

The crew fell to mumbling and muttering, exchanging opinions on Carl Denham's reputation, unmindful of the fact that the boastful director was hearing every word.

"It's true, I tell you!" Denham insisted.

Raucous calls, hoots of derision, sneering comments, and other abuse met his sputtering expostulations.

"I saw Tarzan of the Apes with my own eyes. He and that monkey tribe were—"

Denham cut himself off.

"Were what?" Lumpy demanded.

"What's the use?" growled Denham. "I'm playing to a tough crowd."

Ann Darrow called over, "What did Tarzan look like?"

The fire of enthusiasm returned to Denham's brown eyes.

"He was taller than a tall man, with muscles like wiry steel! His hair was black and he wore it in a long mane, like a lion. I didn't catch the color of his eyes, but they reminded me of knife steel. Although he had the face of a white man, kind of high and noble, his hide had been bronzed by the sun, like he never knew any better clothes than his animal-hide loincloth."

"Did he speak?" asked Lumpy.

"Yes, he did. He knew English."

This assertion brought forth a fresh wave of mockery.

"What language did the monkeys speak?"

Denham flushed crimson from thick neck to forehead. "Go ahead, make fun of me. But if I had brought back that footage, none of you would be laughing."

These hot words only triggered more hilarity.

Finally, the filmmaker sat down to finish his meal, and the crew settled down to do the same.

"Aw, I know when I'm licked," Denham muttered.

In the corner where they sat apart from the others, Ann Darrow asked Jack, "Do you suppose any of that is true?"

"I've been all round the world, and to Africa plenty of times," Driscoll said carefully. "I've heard lots of tales of this Tarzan of the Apes. Natives consider him a forest god of some kind. He's supposed to be a white man, but nobody knows anything about him. How much of these legends are true I can't say, but behind every legend is a kernel of truth."

"So you credit them?"

"Englehorn does. And that's good enough for me. I'm willing to believe Tarzan is real. But that's about it. As for Carl Denham, maybe he ran into the fellow, and maybe he just made that up to cover for his failure. He's pretty full of himself now. Denham thinks he's king of the world. Or will be soon. My guess is he traipsed around the jungle until he got too hot and tired and scared and turned tail with his cameraman and made up the yarn to hide his embarrassment."

"I don't see Carl Denham turning tail very much."

Spearing his last morsel of cooked boar, the First Mate allowed, "Now that you mention it, I don't either. But his story keeps changing, and this is the first time I've heard some of these details."

A sleepy silence settled over the weather deck. Lumpy stood up to police the dishes, complaining about those who didn't finish their food, and receiving compliments on his cooking with characteristic ill humor. Lumpy liked compliments; he just couldn't be bothered to acknowledge them.

When he came to take Jack and Ann's dishes, Ann asked, "How is Ignatz coming along?"

"He's snoring off his troubles," growled the cook.

Ann laughed musically. "I wouldn't think a monkey would have any troubles!"

Lumpy made a face like a fist clenching. "That monkey has nothing but troubles. But he's still sleeping off his case of the vapors, if that's what you mean."

"That's a phrase I haven't heard in a good long while!" Driscoll said, standing up to help Ann to her feet.

"Well, what else would you call what happened to the fool monk?" Lumpy groused.

Changing the subject, Driscoll said, "We haven't fed Kong all day. It's high time that we do."

Lumpy groaned, saying, "My job never ends. What kind of hash do you want me to sling for him?"

"We'll ask Penjaga that. But first I want to take some men down to the hold and check on his condition. See how he's holding up. I'll let you know."

"You do that, Mate. But he's not getting any wild boar. The

crew will string me up if I don't serve the rest as leftovers tomorrow."

"Right," said Driscoll. Turning to Ann, he suggested, "Why don't you run along? I'm going to be busy on this watch."

"Good night, Jack. Be careful."

"Don't worry, honey. I will."

Going among the crew, the First Mate found Beaumont the boatswain and said, "Let's go below and check on the big gorilla, Boats."

"Yes, sir."

They collected two deckhands on their way. No sailor looked pleased to be selected for the duty, but they followed obligingly. Jack Driscoll threw open the steel door to the companionway, then led the way down, deep into the Number Three Hold.

Kong slept, oblivious. The rising and falling in his bristling black chest was rhythmic and regular, but the brute otherwise showed no signs of distress or discomfort.

The air coming in through the open hull hatch was cool and sweet, full of pungent jungle smells.

These odors passed over Kong's twitching face, entering his nostrils with each sonorous breath, calling to him like an ancient summons.

"Let's examine his shackles first," Driscoll instructed.

They started with the left ankle, and found this makeshift steel ring intact—if a bit snug.

"Looks secure, Mate," decided the boatswain.

Going to the other ankle, they discovered it to be too tight.

"We better loosen this one," Driscoll decided. "It's digging in too deep, might even be cutting off the circulation to his foot. Denham will have blue fits if he finds out."

"Did I hear my name?" a boisterous voice called down.

The stocky filmmaker came tramping down the stairs, and

soon reached the bottom. Sizing up Kong, he said, "How's my million-dollar monkey fairing?"

Jack Driscoll said, "Checking the shackles for slippage, but this right one seems to be too tight."

Stepping over, Denham knelt down and examined the steel ring for himself.

"I'll say it's too tight. Looks like the big boy's been putting on weight. Must've been all that fish we fed him."

"Well, we've got to loosen it," said Driscoll. "Just enough to ease up on the pressure."

Tools were fetched, and the work commenced.

While this was underway, Driscoll and Denham examined the wrist shackles, and noticed that they, too, were tighter than they should be.

"Say," declared Denham, "we're going to have to loosen both wrist shackles, as well."

Driscoll frowned. "Maybe we should hold off feeding him. First he loses weight, then he gains it back. We can't be fiddling with these shackles every time this happens. The machinist jury-rigged these contraptions. They won't stand up to much abuse."

Denham scratched his head and murmured, "Let's loosen them and worry about the future when it happens."

Unspoken between the two men was the open question of whether Kong would be carried all the way around the lower half of Africa and off to America.

The right ankle shackle was proving stubborn. They had to bang at it, merely to get it loose enough for readjustment.

The banging went on for some time. Fortunately, the wind coming into the side hatch filled the spacious steel-lined hold, keeping them cool.

Commingled scents of open water, humid jungle, and wild creatures came and went with vagrant shore breezes.

Unnoticed, Kong's nostrils twitched.

"Ease up on that!" Driscoll ordered the man banging at the ankle shackle. "You don't want to break it!"

Carl Denham shoved in, saying, "Here, give me that. I'll do it."

The knot of men stood around the huge creature's bristling right leg as the work progressed. The cavernous cargo hold echoed with the resounding ring and clang of steel on steel. A blacksmith working on an anvil could hardly produce a greater clangor.

As they worked, Kong's nostrils quivered, dilated, and his eyes sprang open, a smoldering anger flaring in their dull amber depths.

Without warning, the black-haired monster made fists the size of automobile engines, and when he lifted them, huge chains rattled loudly, straining at ringbolts welded to the floor.

Every human head in the hold turned. Without warning, Kong let out a bellowing roar that shook the entire ship.

Chapter 29

KING KONG'S head and shoulders came up, and the hideous thing that was his face gathered into a malevolent mask of annoyance. Orbs like tawny moons looked down on the tiny humans working at his foot.

Snapping his head back and retracting a leg, Kong pulled free of the open shackle.

"He's loose!" the boatswain howled.

The crew of the *Wanderer* was not without courage, but two men broke for the companionway steps, while Jack Driscoll and Carl Denham grabbed the nearest sailors, and pulled them to their feet.

"Get topside!" Driscoll ordered. "We'll call you when we need you."

One sailor looked to him incredulously, "Don't you need us now?"

"We can handle this," snapped Denham. "Scat!"

"You, too, Boats," Driscoll added for the benefit of the hesitant boatswain.

Reluctantly, the three seamen bolted for the companionway.

Denham and Driscoll backed away, slowly, carefully, and they seemed to be of the same mind.

Under his breath, Denham said, "I hope you're thinking what I'm thinking…."

"I'm thinking our best chance is to grab those gas grenades and fling them hard."

"Exactly my thought. Just don't make any sudden moves until we have to."

Kong peered at them with his strangely human gaze, stared upward, failed to see sky, and then looked to his immediate right. He saw open water and the fringe of jungle only a few hundred yards away.

The myriad jungle smells filling his nostrils, Kong lurched toward the opening, only to discover that his burly arms were stayed by steel manacles linked to heavy chains.

Bringing up his hands, Kong glared down at them, saw the problem, and whether he understood it or not, responded through bestial instinct.

One bristling fist wrenched up and around, and the great iron ringbolt that anchored the chain to its deck plate broke free. Now freed, blunt fingers dug at the opposite wrist, peeling apart the broad band of steel. First one, then the other restraint was torn loose. The superhuman ape made it look effortless.

As broken linkages of chain went flying, Kong reared up, throwing his hands over his head and beating at the hatch doors above.

One held, but the other flew up with great violence—only to come crashing down again, cutting off the light streaming down into the hold.

Far above the voice of Captain Englehorn called out, "Mr. Driscoll! Mr. Driscoll!"

Whatever else the Skipper might be saying was lost in Kong's bestial roaring, for the gargantuan terror gorilla was gathering himself together, as yet unaware that one leg remained shackled.

Driscoll and Denham turned and lunged for the wooden crate that held the great gas grenades. Together, they fought to get the lid up.

A leathery-soled foot shot out, looking like a monstrous black hand with its crooked big toe suggesting a broken thumb, forcing the two men to leap aside in opposite directions.

Frustrated by his inability to fully stand up, Kong rolled in the direction of open air and freedom. A flailing limb of hair and muscle was briefly inhibited by the final restraining chain, which Kong immediately seized and began worrying.

The chain fought him, but the great prying fingers twisted, warped metal and finally two connected links snapped.

"Unbelievable!" Denham shouted.

"Well, I believe it!" Driscoll retorted. One hand flashed to his sidearm. He yanked out his revolver, bringing the sights in line with Kong's enormous skull.

"No!" Denham shouted. "The grenades! We can stop him with the grenades!"

"What are you waiting for? If you can do it, do it! But if you can't, I'll have to empty all six chambers into him."

Scrambling, Carl Denham lunged for the box, got it open, and fumbled out a cast-iron grenade. Before he could lift it over his head to fling the cumbersome gadget, Kong lurched to one side, and the ship listed violently.

Snarling, the brute flailed about, clearly disoriented, still in the throes of a semi-stupor from his long slumber. Hairy head swiveling on his truncated neck, he sought a way out of his baffling predicament.

Seeing daylight, Kong groped toward it. The vessel rocked violently, causing him to slide closer to the open access hatch. A clutching hand reached out, took firm hold of the hatchway edge. The padded sole of one foot banged against a stainless steel bulkhead, pushing back reflexively. Kong's head slid out, and his blazing eyes fell on the heaving water below.

Struggling for his freedom, the titan rolled about convulsively. The *Wanderer* shook and groaned in sympathy, hull plates straining.

Thrown off balance, Driscoll and Denham fought to keep from being crushed by the monster's limbs or violently pitched overboard.

Stepping back, Denham encountered an object rolling about

the steel floor. He lost his footing, grabbed the grenade in both arms, and shielded it as he fell backward.

"You had your chance!" Driscoll yelled.

"Don't!" shouted the filmmaker. "I'm begging you, Driscoll!"

Jack Driscoll steadied himself, lined up his shot, and began squeezing the trigger.

Whether his shot would have sped true, what effect it would have on the enraged anthropoid, was never to be known.

Down from the partially wrecked deck hatch dropped a small, hairy form, chattering angrily, which sprung for the First Mate's head, knocking off his cap.

For a wild moment, Jack Driscoll thought that one of Kong's unbelievable fingers had seized his head. He spun around, trying to throw the thing off. His revolver discharged, bullet rebounding off a bulkhead, ricocheting twice before it shot out the open hatch.

When the clutching thing let go, Driscoll saw that it was Ignatz the monkey, who sprang away in the direction of Kong, nimbly alighting on one monster shoulder, just as the stupendous ape threw himself out the hatch, managing to hit the water with a great splash.

The water was relatively shallow, and Kong was soon up on his feet, roaring.

Turning, he gave the *Wanderer* an annoyed shove—one that rocked the old freighter alarmingly. Drawn by the sights and sounds and smells of the African jungle, Kong pivoted disdainfully, presenting his much-matted and scarred back to his former captors, and strode like a beetle-browed colossus toward the shimmering beach.

Driscoll ran to the hatch, steadied himself against the edge, and brought his pistol in line again.

"What's the use?" he muttered, lowering the weapon. "Let him have his freedom. It's nothing to me."

Searching, he found Carl Denham flat on his back, holding

onto the gas bomb as if it was a deadly hand grenade whose pin had been pulled.

Heavily, the First Mate told him, "Well, he's gone now. Took Ignatz with him, too."

"Take hold of this thing for me, will you?" requested Denham finally. "I'm afraid to stand up."

Holstering his revolver, the First Mate reached down carefully and lifted up the cast-iron shell, carrying it over to the wooden crate where he replaced it in its excelsior bedding as if putting a baby to bed.

Carl Denham was on his feet by that time, looking pale and shaking. One foot encountered the rolling object that had tripped him. Features gathering in perplexity, he stopped, lifted the heavy thing to the light.

"What is this?" he muttered. "Looks like a knot."

Driscoll looked over, and half laughed.

"It *is* a knot. I made it for Ann. It's called the monkey's fist."

Dropping it with disdain, Denham snapped, "Well, it tripped me up as I was about to give Kong his dose of sleeping gas."

The showman strolled over to the open hatch, and watched King Kong push through the waters, hairy legs churning, leaving a monstrous wake behind him that disturbed the combers surging for the beach.

"Well," said Driscoll, clapping him on his broad back. "I'm only half sorry to say this. But Kong has his freedom back."

Denham shook his head as if to clear it. His brown eyes had a glazed look to them, like kilned pottery.

"Sure, sure, he does." Flint came into his tone. "For now. But we'll get him back. Mark my words. I'll have the Beast eating out of my hands before I'm through with King Kong."

Chapter 30

CAPTAIN ENGLEHORN would have none of it.
His mature face was shaking with some barely-controlled emotion as Carl Denham exhorted him to assemble a shore party and pursue Kong into the African jungle.

"No, Mr. Denham," Englehorn bit out tightly. "We will not do that."

"We have to! We got to get him back. Everything depends on it."

"And my ship and my crew depend upon me to make sound decisions, exercising the good judgment of the ship's master." Englehorn shook his head firmly. "No, we will not pursue Kong. Our problem with that *menschenaffe* has solved itself. Despite our best efforts, it is now clear that it is impossible to convey such a monster to home port."

The demolished deck hatches around which they had assembled bore mute testimony to the truth of the grizzled old salt's judgment.

Jack Driscoll stood nearby, Ann Darrow tight by his side.

"It's over, Jack," she whispered. "The nightmare is over. Tonight I will be able to sleep soundly for the first time in weeks."

Driscoll nodded, squeezing her arm, adding, "I want to hear this. It's been a long time coming."

"Don't be so stubborn," Denham was saying. "We'll ask for volunteers." He turned around energetically, eyeing the assembled circle of merchant mariners, exhorting them in a bluff voice. "Who's with me? There's a million in this venture. Maybe three. I'll split it with all of you!"

The boatswain said sourly, "You promised us that before. And look where it's got us."

Another sailor burst out, "We're just lucky that overgrown chimpanzee didn't capsize the boat and drown us all."

A belligerent expression washed over the excited showman's reddening face. He looked as if he wanted to make an argument out of it, but quickly subsided. As aggressive as Carl Denham felt, he knew he wasn't getting anywhere with the crew in their current mental state.

"All right, all right," he said begrudgingly. "I know when I'm licked. And I'm licked—but good."

The burly filmmaker trudged to his cabin, disappearing within like a retreating storm cloud.

Jack Driscoll walked up to the Captain and said, "Been waiting a mighty long time to see this."

The Skipper eyed him thinly. "See what, Mr. Driscoll?"

"See you get the better of Carl Denham."

"In this case," Englehorn said slowly, "it is not I who got the better of Mr. Denham, but circumstances. This was a doomed enterprise from the start, and we were lucky to survive the foolhardy venture. Now let us get about our own business."

"Yes, sir," said Driscoll jauntily. Turning to the crew, he directed, "Let's take stock of this old rust bucket. We'll spend the night here and look to making repairs in the morning."

Practically the entire complement of the *Wanderer* prowled the weather deck, examining the state of the rusty old vessel, from forecastle to poop deck. After that, individual mariners filtered below deck, to investigate various compartments and holds.

The freighter proved to be shipshape and seaworthy. The starboard Number Three Hold hatch had taken a beating, and would need repairs in the likely event of a tropical storm.

Otherwise, the cargo space would soon become awash from a typical monsoon downpour.

The giant turtle eggs nestled amid bunches of blackening bananas in the forward tween decks hold were inspected and proved to be undamaged.

When Driscoll heard this, he grimaced. "When he gets over his blue funk, Denham will remember them. Make sure nobody spills the beans. Until we dock, let him think they're dinosaurs waiting to hatch. That should mollify him."

"The crew's lips are sealed," the reporting boatswain assured him.

At the stern, Penjaga stood alone, staring out into the jungle, listening for sounds of Kong. Her shoulders drooped and the wind blew her rawhide skirts around her thin legs.

Ann Darrow drifted up to her, took hold of one withered arm and whispered gently, "Perhaps it is better this way. Kong is free again."

"Free in a land he does not know," Penjaga intoned dully. "A monarch without a throne, an emperor over nothing and now cast into a futile exile."

"Africa is much larger than Skull Island," Ann reassured the old woman. "Kong will have a vast jungle in which to roam. Perhaps he will be happy here."

"This jungle is not his home," hissed Penjaga with low vehemence. A salty tear rolled down one pain-squeezed eye, to disappear into the webbing of a wrinkled cheek.

"Nothing could be done now," said Ann softly. "It's fate. That's all. Fate."

"Fate favors Kong," murmured the old woman. Her arid voice croaked like a frog's. "Fate had always favored Kong. We will see what fate will decide to do with him… as well as with those who stole *Tuane* Kong away from his rightful home in the world…."

Chapter 31

KONG MELTED into the African jungle, his broad feet gouging the moist earth with each step. This was the season of the "long rains"—tropical downpours that punctuated every steaming afternoon without fail. It was pouring steadily.

Around him, towering palm trees and spreading eucalyptus shook and shivered, disturbed by his crushing tread. Droplets of moisture pattered down, creating syncopated jungle music.

Watching under the rain shelter of a broad leaf, little Nkima smelled Kong before his tiny ears perked up at the monster's earth-shaking approach. The monkey was reluctant to leave the protection of his palm leaf, for he did not like to get very wet. So he crouched, head switching back and forth, beady black orbs watchful.

The odor his nostrils absorbed reminded the diminutive creature of the great apes who lived in the deep forest. But this wild smell was greater, rank in a way that was new to Nkima, and so unpleasant that a vague unease began to grow in the center of his chest. His tiny heartbeat picked up its pace.

Nkima had lived in this part of Africa all his life, and knew every natural smell. This odor had characteristics that were unnerving.

Presently, the little monkey's curiosity got the better of him. Reaching around, he snapped a palm leaf off its crisp stem, carrying it along like a bright green umbrella.

This action was not conducive to arboreal gymnastics. When

Nkima launched himself into an adjoining tree, he almost missed the inviting limb. One hand grasped rough bark, and he was forced to drop the palm leaf and scramble with all four limbs and his prehensile tail to keep from tumbling to the sodden ground far below.

Chastened by the near calamity, Nkima crept along the jungle lanes, crawling from branch to branch, hopping from tree to tree, steadily moving in a broken path toward the smelly thing that advanced in his direction.

When he saw the bristling black head pushing through the upper branches before him, Nkima gave out a fierce screech of alarm.

This sound caught the attention of the approaching monster; its amber eyes rotated in his direction.

Nkima scuttled into a clump of leaves, more than ever wishing that he'd held onto his palm-leaf parasol. He shivered along with the trees that were shaking in sympathy with the great hairy beast whose height was greater than any giraffe, and whose size was vaster than the largest bull elephant Nkima had ever encountered.

The bloodshot eyes of the simian colossus looked down on the huddling monkey, and his nostrils quickened. The immense head tilted to one side, like a curious dog.

Nkima spoke up in the language of the monkey folk, and the terrifying giant growled in return. Was this a growl of anger? Of curiosity? Or acknowledgement? Nkima did not know. When the ape-monster lumbered toward him, he instantly regretted speaking up.

Dropping down to a lower branch, Nkima swung around, launched himself at an adjoining tree, scampered up to its crown, and waited there as the brute blundered about.

By this time, the rains had abated and night was coming on. A waxing moon commenced climbing the sky, and the creatures that went abroad in the night were prowling now.

Pushing against a great tree, the monster caused the fat bole to groan under the enormous pressure of his arm.

From a hole in a dead part of the tree spurted a cloud of bats, squeaking and seeking escape from the frightening disturbance.

The black beast recoiled from this sudden onslaught of fluttering things. Thick fingers swept up, clamped down on the cloud of wings, and when he opened his broad palms, the crushed bats writhed in their own blood.

The bull gorilla—for that is what Nkima perceived Kong to be—looked down at the smeared things dying in his hands, lifted one palm to his face and sniffed curiously.

The metallic smell of blood was all the monster needed to detect. It brought the hand to its mouth, and a great tongue began licking the creatures off the leathery palm, until they were all gone. Then he transferred his attention to the other palm, lapping up broken bats and blood with great relish.

Nkima watched all this, fascinated. But also fearful. A gorilla such as this would have a tremendous appetite, he realized. And while a little monkey like himself would be but a morsel, he would be a tastier morsel than a bat. That gorillas did not eat monkeys was a fact of life that momentarily escaped him.

Nkima hunkered down, closed his eyes and hoped the monster would pass him by. His shivering was continual.

Grinding sounds, suggesting broken limbs, caused his eyes to snap open again. Nkima had been holding his breath, but now he released it as he saw the great shadowy bulk of the shambling creature move on into the night.

From his broad, bristling back clung a tiny monkey of a species similar to Nkima, but also different. This monkey was holding on for dear life, and the lumbering brute seemed oblivious to his minuscule passenger.

Risking his own life, Nkima sent up a series of cries which, in his own tongue, meant: Jump! Jump! Or he will eat you!

The little monkey seemed to understand, for he climbed higher, and just as the monster who resembled a giant gorilla turned to see what was tangled in its matted fur, the nimble monkey landed in a branch of a fern-leaf tree, scampering up as high as it could go.

Kong caught a glimpse of a fleet form, turned his head, and began feeling through the still-dripping branches, seeking the long-tailed thing that had escaped him.

But the tree was a great spreading goliath and the nimble monkey was clever. It found a hole, wriggled in and rolled up into a ball inside it.

As the moon continued its slow rise, bringing effulgent light to the moist jungle, Kong lost interest and resumed his impatient quest for food.

Feeling safe, Nkima flashed through the trees, reaching the place where the unfamiliar monkey had inserted itself.

It took considerable coaxing before Ignatz relinquished his hiding place, and sat shivering on a branch.

The two monkeys stared at one another, and attempted to converse in the universal tongue of their kind. Much nervous gesticulating accompanied this exchange, during which the little monkey kept pulling on his tail nervously—a trait that Nkima found himself copying without realizing it.

The story that the strange monkey told was brief, and when he had absorbed it, Nkima had but one comment.

"We must tell Tarzan," he chattered.

"Who is Tarzan?" squeaked Ignatz.

"Tarzan of the Apes, the ruler of this jungle. He must know that a gorilla larger than any other is loose in his domain. We will go to Tarzan. He will know what to do."

The nervous monkey peered around in the overwhelming darkness, hesitant and uncertain. But when Nkima shot off into the trees, Ignatz followed.

They raced inland, deep into the jungle, where lay the kingdom of Tarzan of the Apes.

Chapter 32

WITH EVERY step, Kong's muscles creaked and groaned. The stupendous anthropoid ached at every joint. The catgut stitches binding his recent wounds were straining, and attracting flies. As he walked, low growls escaped his bestial lips.

These were unaccustomed sensations to the former Monarch of Skull Mountain Island. Kong understood that he had been asleep for a very long time. Inaction had atrophied his muscles, and leached a sizable measure of innate power from his great vital form.

But he was still Kong, still powerful. The bristling beast-god towered over all but the tallest of trees in this unrecognizable jungle. Monkeys scampered from their sleeping perches and night-roosting tropical birds fled in advance of his thunderous approach.

The soggy earth shook with each halting step, but with each footfall the stride of Kong grew less halting and more purposeful.

Coming to a watering hole, the black-furred beast stopped, and laboriously dropped to his knees, whereupon he leaned in to scoop water up in the palms of his hands. He drank greedily. Aching thirst was a sensation unknown to King Kong. But he felt it now—felt as if he had not imbibed water in a long while. Alien tastes in his mouth were only now fading since he had eaten the smashed and bloody bats.

Guzzling his fill, Kong struggled back to his full height, searching his surroundings with curiously human eyes. A range of expressions crossed his simian features. Kong was scanning distant sights. He was seeking the familiar.

But nothing the immense ape ever beheld greeted his questing orbs.

Turning about, he sought the bald stone prospect that was Skull Mountain, which for as long as he had known life, had brooded over his feral existence.

But there was no sign of the age-old granite death's-head looming over the trees of this place unknown to him.

Lifting his head, Kong sniffed, inhaling the ripe odors of this strange jungle. The stink of giant lizards and roosting pteranodons was absent. Nor was there the familiar smells of other inhabitants of his distant home.

A slow and low growl escaped from his parted lips. As it trailed off, the noise contained a forlorn note. A human being, had there been one close by, might have detected a note of anxiety in that trailing sound.

For the first time in his long existence, Kong knew the pangs of being lost. Dimly, he understood that he had been conveyed to this new place. All his life, he had known but one jungle. The concept that there were other jungles was foreign to him.

One sensation was not, however. Kong's stomach rumbled in its emptiness. He was hungry. He had experienced hunger before. Many times he had felt its aching pangs. And Kong knew how to quench the dull but growing sensation.

Another growl came, this one swelling in volume and ferocity.

This jungle might be unknown, but it teemed with life. Unfamiliar life. Pungent smells intriguing to Kong tickled his dilating nostrils. Some of these scents meant fruit. Others smacked of strange, yet-untasted meat. Having tasted of the blood of bats, Kong desired meat above all. Iron is what his body craved most. But Kong did not know that.

Plunging into a thicket of crackling trees, the determined beast-god began following a scent spoor that smacked of living flesh. The hungry monster did not know whose living flesh he tracked, only that it was just a matter of time before he caught up with it....

Chapter 33

FIRST MATE Jack Driscoll found Carl Denham down in the Number Three Hold less than an hour after midnight.

The dank hold was dark, and Driscoll went down the companionway, stairs shining in the beam of a flashlight before him. The First Mate was intent on making a safety check of the great stainless steel-lined chamber. He had no expectation that the oversized hold was occupied.

Reaching the bottom step, he flashed his beam around. It illuminated a hunched shape squatting on the shattered edge of the great timber-and-bamboo raft that had served to convey Kong aboard the *Wanderer*.

Driscoll paused, and a pang of sympathy touched his salty soul.

When he was last in New York City, Driscoll had seen several New Yorkers seated on curbstones, their bowed heads in their hands, features morose. These were unfortunates who had been thrown out of work and very often out of their flats by the deepening economic depression.

Carl Denham looked like that. Even in the weak light, he was an image of human dejection.

Driscoll cleared his throat, but the showman did not move. Cautiously, the First Mate walked over to him, keeping his light out of Denham's downcast eyes.

"Didn't expect to find you here, Mr. Denham," he said gently.

"Just contemplating my fate," mumbled the filmmaker. "What's left of it…."

He patted the shattered tube of bamboo upon which he was seated. "This is all I got left for my pains and troubles," he continued thick-voiced. "This broken raft and the last three gas bombs."

"Well," observed Driscoll, "you had to know that getting Kong clear across two oceans was a mighty tall job of work."

"And I still say it can be done," grumbled Denham in half-hearted defiance.

"I won't argue the point," allowed Driscoll, "but it hardly matters now."

"I'm sunk. Plain sunk. No point in even kicking my feet and straining upward for a last gulp of air. Me and Davy Jones are cold company."

Throwing his flash ray around, searching for leaks, the First Mate said, "Buck up. Don't take it so tough. You've still got some of that footage you shot of Kong, haven't you?"

"What of it?"

"Well, people paid a pretty penny to see your films of tigers and other wild animals. What you shot of Kong will still be a sensation, won't it?"

Denham grunted, "I got enough for a short feature. I came all this way to film a movie. A short feature won't make me millions. It might pay for all our efforts, but where's the profit in it?"

"These days," drawled Driscoll, taking his eyes off the battered ceiling hatch, "just to break even is enough."

Denham shot to his feet, eyes suddenly aglow with a vision.

Slamming his chest with one fist, he roared, "Not for me! Carl Denham doesn't settle for breaking even. For an ordinary guy, yeah. I suppose it will do. But not for me. I'm accustomed to being somebody. I'm used to doing big things. All my life, reaching for bigger and bigger things. Naturally, that led me to the biggest thing of all time. Kong! A million-dollar wild animal.

And I let him get away from me. Like a chump. A common, ordinary chump."

Driscoll hurled back, "That's a lot of hooey, and you know it. Dream big, sure. But not all dreams come true. Yours came half true. You might want to think of settling for that."

"A short subject," spat Denham. "I'll be lucky to clear five thousand bucks. You might say that's more money than I deserve, but I say different. Carl Denham deserves millions. For what we went through, we all do. How many crew did we leave behind on Skull Mountain Island?"

"Too many," admitted Driscoll.

"I counted an even dozen. They died for nothing. Doesn't that gall you?"

The Mate had to consider that for a moment. He said slowly, "I keep thinking it could've been worse. We should have lost a lot more."

"We left twelve wooden crosses back on Skull Island. Their lives should've stood for something more than a failed expedition."

Driscoll lapsed into silence, his gaze turning inward and reflective. Denham scrutinized him, and a crafty gleam came into his brown eyes.

"Say, we're going to be laid up here for a while, aren't we?"

"At least a day. Could be three. Why?"

Denham snapped his fingers, as if suddenly getting an idea. Had the First Mate been watching him closely, he would have recognized that the notion had already been formed. It was only now being revealed.

"Two or three days, you say! Why, that's enough time to get more footage of the big gorilla. I could turn my short subject into a real movie! Something that would buck *Trader Horn!*"

The expression that came over Jack Driscoll's face was strange. Denham's words seemed to sting him, and his emotions fought between horror and possibly disgust.

"Have you come down with tropical fever?" he burst out. "Do

you want me to take half the crew into this Hellforsaken jungle just so you can capture another forty minutes of Kong on celluloid?"

"Damn right I do!" Denham was now fully alive once more, stocky body crackling with animated vitality. "Thirty or forty minutes of film would turn this fiasco into a going proposition. Pull us out of the hole. Pay for the repairs for the ship. Leave enough left over to put a tidy sum in everybody's pocket. What do you say, Driscoll? Are you game?"

"You mean, am I crazy?" retorted the Mate. "The answer to that is, no, I'm not. And neither is the Old Man. Englehorn will never go for this mad scheme. We're rid of Kong at last, and good riddance, I say. Those of us who still possess skins are lucky to have them to hold their bones together. Why risk a second row of wooden crosses in another backwater jungle?"

But the dynamo of a director was unmoved. "Where's your spirit of adventure? Where's your sense of enterprise?"

"Safely tucked under my common sense," drawled Driscoll. "And I recommend you stow yours in the same place. Forty minutes of footage isn't worth your life."

Seeing that he was getting nowhere, Carl Denham stuck his hands into his trouser pockets and half turned away, saying, "Maybe you're right, Jack. Maybe I got tropical fever. It happens to the best of men who tramp around this part of the world. It's just that I don't like to be beat. I can't stand it. It sticks in my craw. I see any way out of a deep hole, I just want to rear up and scratch and claw and dig until I see sunlight again."

Finishing his flashlight inspection of the Number Three Hold, Jack Driscoll suggested quietly, "Might want to turn in for the night. You slept in for too many days. I think it's affecting you. Get some solid shut-eye, join the rest of us on the weather deck when the sun is shining and the air is fresh and clean. All of us have been stuck down in this dank hold too much. It's full of the stink of the jungle. The musk of Kong. It's a beastly smell, and it has no business befouling a good ship like the *Wanderer*."

The deflated showman grunted noncommittally.

Climbing the companionway, Driscoll called back, "Take my advice, Mr. Denham. Why don't you rejoin the human race and try to live like the rest of us poor souls? Times are hard all over, and just getting by is something to be grateful for."

After the First Mate had gone to the top and closed the door behind him, Carl Denham stood in the gloom that was illuminated by moonlight streaming down through the fractured cargo hatches. He was all alone, so no one heard his muttered words.

"You don't know Carl Denham very well, do you, my fine bucko?"

Chapter 34

A PRIDE of lions was slipping through the jungle, seeking prey. Great padded feet stepped carefully, making only the softest of sounds in the luxuriant grass, their golden orbs lambent in the moonlight streaming down interlacing branches of the jungle canopy.

These big cats displayed lean and tawny flanks as they sifted among closely-packed tree trunks. Most were female, but three wore the flowing manes of male lions. This formidable trio led the pack, and the scars on their faces and flanks showed them to be veterans of the hunt.

From time to time, they sniffed the humid night air, seeking the heady smell of antelope and zebra. As they worked their way along, the patiently-padding felines carefully spread out. For the tantalizing odors of living food was not yet within the range of their sensitive noses.

Before long, another scent came wafting down the wind. Heavy, tangy with a foulness redolent of the gorilla and other apes, it assaulted their senses in an unusual concentration they had never before inhaled.

A male, ranging far to one limb of the stalking pride, came across a paw print that caused him to pause and lower his heavy head curiously.

The print was as large as five lions. What went through the lion's intrigued brain was difficult to describe. This particular specimen recognized the footprint as that of a gorilla, but the unexpected size of it caused him to fold his twitching ears back against his tawny skull.

His tufted tail began swishing in agitation. A lion who would attack a full-grown gorilla was rare. A bull gorilla was the equal to a lion in battle, possessing fangs as formidable as any lion, if not more so. But a gorilla that could make such a gigantic track was an order of magnitude more impressive than anything this particular lion could conceive.

The big cat gave out a warning growl. Within an instant, two of the females flashed to his side, fell to sniffing the same enormous footprint.

The rank odor caused them to lift their heads skyward. They dropped their chins as if in disdain. They also sniffed the air, tasting it, attempting to ascertain in what direction the maker of this massive track lurked.

On an easterly breeze came more of the powerful odor.

Another growl issued forth. Suddenly, the pride was shifting in a new direction, seeking the line of footprints, then following after them. Nostrils quivering, they silently stalked the creature that produced the scent spoor that both repelled their noses and made their jaws slaver in anticipation of a coming kill.

Long into the night, they patiently, stealthily tracked their quarry. If there were other prey about, their scents were smothered by the overpowering musk of this beast that had drawn their attention as had nothing ever before.

Across rivers which they forded with distaste, they methodically tracked, pausing often to sniff the deep impressions in the moist earth, which smelled fresher than before.

So strong was the scent, and so dark the shadow-clotted spaces beneath the jungle canopy, that the prowling pride unexpectedly happened upon the creature before they were ready.

The eyes of the lion are sharp and keen by night, but even they were fooled by the magnitude of the unexpected monster.

The giant had stopped and sat down, pausing to rest. When their eyes first fell upon it, they mistook the huge creature for a particularly dark hill bristling with brush.

Creeping toward this bristled hill, entirely unaware that it breathed, their feral eyes continued switching about, seeking signs of movement that would impel them to spring into action with electrifying alacrity.

Shifting winds brought their own scent toward the furry hill that was not a hill. Monstrous nostrils expanded, catching the feline scent, reacting to it. A low moaning became a prolonged growl, followed by a series of grunts.

The slow-moving pride froze. Before their amazed orbs, the low dark hill reared up and turned, and eyes as amber as their own looked down upon them.

Individual reactions among the pride were as varied as might be those in a human crowd. The males bared their teeth, wrinkling their broad noses, growling in warning. They recoiled, then advanced. The females hung back, nudging the juveniles to safety, then joined the males.

One lion, an older male, and perhaps wiser than the others, realized the true size of the threat standing before them. He began backing away, hackles rising.

When the two males lunged for the monster, they presumed that they were not alone. But they were.

As soon as they were in mid-spring, the awful realization of their mistake dawned. Accustomed to pouncing on animals no larger than they, they misjudged the strength needed to reach their goal. Their powerful leaps failed to bring them to the brute's squat neck and its pulsing, vulnerable jugular vein.

Instead, they slammed into the lower limbs. One lioness was swiftly captured in a mighty leather finger-vise, was raised high, and began screaming before it was dashed to the ground as if it were a mere cub.

The brave lion had attached its curved claws into the giant gorilla's upper thigh. It attempted to climb as if attached to a tree, gouging flesh as it did so, seeking the creature's exposed hairy belly in the hope of disemboweling the invader beast with its powerful hind claws.

This lion succeeded in reaching the hairy hip. Then one horrible hand took hold around his ribs, while another plucked at clinging limbs until the sharp claws popped free.

This unlucky feline found itself being held in two monster paws. He struggled. He roared. He growled. Twisting his supple body around and around, the lion attempted to wrest free of the clamping grip.

By reputation felines are among the most supple and flexible animals that go about on four paws. This sly feline almost succeeded in wriggling free. But blunt fingers squeezed down. Hard. Ribs crackled. The lion could do nothing about it.

Kong inserted his free fingers into the great spreading mane, found the small neck, and began wringing and twisting the head back and forth until there came a distinct crack of sound.

The lion went limp. Kong lifted it up, examining the pitiful thing, turning it in his hand, examining it from all sides. Then he took an experimental bite out of a haunch.

The raw flesh he tore loose was too stringy for his taste, for there is not much meat on a lion compared to a dinosaur. Still, it was meat. Kong broke off the legs, pulled the tail out, and discarded it, then ate all but the head, throwing the latter morsel away with disgust.

Blood running down his massive chin, the terrifying beast turned his attention to the remaining pride, which had observed all in gape-mouthed consternation from the flimsy shelter of thick brush.

For a moment, the other felines watched with furled faces, their pale fangs gleaming in the moonlight. They stood about with attitudes poised between imminent attack and abject flight.

Their tremendous adversary roared at them again.

Then he charged.

The pride had no choice then. They sprang to the counterattack—even the old male who had shown an understandable trepidation.

The black-haired monster was suddenly beset by myriad assailants. He cuffed one of these away in mid-leap, slamming it against a heavy tree trunk. A horny-knuckled fist met another lion in midair, driving it backward to an ignominious end.

No retreat was possible now. The lions sprang upon Kong's ankles, seeking the massive tendons, hoping to pull down the mighty tower of muscle and wiry fur to their level, where they could get at the squat neck and the jugular vein they instinctually knew throbbed there.

But King Kong was more than they could imagine. He lifted one foot, shaking off a lion hugging it in a brave attempt to chew into the Achilles tendon. Kong brought down another foot and crushed the life out of the hapless cat, whose tufted tail jittered in death.

Roaring, bringing both fists down, Kong pummeled his remaining attackers into submission. A gory slaughter commenced. Bones fractured, skulls were crushed and horrible death howls reverberated out of bloody mouths.

One industrious feline, slinking around behind Kong, leapt up on its haunches, energetically climbed Kong's hairy back.

Wavering on his feet, the great simian twisted and turned, attempting to reach the small of his back in a half-blind effort to pluck free the needle claws digging into his thick hide for purchase.

The lion proved swift. He reached the middle of Kong's back. Growling, he lunged for the back of the ape-thing's neck.

But there was so little neck there, there was nothing to bite into. Kong's right hand swept up, captured the flailing feline by its dark mane and swung it around until the lion was helpless in Kong's swiftly-moving fist.

Without fear, the gorilla-like behemoth's amber eyes stared into the yellow orbs of the angry lion. Its paws swiped out, but extended claws failed to make contact. Twisting, it attempted to swing sinewy lower legs up and clamp onto Kong's forearm. All to no avail.

Kong seemed to enjoy taunting the lion. He held it out of range of his face, swung it about to keep it off-balance, demonstrating its utter helplessness until the defeated feline's answering roars grew weak and pitiful, its broad paws swiping futilely at empty air.

Finally, the powerful cat hung limp and helpless in Kong's hand, its energy expended, its sense of helplessness complete and abject.

Seeing that his foe lacked any power or will to fight, Kong brought the lion's head into his gaping mouth, crushing the furred skull between his strong teeth. The taste of warm brain was intriguing, but not sufficiently so for Kong to take another bite.

Grunting, he flung the dead thing as far as he could.

Looking around, the beast-god saw that the pride was no more. It lay about broken and bleeding—and dying. Not even the cubs survived.

Having tasted of their flesh, the mighty monster disdained these meagre morsels.

With a low vocalization denoting self-satisfaction, Kong continued his hunt, seeking more appealing flesh....

SOUNDS of the grisly slaughter woke up the sleeping jungle. Animals that were safely in their lairs, or sleeping out on the open grassland, came awake, eyes and ears alert, heads turning in the direction of perceived danger.

The sky became filled with panicked birds that a moment before had been peacefully asleep.

Giraffes lifted their long necks; antelope froze. Disturbed crocodiles sought to immerse themselves in a nearby river.

All because they heard in the aftermath of the fearsome battle the pathetic whimpering of dying lions.

And far to the west, a pair of mismatched monkeys paused, turned and absorbed those terrible sounds.

After the symphony of death had died down, little Nkima, accompanied by Ignatz, continued on their imperative quest for the Lord of the Jungle.

Chapter 35

Captain's Log
Monday, April 10, 1933

It is with great relief that I record this entry. Overnight, Kong broke free of his shackles and escaped Number Three Hold, causing relatively minor damage to the ship, all things considered. No crew were injured, a fact I consider miraculous.

Mr. Denham is inconsolable. But nothing can be done about the situation, for it is hopeless. The accursed teufel-affe *has been banished to the jungle. That it is a jungle foreign to him does not matter. Kong is a wild animal and will learn to fend for himself, as all wild creatures must. His ultimate fate is up to him. My concern now is—*

An insistent knocking interrupted Captain Englehorn's recording of recent events.

"Enter," he invited.

Jack Driscoll stepped in, looking grim.

"Skipper, bad news to report. Miss Darrow has been looking around for the old woman from the island all morning. Couldn't find hide nor hair of her. So I had a few men scour the ship. No soap."

Englehorn's wintry eyes flickered in concern. "Do you imagine that she fell overboard in the night?"

"Possibly fell—but it could be she jumped overboard on her own hook. According to Miss Darrow, she was acting mighty queerly when they spoke last." Captain Englehorn took up his pipe, which was giving off aromatic fragrance. He replaced this between firm teeth.

"I had been considering the problem of the old woman. Having taken her aboard, it would be our duty to return her to Skull Mountain Island. Now it appears that we have been released from that duty."

"The night watch didn't hear a splash," Driscoll commented. "She might've slipped overboard and swam for shore."

Englehorn's greying eyebrows shot up slightly. His equally grey eyes grew troubled. "Going after Kong, do you think?"

"It's one possibility. One we can't discount. She and Kong are inseparable, you know."

"Since we will be anchored here a while," returned the ship's master, "I give you leave to take a small shore party to the beach and look for footprints in the sand there."

"There's a small problem with that, Skipper." Driscoll hesitated.

"Go ahead," invited Englehorn. "Out with it. No need to hold back."

"Denham has hatched another wild scheme. He thinks he can salvage this sorry expedition if we will let him go ashore to capture footage of Kong tearing the jungle apart."

"Out of the question," snapped the Skipper.

Jack Driscoll grinned. "I was hoping you'd say that, sir. But you know Denham and his wild ideas."

"Yes, the man can be as mad as a March hare."

The Mate's expression grew sober. "But if we let a shore party set off, Denham will demand to be part of it."

"I see." Englehorn took a few puffs of his pipe, then said, "Put the dory off quietly, and have Miss Darrow distract Denham. With any luck, you'll be on the beach before he knows any different."

Driscoll nodded. "But if I know Carl Denham, once he realizes what's up, he'll jump into the water after us."

"That will be his own lookout. Carry on, Mr. Driscoll."

"Yes, sir," said Driscoll, easing out onto the deck, closing the door quietly behind him.

The sun was climbing and it was already blazing hot. The air steamed from the previous day's rains, which had been prodigious.

Going to the mess, the First Mate poked his head in and spotted Lumpy clearing the dirty dishes of breakfast.

Stepping in, he said, "How would you like to go ashore for an hour or two?"

The wizened old cook cocked his bald head, clucking, "I deserve it. I'm a hero now."

Driscoll eyed him speculatively. "I don't get you."

"I'm a hero for my eggs. I scrambled up one of those turtle eggs that we were saving for Denham. They went down pretty good with the crew and the passengers."

Driscoll chuckled. Then he grew more serious. "The old woman's off the ship. Don't know if she jumped, or swam for shore. Skipper says we should make a good-faith effort to find out which it is. Are you game?"

Lumpy brightened. "Game? I'm halfway there already! Give me a minute to change my duds, and rustle up a basket, or something."

"What do you need a basket for, you old sea dog? Your knittin'?"

Grimacing, Lumpy rubbed his bald pate. "While you're looking for the old bat, I'm after catching that faithless scamp, Ignatz. If I find him, I'm going to stuff the rascal in a basket and bring him back. That little monk should know better than to run off with a big ape like Kong. No telling what might happen to him."

A bleak light showed in the First Mate's eyes. "Listen, Lumpy, the chances of finding Ignatz must be pretty slim by now."

"Slim or none, I need to do my best."

"Have it your way, then. Just don't drift too far from the shore party. We may not be on the beach long. The poop deck. Ten minutes from now. Got that?"

"I'll beat you to the poop deck," promised Lumpy, tearing off his apron.

Back topside, Jack Driscoll roamed the shelter deck fore and aft, sidled up to sailors who didn't appear to be too busy and gave them the word. He received nods in return.

Stopping by Ann Darrow's cabin, he knocked. When her blonde head appeared, he asked, "Seen anything of Denham?"

"Not since breakfast. Weren't those eggs scrumptious?"

"Haven't got around to breakfast yet," he said gruffly. "Too busy. Look, see if you can't find Denham and distract him. We're putting off a boat and we don't want him to know about it."

"A search party?"

"Burial detail is more like it. My hopes are not high."

"Oh, Jack," she said, folding her arms to keep her bare forearms from shivering. "Don't talk like that."

Driscoll pressed Ann's trembling arms reassuringly. "Keep Denham occupied. We won't be long."

With that, Jack Driscoll surged to the poop deck, gave the weather deck a quick inspection and found no sign of Carl Denham.

"Good. All right, men. Let's get this dory over the side."

The men fell to the task, swinging the davits out and running the fall lines down with expert ease.

The dory plopped into the water smartly, and they began climbing down the accommodation ladder.

Once every man was at his station, they fell to rowing.

Looking over the side, Jack Driscoll directed, "These waters are pretty clear. Keep an eye peeled for the old woman. In case she drowned."

But no sign of any body did they discover. Just a solitary bull shark, cutting the calm water with the sharp grey blade of his dorsal fin. It ignored them, and they returned the favor.

The party soon beached on the white sand, hopped out and pulled the dory up onto flat rock, its keel grinding a broad gouge in the pale sand.

"Fan out," ordered Driscoll. "Look for any sign of footprints. Sandaled footprints. Make it snappy, too. We don't want to be here any longer than we have to."

The men split up, eyes intent on the crystalline sand. Everyone carried a weapon, ranging from revolvers to Springfield rifles. Driscoll toted his Nitro Express elephant gun, as well as a sidearm in a cartridge belt, along with a bandolier of fat mercy bullets looped over his chest.

Ten minutes later or possibly less, a sailor called out, "Mate!"

Driscoll came running, and found himself in a clump of the brush. There, impressed into the earth, lay what appeared to be a gigantic handprint. But the deep depression was made by no hand. This was the footprint of a gorilla of unbelievable proportions. Most disturbingly, a flatted carcass lay crushed in the outline.

"Hyena," muttered Driscoll. "Kong probably crushed him flat without even noticing that he did so."

Pointing into the jungle, the sailor said, "He went that way."

Driscoll nodded grimly. "Where Kong went, the old woman would follow—if she were able. See if her tracks are anywhere about here."

They began walking along, and the comparative size between their shoes and the monster's prints brought back to their minds the terror of Kong. Although the huge beast had lain a captive in the steel-reinforced hold, he had been supine and out of sight to most of the crew during the voyage thus far. Standing next to his empty footprint seemed to conjure up the superstitious fear that often inhabits sailormen around the world.

Kong in the flesh was terrifying enough. Kong standing erect was horrifying. There was something about the broad finger-toed depression made by the blundering hulk that excited the imagination, and created a cold dread in the pit of each man's stomach.

"How far are we planning to follow these tracks?" muttered one seaman.

"Not far," reassured Driscoll. "We want to be thorough. But Kong's seven-league strides tell a pretty clear picture. He was moving inland, and making good time. We're not likely to catch up to the brute even if we wanted to."

The shore party heaved a collective sigh of relief, not ashamed to do so.

Eventually, after they discovered no clear sign of the old woman's footprints, Driscoll called a halt to the search.

"That's enough," he decided. "If she made it to shore, there's no sign of her. Probably perished in the water. Let's try looking for her there."

With tight grins of relief, the shore party turned around and trekked back to the white sandy beach, and prepared to reclaim their dory.

Driscoll was nonplussed to see a second dory being lowered from the stern of the *Wanderer*.

"Wonder who that is?" a sailor muttered.

"I can't see clearly," said Driscoll, setting hands on his hips. "But if I were a betting man, I'd bet on Carl Denham."

The lines were dropped, the dory pushed away, then pointed her prow at their precise position.

The shore party waited patiently. When the dory began to heave into clear view, no one was surprised to see Carl Denham stand up in the bow, and wave his arms over his head excitedly.

"Ahoy!" he yelled, hoisting his clumsy camera into view. He was grinning, almost beside himself with glee.

The keel grated onto sand, and two seamen rushed up to pull the craft onto firmer ground, whereupon Carl Denham jumped off, cradling his movie camera, a folded tripod of wood clutched in the other hammy hand. A burlap sack of extra film canisters was slung over one burly shoulder.

Two sailors had accompanied him, one the boatswain, Beaumont.

"Well, what brings you here, Mr. Denham?" Driscoll asked politely. More politely than he felt. For a vein in one side of his forehead was pulsing with restrained agitation.

"Do you have to ask?" grinned the irrepressible showman. "Your skipper gave me permission to shoot whatever I could."

"Well, you might be too late for all that. Kong's tracks lead into the jungle. He's probably miles away from here by now. You might catch up to him—if you can find a horse. Since they don't have many horses in Africa, I think you're out of luck."

Denham grinned cockily, saying, "I'll settle for a zebra if we can rustle one."

"Pardon me for being so forward, Mr. Denham," stated Driscoll tightly. "But I have a hard time imagining Captain Englehorn giving you permission to go traipsing around this jungle."

"Why, *you're* here, aren't you?"

"Search party. Maybe a burial detail. We're looking for the old woman. She jumped ship in the night."

Denham's jolly attitude grew more vibrant. "Oh. That might make a swell scene of my movie. Kong's companion throws her life away in her grief. Too bad she wasn't a young maiden. That would go over big. You boys carry on and pay no attention to my camera."

"Suit yourself, Mr. Denham," clipped Driscoll. "But when we get back to the ship, your story better hold up."

Sudden indignation stung Denham's expression. "Say, who are you to question me? I chartered this man's expedition, now didn't I?"

"You did. But the Captain's word is the law, and you know that."

"Well, I'm obeying the law. Show me any different."

Addressing the two accompanying sailors, the First Mate asked, "Did either of you witness Captain Englehorn giving Mr. Denham permission to come on shore?"

The puzzled pair shook their heads in the negative. The boatswain said, "Mr. Denham came up to us and relayed the Skipper's leave to go ashore."

"Alleged leave, you mean," snapped Driscoll. "Sounds to me like you fell for a line of snappy patter, Bosun."

Beaumont colored in embarrassment. "Sorry, sir. But Mr. Denham is charterer on this run. I never—"

"Let it pass, Boats," the Mate said without rancor. "You were taken advantage of, nothing more or less." Turning to Denham, he added, "Remember what I said about the Captain's word being law."

"Sure," cracked Denham. "On the boat. But we're on dry land now."

Jack Driscoll resisted an urge to step up to the overconfident director and hand him a sock in the jaw. Instead, he said tightly, "We were about to search the waters for the woman's body. No sign of her on dry land."

"Carry on. Pay no attention to the camera. I'll be grinding away right here."

So saying, Carl Denham set up his tripod and began mounting the camera on it.

Turning to his shore party, Jack Driscoll announced, "Having two boats at hand ought to cut our search time in half. Now let's get them back into the water and see what we can discover."

Chapter 36

IN A GRASSY patch of savanna, a herd of ostriches slept close to the jungle floor. At the center of the group, a shallow pit had been excavated, and a handful of pale ostrich eggs were incubating, encompassed by its earthen rim.

Ostrich eggs were much prized in the jungle. Monkeys often raided the nest, as did vultures. Hyenas were particularly persistent. Even wily man was tempted to sneak up on the group, intent on making off with a precious egg or two.

These were among the largest eggs available in the jungle. One would fill the belly of any predator for a day, or longer. And eggs do not fight back. Only their guardians.

The largest of these awkward avian guards stood nine feet tall when fully erect. This was a male, whose feathery plumage was black and tipped with white. Alone of the sleeping herd, his large feather-lashed eyes stood open, watchful for hyenas and other skulking predators.

In a watering hole nearby, a bull rhinoceros dozed. The sounds he made were uncouth and carried far.

The ground shook noticeably. Then shook again. After a third time, the rumbling was no longer slight.

This brought the rhino to wakefulness. Swiveling his horned head about, he sought the source of the rumbling noises.

Few creatures of the jungle shake the ground with their tread. Hippopotamus was one. Water Buffalo. And majestic elephants, of course.

The rhino was familiar with all those earth disturbances. An elephant stampede was the greatest of these. What he heard with his long ears and felt in his massive three-toed feet was no approaching elephant herd. It was something else. Something disquieting. Something that caused even imperturbable rhinoceros to give pause.

Flicking its elongated ears, the rhinoceros realized the sound was coming from behind him. Slowly, ponderously, he turned in place, throwing muddy yellow water about.

The night-clotted trees were shaking in a way that was not responsive to the warm breezes. The rhino stared into those close-pressed boles, curious as to what manner of animal could so shake the solid ground beneath his feet.

At first, the grey brute failed to see the approach of this new thing of the jungle.

For the lower limbs of the monster were not visible in the dense grove, but then a pair of leathery black hands pushed apart two towering trees, and a glowering head burst forth, separating the leafy crowns. Curious eyes looked down upon the rhino shining wetly in the moonlight. They blinked at the half-familiar shape, whose thick hide resembled certain dinosaurs who freely roamed Skull Island.

Kong growled in challenge.

The sound brought the small eyes of the rhinoceros lifting upward. Two pairs of orbs locked and fixed.

The titanic size of the monster did not seem to impress the rhinoceros. Grunting and snorting, it clambered clumsily out of the watering hole, found footing in the mud, and started galloping forward, hook-like double horns lowered.

Releasing the tree crowns, Kong emerged from a break in the forest, and advanced, snarling.

The rhinoceros weighed more than a ton of solid muscles and thick hide. The ground shook in sympathy to its thudding gallop.

Rearing so high, Kong misjudged the unfamiliar beast's ferocity. He shifted his feet. The rhinoceros altered course, blundering into one black-haired ankle with overpowering momentum. The lowered horns struck forcefully.

Staggered, Kong's great arms flew up, and the galloping rhinoceros circled back around, ramming the back of the opposite foot with his horned skull.

Like a bristling black tree, Kong fell, slamming onto his leathery-skinned chest, caught entirely by surprise. Back on Skull Mountain Island, the dinosaur fought face-to-face. This bulky creature did not fight like any of those familiar foes.

Snorting wildly, the rhinoceros charged back and forth, then made a beeline for Kong's skull. Its intent was clear. It was going to butt Kong's head with all his muscular might.

The giant anthropoid rolled over. A monstrous hand descended, seizing the rhinoceros in mid-stride. Momentum carried the rhino along for perhaps eight yards, then Kong picked the snuffling beast off its feet, and shook it angrily, roaring wildly.

To the rhinoceros, this was an entirely new experience. An elephant or perhaps a hippopotamus was capable of uprooting him. Nothing on the earth could lift him off his feet with impunity. To the low brute's simple mind, this was against the natural order of things.

Kong struggled to his feet, shook the rhinoceros, slapped it with his free hand, and seemed uncertain whether to bite into its thick greyish side or simply pummel it into submission.

The thing felt heavy in Kong's padded palm. He shook it again, brought it to his great nostrils, sniffed it with interest. Then he began squeezing inexorably.

An awful moaning groan emerged from the rhino's distended jaws. Its toothless mouth writhed in frustrated fury. Kong grunted with intrigued pleasure. Slowly, agonizingly, his crushing grip pulverized the rib cage, turning the internal organs into a mass of jelly.

Out of the rhinoceros' gaping mouth was propelled an explosive release of air originating from laboring lungs which were being squeezed flat. Small eyes bulging wildly from its head, the rhinoceros died under the terrible crushing vise of hair and leather. Juices ran down from bursting seams in the sodden thing.

Kong brought the carcass to his nostrils, again sniffing curiously, and gave vent to a sound that might have been disgust or displeasure. The smell did not appeal to his appetite, voracious as it was.

With a careless toss, Kong flung the rhinoceros to the dirt, where it landed amid the disturbed ostriches, which had risen to their feet. They looked about wildly, mesmerized by the titanic struggle.

The great carcass landed hard, smashed one ostrich to a pulp, while the others scattered in all directions, their precious eggs forgotten.

Hearing these noises, Kong turned about, and crept toward them, curious. The soft thunder of retreating feet reminded him of the scampering of juvenile dinosaurs back in his home jungle.

When he pushed his way toward the spot where the rhinoceros lay dead, Kong spied the tiny feathered creatures melting into the jungle with avian celerity. He was prepared to follow and scoop them up to see how they tasted.

Then his intrigued gaze fell up on the small mound of white eggs. Semi-human eyes gleamed avidly. Small cheeps of pleasure escaped his leathery lips.

Padding up to the mound, Kong sat down before it and studied the heaping nest. While wide-eyed ostriches watched from the shadows in helpless horror, the former ruler of Skull Mountain Island picked up the eggs one at a time, held them over his back-tilted head, and broke the shells, thus permitting the viscous yellow yolk and surrounding clear fluid to drip into his waiting mouth.

Kong went through each one, enjoying their raw goodness, until there were no more. He smacked his lips with relish.

Licking what was left off his creased palms, the apish giant wandered over to the watering hole, where he scooped up a handful of yellowish water, sipped some experimentally, and quickly decided it was too vile for consumption.

Turning his head, the beast-god noticed the wide dark eyes of the watching ostriches. His low brow wrinkled in unreadable thought. A deep growl his only warning, Kong decided to give chase.

But the flightless birds were fast on their nimble feet. They quickly scattered in all directions—so rapidly that Kong broke off the chase, his jungle instincts telling him that these prey were too fleet of foot for easy capture. It would have been a waste of time.

Kong paused, looking and listening, touching his rounded stomach which, while more filled than it had been, was not sufficiently full to satisfy his gargantuan hunger.

Kong did not move. The breeze played with the wiry fur coating his bulk as if invisible fingers were toying with him, exposing scars both long healed and recently stitched closed. A few of the latter had popped open, attracting interested flies. His broad flat nostrils sniffed the moving air, seeking smells of interest to brain and appetite both.

But it was his ears which collected something intriguing. A splashing in the river nearby drew his attention. Hunched over, Kong slouched toward the slithering sounds, creeping cautiously, employing stealth, the way he used to forage on Skull Mountain Island, when hunting his favorite dinosaurs.

Chapter 37

ALL NIGHT long, little Nkima and Ignatz the ship monkey had scampered and raced along the interlacing forest canopy. They paused often, peering about for signs of danger, picking nits off one another, panting from exertion.

Where the trees thinned out, the two monkeys dropped down into the tall savanna grass and scampered along, trying to make as little noise as possible amid the waving blades of emerald.

They came at last to a broad river where hippopotamus and crocodile coexisted in peace.

This truce was not a product of good fellowship, but the natural consequence of two formidable species being forced to share the winding waterway. The crocodiles might enjoy the taste of hippopotamus meat, but they valued their lives much more, so they did not trouble the great wallowing creatures.

Inasmuch as hippopotami fed on bottom grasses and other vegetarian fare, the horny-ridged crocodiles tempted the hippopotamus herd not.

Thus was order maintained in the jungle of the Colony of Kenya in British East Africa.

Creeping through the waving grass, Nkima led the way to the riverbank where he dipped his hand in and drank as monkeys do, a cupped palm of water at a time.

Ignatz followed suit. The frightened little monkey drank greedily, often staring about him. He was used to the comparative safety of a stout tramp steamer, where there were no natural predators. Possibly he had lived in a forest when very young, before Lumpy the cook acquired him. But that was long ago in monkey time.

So Ignatz stayed close to his new friend who, while not himself a brave creature, knew his way through the jungle.

After they had filled their tiny bellies with cool drinking water, Nkima gestured for Ignatz to follow. The nervous ship monkey naturally obeyed, but when he saw what Nkima did next, a deep fear gripped him.

A crocodile was slipping off the muddy river bank to cross the waters with paddling claws.

Displaying no fear, Nkima ran for its heavy tail, leapt up on it, and so gained the middle of the saurian's bumpy back. Turning, he signaled Ignatz to follow quickly.

Ignatz hesitated, a deep terror welling in his dark eyes.

Venting a sharp screech, Nkima urged the frightened monk to hurry up.

Fear is a strange thing. It comes in shades and degrees and weights and other metaphysical measurements. Ignatz was afraid to follow—but he was even more fearful of being left behind, he finally decided. Venting a screech of his own, he raced on all fours, and leapt from the mud to the back of the crocodile just after the sinuous thing splashed into the water.

There, on that nodular surface, the two monkeys squatted, tails curled at their backs like mirror images, while the oblivious crocodile patiently crossed the river, and reached the opposite bank, employing its foreclaws to pull itself up onto the muddy embankment.

There, Nkima gave Ignatz a hard spank to propel him away.

The two comrades made a mad dash for the nearest tree, climbed it easily, and immediately started looking around for a more substantial tree within jumping distance.

There was none. So there they sat, huddling together, panting with fear as much as from exertion, while they contemplated their next move.

One would think that a tiny monkey would not know its way through great distances of jungle. But Nkima was a far-ranging creature, having enjoyed the protective company of Tarzan of the Apes on many adventures. He may not have known exactly where he was in the way a civilized man would recognize a city street, but Nkima recognized natural landmarks—even if he did not comprehend the civilized names for those landmarks.

To the west and the south shone the moonlit peak of Mount Kilimanjaro, a great flat massif topped by ice and snow. To the west, but more toward the north, reared up Mount Kenya, which was not visible at this distance.

The plantation where Tarzan of the Apes dwelled lay between those two mighty mountains. But it was far away. Farther than any solitary monkey could travel in one week, much less a day.

Turning his head to the east, little Nkima scanned the tree-tops, seeking any sign of the gargantuan gorilla who was taller than any tree in this immediate jungle save the mighty bottle tree, which alone towered almost to the sky.

No sign of Kong was revealed, nor was his mighty roaring heard.

Nkima and Ignatz, exhausted beyond measure, decided to curl up in the sheltering crotch of a tree and sleep until their sinewy strength was replenished. Troubled by nightmares inspired by their recent experiences, their furry bodies twitched and jerked, as if poised to flee the conjurings of their slumbering imaginations.

Chapter 38

THE TWO dories off the *Wanderer* crisscrossed the waters of the tranquil cove while the blistering sun climbed to its noonday zenith.

No sign of old Penjaga did they discern. The search became so frustrating that Jack Driscoll stripped off his chambray shirt and plunged into the water. On the other dory, another sailor did likewise. They swam about, diving often into the clear blue waters, but all they discovered was the solitary bull shark gliding about lazily several yards distant, seemingly aimless in its wanderings.

The sight of the sleek, sharp-finned monster motivated them to seek the safety of their respective dories without delay.

Toweling himself off with his own shirt, Jack Driscoll sat in the bow of his boat and complained loudly, "If she's down there, sharks likely got her by now."

"There would be blood, Mate," reminded a sailor nonchalantly.

Driscoll frowned. "You're probably right about that. So where is she?"

"Process of elimination says the old witch disappeared into the jungle."

Driscoll swung his gaze toward the white beach fringing the cove, and let out a yelp of annoyance.

"Where did Denham get to?"

"Ain't seen him."

Calling over to the other boat, Driscoll yelled, "Where's Denham?"

The boatswain hollered back, "I thought he was filming us!"

"Putting one over on us is more like it," growled Driscoll. "We're done here. Let's go fetch him."

After beaching both boats, the shore party started working through the jungle. They soon picked up the director's tracks. Not surprisingly, they were trailing the nightmare prints of King Kong, which made them think that an immense Paul Bunyan had been pressing his deformed palms into the soft soil.

A seaman yelped, "What! You don't suppose he's gone after that big black gorilla?"

"If he has," promised Driscoll, "I'm going to drag him back by his sunburnt ears."

Despite the terrific heat, they broke into a trot, anxious to catch up to the wily old showman.

An hour of this exertion got the better of them and they stopped to take stock of the situation.

"What's got into him?" demanded the boatswain.

Jack Driscoll took off his peaked cap, swiped perspiration from the inner band, then mopped the residue off his sweat-shiny forehead.

"That ornery reprobate probably has it figured that we wouldn't dare desert him. At least, the Old Man wouldn't give up on him. Going to get his footage of Kong, leaving us to take up his slack."

"So what are we to do, Mate?"

"Well, his tracks are plain as day. We'll see what following them does. Maybe if we get lucky, a crocodile will have gotten him before we do."

"We wouldn't get off that easy," chuckled Lumpy, still toting his woven basket in hopes of snaring Ignatz.

"You have that right," growled Jack Driscoll in a low and

menacing voice. "I've lost enough crew because of Denham's crazy ideas. Now look at us. Tramping through the jungle like a damn safari of fools. All right, single file, men. Don't let any of these Kong footprints swallow you."

ANOTHER hour brought them to the first scene of Kong's depredations.

They broke through to a clearing and came to the spot where numerous black flies buzzed around the carcasses of a pride of lions. All were dead. Most were battered beyond recognition.

"Kong done this," a man mumbled thickly.

"Well, it sure wasn't Carl Denham," muttered Driscoll.

The boatswain grunted, "Well, in a way it was, wasn't it?"

"I guess it was, at that," admitted Driscoll wearily. "Let's press on."

Another twenty minutes brought them to the clearing of the smashed ostrich eggs and the even more smashed rhinoceros.

Gathered around the raw and ruined carcass of the latter, their imaginations began to work. The eyes of the defeated beast were open, and leaking fluid, as if crying in death. Black flies were crawling all over the muscular hulk.

"Looks like Kong threw him like a baseball," a sailor said wonderingly. "As if he weighed next to nothing."

"That's what it looks like," admitted Driscoll. "Maybe it's time to turn back."

"You thinking Denham's a goner?"

A frown made a meaty fist of the Mate's sweaty features. "No, I'm thinking that we're two hours from the ship, with no food, one canteen of water, and only a couple of rifles. If we're to make a manhunt for Carl Denham, we're going to need the Skipper to weigh in on this. I've taken as much risk as I can on my own authority. Let Captain Englehorn decide what's to be done about Denham."

Not a man of the crew showed any reluctance in turning

around. Carl Denham had not engendered a great deal of love from the decimated crew of the *Wanderer*.

Following the great tracks of King Kong back to the beach took a lot out of the party. They paused twice to rest, and refreshed themselves with jungle fruit.

Lumpy found a hefty coconut, and took his knife to it, cracking the drupe's hard, hairy shell and splitting it open.

The coconut was passed around, but there was only enough of the thin, sweet milk for three men.

During this rest stop, they failed to hear stealthy footsteps that were creeping up on them….

Chapter 39

THE AFTERNOON rains came once more.

Leaves in the jungle began to twitch and pop as the first pattering of moisture commenced. Soon, they produced a steady, monotonous drumbeat.

Moving through the tall savanna grass, little Nkima and Ignatz the ship monkey put their furry paws protectively over their heads, shaking the first intrusive drops out of their fur.

Seeking shelter, they moved to the north, led by Nkima, who made impatient gestures for the ever-hesitant Ignatz to follow.

Nkima led his furry companion to a clearing by a grove of gum trees. Baking in the sun, a profusion of half-buried white bones lay scattered. Only now they were no longer baking. They were steaming. A warm rain was bathing them, producing a steamy mist.

These were enormous rib bones and leg bones and monster skulls. Some skulls displayed great curved tusks, but others were absent of those elements. Pilfered by poachers, before being run off by guardian elephants.

For this was the Elephant's Graveyard.

Scampering into this natural ossuary, Nkima pulled a reluctant Ignatz into the hollow skull of one great bull elephant carcasses. And there they took shelter, letting the greying old braincase withstand the rain in their stead.

This downpour went on for hours, seemed unrelenting. Despite the urgency of their mission, neither monkey cared to stir from shelter and brave the elements.

A rumble of thunder followed by a stab of red lightning punctuated their mood. This rumbling continued intermittently, and at one point the jungle floor shook.

When it did, Nkima grew anxious. Yes, he feared the lightning. And thunder was disquieting to his sensitive ears. But he never knew the earth to shake in sympathy with a tropical downpour.

The rains continued endlessly, and the ground became soaked and spongy.

Then, there came a crashing of brush as if elephants were stampeding. Little Nkima began to worry that he would be accused of stealing the sacred bones by the elephants known to graze peacefully nearby.

He poked his furry head out of the empty socket of one long-disintegrated eye while Ignatz stationed himself at the other, copying his action. Since the sounds were coming from the direction of the sky above them, they naturally looked upward.

Their tiny jaws dropped in alarm when they saw striding out of the jungle the great gorilla beast they feared most of all.

Trembling, they did not know whether to hunker down, or flee.

Immense amber eyes swept the Elephant's Graveyard. Intrigued glints like diamond sparks came into those simian orbs. With a low rumble of sound, Kong advanced.

Fate had it that the beast-god reached down into the disordered clump of bones and seized the very elephant skull in which Nkima and Ignatz shivered.

They sprang in opposite directions, scattering. But Kong paid them little heed.

Lifting the skull, he crushed it in one massive palm and, finding nothing of interest within, directed his attention toward other bones. A gleaming thigh bone looking fresher than the rest caught his quickening eye, its fresh aroma triggering throaty sounds of pleasure.

Kong took it in both hands, snapped it into two. Lifting the splintered ends, he sniffed, interested. The sweet smell of marrow came to his nostrils.

Inserting his tongue, Kong located the tasty stuff. Pleased sounds came from deep within his throat. After he had licked and sucked as much as he could, Kong threw the broken bones away, and bent down to retrieve more.

The next specimen proved to be equally delicious as to its interior matter.

Enjoying himself, Kong sat down on the veldt, and began picking through the close-clustered bones of the Elephant's Graveyard, heedless of the two little monkeys that sat high in thick trees on opposite sides of the clearing.

Nkima and Ignatz signaled to one another frantically, and when they were satisfied that Kong was fully immersed in his meal, they dropped down to the ground, carefully rendezvoused with each other, far out of sight of the ravenous ape-monster.

Warm rain continued to pour down, but they were all but oblivious to that discomfort, for they knew they had to get word to Tarzan of the Apes as soon as possible. The Elephant's Graveyard was not only sacred to the pachyderm population ranging this sprawling jungle, but Nkima's master considered it inviolate, too.

A certain punishment lay in store for the gorilla-like invader that sucked marrow from honored ancestral bones, ignorant of its terrible transgression.

Chapter 40

WHEN THE long rain commenced, Jack Driscoll and his shore party were oblivious to the softly padding feet drawing very near to them.

"Oh, hell!" Driscoll exploded when the rains began kicking up.

They were soon drenched—even after they found shelter under the interlacing branches of the jungle canopy where it was thickest. Myriad leaves dribbled raindrops off their bouncing stems.

"Guess we're stuck here a spell," grumbled Lumpy. "And no sign of my monk anywheres."

"Ignatz is the least of our worries," grunted Driscoll, yanking down the bill of his cap to protect his face as he sat with his back to the scarred tree trunk. He might have been trying to shut out all sight of the world.

It wasn't long before they were hunkered down and miserable, faces downcast.

The foliage above grew heavy with accumulating moisture and released dollops of warm water onto their heads. Rainwater pooled all around them.

When Penjaga the Storyteller stirred in their midst, at first they did not notice.

She spoke up unexpectedly, her wise old eyes two black jewels beneath the soggy milkweed cloud of her hair. "Driscoll. Heed me."

Jerking erect, Jack Driscoll swept up his Nitro Express elephant gun. Before he could aim it, his men were on their feet, blocking his aim.

Revolver muzzles sweeping in her direction, Penjaga padded toward them unafraid.

"Thought you had drowned," grunted Driscoll, lowering his weapon.

The Storyteller's eyes were bleak. "Would that I had. I have been pursuing Kong. But the length of his stride is too much for me. I had to stop, to sleep."

"We didn't find your footprints anywhere."

Her agate-dark eyes flashed knowing glints. "On Skull Mountain Island, neither did the death runners and other hungry lizards."

"Oh, so you know your woodcraft, do you?"

Penjaga nodded solemnly. "I know how to survive."

"Well, Carl Denham is loose in these woods, but we've given up on him, too."

The ancient crone inclined her head again. "He passed me twice, unaware. I can take you to him."

Driscoll brightened. He blew rainwater off his lips.

"That would be swell. Save us a lot of trouble."

"One condition. That you also return Kong to his home."

"Impossible! How are we going to get that big ape under our control?"

"You captured him once. Do this again. Return Kong to his skull throne."

Driscoll scowled. "I can't promise that. It'll be up to the Old Man, anyway. Take us to Denham and we'll see what we can work out."

"Follow me, then." Turning, the Storyteller started off, seemingly oblivious to the drenching rain.

Shrugging, First Mate Driscoll signaled his men to follow along. As they walked in the old woman's rustling wake, they saw that she left no footprints, but that was because the soaked ground absorbed them.

Running up, old Lumpy accosted the old woman. "Did you see my monkey anywheres around here?"

Penjaga shook her head. "There are many monkeys in these trees. One is the same as another. We seek Kong. There is no other like him."

"Thanks a banana bunch for your help," said Lumpy sourly, dropping back to the shore party.

When the relentless rains at last dwindled down, Penjaga led them to a towering gum tree whose spreading branches stood alone in a grassy clearing. It smelled faintly of lemons.

The old woman appeared to be lost. At least that's how they took her sudden halting beneath the lemon-scented tree.

"Something wrong?" asked Driscoll.

"Denham is here," she intoned.

Everyone looked around. "Where?"

Then Penjaga lifted a wizened finger, pointing straight up.

Throwing their head back, they stared up, and to their amazement, high in the spreading tree, straddling interlacing branches, perched Carl Denham, bulky Bell & Howell camera at one side, his folded tripod across his legs. In some manner, he had looped a vine around the tree trunk, and tied himself there so he wouldn't fall.

"What are you doing up there?" demanded Driscoll.

"Haven't you heard the expression 'up a tree'?" called down Denham.

"Did you climb, or were you chased up there?" wondered Lumpy.

"A little of both. This is the highest spot I could find. I figured I could get a shot of Kong if he pokes his head out of the trees."

"Did you?" asked Driscoll.

"Not yet."

"Well, the safari's over. We're going back to the ship. All of us. You're through shooting for the day."

Carl Denham's grin was challenging. "Motivate me, sailor-man," he taunted.

"Mutiny, eh?"

"No, just ordinary insubordination. Take it up with the Captain later."

Borrowing a Springfield rifle from Coldwell the coxswain, Jack Driscoll lifted the hard stock to his shoulder, took careful aim, and fired a warning shot that caused a brief shower of leaves to come falling down on the director's head. His campaign hat fell to the dirt. He almost lost his tripod, too. But he held onto his camera—which almost caused him to lose his perch.

"You wouldn't dare shoot me."

"I'm not aiming at you. Doing a little landscaping, that's all. Watch."

The rifle cracked again and another branch splintered, flinging leafy debris everywhere.

"I'm liable to fall," warned Denham.

"Don't expect us to catch you," drawled Driscoll, jacking another round into the chamber.

Carl Denham looked down without humor. "I'll make you a deal, Driscoll. If you catch my camera, I'll come down peaceably."

"Let's see the camera drop."

Carefully, Denham took the camera in both hands, aimed with one brown eye shut, and let it fall. Two men caught it, showed that it was intact. Next came the burlap sacks of extra film. Lumpy captured this in his basket. Down came the tripod. No one caught that.

However Carl Denham had managed to climb the tree in the first place, coming down was no easy task. He moved carefully from limb to limb, nearly losing his footing once, shed a shoe which Lumpy caught, but eventually he scrambled down to the jungle floor, somewhat the worse for his experience.

Handing the camera over to the filmmaker, Driscoll asked, "Capture any decent footage?"

"Footprints. Dead lions. Broken trees. An ostrich nest that had been raided, with broken egg shells scattered everywhere. But not a glimpse of Kong. But he's making his presence known. He's got half the jungle terrified. Notice the absence of jackals? It's not natural, I tell you."

"Well, let's get back to the ship before the wild ones come back."

"Fair enough," said the director agreeably. "I'm so hot and hungry, a pile of Lumpy's powdered eggs would look good to me."

Noticing old Penjaga, the two antagonists exchanged glances, but not a word passed between them until they turned back in the direction of the water.

A venomous glint came into the Storyteller's ancient eyes as they fell into the rolling cadence of their trek.

"You thought to conquer Kong, white man," she said with thinly-veiled distaste. "But the gods sent a storm to free him. I warned you of their wrath."

"Humph!" grunted Denham. "You don't understand what's at stake."

Her mouth curled into a thin sneer. "I understand willful stubbornness, which you possess in abundance."

"What of it?" countered Denham. "I'm a showman. And the show much go on. You probably never heard that expression, living in the bush the way you have. But back on that godforsaken island, Kong was dying anyway. The last of his kind. Doomed to extinction. Until I happened along."

A feverish light came into Carl Denham's eyes then, and his face flushed with more than the stifling heat of the jungle.

"If we could have ferried Kong across the Atlantic to the big town," he expounded, "he would have become famous, I tell you. Not some prehistoric survival doomed to extinction. But a celebrated creature. King Kong, the Eighth Wonder of the

World! No one's ever seen anything like him. And after this, no one ever will. Don't you see, you shriveled-up old crone? Kong can't live forever. But taking him to civilization would have given his lonely last years meaning. Why, scientists would come from all over the globe to study him. After he's gone, they'd probably stuff and mount him in a museum. That way, he'll be immortal. A Beast for the ages."

"You speak with great passion," murmured Penjaga.

"I'm a passionate man."

"Passionate, but no wisdom." The Storyteller shook her head sadly. "All passion but no heart."

"What's that?" flared Denham. "No heart, you say? Say, I have the heart of a lion." Seeing the blank expression on the old woman's wrinkled features, the showman seemed to shrink. "I forgot. You don't know what a lion is, do you? Never been off Skull Mountain Island in your life. You only know dinosaurs. Let me put it to you this way. I have the heart of a dinosaur."

Contempt made the Storyteller's wizened features gather and twitch. "Dinosaurs are lizards. Less than man. Less than Kong. If you possess the heart of a lowly lizard, it explains why you fail to see your own folly."

"Folly, is it? Folly! Kong will make us all rich. You call that folly?"

Penjaga made a disgusted sound. "No, worse than folly. You thought Lord Kong would fill your days with gold. But he will not do that. He will instead fill your days with terror if you do not abandon your wicked scheming."

"Well," Denham said morosely, "that's all water under the bridge now. Like you say, Kong is loose. He's got his freedom now. And more power to him. Why, in no time he'll shove the lions aside and make himself the new King of Beasts in Africa."

"Do not think you can fool Penjaga," warned the Storyteller. "Your schemes are not yet dead. Not while you breathe."

"Stow all talk of Kong," grumbled Jack Driscoll. "I'm tired of it. Kong belongs to Africa, now. Let him have it. And Africa can have Kong. I wash my hands of both."

That concluded the heated exchange.

They were a miserable, bedraggled sight as they picked their way back to the beach, soaked to the skin, clothes steaming as the returning jungle heat ignited the strength-sapping process of evaporation.

As the sound of combers washing the beach came to their ears, Carl Denham perked up.

"Say, Lumpy. I don't suppose you'd be up to fixing some of that hash of yours once we're safely on board. My belly feels like an empty keg."

"You're in a hell of a lot of hot water, Mr. Denham," said Jack Driscoll as they trudged along. "You might want to set your sights lower—to bread and water."

"Would you have found the old woman if you hadn't come after me?"

"No, I suppose not."

Carl Denham grinned broadly. "Be sure to tell that to your skipper when you haul me onto the carpet, or swing me from the yardarm, or whatever it is you plan to do. The way I see it, I helped save the old bat by my resourcefulness."

Jack Driscoll said nothing. He could already picture in his mind's eye the wily showman wiggling out of yet another tight spot. It rankled him.

Chapter 41

RANGING FAR inland, Kong continued his exploration of this unfamiliar jungle.

A great hunger impelled him. He had barely filled his great belly with what food he could forage.

Night was approaching, and the natural tempo of the jungle shifted from the hunters of the day to those predators who prowled by night.

The fresh scent of running water came to Kong's pulsing nostrils. Mixed in with it was another, half-familiar, odor that reminded the beast-god of prey he stalked on his home island.

Moving in the direction of this tantalizing odor, Kong pushed aside blocking trees, causing myriad screeching monkeys to leap away and flee to higher branches, out of reach.

Kong saw them not. The edible animals he had thus far encountered had not proven very tasty. Once, a zebra had flashed by, starkly striped, making frightened noises as its hoofs beat out a wild tattoo.

Attracted by the unusual creature, Kong had swerved in its direction, but the agile animal ducked into the underbrush and soon eluded him.

Frustrated, Kong pressed on, grunting to himself, deep-set eyes questing about warily.

Soon the great prehistoric anthropoid came to a winding river where hippopotami dwelled. It was not those fat beasts that attracted Kong's interest, however. Other creatures, much smaller and more sinuous, made his pulse race. For coexisting with the languid-looking hippos, crocodiles baked in the dying rays of the sun. One slipped in and out of the water with reptilian ease.

It was the saurian scent of the latter that had stirred Kong's appetite.

The crocodiles, seeing Kong heave into view, blinked rather stupidly, then backed clumsily to the riverbank as a precaution, seeking the security of muddy water.

Nothing the awesome size of Kong had ever come into view before. No creature in all of Africa had ever towered so high over the riverbank they called home.

Goblin gaze shifting, Kong sought the nearest crocodile, and moving purposefully, stepped out into the clearing and made for it without delay.

Feeling the ground shake around him, the croc turned to crawl off a nervous jerk.

Too late. A huge paw reached down, captured the thick tail, and lifted it off its splayed and straining feet.

Jaws yawning, the croc twisted and flopped about, held helpless. Lifting it high, Kong examined the thing, noted the nodular skin, the reptilian slit-pupil eyes, and other distinct features that brought to mind the prehistoric denizens of Skull Mountain Island.

The specimen was small compared to those formidable dinosaurs. But the look and smell of the squirming reptile smacked of a tasty meal. Kong took the flat skull of the thing between thumb and forefinger, and as the toothy jaw snapped helplessly, he pressed down inexorably, indenting the long skull, ultimately crushing it.

Tearing off the head with a quick wrench, Kong dropped the headless carcass, still warm and flopping, into his enormous cavern of a mouth. Great teeth commenced gnashing noisily. The croc was soon pulverized, going down Kong's throat in bloody gobs of meat.

Crocodiles, like lizards around the world, have a reputation for being sluggish and slow-witted. This may be true by human standards. But the crocodiles whose heavy-lidded orbs absorbed the tableau of one of their brethren being plucked off Mother Earth and treated so cruelly caused them all to plunge madly into the river, seeking the safety of its muddy bottom.

This sluggish river was discolored in a yellowish way, and the crocodiles got busy switching their great tails and digging up more mud with their splayed talons.

Soon, the river water was impenetrable to sight. Snorting hippos began backing off, seeking to put distance between them and the looming monster.

Undeterred, Kong strode forward. A slow-moving croc, unable to reach the water in time, turned and brought about his great sweeping tail to slam it into one of Kong's hairy ankles.

The blow was substantial, but Kong was greater still.

Reaching down, the beast-god caught the thing by the head, clipping the long jaws shut, then seized the croc by the tail with his other hand. Holding the reptile horizontally, the great ape pulled in opposite directions. The long neck strained, elongating away from the body while the tail stayed in place. The latter was much more firmly rooted.

With a careless twist, Kong removed the head, throwing it to the side, and began gobbling up the tail in quick, snarling bites. These first bites he chewed experimentally, spitting out pieces of bone. Then he went to work on the main body.

Not much meat to these flat creatures, the simian monster decided, but the taste appealed to him.

When he was done, Kong stepped into the river. A great splashing and threshing commenced as the bottoms of his feet came into contact with resting crocodiles, crushing skulls and ribcages, and arresting fleeing tails. The yellow-brown water roiled madly, sprouting billows of crimson.

Digging down, Kong began removing the struggling saurians where his probing fingers found them, lifting them high, smashing them together, tearing off their heads and eating what portions appealed to him.

After Kong had consumed every crocodile he could find, the river was red with an ugly mixture of blood and mud. The startled hippos had vacated the vicinity. His belly was still not yet full, but it was full enough to satisfy Kong for now.

Night was coming on. The beast-god looked around. Unlike his smaller African brethren—the mountain gorilla—Kong did not usually sleep on the hard ground or cushiony grass. The great lizards of Skull Mountain Island made such behavior too dangerous in practice. Kong invariably had slept in the colossal granite vault that was the braincase of Skull Mountain. But no such natural bed chamber presented itself in this jungle.

So it was that at last Kong cleared a space by uprooting bushes and trees, and lay himself down upon the grassy swale by the bloody river.

In time, a great moon rose and the hooded eyes of Kong grew heavy of lid.

Sleep soon came. Kong slumbered.

As he dozed, the natural night predators stirred. Deep within the jungle the unique odor of Kong's bristling fur, wet with rain and river water, combined with the metallic scent of blood on the wind, attracted the curious.

IN THIS portion of the jungle on either side of the winding river dwelled the tribe of To-yat, whose ape name meant Purple-eyed.

This To-yat was the king of the great apes—one of many such bands ranging the jungles and grasslands of central Africa. To-yat and his bulls were going about the business of their evening feeding, plucking beetles and grubs off the bark of trees, loafing through the forest with their shes, their clumsy little balus—as they called their young—following close behind.

A powerful musky smell came downwind. They lifted heavy heads, and their broad nostrils quivered in response.

"Bolgani!"To-yat grunted. In the language of the great apes, a Bolgani was a gorilla. The great apes were not Bolgani. They were Mangani, an entirely different species of lowland anthropoid, which was arboreal as much as terrestrial in nature.

One bull, named Go-yad because his ears were charcoal black, snapped, "Not Bolgani. Smells like Tongani." A white man would call a member of the Tongani tribe a baboon.

"Not Tongani!" screamed To-yat. "Bolgani!"

An argument seemed about to break out when To-yat abruptly knuckled forward, sniffing the air and following the unusual scent spoor. The further along he ambled, the less confident To-yat became that he was smelling the wet fur of a common mountain gorilla.

Unlike the great apes, the Bolgani tended to be solitary. The overwhelming odor of musk suggested a band of gorillas, many in number.

Thus, To-yat and his bulls advanced cautiously.

The stink of blood soon came to their nostrils, vaguely at first but more distinctly the closer they got to the winding river, whose liquid purling sounds they began to perceive.

Clutching their balus, the females stayed behind as the males pushed through the forest on all fours, dark eyes under their heavy brows attempting to pierce the increasing dusk.

Sounds soon reached those ears that were not suggestive of water. These noises were those of an animal deep in sleep.

To-yat halted, the others falling in line. Carefully, he listened. Having lived all his life in the jungle, To-yat knew the snuffling grunts of sleeping water buffalo, elephant, hippopotamus and rhinoceros. These strange sounds were none of those.

After listening for a time, To-yat resumed his knuckle walking, and threaded through the trees, carefully approaching the source of the sounds, which included a rumbling and gurgling. A gorilla digesting his meal, he decided.

The sound seemed louder than possible, akin to a rumble of near thunder. Still, To-yat was king of his tribe, so he pushed ahead fearlessly until at last he came to the verge of the forest, near where it transitioned to grassland. Hunkering down, he beheld a sight that caused his heavy jaw to sag downward in amazement.

The others came to a halt, sticking their shaggy heads forward, craning necks and straining eyes to make out what their king beheld.

"Bolgani," grunted Go-yad.

A hairy hand came out and smacked Go-yad to silence him.

"Not Bolgani," To-yat hissed.

"What is it?" demanded another bull.

The king killer ape had no idea. This great hairy sleeping giant was greater than any ape in his conception. Tall as a tree. Indeed, taller than many trees, yet it lay sprawled and insensate.

Observing its stupendous size, grey-shot fur and myriad scars accumulated over what must have been the equivalent to many Mangani lifetimes, To-yat dimly comprehended that the creature must be incalculably ancient, much the way mountains and trees are long-lived.

Among ape folk, there existed a name applied the bestower of life. Their brutish brains held no firm conception of Mulungu, as they called their creator. He was just an idea given a name. To-yat wondered if this monstrous mountain of a slumbering anthropoid was a personification of the mysterious Mulungu.

Another bull grunted, "Where did it come from?"

To-yat did not know that, either. He kept muttering, "Not Bolgani, not Bolgani," as if not believing the evidence of his own senses.

"What is it?" another bull pressed.

In the language of the great apes there existed words for most things, but not all things. For the world in which the great apes foraged for food was a simple one. It was a realm of nature. Having encountered man and his deadly rifles, they called the latter "thundersticks." For they have no word meaning "rifle" in their apish tongue.

Struggling to name the huge black anthropoid, and knowing that the thing was not a great ape, nor a mere gorilla, To-yat fell prey to the same delusion that mankind often does when contemplating the inexplicable.

"Go-pand-usen."

In their rude tongue, this construction of grunts and barks meant Black-thunder-god.

Hearing this unusual coinage, the other great apes fell to muttering and grunting in tentative agreement, and their agitation caused them to shake and scratch themselves nervously.

These noises reached the ears of the recumbent monster, and although his eyes did not fly open, he began snuffling and vocalizing, as if in response.

Hearing these rumbles, To-yat and his bulls commenced a slow and careful retreat, not taking their eyes off the creature they thought was a god of their anthropoid kind. They did not turn around and take headlong flight until they were certain Go-pand-usen would not awake and visit his holy wrath upon them for daring to disturb his slumber.

Chapter 42

D EEP IN the night, a dull booming started up. It swelled in tempo, shook the jungle with every rising beat.

These sounds carried, rising steadily, seeking savage crescendos, from which they fell sharply or trailed off. All of the jungle heard them. Animals prowling close to the center of the primitive orgy of noise slunk away, understanding its portent.

Lions altered their course. Giraffes fled. Even the mighty elephants sought higher ground.

No listening ear failed to capture the syncopation. It reached the shore party off the *Wanderer* as readily as it frightened the night-roosting birds from the trees.

When this drumming rolled across them, said party was winding along a jungle trail. Toting his Nitro Express elephant rifle, Jack Driscoll, in the lead, halted.

Lumpy gasped, "What is that heathen racket?"

"Probably native drums," offered the First Mate. "Well, let's hope they're the friendly sort."

Shoving ahead from the middle, Carl Denham pushed around and accosted Driscoll.

"Maybe those aren't native drums."

Driscoll eyed him speculatively. "Speak your piece, Mr. Denham."

The director's hushed tone became urgent. "I've heard African drums before. The last time I was out this way. But they weren't simple natives pounding on skin drums. Take my word for it."

"You'll have to do better than that. If not natives, what's making that thunder?"

Carl Denham began perspiring and pulled out a soiled hand-kerchief which he applied to his forehead and cheeks. "Maybe I'd better not say until I'm sure."

Driscoll snorted. "Damn right you'd better be sure before you speak."

"Don't look at me that way. I might be wrong. Maybe those drums are local boys, banging out a warning about Kong. But it might be something else, too. Don't ask me to explain it, either, because I can't. But I came across one such ceremony last time. It almost cost me my life."

"Voodoo stuff?"

"No, not men. Nothing human."

Lumpy grunted, "That's crazy talk!"

Turning on him, Denham said savagely, "Crazier than Kong? Crazier than this whole expedition?"

The First Mate had to think about that for a moment. "Call me skeptical, but let's make a wide berth of whatever it is."

To Driscoll's surprise, the showman said, "For once, I'm with you."

"All right," the Mate told his party, "we'll change direction. They won't hear us over their own drums—whoever they are."

"Whatever they are," muttered Denham darkly.

The party melted into the jungle toward the east, skirting the sound of drums, which were changing in pitch and tempo in a feverish way that made the sailors of the rusty tramp ship doubt that human hands were producing them.

"Not like you to pass up some swell footage," Driscoll remarked to Carl Denham as they eased along under the thick jungle canopy.

"Long story. Tell you about it later," returned Denham, a rare nervousness threading his voice.

Driscoll nodded, keeping his attention fixed on the way ahead. The jungle was surprisingly free of night-prowling creatures.

To their nostrils came a wet, musty smell. Rank and powerful. Penjaga caught it first.

"Kong!" she hissed.

The party stopped, sniffing the air like animals. One by one, the familiar odor of the mighty anthropoid distinguished itself from the surrounding smells of the jungle.

The Storyteller pointed with a withered finger, saying, "Kong lies in that direction. He sleeps."

Driscoll asked, "How can you tell?"

"I know what I know," she said cryptically. "Come."

The tightly-packed group resumed their trek, the mad pounding punishing their eardrums, Lumpy grumbling, "If he's sleeping through that infernal noise, the big monkey must be awful tired."

LITTLE Nkima and his companion raced through the night, intent upon their mission.

The deeper inland they traveled, the closer they would come to the area where Tarzan of the Apes dwelled.

Every so often, Nkima paused to rest and, in resting, lifted his pink hands to his tiny mouth, cupped them there, and commenced calling out.

"Kreegah! Kreegah! Tarzan come! Kreegah!"

In the language of the ape folk—which was understood by monkeys, baboons, orangutans, gorillas and the great apes alike—Kreegah was a word conveying the all-important idea of "danger."

All night long Nkima traveled, pausing and calling out to the great Lord of the Jungle.

"Kreegah!"

But Tarzan of the Apes did not reply. And so, the nimble-pawed monkey pushed farther inland, the terrified Ignatz scampering closely behind.

Chapter 43

THE SHORE party came upon Kong sleeping in the clearing by the river where vultures were feasting upon what little remained of the crocodiles that had formerly besported by its plentiful waters. Decapitated heads predominated, their long, toothy jaws clamped tight in death, slit eyes strangely sleepy.

As they drew near, the smell became overpowering. They advanced with extreme caution, until Driscoll warned, "Everyone stay back. I'll scout ahead."

While the First Mate went about that, Carl Denham methodically assembled his camera on his folding tripod. A canister of film was already in the mechanism. His face was twisted in some emotion that combined raw excitement with eager anticipation.

Driscoll crawled the last of the way to keep his head low to the ground and out of sight. He scarcely inhaled.

Kong was a dark shape silhouetted against a full moon whose bristling chest rose and fell regularly, and the sound of his breathing was like that of the *Wanderer's* engines—powerful and disquieting.

Recoiling at the familiar nightmare sight, Driscoll retreated as carefully as practical. This time, he breathed with a ragged rhythm.

When the First Mate rejoined the others, he was walking upright.

"It's Kong, all right. He's fast asleep. Mr. Denham, do what you have to, but don't wake him. Whatever you do, do not wake the brute up."

"Got you," grinned the gleeful director.

Carl Denham advanced carefully, and when his eager brown eyes fell upon Kong, he slowed down and looked around for a spot where his tripod would stand properly. When he found it, the showman carefully set the wooden legs into the soft loam, and energetically cranked away.

He panned from the creature's bullet head to his hairy feet and back again. His face grew dissatisfied.

"Static shot," he muttered. "Good, but not good enough...."

Pausing, the crafty director looked about him, and his eyes fell upon a heavy stone nearby. Creeping over to it, Denham picked it up, tossed it skyward and listened to the smacking sound it made landing in his meaty palm.

"This oughta do the trick," he told himself.

Returning to his camera, Carl Denham brought back his arm and prepared to pitch the substantial stone in the direction of the slumbering anthropoid.

The rock failed to leave his hand. For something new had entered the scene.

On the other side of Kong, a sparse clutch of giraffes came striding along the river bank, driven by the unnerving sounds of the drumming coming from the east.

Seeing their narrow heads set upon tall spotted necks, Denham pocketed the stone, and turned his camera lens in their direction, cranking away once more.

The giraffes were at first oblivious to the hairy monster, for, despite it being larger than any predator they had known, it was not moving.

Their hooves made soft sounds in the earth, and the heads were swiveling back and forth, for the bitterness of blood was in the air. So, too, was the musky odor of Kong. Its unfamiliarity evidently spooked the long-legged creatures, for their eyes grew wide and staring. But they perceived nothing unusual.

As the giraffes drew near, Denham stopped shooting, reached into his pocket, and held himself ready to violently release the rock.

Never dreaming that they were stepping toward unimaginable danger, the grouping of giraffes walked in their stilt-like way, and while their sympathetic, heavy-lashed eyes were elsewhere, Carl Denham pitched his rock.

The stone bounced off Kong's forehead. At once, the great eyes snapped open like plates the hue of honey.

Faster than it seemed imaginable, Kong sat up, looked about, and spied the giraffes. The creatures saw him. The herd froze in their tracks, ears like folded leaves twitching in sudden distress.

At this point, Kong had merely sat up. His phenomenal stature was not yet fully apparent.

With a thunderous roar, the beast-god climbed to his feet and stormed in the direction from which he mistakenly believed the tormenting stone had come.

The sheer size of the apelike giant momentarily stupefied the herd. They still failed to give ground. Not out of bravery, but the paralysis of amazement had seized them, holding the animals fast in a stunned fixity.

For his part, the black behemoth took their fearless stance for a challenge. These were the first creatures he had encountered in this unfamiliar place whose height rivaled his own—although the giraffes' oddly-formed heads barely came to his waist.

Roaring, Kong fell upon the creatures, seizing two by the neck. Holding one in each hand, he began squeezing and wrenching their heads about.

Bones cracked, hooves left the ground, or kicked madly in their death throes. High-pitched sounds of mortal distress were squeezed from their throats, only to be throttled by punishing steel-strong fingers.

Flinging away the first two, Kong caught another in both burly arms, lifted it up, then began squeezing the long-necked animal in his powerful paws.

Kicking wildly, the creature emitted horrible screams as the brute caused its thin bones to break and its ribs to splinter noisily.

That giraffe, Kong slung about contemptuously. It landed in a pathetic heap of broken limbs from which raw bone shards protruded. Then he went charging after a fleeing fellow. The grumbling monster quickly caught up with the frightened creature, grabbed a kicking rear leg, and swung it about, dashing it bodily against a tree.

Two giraffes remained. One, seeing the fate of the others, made a high nasal noise of rage and frustration, and kicked furiously at Kong, using his fore hooves to smash against the great beast's thighs.

With a backward swipe of one hand, Kong struck the thing on the side of the neck, all but snapping the spotted column in two.

One giraffe managed to escape, making unearthly sounds. Kong looked about, and considered what he had wrought.

Bending, the hulking colossus picked up a giraffe carcass in both arms, brought one haunch up to his mouth, and excavated an experimental bite. He decided that the meat was acceptable, and continued his meal.

At his back, concealed by jungle foliage, entirely unsuspected, Carl Denham ran through the last of his film, and then quickly packed up his tripod and equipment and faded back into the jungle, whose greenery closed nervously behind him.

Driscoll met him, after first ordering the others to retreat for their own safety.

"What happened?" the Mate yelled.

"Happened?" Denham said exultantly. "It was like Almighty Zeus started throwing thunderbolts around. Kong woke up and tore into a herd of giraffes. I got it all on film. It's stupendous stuff! All we need is a few minutes more."

Glowering, Driscoll bellowed, "Are you crazy? You're damn lucky you didn't get eaten whole. Now come away. Kong is on his feet and this is no place for mere mortals."

Denham scoffed, "He's busy feeding. If I tread carefully, I can sneak around to catch him from another angle."

"Not a chance! Follow me. We're done here."

Carl Denham followed only because the First Mate snatched his camera out of his hands and disappeared into the jungle with it.

Grabbing up his tripod, the showman reluctantly blundered after him, cursing under his breath, yet in his filmmaker's heart, overjoyed.

Chapter 44

THE JUNGLE is a living thing. A web of life which stretches in all directions, not ending even at the water's edge, but encompassing land, sea and sky in its far-flung strands, both seen and unseen.

Nothing that happens in one quarter of this jungle does not reverberate to all other compass points. All skeins are connected, like trees lashed together by liana creepers.

The colossal marauder that was King Kong disturbed this web as had nothing since the days of the dinosaurs, and sent every connecting strand quivering.

So it was inevitable that knowledge of a strange invader abroad in the jungle should reach the ears of Tarzan of the Apes.

From a great distance, the jungle telegraph system of native tom-toms carried deep into the interior, summoning Tarzan, and warning all who could understand them that the coastal forest was in the throes of a great disturbance.

The word beaten out on stretched antelope skins was: Invader… invader… invader….

Hearing this drumming call, the Lord of the Jungle rushed to investigate.

Movements of wild animals away from their natural preserves were the first signs the ape-man perceived. Unusually thick formations of vultures circling the air and dropping down to feed was another. Their behavior spoke of death on an order of magnitude not common among the creatures of the rain forest.

Tarzan moved rapidly along the jungle path in the direction of the circling vultures. He was a bronze-skinned giant of a man possessing sinewy, pantherish muscles that rippled in the moonlight as he paced along. Naked but for a leopard-skin loincloth whose attached tail whipped in his wake, he looked every inch a figure of legend come to life. His hair was a short-cut mane of black, and his eyes—at once feral yet as intelligent as any civilized man's—gleamed a clear, untroubled grey.

At his side slapped his sole weapon, and the only evidence that he was in some way civilized—a large hunting knife snug in a leather scabbard. It was no jungle artifact, and showed modern workmanship in its well-worn handle of horn. The hidden blade of Sheffield steel—fully twelve inches long—was formidable. If it could speak, the weapon would tell electrifying tales of the copious amounts of blood that it had drunk—of both man and beast.

Behind the tireless Tarzan trotted a magnificent golden lion, whose full mane was as black as ebony. This regal feline was not pursuing the ape-man, but following at his heels in the manner of a faithful dog.

Great was the distance Tarzan needed to travel, so from time to time he launched himself into the close-packed trees, his muscular bronze form flashing from branch to branch, as he endeavored to make the quickest time practicable.

On the ground, the golden lion kept pace, reflecting a shared goal, its fearsome yellow-green eyes sharp upon the trail ahead.

Well along, a tiny screech reached Tarzan's ears.

"Kreegah, Tarzan! Kreegah!"

The ape-man recognized the quavering voice of his friend, little Nkima the monkey.

In the common language they shared, Tarzan called back, "Where are you, Nkima? Show yourself!"

"Here!" Nkima called back. "Hurry, Tarzan! Kreegah!"

The bronzed giant flashed to the south, and below him, the faithful golden lion altered course in concert.

Soon, Tarzan had dropped into the branches of a tree while
Nkima climbed higher to meet him, waving a pink-palmed
paw frantically.

"Great danger, Tarzan!" Nkima cried piteously.

Tarzan admonished, "Calm down, Nkima. Tell me of this
danger. But first, who is your little friend?"

The ape-man was pointing toward the other monkey, who
was afraid to move from his sheltering branch, for he had spied
the great golden lion padding in impatient circles below.

"He is a lost monkey, Tarzan," returned Nkima. "He does not
have a name. I found him clinging to the terrible Bolgani."

"Which Bolgani?"

"He is a gorilla never before seen. I call him Zu-jar-bolgani."

"Why do you call him Big-strange-gorilla?" asked Tarzan.

"Because he is very, very big and he is truly strange to behold.
He does not walk like a gorilla on all fours, but upright like a
man. Upright like Tarzan. Yet he wears the fierce face of a
Bolgani."

"Zu-jar-bolgani is not a great ape?"

Nkima shook his furry head vigorously, saying, "He is too tall
to be a great ape, too large to be an ordinary Bolgani. He is so
tall that he is destroying the forest by the water."

Tarzan knew that Nkima was prone to exaggeration, and was
also easily alarmed. So the ape-man took the monkey's chattering with a liberal dose of sodium chloride.

"How tall is this Bolgani?" he asked.

"As tall as a monkey bread tree," insisted Nkima.

"No Bolgani stands as high as a tree—unless it is a very young
sapling," reproved the ape-man. "You exaggerate, Nkima. Now
tell me truthfully: Is he taller than Tarzan?"

Nkima lifted one paw over his head as high as it could go
and stretched the other under the branch upon which he perched,
and squeaked, "This terrible Bolgani is taller than many Tarzans."

Tarzan frowned at his monkey friend, whom he had known

for years. "Zu-jar-bolgani must be very tall to frighten you so, Nkima," Tarzan returned patiently. "Nevertheless, no creature, much less a gorilla, could be as tall as you claim. It is impossible."

"But this is an impossible gorilla," chattered Nkima. "When Zu-jar-bolgani is standing up, his head swims as high as the moon, blocking Goro from sight."

Tarzan all but laughed, saying, "Perhaps you should call him Goro-bolgani—Moon-gorilla."

"This Bolgani came from the sea," added the monkey. "Perhaps he is a creature of the ocean."

"What does your monkey friend say about him?"

"He does not know much. He is from another land, too, Nkima thinks."

Tarzan dropped down to the lower branch and eyed the little monkey carefully.

"What is your name, little Manu?" he asked gently.

The monkey chattered excitedly, and amid his toothy utterances, Tarzan of the Apes detected confusion, but nothing understandable.

"He is very frightened now," explained Nkima. "Terror has driven all speech from him, and his tongue no longer works properly. He is not brave like Nkima."

"I believe that this monkey is tame," Tarzan told Nkima. "He does not appear to belong in the wild. And he smells of the Tarmangani," added Tarzan, using the ape-folk phrase for white men.

Nkima nodded eagerly. "You are probably right, Tarzan. He came with the great Bolgani. The Bolgani arrived on a very large boat. I beheld it, truly. Zu-jar-bolgani must have escaped the white men who brought it."

"Where is this monster gorilla?"

"In the Elephant's Graveyard by the great salt waters, desecrating the bones of those Tantors who have gone before."

At these words, a ragged scar coursing along the ape-man's sun-bronzed forehead pulsed lividly scarlet, as it did whenever the ire of Tarzan was roused.

Seeing this, Nkima added, "By now, he must have sucked all of the sweet marrow from the freshest bones. Perhaps Zu-jar-bolgani will decide to eat all the Tantors next. What will we do then? Who will stop him, if not Lord Tarzan?"

"No Bolgani will be permitted to disturb the bones of the dead unpunished," promised Tarzan.

"He may be marching this way, taking strides that cross swollen rivers," insisted Nkima. "For Zu-jar-bolgani is truly as tall as nine Tarzans."

Taking the tame monkey onto his brown shoulder, Tarzan said, "We will investigate your story, Nkima. But know that Tarzan does not entirely believe it."

"Nkima does not entirely believe his own story, either," said the faithful monkey, settling on his familiar bronze-muscled perch. "But know that it is true."

Tarzan motioned for Ignatz to follow, and the tame ship monkey was too frighted of his surroundings to do otherwise. Also, there was something instinctively reassuring about the sinewy presence of the Lord of the Jungle.

The three arboreal companions worked through the upper terraces of the jungle lanes, while below them the sharp-eyed golden lion paced ahead with single-minded purpose.

Chapter 45

KONG WAS on the move again.

The brooding beast-god was pushing his way through the strange-to-his-eyes jungle, seeking a peaceful place to sleep. Unlike terrestrial gorillas, Kong was not comfortable ranging the lowlands without respite. Back on his home island, the ancient hollow chamber that formed Skull Mountain served as his retreat and resting place. Through its vacant eye sockets, he could observe the terrain below him, like the lord that he was. It had been his fortress since the day when Kong was much younger and he ascended its stony cliffs to battle a carnivorous prehistoric lizard known as Gaw, who lived in a cavern at the mountain's base.

Here, no such prominence showed itself. But Kong was a creature of instincts, no matter how rudimentary. He was accustomed to sleeping high above the jungle canopy, safe and secure in his primitive throne room, whose forbidding death's-head countenance and difficult-to-climb crags discouraged all rival predators.

Tramping through the jungle, knocking aside trees that clumped too close together to permit passage, the towering creature disturbed all that he passed. Hyenas howled and slunk away. Roosting bats launched themselves into the sky, as did nesting birds. Even the droning insects made way before him.

The earth shook with his impressive tread. Tree branches

trembled in anticipation of his approach. Vegetation lying in his wake was mercilessly crushed and mangled.

At length, Kong burst out of the rain forest and into open grassland. The savanna stretched for countless miles inland. This unexpected sight produced in the shambling behemoth a low grunt of surprise.

For a moment, he surveyed the moonlit field of waving grass. Patches of veldt were of course known to him. They dotted the lowlands of Skull Mountain Island. But nothing so vast and open a prospect had ever presented itself to Kong on his natal island.

Its sheer emptiness and flatness was disconcerting. Apish nose wrinkling up, Kong bared powerful fangs, growling as if to threaten the intimidatingly empty expanse facing him.

The immense anthropoid understood that if he stepped out into this openness, any lurking predators would spy him easily. But as he absorbed the details of the wind-whipped grassland, it dawned upon his simian brain that no predator powerful enough to attack him could possibly lurk hidden in such barrenness.

That realization sinking in, Kong stepped out onto the grass of the veldt, took several tentative steps, and kept on going.

It was strange to tramp this verdant openness where no shelter existed, and all was illumined by unfiltered moonlight.

Hairy arms swinging, Kong strode forth, and as he did so, his stride and confidence increased. Nothing, no beast nor sentinel tree, reared up to rival his domineering height.

And as he progressed, Kong gave forth a mighty roar that set nearby leaves to quaking.

Back in the shadowy jungle falling behind his hairy, hunched back, cowering beasts shrank or screamed out their own vocal defiance, depending on their temperaments. Yet nothing, not even the droning insects on the wing, dared to follow the bristling ogre that had laid waste to the primeval jungle that, until this night, had seemed eternal and unchanging.

His massive feet becoming accustomed to the carpet of cool grassy blades comprising the moonlit savanna, Kong's ever-searching orbs sought the horizon before and around him.

Far to the west, something gleamed. Amber eyes fixed upon it.

It was tall, this silvery prominence. In his bestial brain, Kong understood the great distance only dimly. For his lost realm on Skull Mountain Island was not vast. He could cross the island in less than a day. Concepts beyond a few miles were foreign to his experience.

But that gleam that floated just over the horizon stirred in his savage breast a sense of familiarity. Kong understood that it represented a mountain peak of some kind. Perhaps it was the way it shone, so reminiscent of Skull Mountain bathed in moonlight, but once his attention became fixed on that far beacon of light, Kong resolved to seek it out, to climb it, to make it his own.

With renewed purpose, the imposing anthropoid shifted his direction and strode tirelessly toward Mount Kilimanjaro, not even remotely comprehending how many miles or days march it would take to reach its base.

Kong did not care. He would not have cared even if he understood. For in this strange, unfamiliar jungle he had at last found a goal that called to him, an object of desire that drew him. And nothing would stand in his way until he reached that majestic mountain, conquered it, and made it the new seat of his power.

If any animal guarded its alluring summit, Kong would conquer it, just as he had broken the devil-lizard, Gaw, so long ago....

Chapter 46

THE TREK back to the *Wanderer* was an arduous one.

The jungle stood in a state of repressed uproar. Lions paced like agitated kittens. Hyenas shifted about and slunk through the underbrush, while wide-eyed monkeys flung themselves into high tree limbs.

Now the jungle at night is normally a quiet place. Between the animals who sleep and those who prowl in search of prey upon stealthy feet, little sound disturbs the shadow-clogged forest lanes, except, of course, on those not-rare occasions when a pouncing predator falls upon his hapless prey.

Kong had changed all that. The gigantic anthropoid had blundered about, laying waste to ancient trees, crushing creatures both powerful and humble beneath the leathery pads of his monster feet.

The jungle could not sleep. Nothing slept. From the forest floor to the highest treetops, feral eyes searched the surroundings, and animal brains forgot all thoughts of food, or even of the natural predators that stalked at this moonlit hour.

All eyes scanned for Kong; every ear strained to hear his indomitable approach. The ground—which formerly had quaked in sympathy with his awesome tread—finally settled down.

Dawn was coming. It was yet an hour off. When the solar orb finally shouldered above the leafy horizon, illuminating the blue coastal waters and making green again the forest foliage, the mood of the jungle would shift anew.

But that was an hour yet to come. The jungle remained tense, anticipatory—unsettled.

Through this weirdly palpable atmosphere trudged Jack Driscoll and his fatigued shore party.

"I've tramped a lot of wilderness paths," Carl Denham was saying, "but I've never known a jungle to be like this."

"Like what?" called back Jack Driscoll.

Denham studied the shadows suspiciously. "Like something took hold of everything by the throat at the same time and squeezed the Moxie out of them."

Above their heads, simian eyes peered down, but did not react to the passage of mere men. Black shapes trimmed in white fur hunkered in silent alarm.

"See those Colobus monkeys up above us?" directed Denham. "Those troublemakers should be fast asleep. But they're not. They're all keyed up. Kong did that. Kong's got them all by the throat, I tell you."

"Do you blame them?" asked Driscoll.

"Not much, I don't," admitted Denham, lugging his tripod over one shoulder and watching where he stepped. "There are snakes that come out at night, venomous ones," he mumbled. "I haven't seen a one. Kong's got them coiled up in their holes. Can you beat that?"

Driscoll barked, "Save your breath for explaining the situation to the Skipper. If we're lucky, we'll make shore before daybreak. Much as I don't like blundering through these woods at night, I don't want to be caught flatfooted in broad daylight."

Denham nodded. "Once this spell Kong poured over on them breaks, these animals will turn on anything that looks or smells vulnerable."

"Not to mention tasty," Driscoll growled. "Now kindly clam up and walk soft."

Another two dozen minutes of plodding along, circling around fallen and shattered trees, and skirting the distinctive smell of crouching lions and other denizens of eastern Africa, made them feel as if they were going to make it.

Mouth clamped tight, Driscoll looked to Penjaga plodding along, more tireless than the youngest of his men, noticed that tied to her waist was the hard round knot he had fashioned for Ann—the monkey's fist. It brought a grunt of surprise to his firm lips.

"But for that lump of cordage," he muttered, "we might've been done and finished with Kong by now."

Hearing this, Penjaga turned and bestowed upon the First Mate her cool regard. "What is this you say?"

"Nothing. Skip it." His voice lifted. "Keep moving—all of you."

The men looked at Jack Driscoll dubiously, wondering if the strain was getting to him.

Then the drumming began.

At first, they didn't hear it so much as they felt it. Their nerves were tense, and every sense was heightened. Yet, the first sensation created by the pounding was one of anxiety, an itch that crawled along their skin, a throbbing in the skull that had not yet impinged upon their ears.

The drums seemed to be distant, but as they made their way eastward, its reverberations took hold of them. There was something wild and uncanny about the frenzied pounding. The beating was barbaric, disjointed, unpleasant. It raised the hackles of the most susceptible among them.

Lagging in the rear, several paces behind the others, Carl Denham stopped suddenly, swiveled his head about. His brown eyes became round with wonder.

"Listen!" he hissed. "Do you fellows hear that?"

"Keep moving," Driscoll ordered.

Then the wild beat hit the First Mate. "What's that?" he asked suddenly.

A sailor trudging by his side ventured, "Native tom-toms, starting up again."

The shore party slowed down to a cautious crawl. Eyes growing anxious, they began looking around, ears hunting, trying to get a fix on the direction from which the drumming came.

Driscoll noticed that Carl Denham had stopped in his tracks, and was listening intensely.

Sufficient moonlight filtered down from the interstices of the forest canopy for all members of the party to keep track of one another. Driscoll gave out a little whistle, which caught the showman's attention, and gestured for him to follow.

Shaking off his reverie, Denham caught up with the Mate and said urgently, "I know those drums, Jack."

Driscoll eyed him doubtfully as he responded, "Spit it out. Just don't expect me to believe it."

"Those aren't witchdoctor drums. I'm sure of it this time. Damned sure. These are different drums. Different drummers. I'll swear on my grandmother's grave."

"Well, they sound like native drums to me."

"Drums, sure," agreed the director. "But the local tribesmen aren't making that racket. Listen, Mate, I've heard that exact wild cadence once before."

Driscoll stopped, turned, placed his hands on his rangy hips, and bestowed upon the dynamic director his most dubious expression. The rakish angle at which the First Mate's cap sat upon his head added to the impression of extreme skepticism.

"Go on," he said in a surly tone. "I know I won't like it, so let's just get it over with."

Carl Denham looked as if he didn't know whether to speak or hold his tongue. His tongue won.

"Remember I told you about the last time I was in this neck of the African woods?"

"Yeah," returned Driscoll, his voice dripping with sarcasm. "You met Tarzan of the Apes."

"That I did. Honest. That maddening jungle jazz that you're hearing? That was the same racket the apes of Tarzan were making when I stumbled upon their little confabulation. It couldn't have been more than five or ten miles from this very spot. Men aren't making that racket, I tell you. It's apes. Wild apes!"

"You don't say," said Jack Driscoll. His voice was flat.

"Listen, Mate, you and I have had our differences. But I wouldn't lie to you. Not about this."

Driscoll reached over, took the battered campaign hat off Carl Denham's sweat-plastered hair, crumpled it into a ball and stuffed it into one of the showman's commodious jacket pockets.

"Not about this, maybe," growled Driscoll, "but about plenty of other things. So why not this, too? What have you got up your sleeve this time? Do you want to go film these wild apes of yours, catch another few minutes with King Tarzan? Let's hear it. I could use a laugh. Maybe two."

Denham set down his tripod, fished out his ruined wad of a hat, and began reassembling it into some semblance of normal shape.

As he was doing this, the director considered his words carefully. "All right, Jack, maybe I deserve some of this tongue lashing. But I don't have a scheme in my back pocket. I don't even have one in the back of my noggin. I just want to get back on that ship, in one piece, just like you. No different. But those are wild apes carrying on, and we would do well to give them a wide berth. Get me?"

"I get you," said Driscoll. "Now step lively. Stop dragging your anchor. First light isn't far off."

They resumed their trek, while all about them the nervous jungle and its wary inhabitants seemed to shrink as the sound of drumming escalated in its maddened abandon.

As they walked, Penjaga glanced toward the First Mate and remarked, "Human hands are not making those sounds."

"Not you, too," groaned Driscoll.

"Believe me, or do not believe me," the Storyteller breathed. "But human hands are not behind the drumming that we hear."

"I don't believe a word of what Carl Denham says, and your opinion isn't changing my mind any."

High in the trees on either side of them, baboons and smaller monkeys began to sway in the tree branches, swaying in sympathy with the incessant beating. From their leathery lips came guttural sounds. Screeches, weird howling, gibbering syllables that sounded almost like words, but could not be understandable language.

"Sounds like all these damn apes are talking to one another," a sailor muttered uneasily.

"Apes don't talk," Driscoll snapped. "Get that through your thick skull. Stow your imaginations and put your feet to work. We'll reach the dories in less than an hour."

Chapter 47

TARZAN OF THE APES came at last to the grove which encompassed Elephant's Graveyard, and saw that it lay in shambles in the moonlight.

Something tremendous had rooted around in the ancient bone pile. That much was certain. The disorder amid what had been a revered spot was disturbing to behold.

No elephant would have done such a thing—not even a rogue. The Elephant's Graveyard was sacred to all pachyderms and, for that matter most denizens of the jungle, except perhaps Histah the snake, who was of a colder order of intelligence.

Even Dango the hyena and his brother, Ungo the jackal, declined to scavenge here.

It was sacred to Tarzan of the Apes as well. Among the creatures that inhabited the African jungle, the ape-man held Tantor—as he called all elephants—in high esteem. Only the family of great apes from which he sprang stood higher in Tarzan's estimation.

Padding forward carefully, Nkima perched on one muscular shoulder and Ignatz clinging to the other, Tarzan came to the rim of the graveyard. He studied it with his clear grey eyes turning to moon-brightened steel.

Nkima squeaked, "See, Tarzan? It is as I have said. Zu-jar-bolgani did this."

"Something terrible did," agreed the ape-man.

The magnificent golden lion stepped carefully onto the desecrated burial ground, lowered his broad nose and sniffed curiously. He did not inhale scent for long. Turning to Tarzan, his lambent yellow-green eyes regarded his master with a curious light.

"Jad-bal-ja knows!" Nkima screeched excitedly. "See? The scent spoor is not known to him."

Tarzan had also been sniffing the night air, and the odor that came into his acute nostrils was strange and pungent. It caused his sun-bronzed face to stiffen.

"Like Bolgani, but not like Bolgani," he stated simply. "More pungent than Bolgani—more pungent than a tribe of Bolgani."

"It is one Bolgani," insisted Nkima. "The great moon-high gorilla, Zu-jar-bolgani. Perhaps he fell down from the moon." Nkima pointed upward where the lunar lamp hung like a cool crystal globe above earth's oppressively humid atmosphere.

Tarzan picked his way through the litter of bones, lifted broken shards, and discerned that they had been snapped in two by something immensely powerful. The sweet marrow had been extracted and the bones were still wet from a tongue that rivaled that of a lion. But no lion would desecrate the Elephant's Graveyard. Of that, Tarzan of the Apes was certain.

Sniffing the residue on these broken bone-shards, Tarzan acquired a puzzled look on his noble countenance. Although he had been raised by apes since he was a foundling infant, the ape-man originated from noble British stock. It showed it the natural cast of his features despite the disfiguring scar that bisected his brow.

Dropping the broken shards in disgust, Tarzan walked about, the ancient battle scar on his forehead slowly suffusing red as his anger mounted.

There were unmistakable signs that something large and lumbering had stepped on many of these bones, but no distinct footprints. Tarzan moved about the Elephant's Graveyard until he picked up the tracks that the thing left after it had finished its wanton destruction.

When he came upon the first clear footprint, the ape-man stopped in his own barefoot tracks, and the hairs at the back of his neck commenced rising.

Tarzan of the Apes had ranged far and wide upon the Dark Continent, and had encountered many strange tribes and stranger beasts. Even stubborn survivals of the prehistoric age. None had set his hackles rising like this.

For the footprint of the desecrator of the Elephant's Graveyard was almost as long as Tarzan was tall, and the ape-man stood over six feet tall.

His eyes narrowing, Tarzan walked around the circumference of the footprint. He quickly realized that it was similar to that of a gorilla. Yet there were marked differences, also. The toes were bizarre in their arrangement and configuration, being slightly more manlike than apelike, while still retaining the thumblike big toe sticking out to one side of the broad heel, creating the illusion of a monstrously deformed handprint. This divergence from nature caused the jungle lord's scalp to tingle as few things did. In the long-ago days of his youth, the hereditary enemies of his ape tribe were the lowland gorillas. His first kill had been a Bolgani bull.[*]

Further ahead lay another track. This one had sunk deep into the soft jungle loam, leaving a distinct impression.

Gaze sharpening, Tarzan walked along, following this spoor.

On one shoulder, Nkima trembled. One to boast often when in the company of his lord and protector, the sight of the great footprints did not wring from Nkima's tiny mouth ejaculations of I-told-you-so. Instead, the deep footprints reminded him of the terrible interloper, still astride in the jungle.

Following the fearsome line of handlike footprints, trailed by the golden lion, Tarzan said aloud, "He walks on his hind feet, like a man."

"Like Tarzan," said Nkima.

---

[*] *Tarzan of the Apes.*

"I see no knuckle imprints; therefore this is not a Bolgani. Nor is it a great ape. It is something else. Something other."

Nkima nodded excitedly. "Do you believe Nkima, Tarzan?"

Steely eyes thinning, Tarzan said, "Tarzan believes Nkima now. But Tarzan scarcely accepts the evidence of his eyes."

"Will Tarzan follow the terrible Bolgani?"

"Tarzan must. For this is an abomination loose in the jungles that Tarzan guards. We will follow."

Turning, he murmured half indistinguishable words to the golden lion, which responded by falling in behind him.

The ape-man followed the titanic footprints a fair distance and, when the tang of spilt blood reached his nostrils, he picked up his pace. As did the great golden lion, whom the ape-man had named Jad-bal-ja.

The first giraffe Tarzan happened upon had its neck snapped so severely that the head lay at right angles to the body and three of the four legs were broken, thin femurs protruding from torn flesh.

"Look! Many Omtags lie dead," insisted Nkima. "Zu-jar-bolgani he did this, Tarzan!"

Tarzan said nothing. He walked about the giraffe's cooling corpse and took in the details of its destruction. A charging rhinoceros might have treated a giraffe so cruelly. A hippopotamus, also. But not even a bull elephant could have snapped a giraffe's long neck in such a forceful manner.

Moving along, the ape-man found several more giraffes—all broken and dead, smashed by the creature that left footprints that suggested he was as tall as a coconut palm.

"Zu-jar-bolgani is terrible in his power, is he not, Tarzan?" asked Nkima in a hushed tone.

Tarzan nodded. "Zu-jar-bolgani is terrible indeed. But he must be punished for his misdeeds. For this is not his jungle. He kills, but he does not eat his kills. This is against nature."

Nkima tugged at the jungle lord's ear. "Will Tarzan kill Zu-jar-bolgani?"

"Tarzan will slay this abomination," the ape-man assured the little monkey.

"How will Tarzan slay such a monster, for he is as tall as nine Tarzans? Beside him, Tarzan of the Apes stands as tall as little Nkima stands beside Tarzan."

"Tarzan has slain monsters before. Monsters greater in size and ferocity than Tarzan. But size and physical prowess alone do not make a mighty hunter."

"No?" questioned Nkima.

"No," retorted Tarzan, moving forward purposefully.

"What makes a mighty hunter, if not size and prowess?" wondered Nkima.

"His brain," replied the ape-man, and fell silent.

"Oh," said Nkima, who also fell silent.

The unusual group ranged about the jungle, took stock of the shattered ruins that were ancient trees, lost the trail briefly amid boulders, then picked it up again.

Clinging to a bronzed, many-scarred shoulder, Ignatz held tight to the ape-man, drawing strength from his presence. Head turning about in nervous jerks, he peered above and behind him often, haunted eyes fearful of unexpected danger.

After a time, a drumming commenced.

Tarzan heard this first, for his ears were sharper than those of Numa the lion or Bara the deer.

"What is that?" asked little Nkima nervously.

"It is a Dum-Dum," said the ape-man.

"I thought so," said Nkima, who had not been sure before. "What tribe makes this Dum-Dum?

"These woods belong to the tribe of To-yat and his bulls. To-yat is perhaps celebrating a kill."

"What will you do, Tarzan?"

The jungle lord seemed to hesitate. The trail of the terrible gorilla that was not a gorilla was plain. But a Dum-Dum was usually a matter of great urgency. They were only held on certain momentous occasions, such as deaths of kings or victories over enemies, and always under the light of Goro the moon.

The apish tracks were leading out of the jungle in the direction of open grassland. There, such a monster would stand out. The lions which hunted the antelope and deer that cavorted in the tall grasses would have ample opportunity to spy this towering marauder and so avoid him. Few trees stood in the veldt, and thus there was little to destroy.

"We will go to the Dum-Dum," Tarzan stated at last.

Nkima let out a wild screech. "Tarzan is not afraid of Zu-jar-bolgani?"

"Tarzan is afraid of no Bolgani, no matter how great or powerful," the ape-man said firmly. "But Tarzan understands that, in order to challenge a monster such as Zu-jar-bolgani in combat, allies will be needed. To-yat and his bulls may suit that purpose."

Abruptly, Tarzan changed course and paced swiftly in the direction of the beating of drums.

Nkima and Ignatz clung to his shoulders and hair as Tarzan leapt into the lower branches of the trees, clambered up, and began negotiating the upper terraces, pushing hard in the direction of the Dum-Dum's primitive music.

Without hesitation, Jad-bal-ja the golden lion raced after them. As the jungle seemed to come alive under the reverberant cacophony, Tarzan of the Apes flashed from tree limb to tree limb, the leopard's tail of his loincloth whipping and snapping like a living thing.

The ape-man paused only a time or two to go into the highest branches of the tallest trees, and peer about, seeking any sign of the monstrous gorilla that stood taller than nature normally permitted.

Seeing no sign of the invader, Tarzan resumed his rushing race.

Chapter 48

THE TANG of the Indian Ocean came into their nostrils like salty, beckoning ethereal fingers. The shore party smelled open water before they saw it, and it lent energy to their flagging efforts.

Driscoll picked up his pace, and the others hurried to stay even with him. He had reclaimed the Nitro Express elephant gun, and carried the cumbersome rifle in both hands.

The ferocious cadence of the wild drumming continued unabated. It got into their ears, made their hearts pound in sympathy and their brains ache and throb from the incessant noise.

The jungle was thinning out as they approached the open-water anchorage of the *Wanderer*. But even high in the thinning trees, apes of all kinds cavorted and danced, caught up in the madness of the mindless drumming.

One long-armed baboon, catching sight of the knot of humans working their way to the beach, gave out a screech and leapt from his springy perch.

He landed near Penjaga, and their eyes locked. The wide eyes of the baboon were red with a kind of blood lust. Its bared fangs that were terrible to behold.

The old woman froze momentarily. Then, eyes narrowing, she slipped from her belt the ponderous monkey's fist marine knot.

With a mad screech, the baboon sprang for her. But so quick

that no watching eye perceived the motion, the Storyteller whipped up the heavy knot, twirled it once and let fly.

The hard round ball of cordage bounced off the baboon's forehead, momentarily startling him, and throwing him off his murderous trajectory. The ape stumbled, scrambling to his hairy hands and feet. He emitted a blood-freezing screech.

The gesture of defiance would probably not have saved the old woman had Jack Driscoll not brought up his elephant gun, laid the sights on the center of the anthropoid's hairy chest, and squeezed the trigger once.

Driscoll had no time to set the stock against his burly shoulder correctly, and the kick of the elephant gun literally knocked him off his feet. But the mercy bullet had sped true.

It caught the baboon in the chest, threw him further off his apish feet. Emitting wild screeches as of one who faced imminent and unavoidable death, the anthropoid sat down heavily, his upper body swaying, his eyelids growing heavy as he fought against what he thought was impending non-existence.

Instead, he simply slipped sideways, slammed his right ear against a flat stone and fell fast asleep.

Carl Denham bustled up, studied the tableau and barked, "Quick work, Driscoll. I wish I'd gotten that on film."

"You and your damn film," mumbled the First Mate, gathering himself together. Reclaiming the heavy rifle, he used it as a crutch to regain his feet, pointedly ignoring the showman's offered hand.

The baboon was no longer a menace—that much was certain. As the last fading echoes of the rifle discharge ceased making their ears ring, they recognized that something had changed.

"That infernal drumming," a sailor said darkly. "It's stopped. Stopped dead."

"They must've heard us," husked Denham. "Good thing we're almost there."

"Almost there isn't good enough," snapped Driscoll. "Let's get a move on. No telling what might happen next."

They resumed running. As they sped along, Jack Driscoll said to Penjaga, "You sure know how to handle yourself."

"As a child, I played with young Kong," she said simply.

Driscoll laughed raggedly. "I almost believe you."

"Gold Hair believed me."

Driscoll said nothing. The abrupt silence that followed was getting on his nerves more than the mad beating itself had.

They kept moving, watching for the approach of dawn. For a hopeful spell, they thought they were at the brink of the beach. But even as their anticipation grew stronger, they found themselves continually pushing through the thinning forest whose ancient trees fell farther and farther apart from one another.

"I thought we were almost there," a seaman groused.

"We *are* almost there," insisted Driscoll. "Keep pushing. We'll get there when we get there. Talking won't help. Now snap it up, you farmers."

When at last they broke through a clearing, the party saw painted by clear moonlight a pale crescent of sand, gleaming invitingly. Their hearts leapt, and a sparkle came into their anxious eyes.

Carl Denham spoke the words that made their hearts sink into the pits of their stomachs.

"I don't see the blamed dories. Where are they?"

Plunging forward, they trampled the pristine beach sand, and that alone caused the truth to sink in.

"No footprints here," snapped Driscoll. "This isn't where we beached. We're at the wrong cove."

The First Mate was scanning the placid waters for signs of the rusty tramp steamer, but there was no sign of the *Wanderer*.

"Probably behind that headland yonder," a seaman suggested. "We can't be far from it."

The headland was a rocky prominence, choked with tangled mangrove roots. To climb it would have been foolhardy, so they were forced to backtrack and pick their way south, seeking the *Wanderer's* anchorage. Their mood was dispirited, for they had believed they had been close to their objective.

Trudging along, they made the best of it, keeping quiet, seeking signs of the coming dawn, and watching the treetops warily for predators who might pounce and rend human flesh.

The mossy ground undulated alarmingly, and they realized they had not been this way before. This further disconcerted the shore party, and they wondered uneasily if they were really within reach of their destination.

Driscoll was reassuring them that they were not entirely lost when, topping a ridge that was riddled with the roots of half-dead and toppling trees, they came upon a natural amphitheater.

A steady ocean breeze had been blowing from the opposite direction, so it did not carry any warning smells to their noses until they stood on a ridge and looked down and saw dark eyes looking up at them with malevolent menace.

For hunkered down around what appeared to be an altar made of hard-packed earth, squatted over a dozen apes of a species they had never before seen. They were large and shaggy, more formidable in size and appearance than the common gorilla. The sight took their breath away, and made their mouths go dry.

Driscoll undertoned, "Everyone back away slowly. Make no sudden moves."

He was clutching his elephant gun hesitantly, for he knew that the number of apes far outweighed his meager supply of ammunition, even if he could open fire rapidly enough to tranquilize them all.

"What did I tell you?" breathed Carl Denham excitedly. "This is the place. The exact spot where I saw the apes of Tarzan pounding away. Do you believe me now?"

"I believe my eyes," murmured Driscoll, stepping backward.

The shore party broke out into a productive sweat as the sullen apes below began to clamber to their feet, their eyes studying the humans with unreadable intent.

"If we are careful, maybe they'll leave us alone," Driscoll was saying.

Then he noticed Carl Denham. The showman had planted his tripod on the ridge, and was dropping the camera into the mounting.

"Denham!" he hissed. "Are you crazy?"

"This is the chance of a lifetime, for the second time," the director said exultantly. "I'm not gonna lose out again. You boys run along. I'll catch up. Those monkeys down there don't look too active to me."

As if he had been clearly understood, the shaggy assemblage below broke out in a great howling and screeching that shattered their remaining nerves.

Crying, *"Kreegah! Bundolo!"* they charged up the ridge, whereupon Jack Driscoll and his sailors broke in all directions.

"Denham!" yelled the Mate. "Come on! Run for it! Run for your life!"

But Carl Denham held his ground. Hunched over his camera, he was grinding away, panning from left to right, intent upon capturing the savage attack as it was on the threshold of overwhelming him.

Seeing there was no reasoning with the man, Driscoll turned, raised the elephant gun and fired once.

The round struck Carl Denham high in the left shoulder, and he was thrown forward, upsetting his camera equipment, which went tumbling down the ravine with him.

"Why'd you do that, Mate?" a sailor yelled.

"Those apes are sure to tear him limb to limb," snapped Driscoll, resuming his flight. "Better that he's out of his misery than suffer through such a horrible ending."

Behind them, screaming apes surged up to overwhelm the stricken director. But no one dared look back to see his fate. The mad anthropoid howling fed their imaginations enough. No one needed to witness the horrors such sounds conjured up in their minds.

Chapter 49

TARZAN OF THE APES covered a great distance in an astonishingly short time.

The trees of the rain forest were his natural element, and he sprang from one branch to another, traversing open space in a manner that a circus aerialist would have envied, but never dared attempt to emulate. Circus performers left nothing to chance, stringing their strong guy wires between stable poles. The ape-man launched himself from groaning bough to springy receiving branch purely by instinct, never faltering, never missing his mark or losing his uncannily sure footing.

Time and again, Tarzan leapt from one sturdy tree to another, running the length of swaying branches, springing free when they showed signs of no longer bearing his weight, and landing unerringly in adjoining woody crowns.

Not far behind, but panting noticeably, the golden lion followed like a loyal dog.

Tarzan had raised this magnificent creature from a cub, having found its mother dead in a stretch of jungle far from here, in the heart of the Dark Continent.* Although still wild, Jad-bal-ja—whose name meant Golden lion—was obedient in every respect to the ape-man's commands.

Lions are not by nature creatures that run great distances, saving their energy for stalking and pouncing and sprinting antelope and deer to ground. Yet through some unknowable

---

* *Tarzan and the Golden Lion*

287

mastery, the Lord of the Jungle had taught the powerful feline obedience, and also instructed him on how to pace himself so that he could run and keep up with the bronzed Tarmangani who was his master.

The tom-tom beating of the Dum-Dum grew louder and louder as they moved through the predawn darkness.

Goro the moon was beginning to shine less brightly, but the sun had yet to creep above the watery horizon beyond the trees. The lunar light allowed Tarzan to navigate the upper terraces of the jungle until the saltiness of the ocean air alerted him that he was approaching shore.

The pounding earthen drums told him that the Dum-Dum ceremony lay just beyond the ridge yonder.

Tarzan sought the highest tree and, using this as a vantage point, peered out like a primitive sailor conning the horizon. He had already smelled Tarmangani, which was the word in his ape kin's language for white men. The rough smell of Mangani—the great apes—was also unmistakable.

Climbing down carefully, Tarzan found the lower branches and dropped lightly to the ground, his bare feet landing on the soft earth with hardly a sound.

Through these gyrations, little Nkima had clung to his sun-bronzed shoulder and black hair without losing his grip. But the way had been long and hard, and the little monkey was beginning to fatigue.

"Nkima is tired," he whispered.

"Hold on, little Manu," said the ape-man.

On his other shoulder, the little tame monkey also clung in mute fear. He had learned to trust Tarzan, but the events of the last few hours had been for him terrifying ones. Ignatz longed for the rolling comforts of the ramshackle ship that he called home.

As Tarzan crept along the jungle floor, he moved toward the rise that formed the ragged edge of the shallow crater. The origin of this depression was not known, for it was very ancient.

The jungle lord knew that the tribe of To-yat had been using this natural amphitheater for its Dum-Dums for some years now.

Tarzan had encountered To-yat's tribe before, and had ranged with them for a time. Peace existed between them. Peace among the great apes was an uncertain thing. To-yat had once possessed a deep enmity toward the ape-man, but had gotten over it long ago. Nevertheless, Tarzan approached cautiously.*

Topping the ridge, the bronzed giant's grey eyes searched the floor of the amphitheater, where he saw the wild dancing and cavorting of a Dum-Dum in full cry.

In his savage breast, powerful stirrings arose. Tarzan had been raised by apes since he had been but an infant, and a Dum-Dum of the tribe of Kerchak had been among his earliest exciting experiences.

In the center of the amphitheater floor stood an altar drum, and spaced regularly around it were other, lesser drums, scavenged from hollow tree trunks.

To-yat was giving the altar drum a severe beating with both hairy hands. Others were doing likewise to the satellite drums. The cadence of the Dum-Dum was wild, and it stirred the blood of the jungle lord as few other things would have.

Tarzan would have called over to the apes of To-yat, but he knew that his voice would not carry over the uproar of maddened drumming.

Staring at the scene below, the ape-man attempted to discern what motivated the Dum-Dum. Had someone died? No, for there was not a mournful quality to the dull tom-toms. Had a mortal enemy been slain? That seemed less likely. For the body of the slain was not on open display.

His noble brow furrowing, the jungle lord found himself at a momentary loss.

The only other reason for convening a Dum-Dum was to

---

*   *Tarzan, Lord of the Jungle* & *Tarzan the Invincible*

celebrate the ascension of a new king. But To-yat was obviously still leader of this tribe.

Then a shot rang out. The wanton drumming died in an instant. Myriad shaggy heads turned this way and that, seeking the source of the man-made thunder.

But no ape, not even To-yat himself, made any move to investigate the noise. All the great apes knew—as did Tarzan—the distinctive report of what they called in their rude tongue, pand-balu-den—"thundersticks." The power of a modern rifle was something the Mangani truly feared, even if they did not normally fear the comparatively weaker Tarmangani who wielded those deadly weapons that struck from afar.

Instead, the ape congress stared up and out into the night, their wild eyes seeking signs of movement, their shaggy limbs poised to leap to evade or attack, depending upon developments. They were otherwise silent as ghosts.

Tarzan, too, trained his eyes upon the rim of the amphitheater of packed dirt.

Presently, pale human faces topped the opposite ridge, close to the water. They crept closer, lifting higher, until they could be counted.

Their eyes fell upon the apes below and, instead of fleeing in terror as they should, they pointed and gesticulated quietly. But not quietly enough. Hushed exclamations rang out.

One watchful ape spied the lurking white men, hunkering low. A hairy finger pointed up and an angry screech resounded. Others joined in.

The next words uttered, Tarzan knew well. He had yelled the same many times before since he was a naked apeling rising in prominence in his adopted tribe.

"Kreegah! Bundolo!" screamed the apes.

In their common tongue, the words meant, "Danger! Kill!"

The white men broke, scrambling back out of sight. But one did a mad thing. He had set up a camera on a tripod and was attempting to film the apes. The sudden outburst should have dissuaded him from continuing. But it did not.

Charging up the inner crater wall, the killer apes of To-yat lunged for this foolhardy individual, who stood there cranking his camera as if he were watching a film, not committing one to celluloid.

Behind him, unseen, a man lifted a large rifle and shot him once, causing his body to spin half about and fall toward the hairy hands of the screaming apes.

The camera and tripod also went tumbling down, and these unfamiliar objects struck the first apes, surprising them and causing them to leap to the side.

At the sound of the rifle's thunderous report, Nkima and Ignatz both leapt from Tarzan's shoulders, and scrambled for cover.

It was well that they did so. Tarzan ran down the inner wall of the crater now, and his voice rang out.

"Halt! Bulls of To-yat. Tarzan is among you!"

It was a miracle that his voice carried over the yelling, but the voice of the ape-man was powerful.

Startled, the great shaggy apes turned their heads, unerringly fixing the sound of that challenging outcry.

Tarzan stood among them, and beside him padded Jad-bal-ja, the golden-furred lion.

"I am To-yat!" screamed the king ape in the customary Mangani greeting that might also be interpreted as a challenge to combat.

Tarzan did not reply in kind, for he was not interested in a fight. Instead, he said, "Does To-yat not know one who has danced the Dum-Dum with him in years gone by?"

"I know you!" yelled To-yat. "You are Tarzan!"

Tarzan nodded firmly and unafraid. "Tarzan of the tribe of Kerchak."

To-yat pointed at the lion standing poised at Tarzan's side, its cool yellow-green eyes regarding the congregation of great apes.

"That lion!" he exclaimed. "I have seen it before! The black mane and golden fur. There is no other lion like that in this jungle."

"Nor in any other," returned Tarzan. "This is Jad-bal-ja, the lion of Tarzan."

To-yat advanced carefully, baring his impressive fangs.

Suspicion made To-yat's muzzle lift, exposing gleaming canines. "What does Tarzan want with the tribe of To-yat?"

"Tarzan heard a Dum-Dum, and its call sang in his blood. So Tarzan came. What is the purpose of this Dum-Dum?"

To-yat seemed to hesitate. He looked to the others. One other ape Tarzan knew by name. Zu-tho, which meant Big-mouthed.

Tarzan fixed him with steely eyes and asserted, "There is always a purpose to a Dum-Dum. Why do you hesitate?"

To-yat answered that, licking his red lips nervously.

"There is something new in this jungle, Tarzan. Something strong and powerful."

Tarzan said nothing, awaiting further speech.

"Go-pand-usen is among us," To-yat said suddenly. "He has made these woods his own."

The other apes nodded eagerly. "We saw him with our own eyes," said another bull known to Tarzan of old, M'walat by name. "He looks like a gorilla, but is not a gorilla. Why Go-pand-usen has come among us, we do not know. But To-yat convened a Dum-Dum to praise and worship him. Even though he looks like a gorilla, but is not."

"You have seen this creature with your own eyes?"

"Did I not say so?" the king ape snapped.

"Describe this being you call Black-thunder-god," invited Tarzan.

To-yat snarled out, "He slept when we first came upon him. His size was greater than any Tantor, and his height taller than the tallest Omtags. He was as large as a small hill, lying there asleep. His face was the face of a Bolgani, but his fur was black and he had other qualities that told us he was no Bolgani, despite his Bolgani face."

Tarzan said, "I have seen signs of this creature. The Elephant's Graveyard has been desecrated. Many Omtags lie about with their necks snapped like sticks."

To-yat nodded eagerly. "We have come upon lions who were crushed by hands the size of boulders."

Zu-tho said, "Truly, Go-pand-usen is the most powerful creature in the jungle, and on earth."

"I hunt this creature, who is also called Zu-jar-bolgani," stated Tarzan.

"Why do you hunt him, Tarzan?" asked M'walat.

"This monster is destroying the jungle, ruthlessly killing all that dwell there. He cannot be allowed to roam freely."

"But he is a god," insisted Zu-tho.

"How do you know this?" countered the ape-man.

To-yat lifted helpless hands. "What else could he be? Nothing like him has ever before been seen. He is a new thing. And so large and powerful that he must be a god. And if he is a god, then we must worship him. Even though he looks like a Bolgani," he added self-consciously.

"I do not think he is a god," insisted Tarzan firmly. "But I do not know what a true god might look like. The only god I have ever heard of is Mulungu, who created all men and apes alike."

"We no longer acknowledge Mulungu, whom no one has ever beheld," spat To-yat. "We worship Go-pand-usen now."

Although virtually naked and dwarfed in size next to the shaggy beasts that were To-yat and his bulls, the ape-man did not flinch in his resolve. His teeth, too, were bared, but they were puny in comparison with those of the great apes.

Not so the recurved knife, which rested in its sheath at the jungle lord's muscular thigh. Perhaps it was this weapon that permitted the ape-man to stand his ground and speak with impunity.

"Know that Tarzan intends to evict this abomination from his jungle. If you are not prepared to join Tarzan in this quest, then it will serve you well to stay out of Tarzan's way. For he will not be brooked in his sacred duty to protect the jungle over which he is rightful lord."

Low growls issued forth from the throat of To-yat. Fangs were bared in the thinning moonlight. Other sets of ape-fangs joined in the baring.

In response, Jad-bal-ja offered an answering growl that wrinkled his broad nose and sent his long whiskers bristling.

With a word, Tarzan quieted the beast, and then turned his attention to the fallen white man, whom the bulls of To-yat had surrounded but not yet harmed.

Padding over to him, the ape-man knelt down, saw that he had been shot in the shoulder. The strap of a camera had been punctured, but there was little blood to be seen.

Turning the heavy body over, Tarzan brought the fellow's face up to the moonlight. His brown eyes were half open, but there was no clarity in them. His features were slack, and his breathing deep.

"I recognize this one," said Tarzan, standing up.

"Is he a friend to Tarzan?"

Tarzan shook his black mane of hair, saying, "No. Tarzan compelled him to leave his jungle long ago. Warned him never to come back. But now he has returned."

Skinning his teeth, To-yat screamed, "For that he must die! We will rend him limb from limb to warn other hated Tarmangani never to trespass upon a Dum-Dum again."

Tarzan reached down and lifted the heavy form of Carl Denham, showing no undue effort.

"No," he said calmly. "For this Tarmangani may possess useful information about this giant gorilla whom you think is a god."

"Why do you say that?" growled To-yat.

Other Mangani made suspicious sounds, as if also doubting the ape-man's assertion.

"A tame monkey was found," Tarzan explained patiently. "This monkey came from a ship that is anchored near here. A very large ship. Tarzan believes that the giant Bolgani was brought here by that ship. This man, too, no doubt came from that ship. When he awakens, Tarzan will question him and learn what he can of this new creature in the jungle."

The firmness with which the ape-man made these statements impressed To-yat, for he said grudgingly, "Good! It will be as Tarzan decrees. But after the Tarmangani talks, he will be killed."

"Tarzan will decide that at the appropriate time. Now I will take this man back to the other Tarmangani before they leave the jungle. If the bulls of To-yat do not care to follow Tarzan on his quest, then so be it."

To-yat's red-rimmed eyes gathered a weird gleam in their depths.

"Tarzan intends to slay Go-pand-usen?"

"Tarzan cannot say. If he must, he must. And if he must, he will. That is Tarzan's decision, and Tarzan's alone."

"If Tarzan slays the god of the gorillas, then who will we worship?"

The jungle lord did not have to think long upon that question. Packing the man's body across one shoulder, he said, "If the great gorilla falls before Tarzan's knife, then it will be proof that he was not a god. And so not worthy of the worship of Mangani."

So saying, Tarzan of the Apes turned on his heel and walked away from the tribe of To-yat, followed by the golden lion, whose sinuous tail switched impatiently, as if eager to turn and pounce upon any who would dare molest his master.

Above, on the lip of the crater, Nkima and Ignatz hunkered down, tiny eyes peering over the rim, for they had been eager watchers of the tableau transpiring in the amphitheater.

Now, as Tarzan approached them, they leapt up excitedly, and awaited his commands.

Chapter 50

JACK DRISCOLL heard the silence as the apes' wild yells tailed off, but he refused to look back.

The shore party was running for their lives, dashing madly toward shore. They could smell it; the roll of the surf came to their ears clearly. But they doubted that they could reach open water in time.

Panting, struggling, they ran and stumbled, and ran some more, until at last they reached the sandy shore, and the two beached dories came into view.

Only then did the sailors taking up the rear dare to look behind them.

They saw nothing. They heard nothing. All signs of pursuit were absent.

Lumpy spoke up. "Looks like we shook the devils!"

Driscoll growled, "There is no shaking off wild animals. Something stopped them. I don't know what, but we've no time to worry about that now. Man your boats, men. Shove off. And stop for nothing short of the *Wanderer's* sides."

Pushing off the dories, they piled in, took hold of the oars, and began rowing backward.

"Looks like we'll make it," Driscoll said, almost not believing his own words.

"Yeah, all except Denham," clucked Lumpy. "Poor beggar. Come all this way and he died for a few feet of film he'd never live to develop, much less show anybody."

Jack Driscoll said nothing to that. It was only now sinking in that he would have to break the bad news to Captain Englehorn. There was no telling how the old seafarer would take it. Carl Denham had almost brought them to ruin, and maybe that would still hold true. For without him and his promised profits, the *Wanderer* and her crew had no clear future.

Driscoll looked over to Penjaga, who sat in the stern sheets of the other dory. The old woman's face was an unreadable web of dry wrinkles. She seemed never to sweat. Her head was turned and her wise eyes were fixed upon the jungle into which Kong had disappeared.

Sunlight was creeping up on the water, throwing the rocking freighter into silhouette. The jungle slowly lost its dead grey hues, and traces of greenery came to life as the low, smoldering rays touched the living foliage.

Suddenly, Penjaga pointed a trembling finger, crying, "Behold!"

Hearts stopped beating for fear that the killer apes had burst out of the jungle and would come scrambling and splashing through the surf toward them.

Instead, they saw a man stepping out of the jungle—but such a man!

He was tall and bronzed, his physique magnificent with lean, pantherish muscles. He wore only a leopard-spotted breech clout. And on either naked shoulder sat a monkey.

Lumpy recognized one.

"Ignatz!"

"I'll be damned," muttered Driscoll.

Then they noticed in the gathering light that the bronzed giant held a man in his muscular arms.

A sailor burst out, "Look at those fancy duds! I think that's Denham!"

"Can't be!" another insisted. "Those apes would have scattered him to the four corners by now."

A pair of binoculars were stowed under a bench. Jack Driscoll brought these to bear on the strange figure standing at the edge of the jungle. The light was still not good enough to see clearly, but the First Mate was able to make out Carl Denham's rumpled clothes.

"That's Denham, all right. And there's not a mark on him that I can see."

"What do we do now?" asked Jimmy.

"Why, we go back for him," said Lumpy. "For him and Ignatz both."

Driscoll hesitated. "Didn't Denham claim that Tarzan lived with a pack of apes?"

"That he did."

"How do we know this isn't a trap?" snapped the Mate. "With Denham as the bait. If we turn back now, step onto shore, those killer apes of Tarzan's might fall on us and rip us to shreds."

It was a sobering thought. And no one offered a contrary opinion.

They were still rowing along, but more slowly. All eyes went to Jack Driscoll, whose rangy features showed that he was thinking furiously.

At last, he said, "Keep pulling. Better to lose one crazy-in-the-head landlubber than all of us honest seamen. We'll talk to the Skipper. He'll help us figure this out."

There was no dissent.

Redoubling their efforts, they sculled harder, and only Lumpy looked unhappy. His troubled eyes were upon Ignatz, and he was waving to the forlorn creature.

The tame little monkey waved back. So did the other monkey on Tarzan's opposite shoulder.

For his part, Tarzan silently strode down to the beach, carrying Carl Denham. He laid him down upon the pearly sand as the sun came up to turn the bronze of his nearly naked body to molten metal. Then he retreated silently.

"He's left him there, Mate," Jimmy said. "Should we go back?"

Driscoll shook his head firmly. "No. We go back when the

Old Man tells us to go back. Not before. I'll not lose any more crew for the sake of Carl Denham. Unless of course it's Cap'n's orders."

That satisfied the others. All except Lumpy, who stared at Ignatz with a worried pain deep in his aging eyes.

"That monk better not've gone native on me," he grumbled. "If he has, I'll tear his ears off, twist his tail loose and cook them so's he can watch me doin' it!"

But the sudden choke in the old cook's voice, combined with the water brimming in his pain-squeezed eyes, told another story....

Chapter 51

CAPTAIN ENGLEHORN had spent a sleepless night pacing the wheelhouse and afterdeck of the tired old freighter, the *Wanderer*.

Many times, he brought his binoculars to his sea-grey eyes, searching the rustling jungle for signs of the shore party led by Jack Driscoll. In the ordinary course of events, the seasoned sea captain would not have hesitated sending a second search party to seek out the first. Indeed, he struggled against that very impulse as the night wore on.

But the *Wanderer* was dreadfully short-handed. Englehorn had lost a dozen able and ordinary seamen back on Skull Mountain Island. The shore party consisted of another nine, as well as the fugitive old woman and Carl Denham, whom no one could find.

"Damn that *dummkopf,* Denham!" Englehorn cursed, not for the first nor last time. "If this keeps up, I'll have no crew at all."

Frustrated but held helpless by circumstances, the old sea master awaited the dawn and whatever it might bring.

A wild but incessant drumming started long after midnight and continued almost to daybreak. This did not add to Englehorn's fading hopes.

Came the dawn, and Englehorn again brought binoculars to his eyes. His expectations were low. As he adjusted the focusing screw, sweeping the sandy beach now coming back to colorful life under the welcome rays of morning, he began to discern moving figures. One wore a seaman's cap.

"Du lieber Gott!" he exclaimed. "Driscoll!"

For his First Mate was leading the shore party to the two beached dories that were now emerging from pre-dawn dark.

The Skipper counted the band. All were accounted for. Except one. There was no sign of Carl Denham, whom Englehorn was forced to conclude had left the ship by somehow inveigling two members of his crew into taking him ashore when his back was turned.

This subterfuge had been undertaken during meal time—when only one sailor stood watch, and who had also been fooled by the brash director's convincing line of patter. Englehorn had discovered the missing sailors only after counting heads. By that time, there was nothing he could do. There had been no other signs of the subterfuge, except for the second dory a crewman spied beside the first on the sandy beach.

"Damn that man!" Englehorn muttered. Shaking himself free of his lonely watch, he rattled down the ladder to muster the crew to receive the returning shore party.

A sailor was dispatched to rouse Ann Darrow from her bed.

A single blue eye peeped out from the cracked cabin door, rimmed in red from lack of sleep. "What is it?" she demanded sleepily.

"First Mate returning with the shore party," the seaman said hastily.

"Oh, thank the heavens!" Ann cried, clapping the door shut in order to dress.

Every deckhand not occupied with his work assembled on the poop deck to receive the dories. Falls were lowered, tied to their anchorages, and brought up hastily.

Sea water made long strings of brine under the wet keels as they were hoisted aboard.

The launch containing Penjaga and the others came first,

followed by Jack Driscoll's boat. These were swung in and dropped to the fire-blackened deck.

After he stepped out onto the weather deck, the First Mate gave the Captain a brisk salute and announced, "Shore party present and accounted for, sir."

Englehorn nodded. "I will take your report in my office, Mr. Driscoll. Follow me."

Pausing only to give Ann a consoling hug, Jack Driscoll followed his captain to the wardroom.

"I will lay it out for you," Driscoll began. "We found the woman all right, but not before Denham showed up, packing his camera gear. He claimed you'd given him permission to come ashore to do some filming."

"I will have you know that that is a damned lie," said Englehorn tartly. "But continue."

Driscoll gave a rapid recital of his actions during the night, beginning with the search for Penjaga and the disappearance of Carl Denham, and all that followed, including their brush with a slumbering Kong.

"We had almost made it to the dories when we stumbled across a tribe of wild apes," the Mate continued. "Denham couldn't help himself. He set up his camera and started grinding away. The apes spotted us, became incensed, and came charging. I'm afraid, Cap'n, I had to shoot Denham before the apes could tear him to pieces. It was the only way to spare him."

Captain Englehorn took the news without flinching. "I would've done the same thing had I been in your shoes, Mr. Driscoll. We can assume that Mr. Denham is deceased, then."

"I was just about to get to that, Cap'n. We thought so, but when we got into our dories, a white man appeared on the jungle's verge. He was holding Denham in his arms. Denham didn't look like he was hurt, but that mercy bullet I put into him had enough dope in it to bring down a charging elephant. I can't be sure of these things, but my guess is it would've killed him anyway, and not merely knocked him out."

"Tell me about this white man."

"He wore a loincloth, and that's pretty much it. Looked like a wild man. Had a jungle monkey clinging to one shoulder and Ignatz on the other. That upset Lumpy pretty much. But there was nothing we could do about it. Cap'n, I think it was that Tarzan."

Englehorn's mustached upper lip quirked upward. "You do?"

"That tall tale Denham told us about stumbling across a tribe of apes led by a white man I never took seriously. But I saw the apes. They were drumming to beat the band until I fired my rifle. We got away from them. Then this Tarzan showed up, holding Denham. I figured it must be a trap—bait to lure us back into the clutches of the wild apes."

Captain Englehorn was so caught up in his First Mate's story that he completely forgot about his morning tobacco. Now, as he absorbed the account's ending, he dug out his pouch and inserted a wad into one cheek. This he began masticating thoughtfully.

It was a while before he spoke. The ticking of the wardroom clock was the only noise. It seemed unusually loud. The sound of the surf against the sides of the ship was a muffled crashing.

"I am not in the habit of leaving a passenger behind," Englehorn said carefully, "much less the ship's charterer."

"You don't expect us to go back, do you? That would be suicide!"

The old Captain's weathered features grew heavy and his voice followed suit. "No, I do not. We have no men to spare, much less risk the loss of another search party. I spent a very troubled watch wondering if I had lost my first officer, as well as my cook and a few others. I am grateful that this is not the case."

A relieved sigh escaped Jack Driscoll's lips. He waited for his skipper to resume speaking.

"Have Lumpy prepare breakfast, Mr. Driscoll. After that, we will hoist anchor and depart these waters. We are free of all our burdens, except perhaps for any guilt we may carry to the end of our days."

"You don't blame yourself for the loss of Mr. Denham, do you?"

Instead of answering directly, Captain Englehorn said gruffly, "That will be all, Mr. Driscoll. You have your orders. Carry them out."

"Aye, sir," returned Driscoll, exiting the wardroom. Once out in the morning sunlight, he sought out Lumpy, and said to him, "Fix us some grub, and try to put that monk out of your mind. At least he's not dead."

"That faithless varmint was more trouble than he was worth," Lumpy sniffed. But Driscoll was not fooled. The sentimental old cook's heart was broken. He disappeared into the galley without another word.

BREAKFAST was a sober affair, and any rejoicing over the safe return of the shore party was masked by the realization that they were sailing home to great uncertainty. Without Carl Denham, there existed no hope of any payday, or the magnanimous splitting of any profits—inasmuch as there were no profits to split. Any footage that might have been captured lay back in the jungle, lost and irretrievable.

In one corner, Jack and Ann dined quietly.

"Ann," he was saying with hushed sincerity, "I don't know how I'm going to do it, but I promise you I will not let what happened stand in our way."

She laid a gentle hand on his wrist and said, "I have faith in you, Jack."

"Don't misunderstand. It's going to be tough. Damn tough. But we'll make our way. Somehow. Maybe the Captain can put into some African port and pick up loose cargo. I'll talk to him about that. It's what we do, anyway. All this Frank Buck stuff about expeditions and capturing wild animals, that's not our line. Never was. Not in the days before he hooked up with that madman, Denham. That's done with now. We're a merchant ship. We'll go back to being a common freighter. We'll haul cargo all the way back to New York, and maybe those bananas in the tween decks holds won't spoil before we can unload them off on someone."

"Will an African port take them?"

Driscoll shrugged. "Probably not. But there's nothing keeping us from taking the Suez passage home. Maybe a Mediterranean port will take 'em. We're going to require cash. And coal, too. Lots of it."

The First Mate's features darkened.

"What are you saying, Jack?" implored Ann.

"I'm not sure we have enough coal to cross the Atlantic…."

Ann's blue eyes widened. This was a thought that had not occurred to her. The *Wanderer* gobbled up an astounding quantity of anthracite to keep her old steam engines running. Without coal, an Atlantic crossing was impossible.

Driscoll concluded, "Englehorn and I will figure a way, don't you worry. We've been in tough spots before. Hell, with Kong off our backs, anything is possible now."

"Kong…" said Ann softly. "I wonder, what's become of him?"

Driscoll shook his head, saying, "I don't know and I care even less. Denham said he would teach Kong fear. Tame him. It didn't work out that way. Maybe Kong will become what Denham called him: King. King of Africa. It's a fitting place for him. He might do all right."

"But what about Penjaga?"

Driscoll seemed momentarily stopped by the question. "Hadn't thought of that. I guess we should be taking her back to the island. If we can. That will be the Captain's decision. Not mine. I've had enough of decisions. Let the Old Man make that one. What he says, goes."

They fell into an abstract silence. It was broken by shouting from the weather deck.

Someone blew a boatswain's whistle sharply, piercingly.

Yanked from his seat by the familiar alarm, Driscoll rapped out, "Sounds like trouble! Follow me! All hands on deck!"

Racing for the door, Driscoll heard an upset voice cry, "Boarder! Boarder!"

Over his shoulder, Driscoll shouted, "Ann, stay here! Lumpy, you watch her."

Then he charged out the door, face determined.

Chapter 52

THE COMMOTION was coming from the bow, and Jack Driscoll led his men in that direction.

Up on the flying bridge, Captain Englehorn called down to him. "It seems that your wild man has climbed up the anchor chain, Mr. Driscoll. Deal with him appropriately."

"Don't worry, I will!" shouted the First Mate, pounding toward the bow.

He arrived in time to witness Seaman Foley attempt to fend off the nearly naked intruder with a belaying pin. Foley was bringing the heavy weapon down from on high, attempting to brain the long-haired giant.

A strong right arm came up, blocked the downward blow, and somehow took hold of Foley's muscular forearm. Driscoll expected a left hook to follow that maneuver. Instead the wild man took hold of Seaman Foley with both hands, lifting him as if he weighed no more than a child, and sent him smashing into the forecastle.

Foley did not rise again.

"That's enough of that!" Driscoll shouted. "Who are you? What do you want on board this vessel?"

The boarder whirled on nimble, naked feet. Driscoll got a good look at his face, and was shocked by its innate intelligence. The clear grey eyes had none of the savagery he expected. His bronzed forehead was high and noble, marked by a jagged scar that pulsed with raw ferocity. That, and the leopard-skin loincloth, bespoke of a primitive soul somehow poured into the body of a demi-god, Pan and Hercules combined in one unique being.

Driscoll was unarmed, but he made his sunburnt fists hard. "What's your business here, fellow?" he demanded, squaring off in anticipation of a fight.

Yet the boarder did not make a move to attack. Instead, he stood calmly, in perfect command of himself. His knife-steel eyes found Driscoll's gaze and a touch of awe brushed the First Mate's soul.

"I am Tarzan, of the tribe of Kerchak. War Chief of the Waziri. And lord of this jungle you have invaded. Why do you trespass where you are not wanted?"

"We have invaded no jungle," replied Driscoll stubbornly, dropping his hands onto his lean hips.

Tarzan gestured with one bronzed arm to the expanse of trees lying off the port bow. "All that jungle, for as far as the eye can see," he said imperiously, "is Tarzan's land. It falls under my guardianship. And my question to you stands."

"Are you Tarzan of the Apes?"

"I have already told you that. Now answer, quickly!"

"We were carrying cargo to America. Do you know what America is?"

Tarzan nodded impatiently. "I am an Englishman by birth. Although I was raised by apes."

Driscoll blinked. He didn't know what to say to that. By this time Captain Englehorn had come down off the flying bridge and joined them.

"I am the master of this vessel," he announced. "Any questions you have, you may direct to me."

Tarzan pointed to the anchor chain, where they noticed for the first time little Ignatz, now clinging in agitation to its rust-fouled links. His tiny teeth chattered.

"This monkey tells me that he came with you."

"The monkey told you that, did he?"

The bronzed giant replied humorlessly. "He also said that you brought the great black gorilla to the lands of Tarzan."

Englehorn nodded briskly. "Well, he's telling you the truth, even though I don't believe a word of what you say. Yes, the great black gorilla, as you call him, is ours. We captured him on an island far east of here. But he proved too difficult to manage and he escaped while we were anchored here."

"This monster is destroying the jungle of Tarzan." The words of the ape-man were edged in steel, and carried with them the weight of accusation.

"We had no choice in the matter," insisted Englehorn. "The brute escaped from us and made his way to shore. We were taking him to America to put on display." The old master shook his greying head ruefully. "All that is over with now."

Driscoll interjected, "Say, what happened to the fellow you saved from those apes?"

"He sleeps in the jungle guarded by Jad-bal-ja. The apes of To-yat will not harm him. I ordered them not to."

"Who is this Jad-bal-ja?" asked the Captain.

"A lion loyal to Tarzan of the Apes."

Driscoll demanded, "You say that Denham is alive?"

Tarzan nodded firmly. "He breathes. He sleeps. He will awaken."

"I shot him with a narcotic bullet powerful enough to bring down a bull elephant. I don't know what it would do to a human being exactly, but I have a hard time believing that Carl Denham will pull out, no matter how strong his constitution."

"The bullet struck a leather strap, and did not penetrate very deeply. Tarzan can take you to him."

While this offer was sinking in, Lumpy bustled up, having procured a rolling pin from the galley, and began yelling vociferously in the direction of Ignatz.

"Is that you, you miserable monk? Hop over here and take your punishment."

Clinging to the anchor chain, displaying rude teeth, Ignatz refused to budge.

Tarzan turned, then began speaking to the monkey in low gutturals. The monkey chattered back, throwing in the odd screech.

To the watching crew, it looked as if they were having a conversation. Their faces looked strange as this sank in.

Pointing at Lumpy, Tarzan gave Ignatz an unintelligible command, and the monkey dropped down off the anchor chain, scampered across the deck and climbed Lumpy's leg until he was perched upon the old codger's sweat-stained shoulder.

Driscoll studied the bronzed giant with newfound respect. "You have a way with monkeys, I'll give you that."

Somewhat mollified, Englehorn asked, "I take it you swam to this vessel and climbed the anchor chain?"

Tarzan nodded. "What is the business of the man I rescued from the apes of To-yat?"

Englehorn answered that. "Carl Denham? In America, he's a famous film director."

Tarzan nodded. "I left him on the beach for you to collect at your leisure. Then you must go. Tell Denham that this is the second time I have evicted him from this forest. If he returns again, I will not be so merciful."

Driscoll made a funny sound in his throat. "So he was telling the truth about the time he got run out of Africa by you and your ape pack?"

"He was. Do not forget to tell Denham never to return to Africa again. For he has brought misery to this jungle—as have you all. It now is the responsibility of Tarzan to hunt down this monster gorilla and settle with him for all time. I must go now."

Having spoken his piece, Tarzan of the Apes turned, strode confidently to the anchor chain. Without a backward glance, he went over the rail, clambered down the heavy steel links, and dropped into the water.

The crew surged to the port rail to watch him swim back to the land. The ape-man did so effortlessly.

"Can you beat that?" Jimmy exploded. "Tarzan of the Apes! He was real, after all. Denham wasn't lying."

"No," said Driscoll thoughtfully, "he was not." Turning to address the Captain, he asked, "You heard every word, Skipper. What's your decision?"

Englehorn considered. "That man Tarzan has a bearing that makes me inclined to believe him...."

"I still wonder if it's a trap," the First Mate reminded.

"Arm your men accordingly, Mr. Driscoll. If Denham is alive, we will have to rescue him."

Jack Driscoll took off his seaman's cap and grumbled, "This is getting to be a habit. A bad one."

"We will make this the last time. Give Mr. Denham a few hours to sleep off his narcotic stupor. You and your search party get some sleep yourselves. If you must go ashore again, I want you fresh, even if you're only penetrating a few hundred yards."

"Aye, Cap'n." Turning to the crew, he said, "You heard Captain Englehorn. Shore party turn in. Lumpy, get Foley down to the infirmary and look him over. And when I tell you to watch over Ann, or anyone else, you do it. Or else you'll be eating Jimmy's cooking for a month."

Ignatz clinging to his shoulder, Lumpy went to work grumbling to himself. He doubled as the ship's doctor, although he was not much of a physician except through practical experience.

Those who were free to do so watched Tarzan swim tirelessly to shore. Standing up, he waded the last few yards, and stepped onto the beach, his leopard-skin loincloth dragging a waterlogged tail behind it.

"I wonder if that tail is real?" a sailor asked of no one in particular.

No one ventured a firm opinion. After the ape-man had

disappeared into the jungle fringe, they returned to their duties, but talk of Tarzan occupied their working morning.

"A white man who made himself a king of the apes!" Jimmy exclaimed. "What a wonder."

"When it comes to kings and wonders," scoffed a sailor, "King Kong wins, hands down. What was it that damn Denham called him?"

"The Eighth Wonder!"

"Right. What exactly does that mean?"

"In the ancient world," explained Jimmy dreamily, "there were Seven Wonders of the World, starting with the Colossus of Rhodes. Kong's Number Eight. Which makes Tarzan the Ninth Wonder."

"Not in my book," snorted the other derisively. "He ain't nearly tall enough!"

Chapter 53

L ITTLE NKIMA sat patiently upon Jad-bal-ja's luxurious
tawny coat as the magnificent golden feline rested, slapping
the jungle floor with a leisurely flexing of his long, tufted tail.

A forest monkey would not normally consort with a male
lion in such a familiar fashion, but the golden lion had been
trained by Tarzan never to harm the friends of Tarzan.

Jad-bal-ja stood sentinel over the sleeping body of Carl
Denham, who was deep in a coma induced by the mercy bullet
fired by First Mate Jack Driscoll.

Denham did not stir. His breathing was deep and regular.
From time to time, a snuffling snort emerged from his pulsing
nostrils.

Whenever this happened, the lion would pad over and lick
at the showman's face, as if to quiet him. The long moist tongue
usually did the trick.

Once, Denham batted at his face, but otherwise did not react
to the animal's ministrations.

While the great lion guarded his charge, Nkima foraged
about, picking grubs from the bark of trees, and otherwise
satisfying his appetite as well as his monkey-like curiosity, both
of which were boundless.

Nkima's perambulations eventually brought him to the natural
amphitheater that had been deserted by the apes of To-yat.
There, he found Denham's motion picture camera, which had

become detached from its tripod. It was very heavy, the monkey discovered. Too heavy to lift, but it could be dragged.

Struggling, Nkima dragged the camera back to where its owner lay.

Seeing the unfamiliar object, Jad-bal-ja padded over and sniffed it. His sensitive nostrils recognized the scent of the sleeping man, but otherwise the powerful lion soon became disinterested in the dull black object.

Patiently, the pair waited for their master, who had waded out into the cove and swum for the great ship that stood anchored not far away.

Until Tarzan of the Apes returned, Carl Denham would be safe. Although he did not know that, of course.

Presently, the Lord of the Jungle padded up from the beach, and gave a low word of command to his faithful feline friend.

"Come. We will depart this place."

Nkima spoke up, chattering, "Do we pick up the spoor of the terrible gorilla?"

Tarzan nodded curtly. "We do."

"The gorilla-monster will soon know the wrath of Tarzan of the Apes," squeaked the monkey confidently.

The ape-man said nothing. Nkima leapt onto the lion's back, and from there onto the bronzed giant's shoulder. The trio started inland, walking with a measured pace which covered territory rapidly without tiring them.

As they walked off, Nkima asked, "Will hyenas not try to eat that sleeping man?"

Tarzan shook his head. "Dango will smell the scent of lion and leave the man alone. His people will collect the Tarmangani and take him far away, never to return."

Nkima chattered, "The Tarmangani has learned his lesson. Were it not for Tarzan of the Apes, he would have been torn to shreds of flesh and fragments of bone and left to the jackals and scavengers to eat."

Tarzan said nothing to that. His attention was focused entirely on the path ahead, and the problem of the stupendous gorilla that defied the laws of nature and desecrated the home jungle of the ape-man.

One who was omniscient might look at this half-naked bronze-skinned giant striding into the forest unafraid, armed only with a hunting knife and supported by a tiny monkey and a powerful lion, and ask credibly: How could this man possibly think he could overcome a thirty-foot-tall anthropoid?

In truth, Tarzan of the Apes' thoughts ran precisely along that trend, but in his thinking there was not a shred of doubt that he could accomplish the task at hand. The ape-man only considered how he might undertake such a tremendous feat of bravery.

Knowing that he would have to work that out in his head before he caught up with his quarry, Tarzan moved in a measured pace, but not in a hurry.

If Zu-jar-bolgani was abroad in the vast, empty grassland beyond the forest, there was little harm he could wreak. Tarzan had plenty of time to catch up with him, and to settle accounts.

Of that, the ape-man was confident.

Chapter 54

KONG WALKED and walked until fatigue began to creep into his muscles and joints.

This difficulty was as much mental as it was physical, for the stumbling anthropoid was unaccustomed to mile upon mile of flat grassland, where few trees grew and nothing much of interest to appetite or curiosity existed.

Pangs of hunger continued to gnaw at him, but not so much as before.

Bending, he ripped up a fistful of grass, and chewed it experimentally. It was not without taste, but it lacked what Kong needed most after his long ordeal. Raw meat. The hot, reviving juice of vital fluids. These were the things that the fallen beast-god most desired.

But this long carpet of grass seemed to lack abundant game.

True, deer and antelope did spring about. But they bolted at the sound and smell of the approaching monster and, while Kong could chase after them for short distances, nature had not designed him for running, much less sprinting.

Lunging in the direction of a nimble springbok, he failed to capture it.

A cheetah, dashing from one clump of brush to another, suddenly froze, took in the sight of the preposterous black creature, then flashed away.

To Kong, the spotted feline reminded him of lions he had

previously encountered, so their stringy flesh did not motivate him to give chase.

Eventually, Kong grew sufficiently fatigued that he lay down on his back in the baking African sun. Drowsy but not truly sleepy, he rubbed his hairy black belly, wondering where his next meal might be found.

As he stared up into the bright blue sky, where fleecy clouds chased one another in a steady wind, his simian thoughts went back to his island home, and the fierce creatures that roamed it. Terrible they were, true. But they were what Kong knew, and what he conquered. More importantly, they were composed of the kind of meat to which the beast-god had long ago become accustomed. Reptilian flesh.

A sadness swept across the broad, leathery chest of Kong as he lay there longing for the familiar. Flies were congregating about the reopened wounds running along his hirsute forearms, but the behemoth barely noticed them. In time, his brooding eyes grew heavy and slowly closed. He drifted into restorative sleep, where the pangs of hunger and the longings for home did not trouble his brain.

Kong slept. And as he slept, the earth quieted down and the creatures that had scattered before him started to creep back, moving in his direction, drawn by many primitive emotions, curiosity and hunger among them.

Hours passed.

A reckless jackal crept up, and began sniffing at Kong's feet. The odor did not agree with him, and the unexpected size of Kong was intimidating. After a few experimental sniffs, he slunk away.

Something moved sinuously through the grass, making it twitch and part as it passed. Had Kong been awake, he would not have noticed it. A long form slithered and made a crooked path toward the massive sloping head, as broad nostrils were taking in the warm humid air and releasing it through his open mouth.

Possibly it was the odors emanating from that mouth—a mixture of saliva and fragments of the meals of which Kong had partaken since his advent in Africa—-drew the unseen stalker.

Kong slept on, entirely oblivious to the approaching menace.

Something lifted out of the green grass. A pebbled brown wedge of a head decorated with unwinking orbs the hue of opals. It waved atop its long neck, eyed the recumbent anthropoid unblinkingly, and seemingly fearless, advanced upon the black-haired neck.

So stealthy was this creature that Kong did not feel its cool touch until the thing had affixed itself to him, and began to settle in.

The sounds of Kong sleeping were varied. Grunts, snuffling snores, even an occasional groan. These last might have been the product of submerged hunger pangs.

When Kong awoke, it was sudden. His eyes snapped open and their amber depths took in his surroundings. First, he saw only blue sky.

It dawned on his drowsy mind that he could not breathe. This was a new experience.

Then he noticed a tightness in his throat. Another new experience.

Sitting up, Kong looked about to see what had gotten hold of him, what powerful animal had seized him by the throat.

But he beheld nothing. Nothing lay in sight.

Still unable to breathe, Kong pulled himself clumsily to his feet, and stood swaying. A choking sensation clogged his throat. His lungs seemed paralyzed.

Turning completely about, long arms flailing blindly, he sought what manner of monster was cutting off his breath.

As he did so, his massive fingers reached for his throat, and encountered something elongated and muscular. It was hairless to the touch, the hide scaly yet smooth.

Growling, Kong seized it with both hands and began exerting pressure.

Briefly the thing resisted, but the power of Kong's anthropoid arms was too great and he wrested it free, overwhelming its constricting embrace.

Suddenly, Kong was holding in both hands a writhing, twisting serpent, as long and powerful as anything he had encountered back on Skull Mountain Island.

It was a massive python. And it had wrapped itself about his thick-muscled throat, although for what certain purpose was hard to fathom. Kong could not be consumed by its yawning maw, no matter how much it dislocated its massive jaws.

The python that had coiled itself around Kong was only now discovering that it had taken on more than it could handle.

Angry eyes running along the scaly pattern that marked the python's powerful sides, Kong determined that this attacker represented an unexpected gift.

The reptilian thing fought hard, wrapping itself around the apish brute's thick wrists, twisting, hissing and doing other gyrations designed to break free of the crushing gorilla grip.

Kong proved too powerful for its muscular contortions, however.

Taking the triangular head in one paw, Kong squeezed it remorselessly, forcing the jaws together, crushing the cool-tempered brain into a shapeless mass in its scaly braincase encasement.

That this action caused the death of the organ, but did not cause the body to cease resisting, did not matter. Not a whit.

Wrenching off the head, Kong took the stump of the decapitated serpent into his mouth and began chewing off long strips of reptilian flesh. He took his time, taking mighty bites, chewing portions and spitting out the vertebrae. Other times, he simply peeled and ripped from the serpent its tasty meat.

When he was done, Kong was less hungry than before, but still not satiated.

Leaving behind the bloody remnants of bone and stripped skin, Kong laid anxious eyes upon the looming mountain shining in the afternoon sun. Mount Kilimanjaro. It still called to him.

Energized by fresh meat, the beast-god continued his arduous journey toward his new home.

Nothing stood in his way. Nor could anything block him from his goal. For he was a striding engine of destruction in gorilla form. He was Kong.

Chapter 55

WHEN CARL DENHAM eventually awoke, he was afraid to open his eyes.

His last memory was looking through the viewfinder of his bulky Bell & Howell film camera. Howling, screaming, fangs slavering, a horde of weirdly gesticulating apes were charging up at him. Something struck his right shoulder with such force that he was turned completely around, after which his memory ceased registering impressions.

The director lay on his back—where, he did not know.

Listening carefully, he heard sounds that reminded him of the ocean. He lay upon something soft, and as he focused on this, the bed in which he lay seemed to be rocking gently.

"I must be hallucinating," he muttered to himself. "Feels like I'm back on the ship."

Of course, that was patently impossible. Denham had been staring into the face of death through his camera aperture.

As he reflected upon his behavior, he recalled that it was his last remembered thought to grab the camera at the last minute and run like hell. But the wild wave of apes moved too fast. Besides, he never got the chance. Something struck him from behind.

That recollection caused him to place his attention on his right shoulder. It throbbed like the wild drumming made by the unknown apes. It felt as if an elephant had butted him from behind.

Now Carl Denham was a brave man, but the fact that he feared to open his eyes was not in fear of death. Rather, it was the fear that he had already died, and he was not anxious to see where he had landed, since it was becoming obvious to his clouded brain that death had not extinguished his thought processes.

"Well," he mumbled, "I'm going to have to do this sometime." His eyes came open, one at a time. The right one first.

An explosive oath shot out from between his dry and cracked lips.

"Hell's bells!"

Denham had for a brief period wondered if he had not landed in the place described in the Bible as the realm of everlasting punishment.

This was not that place. For above his head hung the familiar ceiling of his cabin. Denham could not imagine how he had survived, much less been conveyed back to the *Wanderer's* familiar comforts. Yet for several minutes his amazed eyes shot about the room, seeking further evidence of his true situation.

Finally, he levered himself up to a seated position and his shoulder caught fire. This was the fire of pain and not eternal damnation.

Denham's mind was not in correct working order. He could recognize that. His brain felt sluggish, and a little off-center.

Nevertheless, he mustered up sufficient lung power to yell, "Hey!"

The befuddled showman had to repeat himself before the door fell open, bringing in hot tropical air and a blistering sunlight that made him clap his hands over his sensitive eyes.

"What is it, Mr. Denham?" It was Jimmy, the young ordinary seaman.

"Where am I?" Denham croaked.

"In your cabin, where do you think?"

"Never mind that. How did I get here?"

"The First Mate took a party ashore and fetched you. You're lucky to be alive."

"I remember. Those damn apes!"

"Never mind the apes. You're lucky *Tarzan* of the Apes didn't skin you alive. He's the one who rescued you after the Mate shot you."

Denham's bloodshot eyes went wide. "Driscoll! Driscoll shot me?"

"He sure did. You were about to be torn apart by wild animals. Mr. Driscoll didn't want you to suffer."

"Kind of ol' Jack," Denham said thinly. Then, in a panicky tone, he asked, "What happened to my camera?"

"They brought it back. The Mate has it."

"Tell him for me to treat it like a million bucks."

"Yes, sir."

Fatigue caused Denham to settle back on his pillow, dull eyes closing.

They snapped open again. Suddenly, he demanded, "Wait a minute! Did you say something about Tarzan of the Apes?"

"Yes, sir. Tarzan came aboard the ship and told us to go fetch you. That we did. And here you are, safe and sound."

"Safe at any rate," grumbled the showman. "Sound is another matter entirely. Say, I don't think I've eaten in a while. When is Lumpy dishing up chow next?"

"About an hour. But they'll bring it to you. The Cap'n has confined you to your quarters. Punishment for going ashore without permission."

Denham said nothing to that. Instead, he asked, "What's the Skipper's plan?"

"He and Mr. Driscoll are discussing that in the wardroom. Tarzan told us to ship out. But the Skipper is feeling pangs of guilt over having unleashed Kong on Africa."

Fresh interest flavored the director's gruff voice. "You don't say? That sounds mighty interesting. Let me know what they decide when they decide it, will you?"

Jimmy laughed. "They'll probably do that themselves. I imagine you're in for a bit of a tongue lashing."

"Can't say that I don't deserve it. But thank you for the information."

"Think nothing of it," said Jimmy, shutting the door and giving Carl Denham the benefit of silence and solitude.

As he lay there thinking about his situation, a light rain began falling. Soon increasing in intensity, the drumming of rain on the weather deck and the sides of the old ship became an urgent monotony that gave him a slow headache on top of the painful throbbing he was already experiencing.

This noise made it hard to scheme, but Carl Denham nevertheless put every ounce of his indefatigable will into the operation.

"I ain't licked yet..." he mumbled.

Chapter 56

W HEN THE afternoon rains commenced, Kong was caught in the open.

The first light drop speckled his bristling fur, but he paid them no heed.

Then they began to pour and pound, and soon the gargantuan gorilla found himself in the midst of a torrential downpour falling from dark clouds that arrived with uncanny suddenness.

The rain swiftly turned into an inescapable curtain surrounding him. Kong had been moving west, pushing hard, steadily seeking the icy summit of the far distant mountain that beckoned to him.

But that summit still lay many marches in the future. Soon, the fast-moving rain obscured it from view.

A solitary camel's foot tree showed in shivering silhouette to the east. Kong veered in that direction, picking up his pace, moving clumsily, for rushing was not something the tremendous anthropoid did well.

From a distance it was not evident whether the tree would offer much in the way of shelter, but there was no other shelter in sight.

The rain, of course, did not harm Kong, but its relentlessness soon drenched him, making him uncomfortably sodden. Back on his home island, tropical rains were common, but shelter was always at hand. Not here. Not on this vast grassland that seemed so unnatural by comparison.

Kong pounded toward the lone tree, but the slick grass proved too much to offer proper traction. His feet slid out from under him, slamming Kong onto his matted and much-scarred back.

The earth shook. A lone egret, nestled in the branches of the sheltering tree, gave out a forlorn cry. It launched itself into space, but the rains were so intense that flying was virtually impossible, except for the great spread-winged vultures.

Kong sat up, as if stung. He simply sat there and allowed the rain to infiltrate every interstice of his bristly, grey-shot coat of fur. The look on his broad, apish face was miserable, his grave eyes were anxious in a way that was not so much a reflection of fear as it was of a pitiful hopelessness.

Finally, Kong knuckled himself to a standing position and, more carefully this time, strode in the direction of the sheltering tree, which was being battered mercilessly by the downpour.

This time, he made it. But when he reached the camel's foot tree, Kong discovered it to be a spindly little thing. Its dripping branches offered insufficient shelter for an oversized animal such as himself.

Frustration had been building in his breast, and now it exploded in primordial fashion.

Seeing that the tree was useless for shelter, the titanic beast-god seized it with both mighty hands, began swaying and shaking it, twisting it this way and that until he had uprooted the entire bole from the waterlogged earth.

With a roar of anger and defiance, Kong flung it as far as he could. By this time, the roosting egret had taken flight and struggled to leave the vicinity.

Kong dimly perceived beating wings in the pounding rain, and in his simian mind, he understood that the frightened bird was seeking the nearest tree known to him.

Perhaps that one would offer a suitable shelter. Roaring his rage, shaking one dripping fist, Kong followed in the wake of the fleeing bird, his mind fixated on one thing: relief from the remorseless rain that was beating at his spirit as had nothing before in his experience.

For the first time since he had usurped the terrible demon-lizard Gaw, Kong knew what it felt like to be merely another inhabitant of a jungle, and not its absolute monarch.

The bone-white egret bird beat its wings through a shifting curtain of rain, and soon vanished from view.

Kong shambled after him, walking with the stooped-over hunch that was his natural posture and mode of locomotion. The grass under his feet felt cool and slippery, making for an unpleasant carpet. Stubbornly, the simian colossus plodded along.

Overhead, a rumble of elemental warning stirred the low-hanging thunderheads. Somewhere, the dull boom resounded. Then another. Sky thunder.

Kong understood what those natural sounds portended. Growling in resentful alarm, he shuffled along faster. Lightning was a force he could not battle. It struck and was gone, leaving its unfortunate target obliterated without mercy. It was another reason why the beast-god had taken up residence under the brooding granite dome of Skull Mountain.

Through the obscuring rain curtain, a towering tree with a great leafy ball of entwining branches showed dimly. With an eager grunt, Kong aimed for it. The trunk was massive, its crown sufficient to protect any who sought shelter beneath it.

No doubt the fleeing egret was already safely ensconced within its greenery.

Although expected, a pitchfork of lightning arrived with a suddenness that was a shock. Its flash of light was white and searing, forcing Kong to throw one scarred forearm across his startled features. The explosion that followed flung him backward, and made his small ears ring and ring.

Stumbling, Kong toppled backward, landing hard.

When his vision cleared, he blinked at the towering tree that promised relief from the rain. It was no longer there. The lightning bolt had blasted it apart.

Broken branches were scattered everywhere. One bough had landed nearby, its bark stripped clean, like a snake that had shed its skin. Entwined in its sub-branches was the white bird that had sought refuge in its sheltering limbs. It was a smoking, charred thing now.

Clambering to his feet, Kong fell upon that branch and whipped it skyward in a futile act of defiance. Then he shook a mighty fist at the threatening storm clouds marching along, as if daring them to unleash their elemental fury on him directly.

As thunder rumbled and grumbled all about, Kong raged and raged against the bitter rain of his inexplicable exile, but his defiance went unchallenged and unanswered. All he collected was more cold liquid misery....

Chapter 57

I N THE wardroom of the *Wanderer*, the pounding of the rain had settled down into a kind of syncopated jungle melody. Neither Captain Englehorn nor his First Mate paid it any attention as they discussed the situation at hand.

"You're not serious, Skipper?" Jack Driscoll was saying, just a tinge of disbelief in his voice.

"I've never been more serious," returned Captain Englehorn gruffly. His wintry eyes were bleak. "I have pondered the matter while you were recovering Carl Denham. My decision is firm and final. We have loosed this scourge upon Africa, and it falls to us as good men and able seamen to bring it to a just conclusion."

"You want us to hunt Kong and kill him?"

"Precisely. You have sufficient arms, as well as the remaining gas bombs. Between your mercy bullets and the bombs, you may be able to bring him low, after which a shotgun blast to the brain should settle the unfortunate beast once and for all."

"I hadn't expected this from you, Cap'n."

"Nor would I have thought that it would come to this. That man Tarzan is going after Kong, armed only with a hunting knife. It is unlikely to accomplish much. As civilized men, we must do our part. That is my final word on the subject. Pick your men, and undertake your safari."

"What about Denham?"

"Mr. Denham is confined to quarters, as you know."

"It's his mess. If I were captain, I would insist that he be part of cleaning it up."

Englehorn's greying eyebrows crowded together and his entire seamed face gathered like a great thundercloud.

"Your point," he said at last, "can hardly be dismissed, the way you put it." Englehorn frowned all the more deeply, finally saying, "Very well. It is a risky undertaking, but one additional man, provided he pulls his weight, can only help."

Driscoll asked, "What if he refuses? He might, you know."

"In that case, we have no power to compel him—except the power of persuasion and right thinking."

Jack Driscoll suddenly snapped his fingers, saying, "I think I got it, Skipper. We'll let him tote his camera. That'll motivate him."

"The camera will complicate his behavior. You realize that, Mate."

Driscoll laughed roughly. "As if Carl Denham's behavior is not already complicated by itself."

"Put it to him," said Englehorn. "Persuade him to participate if it is in your power to do so."

"Yes, sir," returned the First Mate, adding, "I'm getting dizzy the way we're running around in circles, accomplishing nothing."

"Destroy Kong. That will be accomplishment enough. Once you do that, we will be free to go, both morally and otherwise."

"If we run into Tarzan, he's not going to be happy with us."

"By the time you catch up with Tarzan of the Apes," advised Captain Englehorn firmly, "he may or may not have caught up with Kong. Either way, I suspect he will be happy for your help. He will need it. He is Mohamed seeking a mountain. A very dangerous mountain. Convince him of the power of your modern weapons. He should see the logic in that. He's not a fool. Foolhardy, perhaps. But Tarzan of the Apes is no fool."

"Yes, sir," said Jack Driscoll, leaving the wardroom.

The First Mate went straight to Carl Denham's cabin, and

did not bother to knock. Rather, he shoved open the door, which brought a yell of shock from the occupant's placid chest.

"Shut the damn door!" Denham howled. "That light is killing my eyes."

Driscoll shut the door and said, "We have a proposition for you."

"I understand you shot me down?" said the showman in a heavy voice.

"I figured to spare you the agony of dismemberment," returned Driscoll stiffly. "It looks like I saved your life, or at least participated."

Denham chuckled. "Jimmy told me about Tarzan. I guess that's two apologies you owe me—one for shooting me in the back, and the other for disbelieving me."

"I shot you in the shoulder," countered Driscoll, "and it's a miracle you're not dead, anyway. The dope in those mercy bullets should have put you down like an injured horse."

"I'm not hearing anything in the nature of an apology," suggested Denham.

"And you won't," retorted Driscoll. "Listen to this proposition. The Captain has decided that we are obliged by the laws of man and God to hunt down Kong and destroy him."

"Is that right…?"

"Furthermore, that every man responsible for this sorry state of affairs should participate and pull his weight."

"I don't shoot big game," said Denham lightly. "Not with bullets at any rate."

"You'll be issued a pistol, along with your camera so that you can capture it all on film. That's the bargain. Understand? Pull your weight and you get to film what can be filmed. But if the going gets rough, we expect you to shoot with your pistol first."

"I guess me and Frank Buck have more in common than I thought," Denham said slowly.

"Is that a yes?"

"If I can get a hot meal in me before we ship out, sure. I'm always game for adventure. You know that about me, don't you, Jack?"

Jack Driscoll growled, "The more I know about you, Denham, the less I'm sure about you. But I am certain about what I do know. I think I know what makes you tick."

"O.K.," said Denham. "I'll bite. What makes me tick?"

"Greed. Pure and simple avarice. And it's gotten us into a fix that we're going to have to unfix. You want to take Kong back to America. Well, that's done with. All that's left is to run him down like a rabid dog."

"You know if I capture that on film, we're all as good as millionaires."

"See here, Denham," Driscoll retorted, "this isn't about that anymore. This is about doing the correct thing in the face of a bad turn of events. Our luck has gone sour. We're just trying to make amends."

"Making amends might just make us rich," Denham allowed, keeping his eyes closed. His voice was becoming mellower, and he seemed pleased with this turn of events.

"Food will be served in the mess room. If you're strong enough to walk to it, you're strong enough to join the shore party. But if you can't, then we'll have to leave you behind."

Denham nodded in the semi-gloom of the cabin. The rains continued to drum on the weather deck, but the rolling sound was lessening now.

"Ask old Lumpy to brew a pot of black coffee just for me. When I get enough coffee in my belly, I'll march from here to the opposite coast of Africa. We'll find Kong, and we'll bring him low. It's not the game I wanted to play, but it's interesting nonetheless. So let's be about this business, bad as it may be."

Leaving Denham to muster up his strength, Jack Driscoll went next to Ann Darrow's cabin. She had retreated to it when the rains commenced, and was waiting out the afternoon downpour.

"I don't know how to tell you this, Ann," Driscoll began.

"What is it?"

"We're not pulling anchor. Not yet. We're going back into the jungle. We're going to hunt down Kong and destroy him. Captain's orders."

"Oh, Jack! Must you?"

Driscoll nodded stolidly. "I was against it at first, but the Old Man persuaded me. We brought Kong to these shores, and now he's wreaking destruction such as Africa has never known. The further inland he goes, the more likely it is he'll encounter natives, not to mention white settlers. Their blood would be on our hands. Kong is not their problem. He's ours. We have to settle it the only way we know how."

Biting her trembling lip, Ann rushed into Jack Driscoll's arms and the two lovers embraced. Finally, Jack released her, took her chin in the cradle of his thumb and forefinger, saying in a reassuring voice, "It shouldn't take more than a day or so to track him. We'll pack enough ammunition to do the job right. Then we're rolling back to America. Rolling back to a bright future."

"Take care of yourself, Jack. We've gone through a lot. I can't lose you now. It would break my... heart."

Driscoll's lopsided grin was pasted on his face once more. "It would bust me up something terrible, too, Ann. Don't worry about it. We'll do the job right, and we won't lose a single sailor."

With that, he left the cabin. But once Jack Driscoll stepped onto the sloppy weather deck, his askew grin collapsed and a grimace took hold of his rangy features.

"I don't have a good feeling about the future," he said to himself. "But a man is a man and has to knock the days aside one at a time. If I can get through the next two days, maybe it'll be clear sailing after that."

His voice was firm, but it carried an undertone that lacked complete conviction.

Chapter 58

THE AFTERNOON downpour did not hinder Tarzan of the Apes in the slightest. He was accustomed to the long rains, which had punctuated his days as he foraged in the veldt miles back from the east African coast.

The ranch where the ape-man lived a semi-civilized existence was further inland, deep in the interior. There dwelled his wife, the former Jane Porter, his son, Jack—known as Korak the Killer—and the loyal tribe of Waziri natives, of which Tarzan was war chief.

Tarzan's first concern was that the monster gorilla would blunder in the direction of that ranch, but the ape-man was confident he could overcome the rampaging titan before that eventuality might transpire.

The bronzed giant's bare feet ate up great distances, as did the paws of Jad-bal-ja. Wise in the ways of the jungle, they did not overtax themselves by running or failing to pause for rest and refreshment. At intervals, they stopped to drink water out of a clear stream, and other times to eat.

Once, they spied a deer sitting under the trembling leaves of a shade tree. Since childhood, and the days when he first came into possession of his father's hunting knife, Tarzan was wont to steal up on the unwary Bara, plunging his knife into its throat, and feasting on the still warm flesh.

On this occasion, it was not necessary. Kneeling beside Jad-bal-ja, the ape-man instructed it quietly.

The golden lion advanced, great paws muddy in the steady rain.

Bara was not without resources, however. The deer smelled the lion, and its head began rotating about as its ears twitched nervously.

"Now!" hissed Tarzan urgently.

With a mighty spring, Jad-bal-ja leapt out of concealing brush and fell upon the deer, taking it by the throat and quickly breaking its neck.

It was over in a minute. The lion backed off, its mouth bloodied by its kill. But it had not feasted. Nor would it. Not until Tarzan gave Jad-bal-ja leave to do so.

Kneeling beside the slain deer, Tarzan employed his stout blade to cut out a section of haunch. This he threw into the lion's waiting jaws. The ape-man then cut a smaller portion for himself. The two of them feasted quietly, enjoying the animal's warm, succulent flesh.

Life at times is a cruel and bloody business. But this was the way of the jungle. This was the way of Tarzan of the Apes and all else who dwell in Tarzan's domain.

Of course, the great apes did not eat meat. Grubs and insects and fruit were their daily fare. But Tarzan had been born a human, even if he had been raised by anthropoids, and possessed a natural inclination toward the carnivorous.

Finally, their repast concluded, they washed themselves by standing in the rain and letting the vital juices run down their bodies, to disappear back into the soil, which was soaking up rainwater at a prodigious rate.

Stomach satiated, Tarzan signaled for Jad-bal-ja to continue their trek. Nkima hopped out of a branch that had appealed to him, and landed atop Tarzan's head. He squatted there as Tarzan moved forward.

In due course, the long rains slackened, then abated. Soon, the jungle became a different place.

Harsh abundant sunlight returned as the racing storm clouds

passed further inland. Steam arose mistily from the newly moistened surfaces. The tropical air once more became thick and hard to breathe. But it was good to inhale, being full of the myriad smells of life.

In this humid atmosphere, they plodded along, not as rapidly as before, for they did not wish to needlessly perspire their strength away.

Along the way, employing only the sharp blade of his hunting knife and what he could scavenge and cut down, Tarzan fashioned a strong hunting bow and made arrows, whose tips he whittled to sharp points. A length of string he produced from the folds of his loincloth, and this he used to string the weapon.

Satisfied with its pull, the jungle lord next cut down a suitable sapling, and, chipping away at a piece of quartz, made a war spear. So great was his woodcraft that the two weapons the ape-man seemingly conjured out of ordinary forest wood took on the aspect of formidable weapons once he took them in hand and continued on his way.

"Tarzan, killer of beasts, is going to war!" cried Nkima.

In time, the ape-man came within range of the Elephant's Graveyard. Noises—rustlings and clatterings and other low sounds—came from that direction. Hearing these, the jungle lord changed course.

He broke from the foliage into the clearing where the bones of dead pachyderms lay scattered and broken.

A group of grey elephants, numbering seven, were moving through the dry debris of their ancestors, repositioning the dead bones with their flexible trunks, and taking care not to further damage the remains clattering hollowly under their great padded feet.

Tarzan of the Apes spoke many languages, not the least of which was the tongue of the great apes. This in itself was fantastic. That elephants as a species possess a language of their own is not known to scientists in the modern world. But they do.

Approaching this group, Tarzan caught their attention. And so they turned their heavy heads, lifting their trunks in recognition of the Lord of the Jungle.

Going among them, the ape-man made low sounds that the elephants instantly understood. These were sounds of sympathy, as well as rumblings of anger.

Little Nkima asked, "What are the Tantors saying?"

Tarzan replied, "They are very angry. I have told them of the abomination of a gorilla who committed this desecration of their ancestors' remains."

"Do they wish revenge, Tarzan?"

The bronzed giant shook his head gravely. "Their grief is too great at the moment. But I will tell them of my quest for the great Bolgani. If I know Tantor, we will soon have company in our quest."

Nkima clapped his pink palms together in delight. He had no doubts but that Tarzan of the Apes would give the terrible Zu-jar-bolgani a fierce battle. But to have allies as formidable as seven elephants would help to equalize the odds. To one who did not know the prowess of Tarzan of the Apes, it would seem that the jungle lord was insufficiently supported to take on such a creature.

Tarzan took his time. He spoke to the pachyderms, stroking their trunks, giving their great wrinkled hides a smack of reassurance while he murmured sounds of sympathy they fully understood.

When the elephants were finished rearranging the bones of the dead, they stepped out of the Elephant's Graveyard and the largest, a scarred old bull, knelt down to allow Tarzan to leap upon his back.

The kneeling was not necessary, but it was an example of the fealty the tribe of Tantor owed the jungle lord, who had always been a friend of the elephants.

Rising to his muddy feet, the Tantor began plodding forward, the other elephants falling in line behind him, all but the lead bull taking hold of the thin tail of the one before him. In this fashion, they formed a formidable train.

Selecting a jungle path, they worked their way west while Jad-bal-ja kept a respectful guard in the rear, from time to time running ahead, scouting, while nimble Nkima hopped from the hindquarters of the lead elephant to the head of the second one in the living train.

Clinging to the wiry bristles that comprised the elephant's hair, enjoying a rare moment of pride as he rode his own elephant into unknown danger, Nkima remarked boastfully, "Great will be the giant Bolgani's terror when he beholds the army of Tarzan coming for him."

Tarzan turned and admonished him thusly.

"A battle is not decided until it is fought to its conclusion, little one," he said firmly. "Nor is it decided by talk. Only by action. Hold your tongue and save your energy for the long march ahead."

"Tarzan will win this battle," insisted Nkima, only slightly admonished.

"Why do you say that?" asked the ape-man.

"Nkima says this because Tarzan has won every battle he ever fought."

Touching the scar on his forehead, a relic of a life-or-death battle fought and won long ago, the bronzed giant said simply, "Tarzan has won every battle he has fought. But some victories came hard, and were not won without paying a price. The price can be very dear. Remember that, Nkima."

Nkima the monkey fell silent. He did not like the foreboding tone in his master's usually confident voice. Nkima had only known Tarzan to be victorious. But he had not known Tarzan as a youth, when his survival was in doubt. And although he knew the story of how the Tarmangani had defeated Kerchak, king of the main Mangani tribe, and recognized that the scar of battle upon the jungle lord's forehead was a relic of a subsequent encounter, Nkima did not ordinarily contemplate how very close Tarzan of the Apes had come to death that day long ago when he was a young man, naked and fighting Terkoz for his position as king of the former tribe of Kerchak.[*]

As the afternoon grew elongated shadows, little Nkima kept his tongue still.

---

[*] *Tarzan of the Apes*

Chapter 59

CARL DENHAM struggled to keep the pleased look off his face as he accompanied the shore party into the tangled jungle fringing the cove where the freighter *Wanderer* rode at anchor.

Fate is an incalculable thing, he considered. How many times on this luckless voyage had all hope been lost? How often had it seemed that his grand scheme had devolved into wrack and ruin?

And here he was again, tramping after Kong. Despite his repeated transgressions against shipboard discipline, he was trudging back into the jungle, armed with his camera and permission to use it at the appropriate time.

Ape tracks led them to the amphitheater, now deserted, and there Denham reclaimed his battered tripod and his sack of extra film canisters.

Arranging them about his person, the showman began to feel the first pangs of regret. Not regret that he had agreed to accompany this hunt, but that they had loaded him down with the rucksack containing the final surviving gas bombs, as well as other equipment deemed necessary to pursue their safari.

With the addition of the film canisters and the clumsy wooden tripod, the director felt more like a beast of burden than a hunter.

"I can't make up my mind whether I'm a burro, or maybe a mule now," he grumbled aloud.

"From where I stand, you're a common ass," Driscoll retorted without humor.

"I resent that!"

"Stow your complaints. You volunteered. You're the only one who's not a fighting man. Not that you won't fight when the time comes. I'll see to that. For now, you'll tote your load and like it!"

Denham said nothing. The rains had abated and the steam of evaporation was soaking him to the skin. His equipment, of course, would not absorb any of it, but it became coated with the film of evaporation. The unpleasantness of lugging pounds of extra equipment through muddy jungle soon wore on his normally buoyant spirits.

Penjaga had insisted upon coming along, but Driscoll gave her a flat no.

"It is a foul thing that you undertake," warned the old woman.

"I know that," said Driscoll helplessly. "But what can we do? We created this mess and now we have to clean it up. That's the law of the jungle, isn't it?"

"The law of the jungle is about survival, not slaughter."

Jack Driscoll had said nothing to that.

Then the old woman had reluctantly handed him the monkey's fist knot, intoning, "It brought me luck. It may bring you luck, as well."

Humoring the old woman, the Mate had tied the dangling cord to his belt. And that had been the end of it.

The relentless rain had washed away all but the deepest of Kong's tracks, but there were enough left for them to follow his trail.

Rainwater had filled many of them, and the wash of erosion had obliterated others.

"Looks like he's headed due west," Driscoll observed at one point.

"Makes sense to me," opined Jimmy. "He's probably lookin' for high ground."

Looking about, Driscoll scanned the horizon to the southwest. There off in the far distance, dazzling sunlight glanced off what looked like a glacier.

"There's a mountain yonder," said Driscoll thoughtfully. "You don't suppose…."

Catching his drift, Carl Denham bustled up as best he could. "That's Mount Kilimanjaro! The highest solitary peak in the whole wide world. Climbing it would take you four or five days, during which you'll go straight from the tropics to the Arctic. I think I know what you're thinking, Driscoll. It's not Skull Mountain; it's much higher. I'll bet my last dollar that Kong is making for the only high ground he can spy."

"Your last dollar has already been squandered," said the First Mate bitterly. "That peak has got to be more than a hundred miles inland."

"Kong is built for climbing more than he is for walking," mused Denham. "He may stand upright like a gorilla, but he's not always erect on his feet. He shambles along, stooped over, back bent over like a hunchbacked neanderthal caveman. That will slow him down. There's an old saying: 'Man stands alone because alone he stands.' If we keep moving, we'll overtake him. I'll bet you dollars to doughnuts."

"Let's hope you're right. The sooner we catch him, the sooner we head home. I've had enough of Africa."

Under his breath, Denham mumbled, "You and me both, brother."

Chapter 60

O F ALL who pursued the marauding Kong, To-yat and his bulls had a distinct advantage.

After Tarzan had scattered them, they had fled inland, their wild Dum-Dum ceremony disrupted.

But To-yat was a canny leader in his way. He knew that even in abject flight, there exist opportunities for victory.

"We will follow Go-pand-usen," he said without hesitation. "We will prostrate ourselves before him, and let the Black-thunder-god know that we are now his subjects."

"But Tarzan is Lord of the Jungle," reminded a long-necked bull named Ta-tag.

"Tarzan is a Tarmangani. And stands no taller beside Go-pand-usen than you do beside an Omtag. Since the advent of Go-pand-usen, the day of Tarzan of the Apes is no more. It has passed. There is a new jungle king, and he stands taller than a towering bottle tree. We must catch up with Go-pand-usen, and offer ourselves as his subjects."

This bull, perhaps wiser than most, said, "Tarzan has always been Lord of the Jungle. It is not wise to risk his wrath."

Hearing this first rumbling of disloyalty, To-yat bared his yellowing fangs and lunged in the direction of the hesitant bull.

"To-yat is king! To-yat is leader of this tribe! Go-pand-usen is the god of To-yat. Go-pand-usen is the god of all apes. There is none mightier, none taller, no one more powerful than Go-

343

pand-usen! If you are not prepared to kneel before the Black-thunder-god, To-yat challenges you to fight to the death."

Of course, the shrewd bull had not been interested in a fight, but he had been challenged.

"I am Ta-tag!" he screamed. "I do not want to follow Go-pand-usen. I do not want to follow To-yat anymore. I will follow Tarzan of the Apes!"

And with that, he let out a scream of defiance that was matched and then overmatched by To-yat.

The bulls charged one another, then fell into furious combat, rending with claws and fangs. Shaggy fur flew. Wounds created. Blood began to run, and in this battle, the disloyal bull lost an eye.

That was the end of him. Blind in one eye, he clapped both hands to his face, attempting to keep the injured orb in its socket. But the eye had come loose and was hanging by the thin motor muscles that were like stretched strings.

Having the advantage, To-yat fell upon Ta-tag and ripped his jugular free, along with a mouthful of pulsing flesh.

Ta-tag groaned, began gurgling and stomping in a circle, and finally keeled over to one side where he bled out his life into the wet grass upon which he fell.

Screaming the weird victory cry of the bull ape, To-yat cried out, "I am To-yat! I am the king of my tribe. I am a killer! I worship Go-pand-usen. All who worship Go-pand-usen follow To-yat!"

He turned and began to knuckle in the direction of the far west—and following behind him trailed the servile bulls and shes of the ape tribe, the latter clutching their squalling little balus to their hairy breasts.

Ta-tag finished bleeding to death where he fell. The tribe of To-yat was now united in their quest of Kong, whom they believed to be the god of their kind.

Nothing, not even the persuasive power of Tarzan of the Apes could dissuade them from that firm conviction. In that way, they were like many supposedly civilized Tarmangani, who, once they got a conception of the creator into their head, no amount of effort or force could dislodge it from their brains....

Chapter 61

THE ELEPHANT train of Tarzan of the Apes at last reached the savanna where the jungle petered out and endless grassland lay steaming in the sun.

Here, the veldt had been crushed by the enormous feet of the apelike animal, but it also had been flattened by the pounding rain. Now that the blazing sun was again uncovered, the greensward was springing back into its natural configuration and would soon wave sharp blades in the breeze.

The downpour had all but obliterated the muddy footprints of Kong, whose true name Tarzan did not yet know.

The ape-man surveyed the flat horizon. He sniffed the air, but the strong scent of his quarry had also been beaten down by the rain, virtually obliterated from the moist air.

There was no obvious direction in which the lumbering creature might have gone. He might even have doubled back. Tarzan did not believe so, but it was a possibility.

At a loss for something concrete to do, Tarzan stood up on the back of the lead elephant, cupped his hands to his mouth and gave forth the war cry of the bull ape, a long and horrible screech that would congeal the blood of any foe.

Hearing this, the elephants lifted their trunks and began trumpeting and blowing, adding to the rolling roar of defiance Tarzan was casting ahead of him in the presumed direction of his unseen quarry.

This challenge kept up for a dozen minutes, and when he was

done, the bronzed giant dropped back onto his rugged and wrinkled pachyderm seat to listen intently with ears sharpened by a lifetime of jungle craft.

There came an answering roar, low but thunderous. It rolled across the savanna and reached them, touching their skins with a threatening sound.

"Listen, Tarzan," squeaked Nkima. "Kree-gor pand—thunder roar!"

Tarzan nodded. The roar did rival thunder. If this were the gorilla-beast, he was miles and miles away, the jungle lord knew. But the intimidating volume of his roaring carried further than the roar of the lion, or the trumpeting of an elephant.

Beside him, Jad-bal-ja issued a growl that turned into a lifting roar, but that feral defy was not answered.

Against the deep-throated roar of the great terror gorilla, the challenge of the golden lion was akin to that of a cheetah cub against a full-grown panther.

Folding his ears back in recognition of that daunting fact, Jad-bal-ja turned his yellow-green eyes up at Tarzan of the Apes, and the bronzed giant met his questioning gaze frankly and without fear.

"He is mighty, this is true. But together we are mightier. For this is our jungle, and Tarzan of the Apes is master of it all." And once more the ape-man gave forth the war cry of the bull ape.

This time it was not answered.

Dropping back into his seat behind the elephant's broad skull, Tarzan urged his powerful train ahead.

"Tarzan is not afraid of the Bolgani monster," chattered Nkima.

"Nor is this beast afraid of Tarzan," reminded the ape-man. "Not yet. But soon."

Chapter 62

DEEP INTO the savanna grassland the bulls of To-yat knuckle-walked, led by the king killer ape himself.

The scent spoor of the black brute they called Go-pand-usen was pungent and unmistakable. There was nothing else in the jungle like it. But to To-yat, the stink of the beast-god was as flavorful in his pulsing nostrils as the juiciest grub or the most delicious green bamboo shoot.

To-yat had been king for many suns, and he was undisputed in his tribe. He had never yearned for anything more than a full belly, a convenient mate, many healthy balus, and the prowess that would enable him to remain king to the end of his days.

But having sighted the towering form of Go-pand-usen, To-yat became filled with a wholly unfamiliar emotion. He had no word for it, but had the ape folk possessed such a word, it would have been awe.

Go-pand-usen was an awesome being. His sheer stature, his intensely animal odor, and a vague sense To-yat comprehended that the thing was older than any creature he had ever before encountered, combined to fill him with a mixture of open-mouthed wonder and worshipful dread.

Deep in his simian brain, To-yat understood that here was a bull he could never defeat in battle. And that unfamiliar thought gave birth to a constellation of emotions that bordered on the religious.

If To-yat could not hope to best the giant gorilla in any

contest, he was determined to lay himself prostrate before the creature, thus ensuring his immediate future, as well as the survival of To-yat and his tribe.

To-yat also understood that such a creature as Go-pand-usen was destined to rule the jungle by dint of his stupendous size, if nothing else. The ape king wanted to be the first to swear fealty to Go-pand-usen. For in the future, possessing the gorilla god's favor could prove to be a powerful advantage in the endless war for survival that dominated the African jungle.

These were the thoughts that To-yat kept to himself as he followed the straightening grass imprints made by the formidable feet of Go-pand-usen. Again, To-yat wondered what manner of anthropoid this was. He walked upright like a man and did not go on all fours like the Bolganis he so greatly resembled—or even like the great apes whom Go-pand-usen generally resembled.

The long rains of afternoon came, and To-yat lashed and hectored his tiring bulls to continue. As the rains eventually dwindled to a trickle and the scorching sun returned, the tribe continued to plod along, seeking their towering deity.

"Go-pand-usen will welcome us," To-yat encouraged as their strength began to flag.

"If he does not eat us," grumbled one of the bulls.

Abruptly, To-yat turned, and snarled at the bull immediately behind him.

"Do not speak ill of the new Lord of the Jungle," he spat.

"It was a jest," muttered the abashed bull. But none of the tribe considered the remote possibility that the mighty beast ate the flesh of its own kind. The great apes did not eat flesh. Bolgani did not eat flesh. Yes, they would rend and tear flesh with their claws and fangs in combat, but they did not eat their conquests.

So it was to their horror, after hours of hunting, that To-yat and his apes discovered their sacred quarry tormenting a Duro, which was their word for hippopotamus.

How the hapless hippopotamus should come to fall into the mighty clutches of Go-pand-usen, they did not know, for they were not witness to the event.

What the tribe did behold, at a place where the savanna gave into a dense thicket of thorny brush, was the tremendous monster standing alone, holding a flailing hippopotamus in both hands and shaking it angrily.

With each titanic shake, the hippo gave out horrible noises, and the sounds of its ribs and bones grinding and crunching could be heard unmistakably.

It was a scene never imagined by the apes of To-yat. Most horrible of all was that, between vigorous shakings, Go-pand-usen would lift a haunch of the hippopotamus to its mouth, and take out a prodigious bite.

This meal he chewed noisily, blood rilling down his slavering jaws.

A cold feeling settled into the pits of the stomachs of the ape bulls. They had already processed a rude conception of the power of their gorilla god, but this was something else. Something terrible. Something that seemed to defy the laws of nature as they understood them.

That Go-pand-usen reared up so tall was scarcely believable, but there he stood. There was no denying his gargantuan stature. But to see him eat flesh, and the flesh of one of the most powerful and formidable creatures of the Dark Continent, staggered them.

Stopping dead in their tracks, the tribe of To-yat sat down to watch while the trembling females cradled their balus and the bulls stared with dazed eyes and gaping jaws.

Showing that he was enjoying the fatty flesh of the bellowing Duro, the monstrous gorilla wrenched off a rear leg and, holding it in the opposite paw, gnawed the meat off the bone. Dropping the redly raw remnant, he turned his appetite back to the floundering animal, stripping the remaining meat off the ribs where his massive teeth could take hold. These morsels he devoured. Then, with a smacking of his rubbery lips betokening relish, he flung the half-living carcass away.

Having done so, Go-pand-usen stretched out his hairy arms and began beating his massive chest vigorously.

Impelled by a shared instinct, To-yat raised his arms, stood up on his hind legs and commenced beating his own shaggy chest. His bulls followed suit, and they gave forth fierce roars.

Hearing these calls, the gorilla god turned, grunted, and its huge eyes fell upon them.

A warning roar was issued. The hot stink of it rolled across the savanna and made their fur tremble.

"I am To-yat!" screamed the killer ape. "To-yat of the tribe of To-yat. I come to honor you, greatest of all Bolganis, god of all apes."

If the king ape expected speech in kind, he was bitterly disappointed. Another roar came—this one sharp and menacing.

To his fellow apes, To-yat barked, "Get down. Bow before Go-pand-usen. Show that you worship him."

The apes of To-yat, including the females, got down on all fours, and lowered their shaggy heads in abject supplication, their brutish foreheads touching the sward at intervals.

The earth shook and their eyes lifted upward in fear. They beheld the monster approaching. He walked on his hind legs, arms swinging, crinkling eyes fixed upon them.

"He has heard us!" proclaimed To-yat. "Mighty Go-pand-usen understands us!"

Another angry sound leapt from the monster's fanged maw of a mouth, and its smell was overpowering, mixed as it was with the raw flesh of hippopotamus.

"We are your subjects, great one!" To-yat yelled.

Instead of any welcoming reply, the creature swept out an arm, collected the carcass of the disposed hippopotamus, and angrily flung it in their direction.

The apes of To-yat scattered, the shes clutching their balus, and for a few moments, it was every ape for himself.

The hippopotamus corpse landed hard, with a terrible thud that broke its spine. But the creature knew not of that. For it was already dead.

Seeing this juggernaut of hair and muscle striding toward him, To-yat's confidence shattered.

"Flee! Flee!" he screamed. "Go-pand-usen will eat us. Flee or be devoured. Flee! Flee!"

So the tribe of To-yat ran for the only shelter available—the patch of forest that lay nearby. They had to circle around the frightful monster to do so, but this proved to confuse the hulking creature. Faced with individual apes scattering around it, the grunting brute could not focus on any one prey, and so instead feinted in one direction, missed capturing one great ape, then doubled around to lunge for another.

By luck or skill conferred upon wild animals by fear of death, To-yat just managed to reach the jungle's edge, and disappeared into the trees, screaming and howling and pleading for their lives.

"Kagoda! Kagoda!" he howled, using the universal ape cry meaning, "I surrender!"

Chapter 63

TARZAN OF THE APES moved through the lush savanna grasses on the trail of Zu-jar-bolgani. He swayed gracefully on his rolling grey mount, confident in his mission, and serenely patient in the achieving of it. For the ape-man had never failed in any important undertaking.

There are no clocks in the jungle, and time was told by positions of the moon and the sun and, more elaborately, by the stars.

Tarzan came upon the rotting carcass of a hippopotamus and saw in its wretched condition unmistakable signs that his gigantic quarry had passed this way not long ago.

Other signs had been encountered along the trail, as well—indications that a tribe of great apes had also traveled in this direction. These could only be the bulls of To-yat, reasoned Tarzan.

Observing the hippopotamus carcass, Tarzan was again reminded of the tremendous power of his foe, whom he had yet to behold clearly. The Duro had been mangled in the most cruel manner imaginable. The raw bones of one leg lay at a short distance where they had been carelessly flung. More terrible still, portions of the animal's bulbous body were missing entirely, and red voids in his fat haunches told of titanic bites taken from the hippo while still living.

Perched on the tawny back of Jad-bal-ja, Nkima studied the demolished hippopotamus corpse with wise-looking eyes. Flies were buzzing about the remains in great abundance, and it was this dark cloud that had in truth caused the bronzed giant to move in this direction.

"See what Zu-jar-bolgani has done to that Duro?" Nkima asked, pointing with a thin finger.

"Tarzan sees and understands," acknowledged the ape-man somberly.

"Is Tarzan yet afraid of Zu-jar-bolgani?" pressed the little monkey.

"When Tarzan knows fear," he replied, "Nkima will see it with his own eyes. Not before."

Satisfied with that answer, Nkima fell silent. But as the train of pachyderms resumed their stately trek, he peered behind him and watched the flies crawling along the carcass, consuming the wreck that had been a full-grown hippopotamus. The sight of the destroyed animal made him tremble in every limb. He would not admit it to anyone, but Nkima was very, very afraid.

A trampling of grass in all directions told Tarzan that some form of confrontation transpired here, where the savanna devolved into the jungle, but no blood, no carcasses—not even bits of hair or flesh to tell that fighting had erupted—was in evidence. This was the spot where the giant anthropoid had stampeded the tribe of To-yat, but the ape-man did not know that.

Tarzan pushed into the jungle, his rolling elephants falling behind in single file. Jad-bal-ja ranged ahead, sniffing vigorously, eager to hunt.

The ape-man sniffed the air as well, and the odors that were coming to his sensitive nostrils were unpleasant in the extreme.

"I smell the giant Bolgani," he said at last.

Nkima said nothing. His trembling pulsed anew.

It was late in the afternoon, and the forest was suffused with a brilliant golden light. Yet the jungle was very still, exceedingly quiet. It was as if Death itself was abroad.

To himself, Tarzan thought that Death had indeed passed

this way. But not death in its myriad manifestations of African life. This was not how the forest usually sounded as the day moved into its final hours. This was different—hushed, eerie, pregnant with a pent-up fear. It was as if the jungle had ceased to breathe.

Every sense alert, the bronzed giant clutched his weapons and studied the golden vista before him. Ahead, the trail dipped into a stony declivity, and the sounds that would normally ricochet between the trees were blocked by cracked granite outcroppings.

Moving down a worn jungle trail, elephants stepping carefully to avoid gnarled surface roots and fallen jungle vines, the pachyderm train prepared to descend into the sun-infused depression.

Tarzan's eyes were scanning the trees, for they should have been full of birds and climbing monkeys, but they were barren of all life—except drowsing insects. The hum and drone of the latter seemed hushed, but that might have been mere imagination creating that uneasy impression.

It was rare when Tarzan of the Apes was caught by surprise in his own element. He could smell a lion crouched in a thicket, preparing to spring. A panther in a high tree limb emits a telltale warning growl before he springs. Even a poisonous viper will rustle vegetation as it moves otherwise silently in for the kill.

The wary ape-man was studying the high jungle terraces ahead, thinking that he might stand up and take to them, in order to achieve a better vantage point, when suddenly something massive shoved up in his path, blocking the way.

The creature appeared with such startling silence that when Tarzan's grey eyes fell upon it, astonishment caused them to widen sharply. It seemed to take a fraction of a second longer to absorb the overwhelming vision before the ape-man reacted.

This was Zu-jar-bolgani, whom the apes of To-yat called Go-pand-usen. His huge leathery hands seized an outcropping on either side of the jungle declivity entrance, as if to bar the way. His mouth hung open, and the fangs that shone within them were prodigious.

Tarzan knew of the saber-tooth tiger of prehistoric times. He had encountered one, once, in a faraway land.* Only the canines of the saber-tooth rivaled those of this monster gorilla that looked at him with oversized orbs that were filled with the blaze of sunset. They seemed to smolder.

The enormous face was black and fierce, its lines gorilla-like, yet also different in uncountable ways. The beast's expression was almost *human,* but in a primitive way. Strangest of all, a livid battle scar gouged one hairy cheek, and it reminded the ape-man of a similar scar creasing his own brow—a souvenir of the day the great ape named Terkoz had laid open Tarzan's scalp.

Frowning eyes took in the sight of the bronze-skinned figure atop his lead elephant, and a growl rolled out that was threatening without possessing alarming volume. The huge black ape seemed to bristle all over, in the manner of a grotesque porcupine. Yet the eyes were not those of an ape, deeply dark and without feature. The irises were an expressive amber. They were human.

Tarzan raised one commanding arm and proclaimed in the Mangani tongue, "Hold! I am Tarzan of the Apes, protector of this jungle. Who are you to despoil it with impunity?"

Hearing this bold challenge, the giant gorilla seemed for a moment taken aback.

Then, seeming to expand in stature, he gathered himself up and lunged forward, moving with a surprising alacrity.

Tarzan had no choice but to take to the trees. The ape-man leapt upward, capturing a limb with both preternaturally strong hands, and propelled himself in a somersault into a higher bough.

The speed with which Tarzan executed this jungle maneuver

---

* *Tarzan at the Earth's Core*

was awe-inspiring. It may be that it happened so fast that the gorilla-beast failed to perceive what had transpired.

Snarling, the apish ogre fell upon the lead elephant, who began trumpeting and screaming as it was lifted high, then higher over the head of the huge ape-thing. There it hung suspended, trapped in crushing hands, flailing and screaming and trying to bring its formidable tusks to bear. All to no avail.

With a tremendous muscular exertion, Zu-jar-bolgani flung the screaming elephant at its fellows, striking one down, smashing it to death, and sending the others scattering back.

With a ferocious roar, the golden lion sprang for the tremendous antagonist. Zu-jar-bolgani showed no fear. But Nkima did. He jumped free of the lion's golden pelt, seeking refuge in a nearby fan palm. Into this leafy refuge he scampered, shaking in every limb.

It was Jad-bal-ja, braver than he was wise, who did not hesitate.

High on his perch, Tarzan beheld the loyal lion, curved fangs bared, racing for the right calf of the titanic animal.

Calling down, he commanded, "Halt, Jad-bal-ja. Do not fight. Flee—save yourself!"

For the Lord of the Jungle knew that if his faithful companion fell into the clutches of Zu-jar-bolgani, he would be torn apart in seconds. Obediently, the magnificent lion broke off from his charge, then plunged into a thorny thicket, where the great anthropoid could not easily follow.

The imposing animal swiped out a hirsute paw, inserted it into the quivering thorn bush, and gave out a short, sharp exclamation of pain.

Withdrawing his hand, he saw that it was quilled with tiny thorns. These he attempted to remove with fingers too big and blunt for the task. Frustrated, he began sucking at them and spitting out the tiny tormentors.

Tarzan wore slung across his back a hide quiver of feather-fletched arrows, and he unlimbered his bow.

Aiming for the center of the brute's leathery barrel of a chest, the ape-man sent one missile flying. It struck, penetrated, but not very deeply.

Making quizzical sounds, the creature looked down, saw the feather-tufted shaft protruding, and his eyes narrowed in annoyance. Plucking at it, the beast dislodged the thorny annoyance, and lifted the sharp end to his broad nostrils.

Smelling his own blood, the bull vented a snarl of anger and flung away the offending thing. He was otherwise unfazed by the arrow.

Tarzan was not surprised. The jungle lord had half-expected his arrow to have little effect. For the first shaft had been merely a test of the brute's resolve.

Methodically, he began stringing fresh arrows, loosing them at his antagonist in a steady fusillade.

The first two were batted aside by a massive paw. A third, aimed at the vulnerable tissues of the monster mouth, splintered harmlessly against an age-yellowed fang.

The bronzed giant redoubled his efforts, swiftly emptying his quiver, knowing that those long, swinging arms could not keep up the pace of combat.

Quickly, one of Zu-jar-bolgani's blocking arms bristled with missiles. They resembled mere quills. Some, the ape-man had dipped in the venom of a viper he had encountered along the way.

Grunting in pained surprise, the animal brought up his opposite paw. Blunt, broken-nailed fingers encountered the stinging things sticking up from his fur. He began twisting them out and flinging them away, at the same time smacking his forearm to staunch fresh blood.

Observing this without outward concern, Tarzan saw that his arrows had so little effect that they were but a useless gesture. Not even the deadly viper venom was potent enough to bring the alien gorilla low. He dropped his bow to the ground, having no further use for it.

On his left thigh slapped the sheath holding his father's hunting knife. Its foot-long steel blade was formidable. The ape-man considered springing to the shoulder of the great beast, and plunging it into its throbbing jugular vein.

It might have worked, that plan, but not before those terrible black hands would surely seize him and, once they did, even the jungle lord would have been crushed to a bloody pulp in a matter of seconds.

The old scar on his forehead pulsed redly as Tarzan of the Apes considered this line of attack. He might, in the end, bring down the creature, spilling its life's blood upon the declivity floor, but his own blood would also be shed in kind.

At this moment, Tarzan was not prepared to throw away his life to defeat the interloper—although great was his desire to do so. For the presence of this bristling black behemoth in the sprawling jungle the ape-man called home was an insult to the forest and an affront to his rule as rightful Lord of the Jungle.

When Zu-jar-bolgani finally plucked free the last irritating shaft and flung it away, snapping eyes sought his tormentor. They fell upon the ape-man, standing unafraid on a high supporting bough.

Reaching down, the long-armed giant grabbed a length of desiccated tree trunk, and flung it in Tarzan's direction.

The ape-man leapt clear, well ahead of the crushing obstacle, and landed upright in an adjoining camphor wood tree. From that vantage point, he watched the beast's behavior.

It was not exactly a gorilla, he could see. Zu-jar-bolgani bore a general resemblance to one. But it was not a Bolgani. Bolganis go about on all fours, and not upright. This thing carried himself like a man—albeit like one who was not entirely accustomed to walking upright. He was stooped and shambling in his gait.

The hair of the thing was deeply black, but it was shot here and there with iron-grey threads, suggesting that it was not young but old. The myriad wrinkles of his ebony face appeared somehow ancient, even primordial.

And in that face, there were signs of intelligence that seemed more than ape, even if it was less than human.

This creature, Tarzan knew, was something that was not known to the learned scientists who study evolution. It was too tall for the family of man, just as it was too massive to belong to any of the anthropoid species known in the Twentieth Century.

Tarzan had little time to study the beast, for it soon found him with its searching eyes. Making fierce noises, it charged toward the tree whose leafy branches held the ape-man above the brute's gargantuan reach.

The bronzed giant was confident that the ape-thing would not climb the tree, for lesser apes were commonly arboreal, and this animal appeared to be a new and unknown species of greater ape. In that surmise, he was only partially correct.

Reaching up, the angry ogre grabbed hold of lower branches and attempted to scale the tree trunk, but its weight was prodigious. Those branches snapped and broke. Soon, there were no more boughs low enough for it to reach.

As Tarzan looked down, sun-bronzed face impassive, the giant stared up and howled his frustration. Making mallets with its fists, he beat upon his leathery chest. And Tarzan in turn beat upon his, giving forth the long, screaming war cry of the bull ape.

The two hurled their challenges, haranguing one another, neither opponent retreating or giving cause to believe that the other feared open combat.

Then, compelled by a mixture of rage and frustration, Zu-jar-bolgani turned his hirsute fists against the trunk of Tarzan's sheltering tree.

These blows were powerful, and the tree trunk shook in shock. Tarzan was forced to grab at nearby branches to avoid being flung clear. There, he crouched like a lithe bronze-skinned man-ape.

His thought was to hold on until the beast's rage had expended itself, but to the ape-man's amazement, the fists continued to pound like pistons, bashing rough bark loose, smashing the trunk fibers into pulp and threatening to uproot it by the unstoppable locomotive force unleashed in its driving arms.

From a nearby fan palm came a shrill scream, "Tarzan, jump! He will eat you! He eats animals. He will eat you as well!" Nkima again.

Once more, Tarzan considered dropping onto the creature's hairy head, and bringing his hunting knife to bear, but the prospects of success—not to mention survival—were not sufficiently reassuring.

Abruptly, the ape-man moved along a springy branch, and soared into space, clearing a great distance and landing safely in an adjoining tree.

Not immediately did Zu-jar-bolgani realize that his hairless foe had eluded him. He continued to pound until finally the great camphor tree toppled with a crackling of breaking wood and uprooted roots.

This was an astonishing sight. The tree had stood for hundreds of years on that spot, growing stronger and more firmly rooted with each passing season.

Now it was a splintery ruin. Once a mighty inhabitant of this primeval forest, it had been defeated by an alien invader, a monster of unrivaled and unimaginable power.

Despite himself, Tarzan of the Apes felt the hackles at the back of his black-haired head lift in near-superstitious awe.

Stepping back, the gorilla-like beast once more beat his chest as if in triumph, but this outburst was short-lived. Tarzan gave out another blood-freezing scream, and the black head turned. Questing eyes found him and the slope-browed creature lurched about, moving in his direction.

Tarzan did not wait for what he knew would come next. Flashing from branch to branch, he picked his way down toward the lower limbs, and dropped onto the back of an elephant that was backing away in horror at the sight of the raging fury loose in his serene forest realm.

Returning to his resolute mount, Tarzan led the surviving elephants out of the jungle path, and back into the open savanna, with faithful Jad-bal-ja and Nkima following, each in their own fashion.

"Do we flee, Tarzan?" squeaked Nkima.

The ape-man did not answer. Perhaps he had no immediate reply.

The lead elephant stepped out of the jungle at a brisk trot and the sounds emitted by his upraised trunk manifested as a noisy cacophony that smote the eardrums like a scolding punishment.

Reaching open grass, Tarzan turned about and beheld the creature shouldering through the jungle. Trees trembled and the sounds of snapping branches told of the destruction he was wreaking in his wake.

Finally, Tarzan gave the command to halt. Under his firm instruction, the pachyderms obediently assembled into a semicircle, magnificent curved tusks forming a formidable defense. At one end of the elephantine bulwark, Jad-bal-ja took up a crouching position, yellow-green orbs defiant in his masklike face.

Nkima found a perch on the lofty back of one elephant, after deciding that he could not trust the golden lion not to leap directly onto the path of danger.

There they waited, silently resolute, while the great stoop-shouldered gorilla blundered about the jungle until, at last, he stepped into view, simian features twisted in blind rage.

Beholding the array of be-tusked elephants with the hairless human seated atop the center pachyderm, the beast-god snarled his defiance and it seemed as if the entire jungle shook and even the bright blue sky trembled in echoing response.

Grey eyes unafraid, Tarzan of the Apes awaited his approach.

The open greensward offered no place in which to hide, but

ample room to maneuver abounded, as well as allowing for a clear path of retreat. Not that the indomitable ape-man harbored any such thoughts. His noble features were as resolute as a statue of a Caesar cast in bronze.

They did not flinch as the squeaking voice of Nkima warned, "Kreegah!"

Chapter 64

L IKE SOME barbaric Hannibal, Tarzan of the Apes stood balanced on the back of his lead elephant, and watched the primeval gorilla-thing push his way out of the forest.

There was something about the shambling creature that, even after being seen close up, evoked a tremendous feeling in the observer when it reappeared. It was as though the sheer incomprehensibility of its size and stature struck a fresh chord of awe each time one's eyes fell upon it.

Beneath his bare feet, the Tantor of Tarzan stood fixed and unmovable as a boulder. But deep inside, it trembled. That quaking communicated itself to the ape-man, who understood it, even if he disapproved of fear in a loyal animal. Here, however, it was understandable.

From his perch of safety on the next elephant, Nkima chattered, "Tarzan! He is coming this way. The monster is coming for us. Gom—run!"

Tarzan nodded. Fear was not a thing unknown to him, but neither was it a friend. He thought of his home, hundreds of miles inland, of his wife Jane and his son, Jack. And his faithful Waziri warriors. Although he did not at the moment taste fear in his mouth, Tarzan deeply wished they were at his side, for he understood that in this gargantuan anthropoid he now faced was something the like of which was beyond his ken.

What this prehistoric ape was seemed less important than what it represented. An uprooting and overthrowing of the daily routine of the jungle. That that routine included sudden death and merciless predators that devoured other creatures was not a mark against it in Tarzan's mind. He was fully a part of the warp and weft that comprised the vibrant jungle web. He participated in it, just as did Numa the lion, or any other animal who ate the flesh of others to live.

As Tarzan watched the Cyclopean creature force aside groaning tree trunks in an effort to push free of the encroaching jungle, he considered how best to stand up to the brute.

To charge the behemoth seemed the obvious course of action. It might be that the broad heads of the pachyderms could be directed as battering rams, and their penetrating tusks employed to hamstring him.

Zu-jar-bolgani might be toppled if this plan was executed swiftly and without mercy, just as towering trees are felled by tiny men wielding sharp axes. But having brought the creature down, could he be vanquished once on the ground?

That was the question in the ape-man's mind. And it was destined to remain unresolved.

For out of another portion of the jungle came a shrill screaming and yelling—harsh words couched in the rude barks and grunts of the ape folk.

Tarzan's head snapped about. High in the trees he spied shaggy To-yat and a group of his bulls. They were pointing and gesticulating toward the ape-monster, and their fear-struck words reached his ears.

"Tarzan! Turn back! This creature is no god in the form of a gorilla. It is a devil. A devil from a far land. It does not belong here. It eats whatever it wishes to eat. It eats flesh. It is no ape. For no true ape consumes flesh!"

That Tarzan of the Apes ate animal flesh appeared beside the point. To-yat had worked himself into a lather. His illusions had been shattered by his encounter with the creature he had called Go-pand-usen, and now the king ape had turned against the very idol he sought to worship.

"Tarzan is the true Lord of the Jungle!" To-yat continued screaming. "Without Tarzan, there is no order in the jungle. Turn back, Tarmangani! Death and danger follow in the foot-prints of this devil who should not even exist."

The bronzed giant called out calmly, "Tarzan is not afraid."

"To-yat is afraid. His bulls are terrified. We have seen this demon eat a living Duro. Nothing can stand before him. Turn back before it is too late."

Tarzan heard these words without a flicker passing over his noble features. His attention turned back to the approaching giant. As the lumbering thing wrestled its way through a thicket of trees, an idea formed in the ape-man's intelligent brain.

Turning to Jad-bal-ja, he instructed, "Remain here." Then he ordered his Tantors to attack.

Unhesitatingly, they charged. The thunder of their tough foot-pads shook the grasslands, and they moved with one mind toward their foe.

Zu-jar-bolgani pushed his head through the treetops, his blinking eyes fixating upon the approaching herd. The earth started shaking. The maw of the monster yawned, and it threw back a roar that shook the trees. It was as if the entire world shook before the converging forces.

With a mighty twist of his mammoth shoulders, Zu-jar-bolgani attempted to burst through the woods, but he moved too slowly.

Impelled by a single command, the elephants of Tarzan drove their battering-ram skulls into the trees that yet blocked the struggling brute. Massive trunks and palm-tree boles splintered and split, and they toppled backward to strike the creature at its head and shoulders, stunning his arms, and causing him to stumble backward.

It was a magnificent stroke of generalship—all the more impressive because it had been executed without a single word uttered in English. The manner in which Tarzan communicated with his elephants passed the understanding of ordinary human beings.

But the power and prowess of the jungle lord became evident as the elephants battered away, pushing back trees which, in falling, became great clubs against which the surprised monster could only struggle and flounder.

The apish thing stumbled backward, turned, and seemed to be gathering itself for a countercharge. His leathery features twisted into a simian scowl of rage.

Amidst the struggle, a storm front rolled in. Suddenly, the air was full of thunder and lightning. Swiftly, the inevitable rains came. These were not the afternoon rains that arrived with the precision of a clock, but a freak thunderstorm. Fast moving, and rapidly passing.

During its skyward march, the procession of thunderheads dumped an enormous amount of rainwater upon all the combatants.

As the elephants fought on, oblivious to the growing downpour, the struggling beast-god, who had suffered through the afternoon rains and was made miserable by it, began howling and growling, not in defiance but in a kind of pitiful frustration.

A thunderous rain drenched him, turning the ground around his feet into warm mud. As he struggled against the very forest that seemed to be fighting him, the bristling ogre lost his footing, stumbled backward and landed in a mudhole that had not been there five minutes before.

There, he became stuck. He floundered about. His cries were angry, yet also pitiful.

Hearing them, Tarzan ordered his elephants to halt. Carefully, they backed away.

Patiently, the bronzed giant watched as the ape-thing struggled in the mud, the relentless rain pelting it. And the sounds coming from the anthropoid stirred something in him that was neither awe nor righteous rage.

These were the cries of a lost and orphan ape—a creature that had found itself arrayed against elemental forces it could not understand or defeat.

Loosening his hunting knife from its scabbard, Tarzan dropped to the grass and advanced cautiously.

Here was the opportunity the ape-man had been awaiting. Creeping ahead, he picked his way through the splintered ruin of toppled trees. Carefully, he insinuated himself into the jungle fringe.

Zu-jar-bolgani lay on his back, his mighty strength spent. He panted raggedly, like a grotesque dog. The effects of his long hunger voyage had finally caught up with him. His scarred arms lifted, then fell, splashing mud. Every iota of his power was low.

He did not see Tarzan approach, for he had insufficient strength to raise his massive head. But pulsing nostrils captured the strange scent of the ape-man. One black-bristled arm flailed blindly, impotently, accomplishing nothing.

Grasping his knife by its worn handle of horn, Tarzan slipped around the prostrate giant, creeping toward the head and the jugular vein, which, although thick as a liana vine, would, if mercilessly severed, doom the monstrosity.

From high tree limbs that were dripping with water, To-yat yelled angry defiance. "Bundolo, Tarzan! Slay him now. Slay him while he is down. He does not deserve to live. He claimed your jungle throne, and now you must drink his blood."

But these words fell upon deaf ears.

Listening to the sounds of utter bafflement emanating from the panting mouth of Zu-jar-bolgani, seeing it struggle for air, and noticing the ancient and terrible scars on its chest and arms, some of which resembled the healed wounds crisscrossing his own muscular physique, and a few showing vestiges of catgut stitching that had popped loose, a strange change came over the ape-man's sun-bronzed countenance.

His traveling gaze fell upon the livid scar on the simian creature's right cheek, so much like the one marring the masculine perfection of Tarzan's brow, but larger and more complex, and came to rest there. A flicker of recognition troubled the bronzed giant's resolute expression. Only a foe as stupendously powerful as this black-faced beast could have inflicted such a scar. Zu-jar-bolgani had fought many deadly battles in his long life, the jungle lord realized, and had survived until this very day, unconquered.

Feeling a sudden sense of kinship, Tarzan of the Apes put a question to the helpless creature.

"Kagoda?" he demanded.

When expressed as a question, the word was universal among the apes of Africa, translating from their rude tongue to, "Do you surrender?"

Knife in hand, unheeding of the pelting rain, Tarzan waited patiently.

Struggling for breath, Zu-jar-bolgani forced halting sounds out of his lungs.

Tarzan never knew if the monster was actually responding in kind, or merely mimicking his animalistic speech as would a lowly monkey. But the syllables were unmistakable.

"*KAAA... god... a....*" I surrender.

Face firm, Tarzan holstered his blade and turned to go, saying, "I give you your life, brave Zu-jar-bolgani."

Returning to the savanna, the ape-man urged his elephants to back up. Obediently, they retreated to the open grassland, where they once again arrayed themselves in a semi-circle, this time subject to the storm, but unbowed by it.

Swiftly, the thunderclouds passed, and the skies cleared again. Not far in the jungle, the groaning beast-god pulled himself to his feet, and shook his entire body like a dog throwing off great sprays of muddy water, soaking To-yat and his bulls, who watched in horror.

Without a sound other that the crunching of splintering wood under his weighty feet, the prehistoric gorilla disappeared into the forest, his appetite for battle quenched by the elemental storm.

He did not look back at Tarzan of the Apes, who had spared his life.

Chapter 65

A S HE LISTENED to the tremendous creature disappear into the fastness of the interior forest, Tarzan of the Apes considered all that he had seen and heard.

The red scar on his forehead, which had been livid, began to fade. The ire of the ape-man was abating. The springy tenseness of his lithe muscles softened, and one knowing Tarzan would realize and understand that the Lord of the Jungle had come to a momentous decision.

Beholding this transformation, Nkima asked, "Will Tarzan track the terrible Bolgani into this forest?"

The ape-man was slow to reply.

"I have fought many battles against many foes," he intoned. "Some were terrific fighters. Others were cowards. Here, Tarzan has encountered a foe who cannot easily be bested."

Nkima squeaked in disbelief, "Tarzan gives up?"

The bronzed giant shook his head somberly. There was a chill light in his grey eyes.

"Tarzan never gives up. Let no one think otherwise."

Without a word, the ape-man turned on his heel, and led his elephants across the vast grassland back to the jungle that belonged to him, and only him.

Jad-bal-ja followed carefully, pausing often to look backward and bare his fangs in the direction of the jungle patch where the sounds of the great lumbering marauder could still be heard, turning trees and their branches into kindling with every step.

Nkima sprang from the back of an elephant, onto Tarzan's shoulder and hung on with tiny paws, as was his custom.

"Tarzan is thinking," observed the little monkey.

"Tarzan is always thinking. That is what separates Tarzan from the lower beasts, who do not always think, but behave according to their instincts."

"Their instincts keep them alive," reminded Nkima.

"Sometimes they do," allowed Tarzan. "But other times not. The brain of a warrior is powerful and useful where muscles and instincts are not."

"Nkima thinks often."

Tarzan smiled thinly, saying, "Nkima often thinks of his next meal and his safety. But not very far beyond that."

The monkey did not deny this, but said instead, "Nkima does not know what Tarzan is thinking."

"A canny warrior and hunter keeps his thoughts to himself—unless it is necessary for these thoughts to be shared."

"Tarzan will not tell little Nkima, who is his trusted friend, of his plans?"

"Nkima will know of Tarzan's plan soon enough. Mark the word of Tarzan. He does not give up. Nor does he flee from a foe."

Nkima chattered into Tarzan's ear, "But Tarzan is fleeing from the great foe called Zu-jar-bolgani."

"Appearances are often deceptive, little one."

"You are not fleeing?"

"No. Neither is Tarzan retreating. Tarzan is moving with firm purpose toward a new objective."

"But is not Zu-jar-bolgani a foe more terrible than any?"

"Zu-jar-bolgani is more terrible than any man or beast Tarzan has ever encountered, it is true. Whether he is truly a foe, is an open question."

"He desecrates Tarzan's jungle. You cannot forgive him for that."

"Whenever there is trouble in the jungle," the bronzed giant said carefully, "invariably there is someone to cause it. Do you understand, little one?"

"Yes, yes. For Nkima has a brain, which he uses to think with. You are not blaming Zu-jar-bolgani. You are blaming the Tarmangani who brought him to your jungle."

"This is so," replied Tarzan.

"But those awful men are gone by now—sailed away in their iron vessel."

Tarzan said nothing. He moved through the vast grassland with a silent purpose, and the elephants and the golden lion that were obedient to him, kept pace with the ape-man every sure-footed step of the way.

The sun was falling from the sky, disappearing behind their backs. The warm rays set fire to the fringe of jungle ahead of them.

Night was coming on. And with it, all the inherent dangers of darkness.

But as the undisputed Lord of the Jungle strode toward the nocturnal woods, he seemed to give no outward care to either the darkness or the dangers surely gathering about him.

Chapter 66

JACK DRISCOLL led his search party through the jungle as night began to creep in.

Shadows began clotting the leafy spaces between the trees and the branches overhead of the jungle canopy, and the world slowly turned from green and brown to dull grey.

It was a different jungle they tramped through than on the night before. Before Kong had torn through the jungle like a demonic tornado summoned by an African witch doctor, scattering the very beasts and creatures.

Now that Kong had moved on, normalcy was returning to the jungle. Normalcy, and the predators who made it their business to prowl nocturnally.

Driscoll was saying, "We may have to make camp soon. We'll need a fire to keep these creatures at bay."

To which Carl Denham replied, "We'll never catch up with Kong if we keep stopping."

"Ever seen what a lion can do to a human being?"

"No," admitted the showman. "But I once had a cameraman who agreed to film a charging rhinoceros for me. I held a rifle, and I told him I would blast the rhino before it got too close. I don't think he believed me. When the rhino charged him, the fool dropped the camera and ran for his life."

"How close did the rhino get before that happened?" wondered Driscoll.

"Oh, I don't know," Denham said airily. "Maybe a couple of dozen feet."

Driscoll grunted. "I would've done the same thing. Dropped the camera and run for my life."

"Well, he ruined a wonderful shot, and that was when I stopped using cameramen. Half of them are yellow."

This conversation took place as they were on the move. Jack Driscoll hadn't turned his head around once, but now he did. He looked at Denham's sweaty face in the dying light.

"When those apes charged up at you, and you were staring at them through the camera lens, what was going through your mind?"

Denham grinned. "What a swell shot I was getting."

"And when were you planning to stop filming and save yourself?"

"Aw, I was going to get around to it."

"So you say," the First Mate spat back harshly. "You were so caught up in what you were doing, you almost threw your life away."

"But it worked out, didn't it? Things have a way of working out."

"On that little adventure, sure," admitted Driscoll. "But now, after all we've been through, here we are hunting Kong again. And this time we're aiming to kill him. That's not working out for anyone."

Carl Denham said nothing to that. He had no good answer. The party fell quiet. No one had much energy for speech. They had been marching through hot jungle for hours, following the trail of Kong and wishing that they could catch up with him and get it all over with, but secretly also hoping they never found the fearsome beast-god of Skull Island.

Finally, by a swollen and muddy river that wound its way through the jungle, they pitched camp. They had to scrounge for the makings, since they were traveling light. As the sun went down, they saw that the river was the color of chocolate milk. No drinking water there. But they had canteens.

As they lay down their packs and equipment, Driscoll ordered the men to gather firewood.

Denham laughed derisively. "What do you think is going to burn during the rainy season?"

Driscoll frowned. "Well, gather what you can. We can give it a try."

The men went off to scavenge while Jack Driscoll arranged the dropped equipment in piles for safety, and so they could be grabbed up in an emergency.

When he had the equipment organized, the First Mate wanted nothing more than to drop into it and catch up on his sleep. Driscoll was dead beat. He laid down his elephant rifle and the bandolier of mercy bullets which he intended to keep handy in case of a lion attack.

All around them, the sounds of seamen charging and tramping through underbrush looking for dry firewood filled the dusky night.

Suddenly, a man screamed. It was more of a howl. Driscoll almost immediately thought of Carl Denham. It sounded like his heavy voice.

"Denham!" he yelled. "Where are you?"

"Due east! Come and cut me down."

"Find him, boys," Driscoll yelled. "See what kind of fix he's got himself into this time."

It didn't take long. They found the showman hanging from a tree, his right ankle wrapped up in a loop of what appeared to be tightly-woven grass.

He was very high up, almost twenty-five feet.

"How the blue blazes did you get up there?" demanded Driscoll, hands on hips.

The dynamic director was swinging like a pendulum, flailing

his arms around to try to stop his gyrations. But that only made matters worse.

"I must've stepped into a snare," he called down.

Jimmy muttered, "Kinda high for a snare. Who could have laid a swell trap like that?"

The answer was not long in coming.

Something moved through the trees, and all heads turned, attempting to track it. Someone saw a flash of movement that suggested a spotted leopard.

"Big cat up there," a sailor warned.

A moment later, he was proven wrong.

A bronzed form dropped down from a lower branch when no one was looking, and landed behind them.

Everyone turned. Hands went toward sidearms, but Driscoll immediately yelled, "Hold your fire, hold your fire!"

Out of the crepuscular gloom stepped the tawny form of Tarzan of the Apes, attired in his leopard-skin loincloth, its tail wrapped around his waist like a sash.

"You!" barked Driscoll.

Above his head, Carl Denham said practically the same thing a few seconds later.

"Was that your snare?" the First Mate demanded.

Pointing to Denham, Tarzan said sternly, "I instructed him to leave and never return. This is his punishment."

"Well, if it's all the same to you, I'm cutting him down."

Hearing that, Denham pleaded, "Don't cut me down if he's going to cut my throat."

Driscoll looked at the ape-man steadily. "Well?"

"Cut him down, if it pleases you," said the bronzed giant. "I have not come to create trouble. Truthfully, that you are still here may be a good thing after all."

While Jimmy shinnied up the tree with a folding knife, Jack Driscoll stepped up to Tarzan of the Apes and invited, "Speak your mind."

"I tracked the creature you brought to these shores," said Tarzan simply. "He was very powerful."

"Was? Did you kill him?"

Tarzan shook his thick mane of hair and said, "Such a creature cannot easily be killed by man nor beast. Why are you still here?"

"Captain Englehorn got to thinking about that speech you gave. And he realized that it was all our fault that we brought Kong to Africa."

"Kong? Is that the beast's name?"

"That is what they call him. Denham dubbed him 'King' Kong because, on the island in which he was the last survival of his kind, he was monarch of the whole works."

As they parlayed, the work of lowering Carl Denham to the ground continued, but did not go well. Cutting the rope caused the showman to fall a dozen feet, with the immediate result that the wind was knocked out of him.

Tarzan ignored this accident. He seemed utterly unconcerned about the fate of Carl Denham.

"Kong may have been the monarch of his world, but in this jungle Tarzan is lord over all," he pronounced.

Driscoll nodded. "As I was saying, the cap'n decided we had to put an end to Kong once and for all. For the sake of the people who live in this jungle."

This statement seemed to satisfy the ape-man, but then he said, "As I fought Kong, I heard him bark words in the tongue of his kind. It was not the language of the great apes, who raised me, but there were sounds in it that were similar. What I heard were not the cries of a destructive monster, but the anguish of a creature who was lost and had no way to get home."

Carl Denham sat up, and these words impinged upon his hearing. He shook his head as if to clear it.

"What are you trying to say?" he asked dazedly.

Tarzan replied. "I do not know if it is possible to kill this alien ape, but I do understand that no fault lies upon him. The destruction he has wrought, Kong created because he was brought here in chains. If he cannot be killed, and I am beginning to doubt that he can, Kong must be conveyed to a place where he will bring no harm to those who live in peace."

Standing up, Carl Denham grinned his broadest. "Now you're talkin'!"

Tarzan looked at him with a mixture of scorn and disdain, then ignored him. Instead, he addressed the First Mate.

"If it is possible to drive Kong to the shore, can you capture him and bring him aboard your ship?"

"It's possible," allowed Driscoll. "We're packing gas bombs to knock him out, as well as drugged mercy bullets, which will do the same thing if we can get close enough. Our supply is low. If we don't do it right the first time, there'll be no second time."

"I will make a bargain with you," said Tarzan. "I will lead you to Kong. Together, we will find a way to lure the creature back to the water, where this can be accomplished."

Eyes flaring in delight, Carl Denham snapped his campaign hat off his head, tossed it in the air and said, "Yippee! Never give up! Never give up! There's always a solution."

He was ignored.

Jack Driscoll said to Tarzan, "We kind of figure from the direction Kong is traveling, he's headed for Mount Kilimanjaro."

"So?" asked Tarzan.

"Back on his home island, he lived in a huge cave atop a granite knob called Skull Mountain. Kong isn't like an ordinary gorilla who will sleep on the jungle floor. He likes to sit up high, where he can look down upon his domain."

"Kind of like Zeus atop Mount Olympus," interjected Denham.

"Mount Kilimanjaro lies over a hundred miles inland," said the ape-man. "If he reaches it, there is no hope of turning him around. If that is so, we will have to destroy him if we can."

"There's no need for that," interjected Denham. "We can turn Kong around, sure. We'll figure out a way to march him back, then knock him out and that will be the end of it. Where you're concerned, anyway."

"You will return Kong to his mountain home," said Tarzan flatly.

Denham swallowed hard. "Well, we kind of figured on taking him on to New York City."

The frank gaze of Tarzan of the Apes turned toward the blustery showman, and there was a flicker in those steely orbs that was cold and remorseless.

"You have seen what Kong has done to open jungle. What do you imagine he would do to an inhabited city?"

Denham mangled his unlit pipe in his hands anxiously. "Hell, Kong'll be in chains. We'll have control of him. And we'll teach him fear. The kind of fear that a man can drive into an animal and force him to do his bidding."

Tarzan shook his head firmly. "I will agree to help you, but only on the condition that Kong be returned to his home where he belongs. Not to any city. This is the word of Tarzan of the Apes. Do we have a bargain?"

The level eyes of the ape-man studied the faces of the shore party in the dying light and heads began nodding—all except those of Carl Denham.

"We've brought him a long way," said Denham stubbornly.

"The way to America is even longer. Can you hope to hold him captive that long?"

Shoulders slumping, face turning slack, Carl Denham walked over to his hat, picked it up and jammed it back on his head. He gave out a long sigh of defeat.

Walking up to the imposing bronzed giant, he thrust out his hand and said, "All right, you have us over a barrel. It's a deal. We're taking old Kong back to Skull Mountain Island. Shake on it."

Tarzan pointedly ignored the outthrust hand, saying, "Then

it is done. Pick up your things. We will waste no more time. We must overtake Kong before he reaches the interior."

With those words, the bronzed giant turned and uttered a strange, indescribable sound.

Out of the underbrush stepped Jad-bal-ja, his great black mane imposing as a thundercloud.

"Lion!" yelped Driscoll.

"Hold your tongue," admonished Tarzan. "That is Jad-bal-ja, the lion of Tarzan. He is obedient to me in all ways. He will not harm you."

So saying, the Lord of the Jungle turned, joined his lion, and together they waited patiently for the shore party to pack up their belongings and fall in behind him.

Chapter 67

KONG WAS wounded.

The former beast-god of Skull Mountain Island stumbled through the jungle, far into the night, and the smell of his own blood entered his nostrils.

There was a fresh wound on his right shoulder. Along his arms, healing tooth marks inflicted by the *Tyrannosaurus rex* he had battled before his capture had sprung open. Elsewhere, tiny rivulets of gore seeped from the minuscule wounds inflicted by the unerring arrows of Tarzan of the Apes.

None of these wounds were mortal, but together they sapped his strength and added to his misery. For everywhere he went, fresh flies followed. They formed a black cloud of buzzing torment about him, and only the approach of evening seemed to discourage their insatiable thirst for his blood.

Through the gathering darkness, Kong continued to forage for food. But all game fled before him.

Hearing the high-pitched squeaking of bats, Kong moved in that direction. Impatiently, he hammered at a tree, and out of its hollow center a cloud of leathery wings flung upward.

Grasping at these, Kong captured numerous unfortunate winged things, crushing them in his palm, and licking their remains off the leathery surface. He continued licking until they were clean, as if to replenish the vital fluid that was seeping out of him at different junctures. With his blunt incisors, he pulled free some of the remaining thorns which vexed him so.

Smelling fresh water, Kong moved in that direction, and came to a muddy river which was both wide and deep. Its hue was yellow. Bending over its banks, he scooped up a double handful of the lazy flowing water, and drank greedily from his cupped paws.

But the water was foul to the taste, and he ended up spitting out the first mouthful, flinging the captured fluid from his cupped hands in annoyance.

Rising to his feet, Kong directed his sorrowful eyes all about. He needed food, but he also needed rest. His belly told him that without food he would find no rest. So he pressed on, moving among the trees, pushing primeval boles aside when they impeded his progress, but finding no substantial forage.

Coming to a stand of green bamboo, he wrenched up handfuls of the stuff and began chewing it to pulp. The taste of it was good. But to Kong, bamboo was like candy to a human being. Succulent, but not fully satisfying after his enforced period of hunger. Depleted of iron and other nutrients, he craved raw meat. He thirsted for blood. He would not be satisfied until he filled his belly with both.

Munching on the last bamboo shoot, the brooding beast-god moved on, and behind him, furtive figures gathered in stealth and commenced following, iridescent eyes avid as their nostrils drank in the smell of fresh blood.

Knowing what that tantalizing scent portended, they followed Kong, unsuspected.

Chapter 68

WHEN THE shore party had gathered together their supplies, they looked to Tarzan of the Apes for direction.

Jack Driscoll asked, "How do you suppose we're going to get Kong back onto the ship even if we can knock him flat again?"

The ape-man replied firmly, "You know as well as I that task would be impossible."

Carl Denham interjected, "Maybe we can lure him to a river and raft him down it to the ship. We've done it before, haven't we?"

Driscoll nodded. "We have. But not down a winding African river, having to battle hippopotamus, rhinoceros and crocodiles every step of the way. It's hopeless."

"I don't care for that word, hopeless," growled Denham.

The Mate snapped back, "You don't like it because it doesn't fit with your cockeyed ambitions. But it's the truth."

"Truth be damned! If we're going to get Kong back to Skull Mountain Island like Tarzan wants us to, we have to try. Isn't that right, ape-man? We have to try."

Tarzan inclined his noble head and said levelly, "It may be possible to raft Kong from the interior, but it will be far easier to bring the ship to Kong."

Every man comprising the shore party stared at the bronzed giant for a long minute. They had been attempting to gauge his intelligence, and not succeeding very well.

Tarzan was dressed like an aborigine, in his leopard-skin

loincloth and whiplike decorative tail, with only a knife for a weapon. But it looked like a good English hunting knife. Tarzan also spoke acceptable English, although it was sometimes stilted and fell on their ears with an alien pronunciation that suggested a speaker of French.

Right now they were taking his measure, attempting to determine whether the ape-man knew what he was talking about.

"Are you serious?" asked Driscoll.

"What is the draft of your vessel?" retorted Tarzan.

It was an intelligent question, so the Mate answered it in a forthright manner. "She can navigate in waters thirty-eight feet deep."

Tarzan nodded. "The Mal-histah River is deeper than that during the rainy season. It is the rainy season now."

Denham nodded. "You must be talking about the Galana, which is the only waterway in these parts that can handle cargo ships. I know a little about that river. It twists and turns like a snake, and runs clear to Mount Kilimanjaro."

Tarzan said, "Where the river runs straight, your ship's engines will do. Where it does not, my elephants will guide it."

Jack Driscoll's face became slack with incredulity. He was not yet sure that he could take the suggestion seriously.

"How do we know we can get Kong close enough to the *Wanderer* to put him on board, even if we can get the ship that far upriver?"

"Kong was near the river when last seen. Once the ship is in position, we will drive him toward it."

"That's the spirit!" roared Denham. "I like this man—even though he's kinda rough around the edges. He finds a problem and looks it square in the eye. Solves it with his brain. I'm all for Tarzan's plan."

Jack Driscoll grimaced, then said, "This will be up to the Skipper, of course. We'll have to lay it before him. If he likes it, we'll give it a try. But I can't guarantee you Englehorn will like it."

Denham grinned broadly. "Tarzan will make him like it, won't you, nature boy?"

"Do not call me that," said Tarzan pointedly. "Here in Africa, I am Tarzan of the Apes, lord of this jungle. Back in the land of my birthright, I am John Clayton, Viscount Greystoke."

The ape-man's speech was so direct and forthright, they did not question him, even though it seemed beyond credulity that he would claim British nobility for himself.

Gesturing to his animals, Tarzan directed, "Come. We will march to the water's edge and parley with your captain."

Having no other choice in the matter, the shore party followed in his wake, taking care to avoid the stately golden lion, who tagged along like a docile tabby cat.

Chapter 69

KONG FOUND no satisfactory food and, as the moon in the African sky showed its waning aspect, he finally came to a littered clearing, swept aside some boulders and brush, and lay down to sleep.

Slumber came quickly, for he was exhausted.

Twenty minutes passed. Thirty. Forty-five minutes. An hour. More.

Through the underbrush slunk stealthy creatures on four careful feet. Their long noses sniffing, their eager eyes appraising the breathing black-furred mountain that leaked blood that they could almost taste.

Some of these stalkers were hyenas. Others were jackals—the dog-like cross between a fox and a coyote. Tarzan would have called them Dango and Ungo, respectively. All were scavengers. And all were drawn by the alluring smell of fresh blood.

Kong slept on, oblivious to the approaching danger. The scavengers were small in comparison to Kong, but together they could bring down a much larger animal, such as an antelope or even a water buffalo.

All they needed were their numbers. And if their prey was comparatively weakened, so much the better for them.

Circling and sniffing, they gradually drew closer to the recumbent anthropoid. Like all who had encountered the beast-god in Africa, none had ever beheld the like of him. The sheer size of the stupendous ape instilled a measure of caution in their wicked and wily brains.

But they knew hunger, and smelled blood. And as Kong slept and snuffled the night away, they closed the circle of their pacing, like a living noose about the throat of an unsuspecting victim.

There is always one creature braver than the others in any pack—although this pack did not consist of a single species of scavenger. It was a lowly jackal that attempted to take the first nip out of the seemingly oblivious giant.

This jackal nipped at a twitching thumb, but accomplished little, for the heavy digit continued twitching and its owner continued slumbering.

Emboldened by the absence of remonstration, the brave jackal took another bite. This time his fangs sank deep into the leathery thumb, and Kong reacted.

Animals who dwell in the wild possess the ability to snap to wakefulness without any interval of incomprehension. No less King Kong.

Kong felt the jackal's teeth, and before he was completely aroused, his great hand snapped around at his tormentor, captured him and began crushing the barking scavenger to a greasy pulp.

The unfortunate jackal managed to emit a single yelp of terror, and suddenly it was being conveyed to Kong's mouth, for the great ape was now lifting his immense barrel-shaped torso vertical.

Seeing that he held a small animal, Kong simply placed the mangy body in his yawning mouth and began chewing it alive. Not that there was much life left in the pulped canine.

Swallowing the jackal—hide, head, bones and all—Kong searched his immediate surroundings with his sullen amber-colored eyes.

Jackals and hyenas cringed. Whining, they prudently retreated, but only as far as the underbrush. The eager glow of their eyes in the moonlight told Kong that he was surrounded.

Giving an angry growl, he forced himself to his feet and lunged at those eyes, sending their frightened owners scattering, then he picked up great stones and flung them at his fleeing antagonists.

The dog-like carnivores retreated only a safe distance, circled around, and remained just far enough away to avoid the wrath of the terrible beast-god, but not so far that they could not keep an eye on him.

Finally, Kong gave up, and began walking in the direction of Mount Kilimanjaro, whose icy peak shone like a frigid beacon in the moonlight.

Behind him, the heterogeneous pack followed, panting, tongues lolling out, foamy slaver drooling from their lips.

Where wiser denizens of the jungle would see a moving mountain of menace, they perceived only warm meat. Meat they fully intended to savor when their prey at last ran out of vitality....

Chapter 70

CAPTAIN ENGLEHORN listened patiently as his first officer laid out the plan to capture Kong.

They were seated in the paneled wardroom of the *Wanderer*, along with Carl Denham and Tarzan of the Apes. The old freighter rocked gently in the monotonous combers washing toward the beach. It was humid, and the paneling was warping.

The Captain had been astounded when the shore party returned in the company of the legendary ape-man, but he did his best to conceal his emotions as he had agreed to listen to their entreaties.

"We are to take Kong back to Skull Mountain Island, is that it?" Englehorn summarized after Driscoll had finished his recitation.

"That's about the size of it," shrugged Driscoll.

The master's wintry eyes went to Carl Denham, who had been uncharacteristically quiet throughout the conference. He turned to the director.

"What are your thoughts on this matter, Mr. Denham?"

Denham said heartily, "I'm with Tarzan all the way. He's got a good plan. And he's got the means and the muscle to help us see it through. We'll capture Kong again and take him away— far away from Africa."

"Back to Skull Island. You are satisfied with that?"

A cloud crossed the showman's broad features and his moist brown eyes grew reflective.

"Well, of course it's not the outcome I was hoping for, but we still have those dinosaur eggs in the hold. Unless they've hatched by now?"

"They have not," assured the Captain.

"Well, if I can't have Kong, maybe I can coax them into hatching and I'll still have something sensational to display. Not to mention footage of Kong's capture."

Captain Englehorn nodded and turned to Tarzan. "You say your elephants can help us navigate the Galana River through the difficult spots?"

Tarzan nodded. "Four bulls will accompany us. Between them, there should be no difficulties that cannot be overcome."

"And you say you can make them do your bidding?"

"They are obedient to Tarzan."

Jack Driscoll interjected, "He's got a tame lion, who also does whatever he says. Only I'm not so sure how tame it is."

Tarzan countered, "Jad-bal-ja is not tame. He is, however, subject to my will. He will accompany us and I will tell him to eat none of your crew during the voyage."

Captain Englehorn stared at the impassive-faced bronzed giant as if suspecting that this was some sort of dry jest, then realized that Tarzan was entirely serious.

Blinking away his disbelief, he said, "Were it not for our grave responsibility, I would not risk ship and crew in such a mad undertaking. But all along, this entire voyage has been mad. Perhaps this is the sanest resolution that could be arranged for."

Denham asked, "So you're saying you're game to try?"

Turning back to Tarzan, Captain Englehorn said, "My vessel is at your disposal, Mr. Tarzan. Within certain constraints, of course."

Tarzan stood up and said, "I will drive my elephants into the water. Have your crew stand ready with suitable towropes. Make certain they are stout."

With that, the stoic ape-man stepped out onto the weather

deck and without the formality of asking the master's leave, leapt over the rail and plunged into the water, where he began swimming for shore.

Ann Darrow happened to be on deck when that happened, and she watched, fascinated, as Tarzan of the Apes swam to shore, and got his elephants moving into the surf with no more effort than coaxing dogs to take a plunge into calm pond water.

Jad-bal-ja, the golden lion, was no connoisseur of salt water, so he lolled lazily on top of one of the elephants' backs, and when the beasts finally trudged their ponderous way to the starboard side of the ship, the great lion sprang for the bow, clearing the rail and landing perfectly there.

Thereupon, Ann screamed and fled for her cabin. Some of the crew wore twisted expressions suggesting that they yearned for the relative safety of their bunks as well.

Jad-bal-ja simply lay down on the warm foredeck and curled up like an overgrown tabby cat while Tarzan called up for appropriate lines to be thrown to him.

The elephants were well disciplined. Two took positions before the bow, and after the great rope hawsers were thrown down to Tarzan, he fixed them around the elephants' massive chests in a way that impressed the watching sailors in the expert tying of the ropy harnesses.

"I'll bet he could tie you a mean monkey's fist if he put his mind to it," said Jimmy admiringly.

"I don't doubt it," agreed Driscoll.

The operation continued with the remaining elephants stationing themselves at the stern without supervision. Tarzan climbed up the anchor chain, and accosted Jack Driscoll, saying, "Hoist anchor. My elephants will guide your ship into the mouth of the Mal-histah River."

Jack Driscoll looked to Captain Englehorn, who said, "Make it so, First Mate."

Driscoll called out orders to the deckhands, and the great

anchor chain began rattling as the steel links were pulled up into the hawse hole.

They had to work around the golden lion, who watched them sleepily and without great interest. The feline seemed rather bored. Flies buzzed about his hindquarters, and his tufted tail knocked them away with casual skill.

Hovering about, observing all, but pointedly not participating in the proceedings, stood Penjaga the Storyteller. Her sharp agate gaze flicked from face to face as each man went about his business, but her seamed features were otherwise unreadable.

At one point, her dark eyes met those of Jad-bal-ja and a look passed between them that suggested a knowing recognition of each other's power. A flash of mutual respect appeared in their depths, then they looked away from one another.

Tarzan gave out a long, terrifying cry that froze their blood because it came unexpectedly.

In unison, the four elephants began to paddle forward, and the ramshackle ship lurched ahead. Plodding along in the shallow coastal waters, they guided the rust-encrusted hull along until they came to a muddy yellow-brown fan of outflow water, signifying the mouth of the Galana River, two pulling in the lead and the other pair swimming against the port and starboard hulls, helping to guide the ponderous vessel, which was not yet under power.

At the bow, Carl Denham grinned and cranked away at his camera, which he had carefully set up atop a windlass while the others were working.

"This'll make a swell scene!" he crowed. "I'll call it 'The Quest for Kong!'"

Chapter 71

L ONG INTO the African night, Kong struggled to keep moving, yearning for rest, desiring food but finding neither.

Pale vultures gathered together in the sky.

They could not smell his leaking blood, as did the pursuing jackals, but their beady, unreadable eyes recognized that below them a wounded creature walked. Where the wounded went, they often fell in death.

Perhaps these vultures circling so high in the sky did not grasp how large Kong was. Perhaps they did not care. For they had no intention of descending upon their prey until it was entirely helpless, if not dead.

So, without fear, they circled and swept along after Kong, who stumbled as he walked, but who refused also to lay down his tired, aching body—to say nothing of his ebbing life.

Kong stayed within sight of the winding river, not because it offered clean water; it did not. He knew from past experience that crocodiles lurked in this water. And of all the things the black brute had tasted in Africa, crocodiles most appealed to him, even if they were puny and not robust enough to satisfy him.

So great was his hunger and so fatigued his brain, the beast-god of Skull Mountain Island gave little thought to the fact that his pounding course was taking him north of Mount Kilimanjaro, which lay far to the southwest.

That shining peak could wait. Wait until Kong was once more

strong. Wait until he was rested and fed and could climb its mighty bulwarks.

Assuming, of course, that such a glorious day lay ahead.

The trailing hyenas and the circling vultures plainly intended otherwise....

Chapter 72

CARL DENHAM had stopped filming, not because he lacked spectacle to capture on celluloid, but because his precious supply of film was limited.

The impatient showman could not sleep, so he paced the deck of the *Wanderer,* marveling in the moonlit scenery. Riverbank poplars paraded past like eerie scarecrows clothed in peeling white garments.

Pushed by swimming pachyderms, the *Wanderer* was being barged up the Galana River, which Tarzan called the Mal-histah-gom-lul, a mouthful of syllables he explained meant Yellow-snake-river.

It was a fitting coinage, for the swollen waterway was a muddy thing, its banks overflowing at many spots. Had this not been the rainy season, it was doubtful that the rusty old freighter could have navigated it safely for, at intervals, they encountered wading hippopotamus, who slowly and reluctantly gave way before the trumpeting challenge of the lead elephants, who swam ahead of the knifing bow.

At one point far into the midnight hours, the elephants in-explicably slowed and, lifting their snakelike trunks, began emitting discordant sounds under the waning moon. The freighter continued along, threatening to collide with their enormous hesitating forms.

Tarzan trained his steely eyes upon the moonlit river, soon spied a lean grey fin slicing the yellowish surface.

Pulling an arrow from his back-slung quiver, the ape-man nocked it, drew back a bowstring that a circus strongman would have struggled to budge, and let fly.

The shaft found its mark, and in the water, a large bull shark fell to threshing about in its death throes, the slim arrow sticking out of its fiercely-fanged face. The muddy water turned the color of wine. The shark's frantic squirming soon turned feeble.

With a weak salute from its broad forked trail, it vanished from sight.

The bronzed-skinned giant made an encouraging noise. The lead pachyderms lurched ahead, just ahead of the freighter's gliding bows, and so the hauling of the *Wanderer* continued unbroken. The pair at the stern caught up, ready to push and steer at the command of the jungle lord.

Owing to the deep draft of the cargo ship, the pachyderms were afloat, but their massive bodies were sufficiently powerful to impel the vessel along the meandering channel until the engines could be safely engaged.

Jack Driscoll had drifted up during this struggle, for he could not sleep either. The Captain had gone to his private cabin, with orders to be called if an emergency transpired.

"Quite a show, eh?" Denham remarked to the First Mate.

"If I live to have grandchildren, I'll have a lifetime of bedtime stories," admitted Driscoll reflectively. "Whoever heard of drafting elephants as tugboats?"

Denham grunted a bitter laugh. Turning to the Mate, he regarded him frankly and reminded, "We've waded through a lot of grief together."

Driscoll grunted, "Hell, and things that are worse than hell. It's a wonder we're still alive."

"You're probably wondering why I'm willing to take Kong back to Skull Mountain Island after all we've been through," the director suggested.

Driscoll said flatly, "I figured you'd had enough. There comes a time when a man's ambitions become like his appetite. They get too big for him."

The director squared his pugnacious jaw. "Well, don't think I'm licked. I still got footage to shoot, not to mention those unhatched eggs tucked in the tween decks. I'm thinking I might have another ace up my sleeve."

Jack Driscoll eyed the showman with a flare of alarm coming into his windy eyes.

"If you got more sleep," he suggested dryly, "you'd hatch a few less reckless schemes. But I guess I don't have to tell you that, do I?"

Looking around to make certain they were alone, the wily Denham pitched his voice low. "I have a notion I'd like to share with you."

Driscoll said nothing. He simply waited. River poplars on either side of the slow-moving ship seemed to stalk past like lean, stark ghosts in the moonlight—ghosts who were shedding their fragile skins with every halting step.

Denham offered, "That Tarzan is a wonder, isn't he?"

The Mate grunted dismissively. "It's a wonder he didn't cut your throat! He considers himself the guardian of this jungle, and you keep trespassing on his preserves."

The filmmaker's warm brown eyes grew speculative. "What if I were to say to you that Tarzan of the Apes might be worth a lot of money if we could convince him to come back to New York with us?"

Driscoll flushed angrily. "Convince him? You mean *capture* him, don't you? And don't tell me otherwise. I know you, Denham. *Too* well."

"Listen, Driscoll, Tarzan's a wild man. I know he talks like a white man, but he's half ape. Just like Kong seems to be part human. Don't you see? If I can't have one, maybe the other will do. Maybe you could accidentally shoot him with one of your mercy slugs. Knock him out for a spell. By the time he wakes up, we'll be far out to sea and there'll be nothing he can do about it. Especially if he's in chains."

Jack Driscoll studied the blocky director for the longest time. His eyes grew as inversely cold as his windburned features grew hot.

"I have a good mind to sock you silly right here and now," he said flatly.

"For what?" Denham asked in an injured tone. "I was just thinking out loud."

"It's kidnapping on the high seas, Denham. And if I hear another word about this, I'll ask the Skipper to clap *you* in irons."

Turning smartly on his heel, Driscoll stormed off, his horny fists hard and white as bone.

"That mug has no imagination, no imagination at all," muttered Carl Denham.

Turning back to the bow, he watched Tarzan of the Apes, who was majestically riding one of the elephants, balancing on its broad back, and occasionally gesturing ahead.

The ape-man seemed to know every twist and turn of the river, where it was shallow and where it was navigable, and for a moment the hardboiled Denham was impressed in spite of himself.

"Pretty savvy for a wild man. Maybe he'd like to visit New York if I put it to him the right way...."

Chapter 73

ALL THROUGH the night, the elephants of Tarzan guided the *Wanderer* up the swollen and sluggish Mal-histah River.

Only once did First Mate Driscoll order the engine room to fire up the engines, and that was to navigate a long stretch of straight waterway at quarter-speed. Feet planted before the wheel, hands steady, Driscoll held the ship firm in the center of the channel.

When the freighter ran out of straightaway, Driscoll ordered the engines throttled and the great screws ceased revolving. Gradually, her forward momentum slowed sufficiently to allow Tarzan to mount the lead elephants, haul up the waterlogged lines, and fling them up toward the bow where they were captured by boat hooks wielded by burly deckhands.

The powerful pachyderms swam to either bank to pace along beside the ship while the trailing pair who had been piloting the ship from the stern and sides surged ahead to take the place of their fatigued fellows.

The fresher elephants took the lead then, their stubby feet propelling them forward with kicking motions. Once they resumed their steady, rhythmic swimming, the animals continued guiding the bulky ship forward. They had churned up a great deal of muddy water, but the riverway was so foul in the first place all that was altered were the ever-shifting hues of yellow and brown and ochre.

Dawn had stolen up on them during this laborious operation, and as the morning sun climbed, the shadowy jungle on either side of the river took on fresh color and new life.

"He got 'em trained well, all right," one deckhand said admiringly.

In the pilothouse, Driscoll surrendered the wheel to the helmsman, then took a pair of binoculars out onto the flying bridge where he scanned the treeline to the south, seeking Kong.

But there were no signs of the towering terror.

Further inland, Driscoll spotted an unusual cluster of vultures circling and wheeling. They looked like fragments of something animated with unholy life. A frown touched his face.

Climbing down the ladder to the weather deck, he ran forward and called to the ape-man. "Awful lot of carrion birds circling to the south. You can't spy them, but I can."

Standing on the broad, rolling back of one of the lead elephants, the bronzed giant stood up and began sniffing the air.

"I do not smell death," he called back curtly, as if that ended the matter.

Driscoll was not convinced. "What do you smell?"

Tarzan replied, "The ape-musk of Kong. He is not many miles east of here."

"If we can find him, we need to lure him closer to the river. It would be impossible to drag his bulk through thick jungle."

"We will find him," the jungle lord said with simple confidence, then turned his attention to the way ahead, signifying the exchange concluded.

Not long after first light, Captain Englehorn emerged from his cabin, and joined the First Mate at the wheel.

"I would like your morning report, Mr. Driscoll."

The Mate said, "Tarzan claims that Kong's a few miles south. I spy a kettle of vultures. They may not mean anything, but they look ominous to me."

Englehorn nodded. "Until we have ascertained Kong's precise position, I will not put off a shore party."

"Understood, Cap'n. Maybe we can find a way to trick Kong into coming our way."

"I am open to suggestions."

"I wish I had any," Driscoll said sheepishly. "Maybe the old woman has an idea."

"When Penjaga awakens, find out for us all. In the meantime, it might be advisable to drop anchor here. No point in over-shooting our mark."

"Aye aye, sir," said Driscoll, taking his leave as the Skipper engaged the telegraph instrument, signaling the boiler room to throw the engines into reverse.

The ship began slowing. At a signal from Driscoll, Tarzan cast off the towropes and released his elephants from pilot duty.

As deckhands ran the waterlogged lines around grumbling deck winches and made them fast, the elephants of Tarzan took to the low banks, climbing ponderously. The animals swiftly vanished into the forest, no doubt to forage for welcome rough-age after their long nocturnal pull.

Slowly, the *Wanderer* lurched to a full stop.

A voice shouted out, "Drop the hook!"

Immediately, the massive anchor began unwinding from the hawse hole to splash into the mucky watercourse. The old freighter was now fast.

FIRST watch found Ann Darrow and Penjaga taking breakfast not long after. They were in the mess room. It was already hot, but would soon be stifling.

"You two are up early," observed Driscoll dryly.

"Couldn't sleep," said Ann, smiling gently. "Those horrid jungle noises kept me awake half the night."

Signaling for Lumpy to bring him some grub, Driscoll plunked himself down beside Ann.

"Tarzan thinks Kong isn't far from here," he advised, "but the Captain doesn't want to send out a shore party until we're certain. Englehorn is wondering if there's a way to entice Kong closer to the boat, so that when we bring him down, there's half a chance we can haul him on board without having to spend a week dragging him through jungle."

Penjaga studied her disagreeable-looking powdered eggs, and finally looked up, saying, "Kong will be hungry. This much is certain."

"I reckon you're right," admitted Driscoll.

"The creatures inhabiting this jungle would not satisfy him," the Storyteller said flatly. "He requires the flesh of lizards nearer to his size."

"Well, he's plumb out of luck. Other than crocodiles, Africa doesn't have much to offer in the way of big lizards."

"The morning is hot," said Penjaga carefully. "By the time the sun climbs to the center of the sky, it will be much hotter."

"Where are you going with this yarn?" asked Driscoll.

"I have walked these steel decks in my sandals, and felt their heat."

"Sure," grunted Driscoll. "Sometimes it's hot enough to fry eggs on—if only we had the eggs to waste."

"The great eggs that were pilfered from Skull Mountain Island," intoned the old woman slowly. "Have they hatched?"

"No, and I'm not sure they will." Suddenly, a wild light leapt into the First Mate's eyes, and he said, "Old woman, I believe I am getting your drift."

Ann looked blank. "Kindly enlighten a sleepy gal, won't you?" she entreated.

Instead of replying directly, Driscoll called over to the cook. "Lumpy, if we clear the poop deck and crack open those monster eggs, do you think they would cook up in this heat?"

Lumpy looked doubtful, squinted one eye, and said finally, "Only one way to find out. You sure you want to waste them?"

"I'm sure I want to waste no more time on this infernal river than I have to," returned Driscoll firmly. "I'll have Jimmy look over those eggs and check their condition."

Carl Denham picked that precise instant to shoulder in through the mess room door, looking characteristically disheveled. He perked up when he heard Driscoll's comment.

"Do we have fresh eggs this morning?" he asked, brightening.

"If you mean ostrich eggs, no. But we may have hatched a scheme to lure Kong to the river."

"I'm all ears," said Denham, drawing close.

"It will mean sacrificing those big eggs we took off the island. We're considering breaking them open on the back deck and letting them fry on the steel plates."

The canny showman flinched. "You can't do that! Those are *my* eggs, my last hole cards. If I can haul them back to New York and coax them to hatch, I'll have a flock of baby dinosaurs to show folks."

Jack Driscoll looked uncomfortable and said, "It's time I leveled with you, Denham."

The director looked the First Mate over and murmured thinly, "Go ahead and level, if the spirit so moves you."

Driscoll looked slightly abashed. "Back on the island, we couldn't get our hands on any dinosaur eggs, so we had to settle for what we could safely scavenge."

"Go on," invited the filmmaker, eyes narrowing until their brown gleams turned nearly black.

"Best we could manage was turtle eggs."

Denham's eyes popped open. "Turtles! Is that what those are?"

"Giant turtles," corrected Driscoll. "Prehistoric monsters. If they were to hatch, they would be a wonder. Once they grow up, that is. But they're not dinosaurs exactly."

"So you hoodwinked me, is that it?"

The Mate wavered. "Oh, I don't know about that, Mr. Denham. We had to improvise."

Carl Denham made an assortment of faces that suggested he was contemplating various possibilities. "What are you driving at, Driscoll? Going to cook up those eggs so Kong can smell them a mile off. You think the big ape would be interested in some scrambled eggs?"

Driscoll toyed with his breakfast. "He's sure to be hungry. The smell of cooking eggs might attract him. We know he ate raw ostrich eggs the other night. We came upon the shambles he made."

Unexpectedly, Carl Denham laughed and burst out, "Well, if you're going to go to the trouble, you might as well make him an omelet! Maybe catch a couple of crocs and throw in some crocodile meat."

Jack Driscoll thought he was being made fun of, but behind him Penjaga inserted, "The flesh of lizards would be irresistible to Kong. And I possess potent herbs to add to the cooking eggs that are sure to catch his attention, for they would remind him of the wild plants of his home."

Denham looked philosophical. "Well, it sounds like a sure-fire plan to me." His voice grew artificially magnanimous. "Sure, I'll contribute my precious prehistoric eggs. You'll get no kick from me on that score."

Surprised that he was getting so little argument from the argumentative showman, Jack Driscoll said, "I'll have to clear it with the captain, of course."

"Of course, of course," Denham said expansively. "You do that little thing. Me, I'll have myself a hearty breakfast. Then we'll all get together for a cookout around noontime."

"It's settled then. I'll let Englehorn know what we have cooking."

After Jack departed, Ann Darrow observed, "You're taking this well, Mr. Denham."

"You have to roll with the punches in life, Ann. If you don't, you could be knocked flat. And getting up is one of the hardest things a man can do."

Ann smiled sweetly. "You're such an optimist, Mr. Denham. Wherever do you get it from?"

As he took a seat and Lumpy dished out hash, cured bacon and toast, Denham said to no one in particular, "Oh, I've been knocked down a time or two in my life. Not flat. Never flat. Rolling with the punches just comes natural to me, that's all."

After that confident comment, the brooding director ate in total silence, as if he were entirely alone. In the privacy of his thoughts, he was.

Chapter 74

WITH CAPTAIN ENGLEHORN'S permission, the great eggs scavenged from the Skull Mountain Island turtle nests were carefully rolled out of the tween decks holds forward of the bridge, and carried in hammocks made from bedsheets and horsehair blankets to the fire-blackened poop deck.

As Jimmy observed, "These deck plates look like they've been used for skillets before this."

"Maybe they have," grunted Lumpy. "This old scow was in the World War."

When the eggs were carefully set in place, Driscoll said, "We'll wait until it's good and hot. That ought to be around the end of the forenoon watch, or maybe an hour after."

Carl Denham asked, "Where we going to get some crocodile meat?"

"Maybe Tarzan knows. We haven't seen a croc yet."

The ape-man, when told of their needs, simply nodded and plunged into the water, leaping off the back of one of his un-tethered elephants who had wandered back to the riverbank.

He swam upstream a fair distance, and was not gone long.

When Tarzan returned, the bronzed giant was dragging a full-grown crocodile by its tail. The saurian left a billowing trail of red in the muddy river waters. It was dead, and the hunting knife clutched in the ape-man's sun-bronzed hand dripped crimson.

Dragging the lizard up onto the banks, he used his blade to butcher it, doing so with such methodical efficiency that it was obvious to all watching the ape-man knew his way around a crocodile carcass. A time or two, Tarzan sampled the raw reptile meat, but seemed to have little taste for it.

Captain Englehorn ordered a lifeboat dropped into the water to collect the growing pile of meat. This was soon conveyed back to the boat, and arranged in zinc buckets on deck.

Once this was accomplished, the bronzed giant signaled to Jad-bal-ja, who had passed the night dozing on the foredeck. The black-maned lion obediently snapped awake and sought to disembark.

Displaying the typical feline distaste for the water, he first made his way down the massive steel links of the anchor chain gingerly, then plunged into the water, swimming to dry land and his master's side.

"Stick close," Driscoll called to Tarzan. "We're expecting company for lunch."

A lifted hand signified the ape-man had heard the admonition. Together, man and beast melted into the brush without saying where they were going. But their intentions were clear: They were scouting for Kong.

As the roasting sun climbed toward the meridian, Lumpy tested the deck plates as they heated up under the baking solar rays.

Middle watch arrived at twelve-thirty, signified by one bell.

"Is she sizzling yet?" Denham asked old Lumpy.

The bare-chested cook nodded vigorously. "Sizzling, alrighty. But not to my liking." Lumpy looked toward Jack Driscoll.

"Give it another twenty or thirty minutes," snapped the Mate. "But no longer. We've got to beat the afternoon rain."

It was just shy of two bells—one o'clock—when Lumpy announced, "This is probably as hot as it's going to get. Commence operations, I say."

Denham said jauntily, "Allow me to do the honors." He took

a fire axe from Lumpy's bony fists and began chopping away at the eggshells.

It was a messy affair. The mustard-hued yolk, along with the broken shards of eggshell, were soon puddled on the deck, making a sloppy mess.

The cooking commenced almost immediately, and the smell was strangely pungent in a way that made them feel queasy in the pits of their stomachs.

As the malodorous mass bubbled and sizzled, Lumpy pitched pieces of raw crocodile meat into the frying matter, while Penjaga took from one of her belt pouches some dried herbs which she tossed into this cooking omelet in generous pinches. The stuff resembled oregano but smelled worse than garlic.

By the time the great agglomeration of yolks was frying up nicely, the smell proved overpowering and they were forced to retreat.

Lumpy muttered, "Sure hope Kong has a taste for that awful concoction. I would hate to have to clean it up the hard way."

Jack Driscoll threw cold water on Lumpy's hopes. "We can't let that big gorilla anywhere near the boat while he's upright. He'll capsize us for sure. The smell is just to get him interested. We'll have to settle with Kong before he gets close enough to do us any damage."

Lumpy's face fell. On his shoulder was Ignatz, and Ignatz was chattering away aimlessly.

Out from the yawning mouth of a nearby deck ventilator popped the furry head of Nkima, the wild monkey. He had slipped aboard with Tarzan but, distrusting of humans, had secreted himself in various nooks and crannies, changing hiding places often, and refusing to associate with the crew of the rusty old freighter.

Ignatz and Nkima commenced scolding one another like angry squirrels. What passed between them sounded like a quarrel, but not one of the crew could decipher what it might entail.

From the moment the jungle monkey had come aboard, Ignatz had flown into a screaming rage and took to throwing various objects at his perceived rival. Nkima had flung some of them back, and a lively running battle had run the length and breadth of the old freighter, entertaining the howling crew.

All except old Lumpy, who announced to all parties within hearing, "Bad enough I gotta contend with one mischievous monk. Now I got two of the crazy-brained varmints bedeviling me. Mark my words, once we reach home port, I'm selling anything with a tail attached to it to the Bronx Zoo! And that's final!"

Chapter 75

K ONG AWOKE to the strong odor of frying eggs.

This was not something that was familiar to him, but mixed in with it were half-familiar aromas. Back on Skull Mountain Island, he had eaten raw turtle eggs, and this heady smell was similar. Mixed in with it was the distinctive tang of lizard. And that smell, as much as the others, sharpened his famished interest.

During the night, Kong had found another place to sleep, and the jackals and the hyenas had made sly efforts to steal up on him, but the canny anthropoid was aware of them. A few pitched rocks and broken tree limbs discouraged them sufficiently for the beast-god to sleep—especially after Kong had uprooted a young palm tree and flung it, breaking the spine of an unfortunate jackal, and pinning it helplessly while it yipped and howled its life away.

Since these scavengers were inhabitants of the night, the rising sun had further discouraged them. They soon slunk off into the forest to sleep the day away, in the hope of returning after sundown for their much-desired meal.

Far above, the black-winged vultures continued to circle and swoop, but they were no braver than were the loathsome jackals. They could afford to be patient. The buzzing of flies about the behemoth's festering wounds told that life was slowly ebbing.

Swatting at these pests as he awoke, Kong showed that he still lived by greeting the morning sun with a growling roar of defiance. Climbing laboriously to his feet, he ponderously turned about until he had oriented himself toward the strong smell that seemed to be calling out to him.

Once his quivering nostrils had identified the direction, the gargantuan ape began blundering toward it, still weakened, still bleeding, but very much eager to satiate his bottomless appetite.

A lone hyena fell in behind him, thirsty tongue lolling. Either hunger or some other species of madness had firm hold of his cunning brain, for once the stalking animal realized that his supposed prey was beginning to outpace him, the hyena raced ahead, and began nipping at one of the monster's heels.

Perhaps in some grandiose corner of its mind, the hungry animal thought it could hamstring the huge creature.

If so, its dreams of fresh meat proved to be fleeting.

Feeling the sharp bite of canine teeth, Kong turned and brought one Brobdingnagian heel onto the hapless hyena, splintering its frail skeleton and provoking a final painful yip that signified sudden, ignominious death.

With a low grunt of satisfaction, Kong resumed his march.

Chapter 76

T HE OVERPOWERING stink of cooking turtle eggs
infiltrated the jungle on either side of the sluggish Galana
River. The sizzling sounds of frying also carried. Combined,
they meant little to most of the inhabitants of the jungle, be
they terrestrial or aquatic.

Yet simian noses—very much like those of Kong except in
miniature—reacted to the strong odor with keen interest.

For the apes of To-yat had been rummaging around the jungle,
seeking edibles, and shrugging off their profound disappointment over the glum realization that the titanic creature they
called Black-thunder-god was not in fact their deliverer, but
instead some demon Bolgani from a distant jungle.

Smelling the unfamiliar odor, To-yat paused in his investiga-
tion of a crumbling old tree, and snarled to his fellow bulls,
"What is that smell?"

None of the bulls recognized it, of course, cooked food being
a thing alien to their daily existence.

Curiously, they sniffed at the air, and their small ears swiftly
determined that the sizzling sounds were coming from the
direction of the great winding river known to all apes dwelling
in this stretch of jungle as Mal-histah-gom-lul.

The succulent smells were making their mouths water, so that
even though they were not recognizable to the tribe of To-yat,
they strongly suggested food.

The great apes, like many creatures of the jungle, were not

above eating ostrich eggs, as well as the eggs of other wild avians. These were not considered meat, but a delicacy prized by the constantly foraging ape folk.

Drawn by this tantalizing smell, To-yat knuckled toward the river, motioning for his bulls to follow. The females and their offspring naturally took up the rear and, even if their senses were not telegraphing to them a possible source of food, the novelty of the sizzling sounds and the pungent odors combined to stir their monkey-like curiosity—not to mention their appetites.

TARZAN crept sure-footed through the treetops, his naked limbs smoldering where the solar rays touched them.

Below him, the apes of To-yat foraged, entirely unaware that the bronzed giant inhabited the crown of the spreading nut tree above their shaggy heads. Earlier in the day, they had fled the horrific confrontation, believing in their dull brains that Kong would crush and consume Tarzan. Possibly, they continued to think that this had been the ape-man's fate.

The jungle lord paid them no heed. He was seeking signs of the destructive invader, Kong.

Loud rummaging sounds came to his sharp ears, along with the unmistakable noises of the long-armed brute clumsily smashing obstacles as he encountered them, for his broad girth outmastered all African trees.

The branches in which Tarzan crouched started trembling intermittently. The earth quaked in unison with that leafy response. The power of it grew. Tarzan knew that Kong was approaching. The beast-god's footsteps created that quaking rhythm.

On the ground below, the golden lion stood his ground, sniffing the air. His fangs bared to the gum-line, he growled low in warning.

The ape-man silenced Jad-bal-ja with a sharp hiss. The feline fell silent.

When the shaking of the trees and the thudding of the earth increased alarmingly, Tarzan knew that Kong was nearing the spot, drawn by the ripe smells that had been prepared to appeal to his anthropoid appetite.

Signaling to Jad-bal-ja, Tarzan retreated, making his way to the riverbank to warn the others that the plan was working.

Kong was coming. Kong was hungry. The beast-god would not be denied. Not without a great struggle.

Tarzan of the Apes intended to be at the heart of that battle. This was written in the determined cast of his sun-bronzed profile, and in the way the ancient battle-scar marking his brow burned with a sullen, inflamed life.

Chapter 77

A S PREPARATIONS were undertaken for the recapture of Kong, Carl Denham went to Ann Darrow's cabin and gruffly announced, "All hands are tied up. I could use some help, Miss Darrow."

Ann looked puzzled. "Help with what?"

"Why, I'm going to film the capture of Kong. You know that. And the best way to do that is from the crow's nest. I've got a lot of equipment to lug up there. Mind helping me out?"

Ann hesitated. "Jack told me to keep to my cabin, with Penjaga. He said it would be safer there."

"He's right, your boyfriend is," Denham said hastily. "But if Kong smashes through our defensive line and gets his hairy paws on the ship, he's sure to start rocking it. It's going to be every man for himself. Up in the crow's nest, the big ape can't reach you. You know he could take this superstructure apart with his bare hands."

Ann's blue eyes widened with growing worry. She bit her lip and seemed at a loss for words.

"Listen," stressed Denham. "If you don't want to stay up in the crow's nest, that's all fine by me. At least lend a hand."

"Very well," the blonde said decisively. "You may be right about the danger."

"Of course I'm right. I'm always right. Or practically always. Now let's go."

Carl Denham had already run a rope up to the crow's nest, and this trailed down from the steel plate hatch.

"You tie the equipment," he directed, "and I'll haul the stuff up to the crow's nest. Once I untie it, I'll drop the line again. Get me?"

Ann nodded gamely. "I get you."

They got to work, but Ann's mind was on Jack Driscoll, off in the jungle not far away, setting up a snare to capture Kong, whose foraging around in the forest was distinctively noisy. It sounded as if the big beast-god was getting closer by the minute.

Soon, they had the cumbersome Bell & Howell camera, its wooden tripod and the remaining canisters of unexposed film arrayed in the round tub of the crow's nest. It became crowded up there. But the view was breathtaking, and it would be possible to film anything that transpired below.

Denham had carried up a pair of binoculars and he handed this to Ann, who nervously started scanning the greenery. She discerned no sign of Jack Driscoll.

The young actress didn't know whether that was a good sign. But she understood the Mate and several of the crew were setting the iron-hulled gas bombs in place, where the rummaging monster was most likely to step on them.

Of Tarzan of the Apes, there was no sign. He had once again disappeared into the woods, along with his faithful lion, presumably to hunt for Kong.

So they waited, Denham peering through the camera viewfinder while Ann held the binoculars up to her haunted eyes.

"Let me know when you spot anything interesting," Denham reminded.

Not a minute later, shaggy forms began blundering out of the jungle, some dropping from the trees, the others knuckling along, hunched and apish.

"There!" shouted Ann. "Look to the south."

Denham could see nothing through his viewfinder, so he took

the binoculars and trained them in the direction of Ann's pointing finger.

"Hell's bells!" exclaimed the showman. "What are those damn
apes doing here?"

"I imagine they smell fresh eggs," Ann said dryly.

"Look at those hairy brutes," said Denham, leaping to his
camera to turn the crank. "Makes the blood run cold just seeing
them rummage around."

As Ann Darrow watched anxiously, shaggy heads turned
toward the *Wanderer*, and the apes ambled toward it, dark eyes
looking almost human.

Seeing those simian orbs, the director's memory flashed back
to the time they had flooded up from the natural amphitheater,
howling and clutching for him.

In spite of himself, Carl Denham shivered. "I think I'm finally
becoming allergic," he muttered darkly.

Ann regarded him blankly. "To what?"

"Apes!" snapped the crusty showman, turning his attention
in another direction.

Chapter 78

CROUCHING IN the tall elephant grass, hunkered low behind a bristling thorn bush, Jack Driscoll lay in wait with his Nitro Express rifle leaning against a rustling coconut palm. He packed a .44 pistol at his hip.

The First Mate's plan was simple. When Kong emerged from the jungle, he would no doubt make a beeline for the smell of frying eggs rising from the aft deck of the *Wanderer*.

The remaining gas bombs were being secreted in the muck of the riverbank where the great gorilla-like marauder was certain to step on at least one of them. Seaman O'Brien, young Jimmy and some others were finishing up that unpleasant task.

Everyone paused often to hold their noses against the cooked-egg stink.

As a precaution, Tarzan of the Apes crouched in the concealing growth of a tall blackwood tree, another gas bomb cradled in the crotch of a stout branch, where he could seize it if necessary.

If Kong failed to step on one of the buried bombs, the ape-man would fling his cast-iron egg, breaking it against Kong's hairy skull, and so bring him down.

This had been hastily arranged on the riverbank after the crew had disembarked. For Tarzan had not ranged far as he scouted for Kong.

For his part, Driscoll was prepared to shoot at the fragile gas bombs with his pistol, shattering them, should Kong manage to step around them without disgorging their noxious contents.

As an additional precaution, the enormous elephant gun would be brought into play to make sure Kong stayed down when he fell.

It was a sound plan and it probably would have worked had it not been for the advent of To-yat and his blundering bulls.

Waiting in concealment for the sounds of Kong rummaging around the jungle to manifest themselves in the form of the terrifying colossus himself, the Mate and his men were alarmed when the great apes showed themselves instead.

"What do we do now?" questioned one.

Reaching for his elephant gun, Driscoll growled, "I may have to bring some of them down with this."

As more shambling apes appeared, another sailor wondered, "Do you have enough mercy bullets for them all and to settle Kong, too?"

It quickly became evident that the First Mate did not. His expression said that better than mere words.

Lowering his rifle, Driscoll closely watched the approaching anthropoids, waiting to see what they would do.

In the pit of his stomach, a sinking feeling commenced. It was like an elevator dropping from the top floor of the Empire State Building. There seemed to be no bottom to its rapid descent....

Chapter 79

Captain's Log
Wednesday, April 12, 1933

*I have just completed the most fantastic passage I ever imagined
captaining. Piloted by a quartet of wild elephants, the* Wanderer
*has made her way up the Galana River. We are now anchored deep
in the African interior, where we hope to lure the great hairy devil
called Kong back into the main hold.*

*It is a mad scheme. I'll not deny it. Mad, and beyond foolhardy.
But the situation is desperate, and so are we. For if we fail to
recapture Kong, the ship and its crew will be stranded in Africa,
with little hope of reaching home port.*

*Dire as that prospect may be, we risk utter destruction in this
latest undertaking. I rue the day I ever met Carl Denham and
pray that success will be ours. Otherwise, this old vessel will lay her
keel to rest in the river bottom beneath my feet.*

PERHAPS IT was appropriate that Captain Wilhelm
Englehorn was the first person to spot the tremendous
head of Kong moving through the rainforest greenery.

The freighter skipper was at his usual station—in the wheelhouse, his helmsman by his side. He was masticating a chew
of tobacco methodically, and his wintry eyes were pinched but
alert. Leaning in a corner was the Thompson submachine gun
he kept under lock and key in his cabin, its ammunition drum
heavy with .45 caliber slugs.

Down in the engine room, the boilers were going full blast.

If the word came, and the enormous ape lunged for the *Wanderer*, Englehorn intended for the freighter to be steaming away before the monster could get those powerful paws on his ship.

At least, that was what Englehorn told Jack Driscoll before the First Mate took a small work gang ashore to lay the trap for Kong. In reality, it would not be possible for the freighter to get up much of a head of steam if Kong ranged too close, but the old ship's master was not about to overlook any possibility that might endanger his vessel. The aging rustbucket meant everything to him. Life, liberty, and—eventually, he hoped—a comfortable retirement.

Englehorn watched as the bombs were carefully laid in the mud, and the crew party retreated to the concealment of thorny brush, where they crouched and waited near a stand of ghost-pale river poplars.

The arrival of a group of smaller apes was not lost on him, but Englehorn did not think they posed much of a threat to the anchored vessel. So he kept his canny eyes on the trees, from time to time employing his binoculars.

Kong's massive head suddenly loomed behind an impressively-branched blackwood tree and a single amber orb peered through its leafy crown, which the master saw as clear as daylight.

"*Gott in Himmel,*" he breathed. A sense of awe overtook him. As many times as he had stood close to the gargantuan creature when it lay in chains, to see it standing upright—even though it was shielded by jungle trees—was breathtaking. At the same time, it made his suddenly pounding heart quail in his chest.

Stepping out onto the flying bridge, Englehorn yelled the much-anticipated yet dreaded words.

"*Kong ahoy!*"

Far above, the anxious voice of Carl Denham shouted down from the crow's nest. "Where? I don't see the blasted beast."

Englehorn called up. "South by Southwest, Mr. Denham. Behind the great tree."

"I see him, I see him!" the director exulted.

Then the old skipper ducked back into the wheelhouse, where he gathered up the cumbersome Tommy gun, pulling hard on the charging handle.

If Kong made it into the water, Captain Englehorn intended to unleash the weapon's battering fury upon the fearsome super gorilla before the thing could manhandle his beloved *Wanderer*. But would punishing lead do the job?

In the growing excitement, no one appeared to notice the first drops of falling rain, which presaged the inevitable long rains of the African afternoon....

Chapter 80

THE FORAGING apes of To-Yat were drawing close—too close for comfort. Jack Driscoll knew he had to make a decision and make it fast. It was not the decision he wanted to make.

Hunched in concealment, perspiration pouring out in the intolerable heat of day, he lined up his gunsights on one of the approaching apes, and carefully squeezed the trigger. The elephant gun kicked so hard that it almost knocked him off his feet.

The strange ape gave a great, screech-voiced upward leap, and for a moment the First Mate thought the potent anesthetic would not do its job.

Nervous strength caused the shaggy creature to charge about blindly. Others apes joined in the confused chorus. Some scattered. Others hunkered in the shivering brush.

Unexpectedly, the anthropoid fell on its face. He jittered in the tall grass, but failed to otherwise stir.

"The stuff works!" Jimmy breathed at his side.

Driscoll fired in the direction of another crouching ape, producing similar results. This creature was knocked backward, its arms and legs flopped and beat the ground as it succumbed to the narcotic solution squirted into its bloodstream by the hypodermic bullet.

The frightful reports caused the remaining troop to leap away, howling.

The commotion naturally drew the attention of Kong, lurking behind a thick shield of trees whose twisting branches tightly interlocked.

Jack Driscoll had heard the Captain's shout of "Kong ahoy!" but he dared not take his eyes off the advancing apes until now. Lifting his gaze, he turned around, and his eyes fell upon the sun-bronzed figure of Tarzan, who was pointing deeper into the forest from his treetop perch.

At first, the Mate could discern nothing. Then he spotted a single terrifying orb the color of golden amber. It swiveled, seemed to center on him. A momentary chill caused his skin to prickle.

Crouching back down, Driscoll warned, "Here he comes, boys. Get set."

With such speed that it almost took their breath away, Kong burst into view. He was a pitiful sight, for he had lost considerable mass through his hunger-ridden trek. Hunched over, his fur tangled, wounds raw and buzzing with black flies, his fierce mask of a face deeply wrinkled, he lumbered forward.

His tremendous mouth gaped open, and from it issued a rumbling growl that grew in volume, rolling out like a prolonged peal of preternatural thunder.

The war challenge of King Kong!

Jimmy yelled out, "He sounds mad as a hornet!"

"Do you blame him?" Driscoll shot back, feeling a pang of guilt at sight of the once-majestic anthropoid. "Now stay out of the way before he swats you dead."

The stupendous monster came striding, stooped and shambling, yet still managing to communicate a frightening measure of his brute power with every halting, ground-shaking step. This was the moment of truth, the fateful hour upon which all their futures would stand. Or fall.

Chapter 81

I N THE THORNY thicket where he crouched, Jack Driscoll redirected his rifle's massive muzzle toward the broad chest of the looming behemoth.

The plan was to use the tranquilizer bullets to keep him down after Kong succumbed to the gas, but beholding the mammoth monster's approach, Driscoll instantly reconsidered.

Everything depended upon dropping Kong close enough to the *Wanderer* to winch him aboard without difficulty. This entailed the unavoidable risk that the hungry creature might wade out and take hold of the ship once he reached the riverbank.

As the Mate thought hard, blinking salty sweat out of his stinging eyes, the apes of To-yat were scattering, shocked at the sight of two of their number falling.

They recognized the bark of Tarmangani thundersticks—even if they did not comprehend their method of operation. They fully understood that the weapons inflicted a sudden and violent death. That was enough to send them fleeing.

The startled Mangani scattered into the brush, clambered into the trees, seeking safety. But one did not.

It was the king killer ape himself—To-yat. It was beneath his simian dignity to flee a foe, no matter how deadly. Smelling burnt gunpowder, he moved in the direction his nose told him to go. A rising cloud of cordite smoke betrayed the First Mate's position in the brush.

So it was that Jack Driscoll, his full attention on the approaching Kong, failed to see hairy hands snap out of the brush, and pluck his rifle from his fingers.

"Hey!" Driscoll yelled, one hand flashing for his sidearm.

To his wide-eyed astonishment, he witnessed one of the great apes taking the rifle in hand and, exerting enormous strength, snapping it in two. Snarling, the angry anthropoid dashed the halves against a large stony protrusion, further destroying it.

The elephant rifle fell to the dirt, forever useless.

From high in the treetops, the powerful voice of Tarzan of the Apes called down.

The syllables were weird and guttural, but the enraged great ape, hearing them, wrenched his dark eyes away from the helpless Tarmangani. Seeing the ape-man above, To-yat hastily retreated into the jungle, looking abashed.

Driscoll immediately apprehended that Tarzan had somehow warned the marauding ape to quit the vicinity. And to a wonder, the shaggy brute had obeyed.

The Mate stared at his numbed hands in disbelief. That heavy rifle was his last line of defense, for he could not work his sidearm until his fingers regained their nerve strength. Now it was all up to Kong. Only he could unwittingly fracture the buried gas bombs waiting to lay him low.

Worried eyes going to the leafy branches not far distant, Driscoll remembered that there was still another factor: Tarzan of the Apes.

Craning his head, he could not locate the giant ape-man. For Tarzan had vanished. Only then did he realize that it was raining. Raining hard.

Behind him, the torrent was striking the omelet frying on the freighter's back deck, making it pop and sizzle, but also dampening its horrible yet alluring aroma, until it could be detected no more.

Driscoll groaned. The plan was unravelling.

Chapter 82

THE RATTLE of gunshots had made the bestial Kong hesitate for the merest of moments. Apish eyes quested about with curious animation, and dark nostrils flared as the bitter stink of cordite reached his nose.

Then out rolled the warning war challenge of Kong once more, a vocal thunder that had terrified the inhabitants of Skull Mountain Island going back to primordial times.

Torrential rains were pelting the soggy-haired behemoth. Kong gazed skyward, then shook one fist as if to threaten the thunder clouds that were rolling in. They resembled celestial elephants, dark grey and massed together, marching overhead.

Soon, a drenching downpour commenced. All visibility was obscured. The steady sound of sizzling gave way to a popping intermittent noise, then died out altogether.

Suddenly, there was no wind or air moving in the lashing storm, and the odor of cooking turtle eggs ceased to permeate the river area.

Annoyed if not angered by the sudden drenching he was subject to, and no longer smelling the tantalizing odors that mixed lizard flesh with cooking eggs, Kong shifted about, barrel chest heaving and deep-set eyes anxious. The brute seemed not to know what to do. Or where to go.

From somewhere amid the rain-punished trees came a weird, bloodcurdling scream—the cry of the bull ape. Tarzan was giving vent to it with all of his prodigious lung power.

To the simian mind, this was an unmistakable challenge, and Kong answered it forcefully. The air again filled with his reverberant war challenge. It made the humid air quiver in anticipation.

Tarzan suddenly showed himself, a bronzed demi-god of the forest attired only in a loincloth of leopard fur, a bow and quiver of arrows slung across his naked back. The ape-man beat upon his chest, making the terrible screeching sound that drew Kong inexorably toward it.

The intimidating monster responded in kind.

As he approached the trees where Tarzan stood haranguing him in an age-old ritual of combatants vying with one another for mastery, Kong recognized his leopard-spotted antagonist.

From his fanged mouth came growling syllables seeming to form a single savage word:

"KA... GOD... AAA!"

Was Kong demanding that Tarzan surrender? Or did he cry out what he believed to be the name of his foe? No one would ever know.

Pushing out from the sheltering trees emerged the elephants of Tarzan, palm-leaf ears waving, curved tusks gleaming, coarse hides impervious to the drenching rain.

Stepping ponderously, they moved around and behind the towering anthropoid, whereupon they attempted to herd him riverward by lifting their sinuous trumpets and blowing mighty blasts.

These sounds were the war cries of the elephant tribe, and they smote Kong's ears like a punishment. Reacting, he turned on his huge feet, swiveling narrow hips, looking about him defiantly. Making hirsute fists, the beast-god was preparing to strike out when Tarzan of the Apes lifted the fragile cast-iron shell of his gas bomb, and flung it in the monster's direction.

The grenade struck Kong on one scarred shoulder, but failed to fracture, and rebounded intact. Falling, it landed in one of the beast's own footprints, which had rapidly filled with water.

It made a great splash in landing, but once again failed to break. No trichloride gas, no greyish vapor arose.

Angrily, Kong snarled defiance.

"Kagoda?" demanded the ape-man.

No reply came.

Tarzan's war spear rested balanced in the crotch of his tree, and this formidable weapon he took up. Throwing one steel-thewed arm back, the ape-man sent the lance skimming down toward the water-filled footprint.

The spear tip was of chipped quartz, but it struck the grenade forcefully, shattering it.

Unfortunately, by the time the gas released, Kong had moved on. The drenching curtain of rain flattened the billowing stuff, dispersed its potency, inhibiting it from spreading.

Observing this phenomenon from his brushy concealment, Jack Driscoll cursed bitterly.

"We're fast running out of traps," he complained to no one in particular.

Then, to their profound disappointment, Kong turned away, seeking the shelter of the forest. Once again, the long rains were acting upon him, seeping into his bristling fur and open wounds, producing the inexorable discouragement that comes of being subject to the unforgiving elements of untamed nature.

Jimmy's voice piped up, "What's the big lug doing?"

From the *Wanderer*, came a familiar female voice. Ann Darrow. Her voice carried as she cried out, "He's getting away."

"There's your answer, Jimmy. He's hightailing it for his own good."

Jack Driscoll didn't know whether to be disappointed, or relieved.

Chapter 83

I N THE CROW'S nest, Carl Denham had been cranking away, grinning from ear to ear, and capturing every moment of the wild scene on celluloid.

Then the rains came, spoiling visibility. This was not a typical rainy season late-afternoon soaking, but an early shower. Only this shower swiftly intensified, pelting them lavishly and making the crow's nest floor drum under the elemental onslaught.

Denham was forced to shrug off his jacket coat and drape it over the camera to protect it from a severe soaking.

"This isn't a downpour," he groused. "It's a *drown*-pour!"

Soon, he was drenched. Beside him, Ann Darrow was already soaked to the skin.

Worst of all, Kong was turning inland, presenting them with his broad hairy back, as if to say, I am done with you all.

"He's getting away!" cried Ann. There was a mixture of fear and relief in her tone, and every syllable carried to the riverbank.

Hearing this, Denham growled, "Over my dead body." Suddenly, his face twitched with an idea. He turned to the bedraggled blonde. "Ann, remember when we were first on this ship and I asked you to scream for the camera. And later you screamed when Kong reached for you on the sacrificial altar back on that Godforsaken island?"

"Of course I do," retorted Ann. "How could I ever forget it?"

"Swell. I need you to scream just like that now. Scream with

430

all your might. Scream for your life. Scream so that old Kong hears you."

Ann froze, fear and shock making the pale oval of her face white as an ivory cameo. "But if he hears me, Kong will come for me. *He knows my voice!*"

Grabbing her shoulders, Denham bored all the intensity of his director's commanding will into her eyes. "Look, I know that. But Jack will protect you. Tarzan will protect you. Hell, *I'll* protect you if I have to. But we've got to get Kong moving back toward the ship. Everything depends on it. So scream, honey. Scream with everything you've got. Scream your beautiful lungs out!"

Blue eyes hardening, Ann Darrow made fists with her bone-white fingers and stood straight up in the drenching rain. There, high in the crow's nest, she took in a long, sobbing breath, and when she released it, the escaping air emerged as a high Banshee wail.

Out rolled that piercing shriek, in wave after wave of nerve-jarring sound. It struck the ears of everyone in the vicinity, making birds evacuate their sheltering tree limbs, and causing the fleeing apes of To-yat to stop and look about them in startled consternation.

OF ALL the ears that heard these rising sounds, those belonging to the beast-god Kong reverberated the most keenly.

Striding into the trees, he stopped, grunted, and looked about, then reversed himself, pushing back into the open, searching for the origin of those familiar cries.

Kong soon found it when his attention was drawn to the rusty vessel on the river. High in the crow's nest, the tallest part of the ship, he spied a pale face he recognized, and even though it was wet and pasted to her skull, Ann Darrow's honey-gold hair caught his avid eye as well.

Strange noises welled up from deep within Kong's barrel chest. A renewed vigor seemed to overcome his bloody and mud-plastered bulk. He moved confidently and eagerly toward the ship, apparently prepared to brave the river to get to the vessel and the beautiful offering it upheld for him to see.

Carl Denham flung aside his soaked coat, and began cranking away at the draped Bell & Howell movie camera.

As he ground away, he exclaimed, "He's coming this way! The big gorilla is falling into our trap!"

"I know," Ann said in a fear-twisted and miserable voice. "I must go below now. You understand."

"Don't let me hold you up," said the showman, not bothering to look back.

Ann lifted the plate-steel trap door, and began climbing downward, her heart pounding, the rain hitting her face mixing with the tears of fear and horror that were welling up from deep within her distressed eyes.

For the musk of the beast had found her nostrils, and smothering memories of his crushing grip made her blood run cold in her veins.

"Oh, Jack," she was saying to herself. "Please don't let me down. Please don't let me down...."

Chapter 84

JACK DRISCOLL crouched helplessly as Kong approached, his shattered elephant gun useless, the fat mercy bullets strung in a bandolier across his soaking chest equally of no value.

Beside him, Jimmy whispered, "Let's hope the big bruiser steps where we want him to."

Kong strode so purposefully it looked as if he were intent upon capturing the ship, not investigating it.

Dimly visible through the downpour, Driscoll spied Ann climbing down the crow's nest ladder, and he was forced to bite the inside of his cheek to keep from crying out in fear.

Kong was no longer interested in the frying-egg smell that had been smothered by the drenching tropical rain. The ship did not interest him, for he knew it had held him captive once, not many days ago.

But Ann Darrow had fascinated Kong since she had been offered up as a sacrifice by the native islanders of Skull Mountain Island, where she had been cruelly chained to two posts in the shape of barbaric totem idols, fettered as the bride of Kong. A human sacrifice entirely different from any of the dark-skinned native girls whom the ancient beast-god had taken in years gone by.

Striding toward the river, the elephants of Tarzan following behind, trumpeting loudly and seeming to herd him in the right direction, Kong reached the muddy river bank, nearly stepped on one muck-covered grenade, yet avoided the other entirely.

Driscoll had his sidearm out, and was lining up on the muddy spots.

"Shoot the bombs, boys!" he shouted. "Lively now. Don't you dare miss!"

A popping fusillade of small arms fire commenced, but only one grenade was shattered.

Sunk deep in the mud, it collapsed, but to no avail. Once again, the battering downpour pounded the escaping gas into uselessness, as shifting mud swallowed the rest of the chemical brew.

Yet some wispy tendrils of vapor arose, found Kong's wide nostrils, and smelling the familiar but hated fumes, the enormous beast hesitated. His bullet head rotated on its thick, truncated neck, looking about for the source of his discomfort.

One foot had slid into the flowing water, and the other was sunk ankle-deep into riverbank mud. The brute became stuck, as if in quicksand.

"Aim for the other grenade!" Driscoll shouted, popping out from shelter.

Suddenly beside him appeared the bronzed giant, Tarzan of the Apes. The ape-man had his bow in hand. Nocking a shaft, he pulled back on the powerful string, releasing a single arrow with a loud twanging.

It sped true.

The brittle iron egg ruptured. Gas began billowing out. As before, the rain beat it down, flattening and neutralizing it, but not entirely. Ghostly grey tendrils of the chemical preparation rose weakly like feeble fingers of ectoplasm.

A curtain of rain pulverized these climbing gases, dispersing them. Spreading outward, some thin rags of trichloride found Kong's pulsing nostrils.

The behemoth staggered. He wavered on his feet. An alarmed

light came into his semi-human eyes, and he grew dazed and uncertain.

One colossal arm reached out, straining toward the anchored ship, groping toward the tiny figure of Ann Darrow, dropping off the bridge ladder to race for her cabin, her features pale as an ivory cameo.

As the blonde girl slipped from sight, Kong gave out a pained, pitiful sound. It combined misery with a heartfelt disappointment that seemed to emerge deep within the creature's submerged soul.

Abruptly, he arrived at a decision through pure bestial instinct. Pulling his great foot out of the river, Kong began backing away, retreating toward what he believed was the relative safety of the jungle. He stumbled once, wavered, but stubbornly lurched on.

"He's going down," cried Jimmy excitedly.

Tarzan shook his head firmly. "No, Kong is stronger than the pitiful fumes reaching his lungs."

Angrily, Driscoll yanked off his bandolier, moaning, "If only I had my rifle. These damn shells are useless now."

Taking the bandolier from his hands, Tarzan stated, "Not useless."

Driscoll started. "What? Are you just going to walk up to Kong and inject him like you're some kind of jungle witch doctor? He'll never let you get close enough. And one bullet alone wouldn't bring him down. It would take a half dozen. Maybe more. How can we deliver these so it makes a difference?"

Swinging from his belt on the opposite side of the empty pistol holster hung the ponderous monkey's fist that Jack Driscoll had carefully knotted, and gifted to Ann Darrow, who then passed it on to Penjaga before it had found its circuitous way back to its creator.

Reaching down, Tarzan took this in hand and remarked, "This is like a mace without spikes. Can you undo this knot and introduce these bullets to make it one?"

At first, the Mate looked blank. Gradually, the possibilities dawned upon him and his slack expression tightened.

"I'd be one hell of a sorry sailorman if I couldn't make a monkey's fist knot do what I wanted it to," he growled.

It took only a minute or two. Driscoll loosened the rounded knot until it lay flat on the ground in complicated interlocking braids, inserted a half-dozen bullets so that the needles pointed upward. With a hard, two-handed pull, he tightened the entire contrivance until it was a stout ball of cordage once more.

Only this time needles protruded from the monkey's fist like spikes from a particularly nasty set of brass knuckles.

Walking it over to Tarzan of the Apes, he said, "It's all yours. You won't have more than one chance to hit your target, big as he is. Better make it count."

Tarzan took the dangling line in one sun-bronzed hand, tied it around his waist so that the makeshift mace hung low at the side opposite his sheathed knife. Satisfied it would remain in place, the ape-man turned and gave a weird sound that brought the golden lion, Jad-bal-ja, leaping out of jungle concealment. Together, they ran in the direction of Kong, who was backing away from the river, eyes blinking, broad features confused, fighting off the acrid anesthetic vapor, but only half succeeding.

"There goes the bravest man-jack in the whole wide world," breathed Driscoll.

"Or the wildest wild man ever," cracked Jimmy.

Chapter 85

VISIBLE THROUGH the pouring rain, the savage countenance of King Kong displayed an ever-changing parade of expressions. Anger was chief among them. So was confusion. Dismay. Rage. Uncertainty.

As Carl Denham captured them all on celluloid, the features of the behemoth settled on an unexpected emotion. One that Kong had rarely registered. But one that Carl Denham instantly recognized.

Seeing this emotion reflected on the indomitable beast-god's simian face through the obscuring curtain of rain, the showman gave out a shout of triumph.

"Fear! That's fear I see. We finally taught the Beast fear!"

It seemed true. Dimly, Kong was grappling with the deepest and darkest emotion any man or monster could face.

Clearly, Kong recalled being brought low by the hairless humans back on his home island. Indelibly, he remembered succumbing to a strangely pungent cloud and waking up later in chains. The prospect of a second loss of his savage freedom made him quake inwardly. Quake in anger, as much as in apprehension.

His long ordeal and the constant battles in the African jungle had withered his anthropoid frame, and his prodigious stomach was still half empty from lack of food. Flies crawling in his burst wounds—along with the perpetually pummeling rain—

437

made him miserable. And here again puny humans were trying to capture him.

This realization brought renewed strength to his weakened arms, and the enraged anthropoid attempted to lurch inland, to flee the vicinity. To seek freedom and the opportunity to fight to live another day.

But it was not to be.

Out of the jungle raced a tawny flash. A great black-maned lion. Roaring, it charged toward him on pounding paws.

Snarling, Kong turned to meet this new challenge. Baring his age-yellowed fangs, he roared out his answer.

The lion was brave. It never wavered. Twisting in midair, nimble Jad-bal-ja narrowly avoided Kong's blunt black fingers as the monstrous ape attempted to bat him aside. A single digit clipped one feline ear, but did no damage.

Jad-bal-ja landed safely, found his footing. He twisted his sinuous form about to face his towering foe anew. Yellow-green eyes intent and unafraid, he began circling the tower of hair and fury.

Like a punch-drunk prizefighter, Kong stamped around, endeavoring to keep the lion always before him. He was hunched over, and although he ached at many spots, Kong was just as determined to meet this challenge unafraid.

Back and forth paced Jad-bal-ja. Snarling, Kong moved with him, reaching out, swiping at the shaggy black mane and tufted tail, only to have the lion escape his clutch time and again.

Four elephants also moved in, causing Kong's head to swivel on his short neck, whereupon he offered them a warning growl. It was as if he was saying: *Stay out of this.*

To all ordinary ears, it was only a rumbling growl of an aroused beast. Fearsome, but unintelligible.

While the pacing lion and the stamping anthropoid mirrored one another, Tarzan of the Apes leapt into a tall tree, found its loftiest branch, and took the long length of cord that he had carried at the waist into both hands.

Drawing this up, he captured the monkey's fist, whose broad head now bristled with hypodermic needles.

The ape-man's keen grey eyes watched as his faithful lion and the slouching beast contended with one another. The gas had slowed down Kong, Tarzan saw. He was not himself. The lion easily evaded him.

The bronzed giant watched carefully, observing the display. In a coconut palm, Nkima the monkey was doing the same, eyes wide, tiny face puckered with excitement.

Suddenly, Jad-bal-ja became a tawny fury as he raced toward Kong, seemingly intending to tackle him head-on.

Hairy fists tightening, Kong stepped forward to meet this new challenge, hooded eyes narrowing with a dull-witted annoyance.

From high in the crown of his palm tree, little Nkima picked up a coconut in both pink paws and heaved it toward Kong, shrieking, "Fall down, Zu-jar-bolgani! Prostrate yourself before the true Lord of the Jungle, Nkima the brave!"

This improbable boast went unanswered. But the hard drupe bounced off Kong's hairy skull with just enough force to distract him.

The monster shifted about, angrily seeking the source of this new challenge, his stance growing more spread-legged.

Jad-bal-ja saw an opening then. Growling, the golden lion flashed between Kong's ankles faster than the creature could react.

The unexpected sensation of feline fur scraping the inside of one calf took Kong by surprise. He lurched, almost lost his footing, baffled orbs searching for his elusive foe.

They fell upon Nkima, who promptly burrowed his nimble body in a clutch of coconuts, crying, "Tarzan, show him your might!"

While Kong was struggling to comprehend the many threats arrayed against him, high in the treetops Tarzan of the Apes was determinedly spinning the weighty monkey's fist in a circle over his head. The makeshift bolas made a dull sound of warning, rather like a bull roarer.

When Kong presented his broad back to him, Tarzan let go.

The flail of cordage flew straight as an arrow. It struck the behemoth square in his fur-tangled back, sticking there, a half-dozen hypodermic needles embedding themselves forcefully in the raw meat of an open wound.

The force with which the knotted ball landed would not ordinarily have staggered the mighty anthropoid, but Kong was no longer himself. He was but a shadow of his former primeval glory.

He gave out a grunt of surprise, twisted about. One hand attempted to reach behind him to capture whatever it was that had stuck him and hung there. The needles were long enough to stick and sting. But as Kong wrestled about, the powerful anesthetic potion swiftly seeped into his bloodstream. Strickened eyes took on a strange look that was at first slightly dazed, then grew clouded. The light of awareness slowly went out of their amber depths.

Even with the powerful narcotic influence creeping through his emaciated frame, Kong struggled to keep his feet.

He might have lurched another step or two, but at a signal from Tarzan, the watchful elephants moved in. Using their broad grey skulls to butt Kong's muscular calves and their ivory tusks to hook him by the ankles, they succeeded in upsetting the reeling brute, for his balance was uncertain and his brain had become fogged.

Like a monstrous tree, Kong toppled, coming to rest on the muddy riverbank, where the buried gas bombs were still releasing their powerfully noxious vapor.

For a few moments, Kong struggled to remain aware, massive hands clawing the mud into which he had fallen. Then one fumbling paw encountered a hidden gas grenade, fracturing it and releasing even more of the knockout brew.

Finally, with a great muscle-racking shudder, Kong became still, as all remaining animation leaked out of him.

From high in the crow's nest, the voice of Carl Denham called out to the heavens, "What a finish! Ape-man conquers gorilla-god! And I got it all! You caught Kong, but I captured every frame on film!"

The overjoyed director threw his waterlogged hat up in the air, but no one else joined in his solitary celebration.

They stared at the hairy mountain that was the former lord of Skull Mountain Island, and for the first time in hours they felt as if they could breathe normally again. All was silent for a time. Strangely silent.

Their hearts jumped into their throats when a piercing cry shattered the silence. Weird, terrible, it caught them by surprise, congealing the blood running through their veins, and made every man wildly looked around for any sign of fresh danger.

They spotted its source almost at once.

High above, Tarzan of the Apes had thrown back his black-haired head and was screaming the blood-chilling victory cry of the bull ape—a savage sound signifying that the triumphant Lord of the Jungle had finally reclaimed his arboreal domain from a rival monarch—King Kong.

After the horrid sound trailed off, little Nkima proclaimed this victory to the jungle folk, poking his tiny head up from the top of the coconut palm, screeching, "Tarzan has conquered Zu-jar-bolgani the terrible. Powerful is Tarzan, mighty hunter, fierce killer of foes, protector of the forest."

From elsewhere in the jungle, other simian voices took up this praise, transmitting it to all points. The loudest voice of all was that of To-yat, who howled, "Tarzan is again Lord of the Jungle! Great is the adopted son the she-ape Kala named White Skin. Greater than any Mangani or Tarmangani who ever lived, or will live. All praise Tarzan of the Apes!"

To Jack Driscoll and his crew, it sounded as if the jungle apes were going mad, making sounds of fear and consternation in sympathy with Tarzan's outcry.

But on the *Wanderer,* cowering Ignatz the monkey knew different. He understood every syllable....

Chapter 86

THE RAINS continued long into the late afternoon, hampering the efforts to salvage the pathetic hulk that Kong had become.

The incessant downpour did produce one positive result. It beat down the residual gas vapors so that it was safe for the *Wanderer* to warp close to the riverbank, and swing out its derrick boom, while the deck crew went about the tedious business of affixing the steel chains and broad cuffs to Kong's shrunken wrists and ankles.

The luxury of building a raft or supporting pallet was absent this time. Instead, stout trees were felled to serve as a hoisting post, once it was bolted and screwed to Kong's fetters, linking them.

Tarzan observed this procedure from the leafy shelter of a high blackwood tree. Beside him squatted Nkima, who timidly emerged from hiding, while Jad-bal-ja, who was unscathed by his encounter with Kong, had sprawled his sinuous form over the length of a lower branch, in the languid manner of felines of all types and sizes the world over.

At a word from Jack Driscoll, the winch commenced whining, and the wire cable lifted the timber bar, bringing Kong's hairy arms up with it. It was a mouth-drying sight, for it looked as if the colossus himself were hoisting his arms skyward.

As the donkey engines banged and worked, Kong was pulled up, first the barrel chest and then the rest of him came out of

443

the mud. His battered head lolled to one side in a pathetic manner, eyes closed, bearded jaw hanging loosely open, tongue distended.

For several minutes, Kong hung from his wrists, feet dangling. Then the boom swung on board—very carefully, for Kong's handlike feet had to clear the high steel side of the well deck amidships.

Stationed on the aft deck where he had relocated his camera, Carl Denham was filming everything, his grin irrepressible.

As Kong was lowered into the Number Three Hold, he was carefully laid out flat on his matted back as he was restored to the long timber pallet assembled from Skull Mountain Island trees and other detritus.

While the hatch doors were mechanically lowered, Jack Driscoll went to the base of the tree where Tarzan of the Apes watched the proceedings in silence.

"We're done here. Thanks to you."

The light of guarded friendship came into the ape-man's grey eyes. He called down, "Go, and do not return."

"I understand," said the First Mate. "We're sorry for all the trouble we brought."

"You are a brave man, Driscoll. And I consider you to be a friend. But not so Carl Denham. He brings trouble wherever he goes. You appear wise. You will part company with him once Kong has been returned to his home island. For a man as reckless as Denham, trouble is sure to follow to the end of his days."

"You'll get no disagreement from me," laughed the Mate. "By the way, Denham asked me to invite you along. He said you might find Skull Mountain Island fascinating."

"Tarzan is not interested," said the jungle lord, reverting to his jungle custom of referring to himself in the third person, as he had when they first encountered him.

"I was about to add that Denham has a cockeyed idea that maybe you'd want to come back to America and see the sights."

Tarzan frowned. "The jungle is my home, and I do not trust that man."

"On that, we are in complete agreement. I think he wants to put you in chains alongside Kong. At least, that's the way his thinking runs."

"Tell Denham if he sets foot in Africa again, Tarzan will slay him on the spot."

"Consider that telegram delivered," said Driscoll wryly. He popped a sharp salute, adding, "I'll be shoving off now."

Having spoken his piece, the bronzed giant did not linger. Abruptly, he was moving through the upper forest terraces, his leopard-skin loincloth a fleeting scrap of color against the lush greenery of the jungle.

Simultaneously, the patient elephants on the ground turned in the same direction, and began trudging along, ears flapping, bulky bodies rolling like ungainly ships of the forest.

Before they were gone, Nkima took a moment and sent a screeching yell in the direction of the *Wanderer*. Back echoed the shrill voice of Ignatz. It sounded as if they were saying goodbye to one another—or perhaps good riddance. Driscoll suspected the latter.

Within thirty minutes of the deck hatch being closed, the *Wanderer* began reversing engines.

Jack Driscoll went to the wheelhouse and reported, "Tarzan is gone. I guess we have to fend for ourselves on the trip out."

Captain Englehorn nodded sagely. "Having navigated this far upriver, reversing course should not be arduous, provided we take our time."

"If you say so, Skipper," said Driscoll. He heaved a moist sigh. "I'm glad this is over with."

"Have you seen Ann?"

"No, where is she?"

"Hiding in her cabin; she is understandably terrified. After Kong came after her again—well, it may not have broken her nerve, but it surely tested it. The poor girl could use some manly reassurance. I will give you an hour to accomplish that task, Mr. Driscoll. Now be about it."

The old ship master's tone was stern, but there was a fatherly light in his sea-grey eyes.

"Yes, sir," said Driscoll, diving for the ladder leading down to the weather deck.

ANN DARROW answered her door reluctantly, but when she saw it was Jack Driscoll, she fell into his arms and began sobbing in jerky spasms.

Jack patted her gently on the back. "There, there, honey. It's all over with now. We're going to take Kong home and that will be the end of it. Another three weeks, and we're done with this insane expedition."

They spent an hour talking in low tones, enjoying the solitude of the private cabin as the incessant rain slackened, swelled again, and then finally died away.

When Jack Driscoll finally took his leave of her, Ann's tears had all dried and she was laughing at his awkward attempts at humor.

"Oh, Jack, you always say the most wonderful things."

Jack grinned crookedly, and soothed, "I hope you'll still be saying that ten years from now, after we've been married that long."

"Promise me that you'll let nothing prevent that day."

"I promise," assured Driscoll. "Now let me get back to my duties. If I know Carl Denham, I'm going to need to keep a weather eye on him."

Ann frowned. "He's got his footage; what more could he want?"

Pausing at the door, Jack said in a dark tone, "Carl Denham would not be satisfied with escaping the hangman's noose. He'd want to take the rope along as a souvenir. And that's exactly how guys like him get their necks broken in the end. By wanting more than any man's needs would naturally allow."

The First Mate took a turn around the weather deck to make sure that all was shipshape. Old Lumpy was at the stern, stripped to the waist in the steamy African heat, along with a grumbling work gang. They were shoveling sloppy egg fragments overboard, which trailing crocodiles swiftly snapped up once they splashed into the water.

There was a lookout with binoculars at the stern, making sure that the *Wanderer* avoided river obstacles. It was the boatswain, Beaumont.

"Carry on, Boats," he told the man.

"Yes, Mr. Driscoll."

Running into Jimmy, Jack asked, "Any sign of that old woman, Penjaga?"

"Down in the hold with her bone needle and a bag of catgut. She's sewing up the big monkey's wounds so he'll be in good shape for his next landfall. Ignatz is helping."

"Good. That should keep both of them out of mischief."

Before long, the Mate found himself in the wheelhouse, where the helmsman was struggling with the wheel while simultaneously having to look backward in order to navigate.

"There's a broad bend in the river half a mile back, where we might be able to turn around," Driscoll reminded the man.

"Can't come soon enough for me," grumbled the sailor.

"Where is the Captain?" demanded Driscoll.

"In the wardroom with that Denham. Wouldn't you figure? Denham came up with another one of his crazy notions."

Driscoll groaned. "Not another one. What is it this time?"

One eye on the stern, the sailor shrugged. "Don't know. Moon talk, as the Skipper calls it. He requested a word with Englehorn in private. You might want to knock. Maybe you could interrupt trouble brewing."

"I'll do just that," said Driscoll, making his way down below.

Going straight to the wardroom, he arrived just in time to hear an argument winding down.

Captain Englehorn was going on strenuously, "Have you not had your fill of troubles, Mr. Denham?"

"That's a harsh way of putting it," said the showman in an injured tone. "I suppose you're still sore at me for tricking your boatswain into taking me ashore that time?"

"I have decided to overlook that particular incident. It's been a hellish voyage. You know that as well as anyone. And I will not hear any more of your mad schemes. That is final."

It sounded as if the Old Man was holding his own, so Driscoll declined to knock and wandered off in search of something more useful to do. They would not be out of the woods until they were off the river, and even then there was still the hard push against the monsoon winds back to Skull Mountain Island.

The prospect of that lengthy leg reminded Jack Driscoll that they were still a long way from being rid of Kong. The thought was disquieting, for there remained the problem of putting off their mountainous cargo out in the reef-fanged breakwaters, but they were committed to do it, and would find a way. Somehow.

Passing the entry door to Hold Number Three, the Mate encountered Penjaga, who was just emerging from her ministrations upon the sleeping colossus below deck.

"How is he?" Driscoll asked.

"Kong sleeps," the Storyteller murmured darkly. "He is far weaker than before, and will need much food if he is to survive the voyage home."

Driscoll groaned. "Here we go again. But at least he's been conquered."

The old woman's eyes flared like angry coals. "Kong will never be conquered. Ever."

The Mate cocked back his cap and remarked, "Denham swore he'd teach Kong fear. I'm not so sure he hasn't done exactly that. The look on that gargoyle's face when the gas got him told that tale. Kong knew it was the end of the line."

"The end is not yet here," Penjaga cautioned. "And Kong fears neither mortal nor monster. You think he knows fear now? Wait and see, wait and see. When Kong's strength returns, so will his courage. He will be furious. What will you do then?"

"I'm too bushed to think about it now," Driscoll admitted frankly. "I just want to get the poor devil home in one piece and be rid of him."

The old woman's stern face softened. "In that goal, you and I are of one spirit, Driscoll. Pray that we are successful, for I fear for all of our futures when the supreme power of Kong is aroused once more."

"Well, you go ahead and pray. I'm off to get some shuteye. After that, maybe we'll swap places."

As he turned to go, Penjaga whispered a final warning. "Kong does not know fear, but he knows how to teach it. Remember my words. More than fear, he will teach terror."

Jack Driscoll grunted, "Don't worry. King Kong has a permanent place in my nightmares."

"And my prayers," Penjaga murmured too softly to be heard.

Chapter 87

THAT NIGHT, Jack Driscoll slept and slept, and ultimately overslept.

When he emerged from his cabin long after his watch was to have begun, he made a round of the deck, and swiftly realized something seemed wrong.

At first, the Mate could not put his finger on the problem. Having overslept, his brain was groggy. Furthermore, he was hungry. Driscoll was walking in the direction of the mess when suddenly it hit him.

The rising sun was to port, not straight ahead as it should be if the ship was on the true heading for Skull Mountain Island.

Grabbing the coxswain in passing, he demanded, "Mr. Coldwell, why are we sailing south and not east?"

"Captain's orders."

Ruddy features darkening, Driscoll muttered, "I have a bad feeling about this."

"If you want Mr. Denham," the other said dryly, "he's in the mess room trying to convince everybody they're all going to be millionaires."

The Mate flushed red. "That silver-tongued scoundrel! I'll see about that."

When Driscoll burst into the mess room, Carl Denham was holding court. He was on his feet, burly arms gesticulating, broad face aglow.

"We've been through a lot together, boys," the showman was

saying. "We shed our blood, buried our dead, suffered and sweated halfway across the world. That's all behind us now. It's just a sweet run around the Cape of Good Hope and across the Atlantic Ocean. Then we'll be home. Why, when they hear what we're bringing into port, the city fathers are sure to give us a ticker tape parade. Won't that be swell?"

"In a pig's eye!" bit out Driscoll, storming in. "Now what's all this about?"

"Why, Jack," the director said expansively. "You're a late riser these days. A man after my own heart, you might say. I was up half the night, talking to the Skipper myself. It took a while, but we came to a meeting of the minds. We're not going to Skull Mountain Island, after all. We're clearing Africa instead. We're headed home, Jack. Home to America."

To the First Mate's consternation, some members of the crew began applauding.

Driscoll growled, "Captain Englehorn would never—"

"Would never back off from a challenge?" asked the effusive Denham. "Is that what you're trying to say? Well, you'll have to take that up with him. We're headed to America. It's Captain's orders." Denham's tone dropped in register. "You know what that means, Jack? You've handed me that line a thousand times. Captain's orders are fixed and final."

Features turning dull red, Driscoll made two hard fists of anger at his side, and it was all that he could do not to stalk over and bring them to bear on the overconfident showman's pugnacious features.

"What changed his mind?" he grated. "Did you hypnotize him?"

"It's a sad story, Jack. Remember all that amazing footage I shot? Damn rain got into that old camera of mine. Into the film canisters, to boot. Ruined everything. Can't be salvaged. There went our movie, our millions—not to mention the ship. When I explained it all to Englehorn... well, it took a lot of convincing, but he finally saw it my way. I think it was the prospect of losing his ship and his retirement that finally got to him."

"You mean that *you* got to him, you conniving—"

"Now, now. Don't berate yourself. You were sleeping the sleep of the dead. And a hard-earned sleep it was, too. I'm sure Englehorn would have sought your wise counsel, but neither of us wanted to wake you."

Jack Driscoll ground his teeth, but said nothing more. Repressed rage already made his face work. Getting control of himself with difficulty, he stormed out of the mess, going in search of the ship's master. But he already knew that his pleas for sanity would fall on deaf ears.

"Yessiree," continued the director, turning back to his rapt audience. "Three months from now, we'll all be in clover. Sitting pretty. The toast of old Gotham. Mark my words. It's been a hard, hard run, but in the end, it will all have been worth it. I can feel it in my bones. As sure as my name is Carl Denham...."

Epilogue

THE SUN was going down on another sweltering African day. The rainy season was over and the long rains lay weeks in the past. It was July, and the beginning of the dry season.

Tarzan of the Apes sat on the veranda of his ranch home, east of Lake Victoria in the splendid backcountry of Kenya.

He did not look like the Lord of the Jungle now. He was dressed in gentlemanly attire and an open-necked shirt that barely concealed his powerful muscles. The cool of the evening was still hours off as John Clayton looked out over his vast holdings.

Nkima was busy investigating a fresh hole in a shade tree, his mind and his stomach, as always, on grubs.

The impressive golden lion called Jad-bal-ja dozed in the shade of that same tree. As Nkima picked out chunks of rotted wood, he threw them down at the lion's skull. But the lion only twitched its ears, and its long tufted tail slapped the sward in vague but tolerant annoyance.

Out of the distant jungle came a line of Waziri warriors on horseback. They were not dressed for war, however.

Seeing them, Tarzan's grey eyes blazed with interest. For he knew they were returning from the trading post at the highlands town of Eldoret. Their saddlebags were bloated with goods, and they smiled to see their bronzed war chief standing calmly on his veranda.

A young lad leapt from the back of a horse his father rode,

and came running up to the great white bungalow yelling, "Bwana Tarzan. Look see! Look see!"

The ape-man smiled. "What have you brought for me, Lion Cub?"

The boy's name was not Lion Cub, but that was what Tarzan called him, for he recognized in the youth a great future warrior of his tribe once he reached manhood.

"Important news!" yelled the boy. "Big doings in America!"

Tarzan nodded, saying, "I imagine that the new President continues to govern forcefully."

"Not about him, not about him," said the boy excitedly. He jumped up onto the porch, and offered Tarzan a folded copy of the *East African Standard*.

Tarzan took the paper, unfolded it, and took in the headline.

KING KONG DEAD!

"Zu-jar-bolgani, whom Tarzan conquered, is no more," panted the boy.

Tarzan's eyes went crystalline as they read the stark headlines.

Prehistoric Ape Falls from Empire State Building
Carl Denham Sought!

Beneath the screaming scareheads was a large photograph of the deceased beast-god lying on the broken pavement of faraway Fifth Avenue.

"Denham…" intoned Tarzan through tight teeth. Deep within him, a low bestial growl emerged from Tarzan's inner being.

Hearing this familiar but frightening noise, his concerned wife emerged from the house proper.

"What is it, John?"

Wordlessly, John Clayton handed over the newspaper. Jane Clayton read the front page in silence.

"Oh, John," she said plaintively. "I am so very sorry to learn this news. All your sacrifice, all your hard work was for naught. What a terrible tragedy."

Tarzan said nothing. Wrapping his strong fingers around the veranda railing, his knuckles turned bone white. He stared out toward the southern horizon. The dying sun sank into the western reaches, making the icy peak of Mount Kilimanjaro blaze crimson in the distance.

On his noble brow, the ancient scar burned a resentful red and remained that way for nearly an hour.

Those who knew him well understood that it was better to leave the master of the house alone with his thoughts, for he had once again shed that perilously thin veneer civilization had laid upon him in adulthood and was no longer John Clayton, Lord Greystoke, but Tarzan of the Apes to his smoldering core....

About the Author

WILL MURRAY

L IKE MANY young boys growing up in the 1960s, Will Murray first encountered King Kong on television, via reruns of the deathless 1933 RKO film and the 1966 Saturday morning cartoon series. He read about Kong in *Famous Monsters of Filmland* magazine, and built a King Kong Aurora monster model kit—along with millions of his fellow waifs of the baby boomer generation.

Twenty years later, Murray found himself on the set of *King Kong Lives,* covering it for *Starlog* and *Fangoria* magazines. He never imagined back in the '60s that he would stand on movie sets and watch them being filmed. But even in the '80s, the now-adult journalist never envisioned that thirty years into the future, he would be a novelist writing about King Kong in epics such as *Skull Island* and *King Kong vs. Tarzan.*

It was the same with Tarzan of the Apes. The jungle lord was a staple of 1960s television, and was still appearing on the silver screen, as he does today. Murray's primary exposure to the ape-man was on TV in the person of Johnny Weissmuller and Ron Ely, and in Dell and Gold Key comic books. He finally got around to Edgar Rice Burroughs' seminal novels in the 1970s, around the time that DC Comics had taken over the Tarzan property.

In those days, King Kong and Tarzan just seemed to go together, fellow simian inhabitants of the untamed jungle and
rival monarchs who had more in common than not.

Way back in 1996, Murray was approached to contribute to
a new series of Tarzan adventures planned by Del Rey Books.
But the project never got off the ground. However, the writer
seemed destined to pen an original exploit of the ape-man, for
in 2015 Altus Press released his novel, *Tarzan: Return to Pal-
ul-don,* a sequel to Edgar Rice Burroughs' 1921 classic, *Tarzan
the Terrible.*

Murray has written nearly seventy books and novels, and if
you were to ask him, he would say all of them are special in
some way. But some of them are more special than others. This
may be one such novel....

About the Artist

JOE DeVITO

J OE DeVITO was born on March
16, 1957 in New York City. He
graduated with honors from Parsons
School of Design in 1981 and studied
at the Art Students League in New York
City.

Over the years, DeVito has painted
many of the most recognizable Pop
Culture and Pulp icons, including King
Kong, Tarzan, Doc Savage, Superman,
Batman, Wonder Woman, Spider-Man,
MAD magazine's Alfred E. Neuman and various characters in
World of Warcraft, with a decided emphasis in his illustration
on dinosaurs, Action Adventure, SF and Fantasy. He has illustrated hundreds of book and magazine covers, painted several
notable posters and numerous trading cards for the major comic
book and gaming houses, and created concept and character
design for the film and television industries.

In 3-D, DeVito sculpted the official 100th Anniversary statue
of *Tarzan of the Apes* for the Edgar Rice Burroughs Estate, *The
Cooper Kong* for the Merian C. Cooper Estate, Superman,
Wonder Woman and Batman for Chronicle Books' Masterpiece
Editions, and several other notable Pop and Pulp characters.

An avid writer, Joe is also the co-author (with Brad Strickland)
of two novels, which he illustrated as well. The first, based on

Joe's original *Skull Island* prequel/sequel, was *KONG: King of Skull Island* (DH Press), published in 2004. The second book, *Merian C. Cooper's KING KONG,* was published by St. Martin's Griffin in 2005. He has also contributed essays and articles to such collected works as *Kong Unbound: The Cultural Impact, Pop Mythos, and Scientific Plausibility of a Cinematic Legend* and *"Do Android Artists Paint in Oils When They Dream?"* in *Pixel or Paint: The Digital Divide in Illustration Art.*

Further exploration of DeVito's Kong prequel/sequel series continues in the forthcoming book, *Skull Island,* with the property also in full development as a TV series. DeVito continues painting covers for the Wild Adventures novels (written by Will Murray), featuring Doc Savage, Tarzan, The Shadow, Pat Savage and King Kong—including *King Kong vs. Tarzan,* the first-ever authorized meeting of the two iconic jungle lords. DeVito is also gradually developing the imagery for his newest creation, a faction world of truly epic proportions tentatively titled *The Primordials.*

Joe is the founder of DeVito ArtWorks, LLC, an artist-driven transmedia studio dedicated to the creation and development of multi-faceted properties including Skull Island, War Eagles, and the Primordials. DeVito ArtWorks is exclusively represented by Festa Entertainment and Dimensional Branding Group.

Regarding King Kong vs. Tarzan, Joe writes:

> First, I would like to restate what I wrote when Will and I first worked on *Doc Savage: Skull Island* together, as I think it captures my point of view perfectly: This was one of those very special projects that comes along very rarely. It's important to keep in mind how few of these kinds of ideas actually become a reality. Anyone who has tried something like this will likely agree that they take a tremendous amount of hard work, luck and timing to see the light of day.
>
> How Carl Denham actually *got* King Kong to New York City—I mean plausibly got him there—has never been explained. Both the book and the film have Kong getting laid low

by gas bombs on Skull Island. Denham gives his "We're millionaires, boys, I'll share it with all of you" speech, and the next thing you know, Kong is on display in Manhattan. I'm sure I'm not the only one to wonder: Just *how* did they get him there?

As a kid, I could not stop daydreaming about King Kong. I was utterly hooked the first time I saw the movie and the more I thought about it, I began to ponder: Whatever happened to Kong's body? Being a boy living in Manhattan, I expected to see it on display in the American Museum of Natural History with all the other dinosaurs, but never did. Years later, under the auspices of Merian C. Cooper's family, I created an entire world around that premise to augment the original story created by Merian C., called *Skull Island*. And I published my first book based on that story, *Kong: King of Skull Island,* followed by *Merian C. Cooper's King Kong,* which folded those discoveries into a thorough rewrite of the original King Kong novel for the Cooper family (both novels were co-written with Brad Strickland, as will be my upcoming book, *Skull Island).*

Even with all that, I still had never gotten around to dealing with *how* Denham actually got Kong to NYC. When Will first proposed his idea not only to tell that story, but also to use it as the premise for the ultimate meeting of Kong with his only rival in the annals of action adventure jungle lore—the iconic original jungle man, Tarzan—I was instantly hooked!

As with Doc Savage's visit to Skull Island, there was quite a bit of back and forth with Will on Kong story details, plausibility factors and general brainstorming as he took on the incredible task of creating a full novel around his original premise. Concurrently, I was working on my Kong book and contemplating cover concepts with Will and our cover patron for this book, Richard Burchfield. I drew up some pretty cool concepts—Kong dramatically lifting an elephant clear over his head is one that came very close to making the cover. Before we knew it, a couple of years had gone by!

From the beginning, it was no easy task trying to project equal visual importance on two characters of such disparate sizes. The obvious approach was to have a closeup of Tarzan up in a tree looking at Kong's head or a distant figure, letting perspective equalize their respective sizes, but that seemed too obvious. I went for something different that focused on the gigantism and power of Kong while accenting the indomitable command of Tarzan over the forest he ruled through gesture and juxtaposition. Tarzan may be much smaller than Kong, but his appearance astride the back of a massive bull elephant placed in a prominent foreground position with the focus being on Tarzan's commanding gesture of "Halt!"—you don't have to hear the word at all—has a dramatic impact all its own. When contrasted with Kong's stupendous size and surprise at finding a phalanx of Tarzan-led elephants blocking his path, the proper attention is established for each. The two great characters are further emphasized by each having their heads subliminally positioned at the point of a compositional triangle, the lines of which draw the viewer's eye directly to them.

I can't help but think that Burroughs and Cooper would have had a grand time working together on such a project, had they done it. I know Cooper had contemplated such a cinematic pairing, but I don't know if Burroughs ever did. That such a meeting would take place in Africa as opposed to Skull Island, I don't think anyone believed would happen, me included. Yet, when it is thought through, it is the most logical possibility! Across the Pacific, with nary an island in sight for vast stretches, only to be faced with the impossible choice between transiting the Panama Canal or undertaking the perilous voyage around Cape Horn, generally agreed to be the most dangerous stretch of ocean on Earth—or to go westward, with the entire African coast available for landfall in case of emergency with such an unpredictable cargo such as King Kong, then straight to New York City?

And so the tale begins. Granted, either way is an extreme gamble. If not for Penjaga, Skull Island's enigmatic Storyteller, neither passage would have been possible. Will had to pull out all the stops and we had innumerable conversations on just how such a fantastic voyage might have been possible. As predicted, what could go wrong did, and had it not been for the proximity of the African continent, all may have been lost. But what occurred when the beast-god of Skull Island discovered himself disoriented and weakened in a strange land populated by creatures so unlike those of his home island? What happened when Tarzan, the Lord of the African Jungle, suddenly found an irresistible force of nature in the form of King Kong wreaking havoc in his domain? Those questions and a hundred others, my friends, can only be answered by reading the first of its kind book that you hold in your hands. But be prepared to flee for your lives when you find yourself caught in the middle of the Confrontation of the Century: *King Kong vs. Tarzan!*

www.jdevito.com
www.kongskullisland.com
FB: Kong of Skull Island
FB: DeVito ArtWorks

About DeVito ArtWorks

DᴇVITO ARTWORKS, LLC is an artist-driven transmedia studio dedicated to the creation and development of multi-faceted properties including Skull Island, War Eagles, and the Primordials. DeVito ArtWorks is founded and led by renowned artist, illustrator and author, Joe DeVito. Mr. DeVito has painted and sculpted pop
culture's most recognizable icons including Doc Savage, Superman and Batman and has had his work exhibited in museums and galleries throughout the world.

DeVito ArtWorks is the home of Kong of Skull Island, its associated Skull Island property, and all its derivative works. Richard M. Cooper LLC owns all copyright rights in the novel Merian C. Cooper's King Kong. The DeVito and Cooper properties work in concert to create, through fully copyrighted words and pictures, the complete King Kong–Skull Island origin property, uniquely endorsed with the name of Kong's creator, Merian C. Cooper, and exclusively authorized by his family's estate and that of Skull Island creator, Joe DeVito. DeVito ArtWorks, LLC and its representatives, Festa Entertainment and Dimensional Branding Group, have the exclusive right to develop and market both properties in all media formats. For more information go to: www.kongskullisland.com

About Edgar Rice Burroughs, Inc.

FOUNDED IN 1923 by Edgar Rice Burroughs, as one of the first authors to incorporate himself, Edgar Rice Burroughs, Inc., holds numerous trademarks and the rights to all literary works of the author still protected by copyright, including stories of Tarzan of the Apes and John Carter of Mars. The company has overseen every adaptation of his literary works in film, television, radio, publishing, theatrical stage productions, licensing and merchandising. The company is still a very active enterprise and manages and licenses the vast archive of Mr. Burroughs' literary works, fictional characters and corresponding artworks that have grown for over a century. The company continues to be owned by the Burroughs family and remains headquartered in Tarzana, California, the town named after the Tarzana Ranch Mr. Burroughs purchased there in 1918 which led to the town's future development.

www.edgarriceburroughs.com

www.tarzan.com

About the Patron

RICHARD BURCHFIELD

I GREW up with three brothers on a hobby farm in central Minnesota, and have been very fortunate to go to school and work in the north, west, south, and east of this great country. Also, I have had the opportunity to hike and camp the magnificent national parks, Grand Canyon, Zion, Sequoia, Yosemite, Yellowstone, Glacier, and more and have great memories of the crown jewels of this nation. Since I can remember, my mother, Rosita, influenced me with her love of reading science fiction. She introduced me to the wonderful worlds of Tarzan, John Carter, and Conan, and more. I can remember escaping to Mars, Venus, Skull Island and the Dark Continent during cold winters in Minnesota during the 1960s and '70s. To this day, when I see Tarzan, John Carter, Conan and others, I think of my mother and how she expanded my thinking and encouraged me to read and learn. In the late '60s, my father got us kids around the TV to watch the Apollo launches. It was a time when anything was possible. I had these great science fiction books and the real world was reaching for the stars. I have had a career in information technology since the early 1980s, and it's been an incredible transformation, witnessing of how technology has impacted our lives.

Lastly, to be the sponsor of the cover for these two great iconic characters, Tarzan and King Kong, is a tremendous honor for me.

TARZAN

Return to Pal~ul~don

"This first authorized Tarzan novel from the sure hand of pulpmeister Will Murray does a fantastic job of capturing the true spirit of Tarzan, not a grunting monosyllabic cartoonish strongman, but an evolved, brilliant, man of honor equally at home as Lord Greystoke and as the savage *Tarzan the Terrible*."

—*Paul Bishop*

$24.95 softcover
$39.95 hardcover
$5.99 ebook

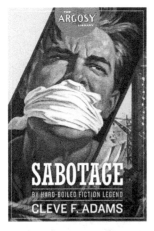

SABOTAGE
BY HARD-BOILED FICTION LEGEND
CLEVE F. ADAMS

CHAMPION OF LOST CAUSES
WILLIAM F. NOLAN
MAX BRAND

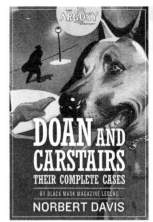

DOAN AND CARSTAIRS
THEIR COMPLETE CASES
BY BLACK MASK MAGAZINE LEGEND
NORBERT DAVIS

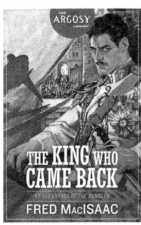

THE KING WHO CAME BACK
BY THE AUTHOR OF THE RAMBLER
FRED MacISAAC

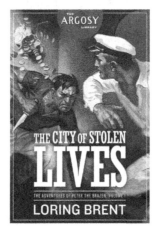

THE CITY OF STOLEN LIVES
THE ADVENTURES OF PETER THE BRAZEN, VOLUME 1
LORING BRENT

THE RADIO GUN-RUNNERS
BY SCIENCE FICTION LEGEND
RALPH MILNE FARLEY

BLOOD RITUAL
THE ADVENTURES OF SCARLET AND BRADSHAW, VOLUME 1
THEODORE ROSCOE

THE SCARLET BLADE
THE RAKEHELLY ADVENTURES OF CLEVE AND D'ENTREVILLE, VOLUME 1
MURRAY R. MONTGOMERY

SEMI DUAL
THE COMPLETE CABALISTIC CASES OF
THE OCCULT DETECTIVE, VOLUME 2: 1912-13
J.U. GIESY AND JUNIUS B. SMITH

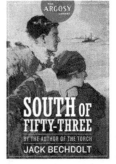

SOUTH OF FIFTY-THREE
BY THE AUTHOR OF THE TORCH
JACK BECHDOLT

THE ARGOSY LIBRARY ™

SERIES 2 INCLUDES:

* BRAND * BRENT * ADAMS *
* MacISAAC * ROSCOE *
* GIESY & SMITH *
* BECHDOLDT *
* MONTGOMERY *
* FARLEY *
* DAVIS *

THE BEST FICTION
FROM THE FRANK
A. MUNSEY LINE

THE ALL-NEW *WILD* ADVENTURES OF
DOC SAVAGE

Doc Savage:
The Desert Demons

Doc Savage:
Horror in Gold

Doc Savage:
The Infernal Buddha

Doc Savage:
The Forgotten Realm

Doc Savage:
Death's Dark Domain

Doc Savage:
Skull Island

WORDSLINGERS

AN EPITAPH FOR THE WESTERN

☞ **WILL MURRAY** ☜

Will Murray's Wordslingers is not only the first in-depth history of the Western pulps, it's one of the best and most important books on the pulps ever written, perfectly capturing the era, the magazines, and the writers, editors, and agents who helped fill their pages. Pulp fans will be fascinated by the rich background provided by hundreds of quotes from the people involved in producing the Western pulps, while writers will benefit from the discussions of characterization and storytelling that prove to be both universal and timeless.

—*James Reasoner*

$29.95 softcover
$39.95 hardcover
$8.99 ebook

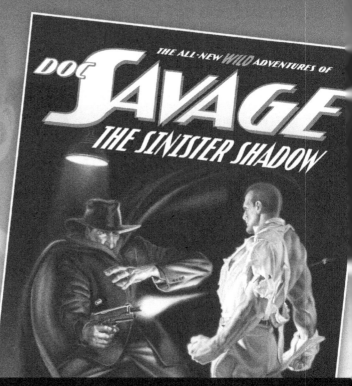

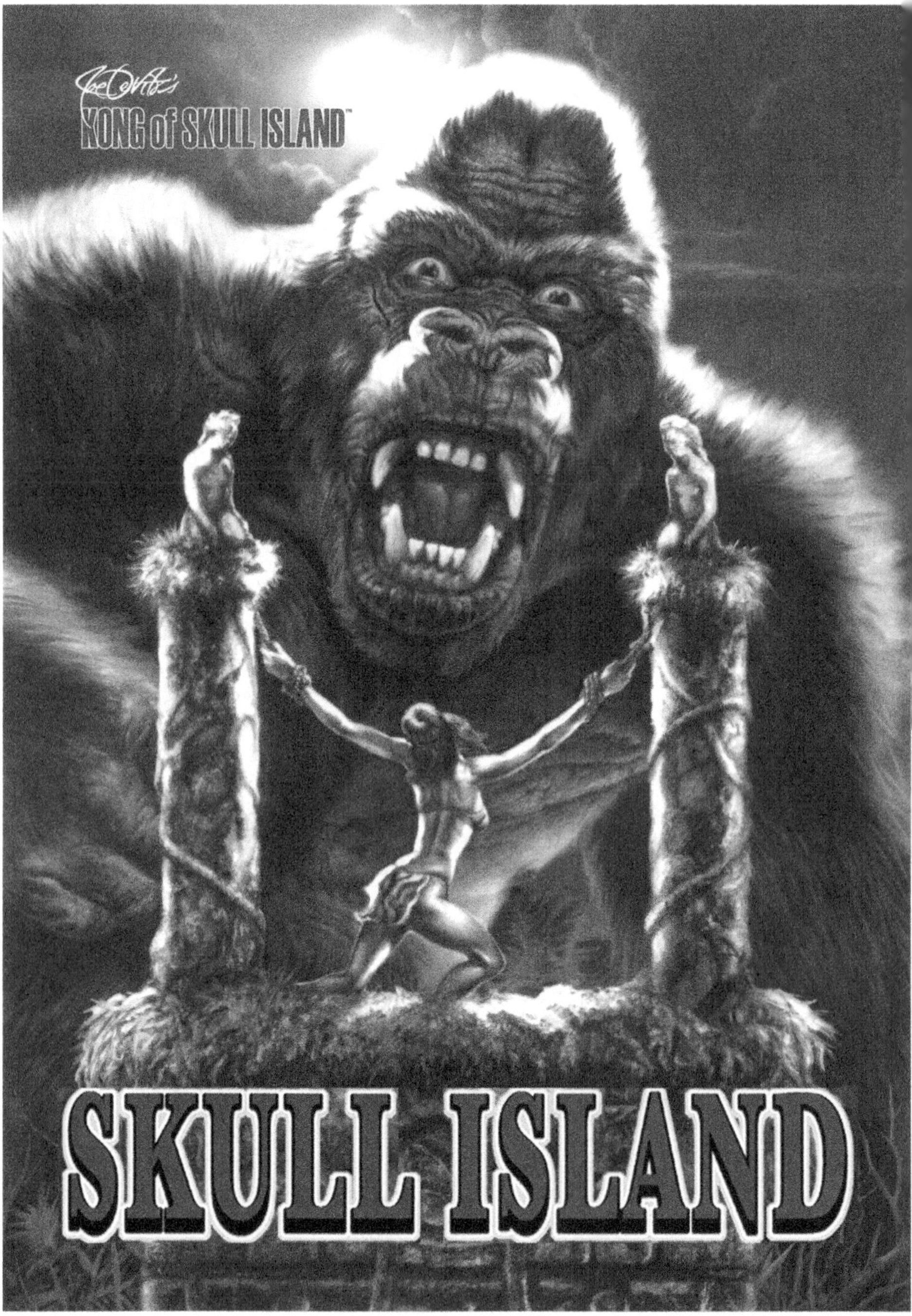
Joe DeVito's
KONG of SKULL ISLAND™
SKULL ISLAND

SKULL ISLAND

The sprawling new adventure novel written by
Joe DeVito and Brad Strickland, with illustrations
by Joe DeVito. It chronicles the origins of the Kongs,
the ancient civilization called the Tagatu, and their fight to
survive in the midst of Skull Island's prehistoric denizens,
culminating in the epic building of the Great Wall.
Untold mysteries surrounding Skull Island's enigmatic
origins and its bizarre natural wonders are also revealed!

Skull Island is the first book in the exciting new series,
"Kong of Skull Island."
Part of DeVito ArtWorks' unfolding universe, "King Kong
of Skull Island", it joins the Cooper Estate's original
storyline "Merian C. Cooper's King Kong" with DeVito's
ground-breaking Kong of Skull Island origin story –
the first and only creator-authorized expansion of the
Skull Island mythos since Cooper created
King Kong!

Watch For It Here:
Facebook: Kong of Skull Island
Facebook: DeVito ArtWorks
www.kongskullisland.com
www.jdevito.com

KONG of SKULL ISLAND

DOC SAVAGE
SKULL ISLAND

The Man of Bronze meets the 8th
Wonder of the World is a historic
matchup untold for 80 years! Before
the world knew them, King Kong
and Doc Savage faced off in Will
Murray's monumental new novel.

$24.95 softcover
$39.95 hardcover
$5.99 ebook

Made in United States
North Haven, CT
01 August 2023

39800654R00271